SHADOWS IN THE DUST

Suzanne Cass

S C
STORM CLOUD
PRESS

If you would like to find out more about my new book releases, free book offers, discounted books and newsletter, then please join my mailing list.

www.suzannecass.com

I've also got a **FREE NOVELLA**, Solar Flare, just for you. Check the last page of this book for the links.

Shadows in the Dust

Storm Cloud Press, Perth Australia

Copyright © 2018 by Suzanne Cass

Cover by Vikncharlie

All rights reserved.

Dedication

To all my invaluable writer friends who've helped me on this journey.
You know who you are.

CHAPTER ONE

'Move will ya!' Puffs of dust billowed up as a large woman shoved past Jenna and jumped down onto the ground beside her. 'Bloody hell, they weren't kidding when they warned us about the red dirt, were they.'

'Sorry,' Jenna apologized, taking a few steps away from the doorway of the bus. Shaking her head, she gave a small grimace. She'd been so captivated by the bluest sky she'd ever seen she'd forgotten where she was for a second.

'Didn't mean to push you, luv, but you were just standing there like a stunned mullet.' The woman reached out a plump hand. 'Hi, I'm Shauna.'

Raising one eyebrow Jenna watched the buttons on the woman's tight blue shirt strain to breaking point over her ample breasts.

She took Shauna's hand and gave her a tired smile. 'My name's Jenna.' The name rolled off her tongue easily now. Her true name, Emily, now a distant memory. Jenna was a completely different person to Emily. Tougher. Stronger. She had to be if she was going to survive. It was two years and two months since that fateful night when her father was murdered, but it was still as clear as if it had happened yesterday.

'Nice to meet ya,' Shauna replied, but her attention was already shifting towards the buildings on the other side of the road. 'I guess we'd better go and see what this little hick country town has to offer then.' Pushing a chunk of flaming orange hair behind her ear, Shauna shoved her red Akubra hat more firmly onto her head and set off in an exaggerated swagger towards the town.

'Bring the bags will you,' Shauna called back over her shoulder.

Jenna snorted. If Shauna thought she was going to start ordering her around, she was mistaken.

'Excuse me.' A long-limbed woman sidled down from the last step of the bus to stand next to her. She was the complete opposite of Shauna, thin and olive-skinned, with dark, straight hair that hung to the middle of her back. She gave Jenna an infectious smile and Jenna couldn't help but flash an answering grin back.

'Shauna meant for me to bring the bags, not you.' The tall lady laughed and held out her free hand. 'I'm Lynne, chief bag dragger.'

Jenna shook the other woman's hand, warming to her pleasant nature. The two seemed a bit of an odd couple. They must be here for the same reason she was; they'd answered the employment ad in the newspaper for station hand's to come and work at the Shiralee Cattle Station.

Lynne chased Shauna across the road, struggling to drag the two enormous bags behind her.

That left Jenna standing on the side of the road alone as the bus roared off in its own self-made cloud of roiling dust. This surely was the middle of nowhere. Her gaze searched the huddle of grey buildings on the other side of the road, darting to the stretch of low, undulating hills fading off into a shimmering red heat haze on the horizon. A wry smile broke out on her lips. It'd become a habit. To observe every detail, take note of every escape route. But it'd saved her more than once in the past few years.

Dragging a hand through her unruly hair, she pulled it up into a single plait. Then she picked up her discoloured duffle bag and placed her dusty grey hat on her head.

Following the pair to the eastern end of town, she approached a large brick building, where the sound of harsh laughter pinpointed the local pub. The sign that swung from underneath the verandah stated *The Elsewhere Hotel*. An apt name, considering where they were. The edge of the Great Sandy Desert, somewhere in the top end of Western Australia. Taking a lungful of hot, dry air, Jenna held her breath for a few seconds and then exhaled slowly.

Rounding the side of the pub, she stopped when she saw a man leaning against the only tree offering any shade from the midday sun.

'You must be, Jenna Smith,' he said. There was a rich deep timbre to his voice. Liquid-amber eyes considered her from within the deep shadow of his hat. When she didn't immediately reply, he continued, 'I'm Dan. Dan Simmonds.' He extended his hand. It was warm, engulfing her smaller one, surrounding it with long tan fingers. His smile was just as warm, showing off straight white teeth.

'You're the one I talked to on the phone the other day, the leading-hand?' she asked.

'Nope, that would've been Lex. I'm just the lucky one who gets to deliver all you charming new jillaroos safe and sound to the station.' He wasn't in any hurry to let go of her hand. Was that a hint of irritation in the quirk of his mouth? Had she just broken some unwritten rule by mistaking him for the leading-hand? Great, she hadn't even made it to the station yet and already she was putting her foot in it.

She tilted her face upwards to get a closer look at him from beneath half lowered lashes, trying to hide the way her gaze raked over him. He was taller than her, slim and cat-like. Sun-bleached streaky brown hair curled enticingly from beneath his hat. His skin had a honey, tanned quality that made Jenna think of butterscotch candy. Perhaps a few years older than her if she had to guess. And good-looking. Very good-looking.

Dan returned her gaze, unhurried in his scrutiny. When his eyes reached her face, they paused to gaze at her lips before looking deep into her eyes. The tips of Jenna's ears flushed with heat.

The touch of his strong fingers felt effortless and inviting, and all of a sudden her body became hyper-aware of how close he was standing.

She took a step backwards.

'Thanks for that,' she mumbled, tearing her gaze away and disentangling her hand from his.

A weather-beaten wooden table and chairs stood on a brown patch of grass a few feet away. She headed towards that and chose the cleaner looking seat, dropping her bag on the ground.

'Don't you want to come inside for a drink before we go?' He raised one eyebrow. 'The other two have already gone in.' Tilting his chin, he indicated the open doorway. 'Come in and we can get to know each other better.' Jenna didn't miss the implied meaning. Peering around him she took in the noisy interior of the pub, filled with loud drunken men. It was Saturday afternoon, and it seemed everyone in the district was here. Too many people in there. People who'd undoubtedly want to talk. Ask questions. The idea made her skin crawl.

'No thanks. I might take a bit of a walk. Have a look around the town.' Pretending to rifle through her bag she turned away from him.

'Suit yourself,' he answered, voice gruff. 'There's not too much to see around here, this is just the same old shitty little outback town you see everywhere.' His puzzled tone said it all. Out of the corner of her eye she could see he still hesitated, but when she gave no further reply, he stalked towards the cool inside of the pub. 'I'll come and get you when the rest of us are ready to go,' he said over his shoulder before disappearing through the door.

Jenna exhaled through pursed lips.

Her gut reaction to Dan had been an unwanted surprise. She didn't usually take much notice of whether a man liked what he saw or not. But for some reason Dan's intense assessment unnerved her.

Wearing the eternal pair of faded blue jeans, finished off with tired brown Blundstone boots, she knew she fit the stereotype of a country girl perfectly. She was petite. Most people dismissed her with one quick glance, which was the way she preferred it. Her long, blonde hair was always tied up out of the way, so she could get on efficiently with whatever job needed doing. It was her clear blue eyes that seemed to bring her most attention from the men, however. Attention she shut down in the same way she'd effectively snubbed Dan. A man would get in the way. Romance was for those lucky women who led normal, complete lives. Not for her.

Jenna sighed and shot a furtive glance back inside the pub. The beers were lining up on the bar and Shauna and Lynne clinked their cold-beaded glasses together, congratulating each other with their smiles. The scene was so inviting; friends sharing a beer and a joke with not a care in the world. It made Jenna catch her breath. If only life could be that simple. She'd almost forgotten what it was like to be happy and carefree. *One day.* One day in the future she might be able to settle down in one place. Be able to stop running and hiding. *Perhaps even fall in love.* The thought came before she could stop it, filling her with a longing so severe she almost doubled over in pain. But that was just idle fantasy. A dream. The way to stay alive was to be alert and keep moving. That was her reality.

The outback heat was stifling as the sun slipped past its midday zenith. Stretching her jean-clad legs, still cramped from her long journey on the bus, she got up and ambled back towards the main street. The harsh sun struck the cluster of low buildings that made up the town of Smokey Creek. Most of them were run-down and unkempt. As she wandered down the road, Jenna decided Dan was accurate in his description. It was typical of any number of scattered settlements she'd seen from the bus window on her trip through Western Australia.

Kicking the dust up into puffs of red, Jenna looked out at the sparse countryside surrounding the township. It stretched for as far as the eye could see in all directions, clear and open, not a single soul in sight.

Turning in a large circle, she realized for the first time how far she'd wandered from the pub. At this end of town nothing moved. It was deathly silent. She was totally alone. Her heartbeat skipped up a few notches, a nervous shiver spreading down her spine. *Shit.* Picking up her pace, she walked a little faster through the heat back down the deserted street.

Arriving at her table next to the pub, once again inside the bubble of humanity she released a slow breath.

Liam didn't like crowds, or the attention they garnered. He'd rather catch her alone and unawares. Pulling a warm bottle of water out of her duffle bag, Jenna lay down on the long wooden seat to wait in the thin shade of the peppermint tree.

Liam.

Just thinking the name was enough to raise the hair at the back of her neck. But she was safe enough from him out here. At least for a little while.

Her fingers went automatically to the ring dangling from the chain around her neck. She held it between thumb and forefinger, rubbing it softly. The ring was set with an opaque stone, a soft milky pink colour, symmetrical and smooth. She dare not wear it on her finger, incase she lost it. Instead it was always kept safe near her heart. It was the only thing she owned that belonged to her mother.

* * *

Pain exploded in Dan's left cheek as George landed a healthy right-hook square in his face. The shock of the blow left him groggy and as he stumbled backward, the man got in a few more heavy punches to his ribs. Rising on his toes, Dan danced back towards the open doorway, forcing his arms to stay up as George advanced towards him again.

The vague sound of voices, interspersed with yells and whistles came from the throng of pub patrons in the background, but Dan's concentration remained on the ruddy-faced man in front of him.

'I saw you eying my girl's legs!' the fat man bellowed.

Dan ducked under another wild swing. 'Hey, she was the one who approached me and suggested I buy her a drink.' He should've known better, but he bought her a drink anyway, while she leaned in extra close to him on the bar. It was the chivalrous thing to do, after all.

George, the local mechanic, was twice Dan's size. And twice as dumb. He came at Dan with a loud bellow and a cracking punch that sent him sprawling to the ground. Right in front of the new jillaroos, who stood at the bar with shock frozen on their faces. He got to his feet, swaying groggily.

Getting the three girls back to the station was his responsibility. Lex trusted him to come and pick them up and he had to think of a way to talk his way out of this. Before he lost his job.

A blur of movement caught Dan's eye, but he was too slow. The publican rushed at him from around the side of the gathering crowd, crashed his shoulder and elbow into Dan's chest and sent him flying out the rear door. Dan landed on his back on the dirt outside. Hard. So hard he was left writhing on the ground as pain speared through his whole body. He took great gasps of air, trying to fill his empty lungs.

'How's that feel, you bastard?' asked George, standing threateningly over him, words slurring.

'That's enough, George.' Wazza, the publican, laid a hand on the irate man's chest, urging him back inside. 'I've taken care of him.' The publican cast a warning glance back over his shoulder at Dan as he spoke.

'I don't take kindly to guys who try and chat up my girl,' the fat man growled. If Dan had been able to speak he might have spat out some flippant answer like, 'Maybe you need to check on who's chatting up who, before you use your fists so easily.' But perhaps it was better he was still too breathless to speak.

'Don't be coming back here for a while, Dan,' said Wazza, shaking his head. 'You seem to be in the wrong place at the wrong time.' The publican closed the door behind him. Why did Wazza always take the other guys side?

'God, are you okay?' The new jillaroo, Jenna, knelt down in the dirt by his side. Her fingers were tentative as she touched his face.

'You're hurt!' He looked into her compelling blue eyes. His assessment of her from earlier was still true. Her lean, fit frame confirmed she knew what hard work was all about. There was none of the make-up or pretence other girls employed, just a fresh beauty that was utterly undeniable. She was perhaps in her early twenties, not much younger than him. But her gaze held reserve, a haunting vulnerability that seized his attention.

'I'll live,' he replied, trying to cover his grimace as he levered himself into a sitting position.

But he didn't hide his expression well enough.

'Let me take a look. You really took a beating from that guy.'

'No, I'm fine,' he repeated and went to push himself off the ground but had to stop when a sharp pain shot through his chest.

She laid a gentle hand on his arm. 'You could have a couple of broken ribs, or internal injuries. Just let me take a quick look.' Her manner was cool and calm, as if she dealt with these kinds of situations every day. If he had to describe her in one word, he would say guarded. And perhaps stubborn. Dan could see a certain tilt to her chin indicating he wouldn't get away until she got what she wanted. He nodded a quick agreement, throwing her a sideways glance of exasperation.

She lifted the corner of his shirt. Her fingers grazed the skin over his hip and he had to hide his surprise when a tingle ran across his skin. She took in his bruises—which were already turning purple—and narrowed her eyes at him.

'You are not fi—'

'Jesus, Dan, are you okay? I didn't think they were going to let us out of there.' Shauna stumbled through the doorway, Lynne hot on her heels. 'That big wanker kept asking me questions, as if I was involved or something. Luckily Lynne was there to hold me back, or else I would've punched the fucker, right in the face. Did he hurt you?'

Jenna shuffled backwards to allow Shauna and Lynne room to kneel in the dirt next to him. Dan had to drag his gaze away from the tantalising smooth run of her collarbone, exposed as she knelt over to examine his bruises, and bring his attention back to the other two women.

'I'm fine, girls. Really, it's nothing.' He ignored Jenna's frown. 'Come on, let's get going.' He stood, resisting the urge to hunch over in response to the pain in his ribs. 'It's well past time I got you back to the station.'

'Aren't you going to do something about that bastard?' Shauna said. 'We should go and report him to the police or something.' She placed her hands on her ample hips.

'Don't you need to see a doctor?' added Lynne, her eyes wide with worry. Taking the corner of his shirt he held it against his lip where a warm trickle of blood ran down his chin.

'No, I don't need a doctor. And I'm not going to the police. It wasn't that guy's fault. His girl got exactly what she wanted from that confrontation. The big guy was just a pawn in her stupid game.' Brushing at the dust that coated his jeans, he tried to hide his anger at his own foolishness. Heading in the direction of his ute, he mumbled to himself once he was out of earshot, 'And I probably got what I deserved as well.'

* * *

Shauna steamrolled her way into the front seat, pushing the other two out of the way in her haste to take prime position. Jenna and Lynne looked at each other and shrugged with amusement before turning towards the back of the old Holden ute.

'Sorry, girls.' Dan gave a weak smile and raised his hands in the air. 'I'll see if I can swap you around later in the trip.'

'That's okay. We don't mind do we, Jenna? It's all part of the adventure.' Lynne gave Dan a winning smile.

'Are you sure you're all right to drive, Dan? We could all take turns.' After seeing those bruises, she could only imagine what kind of pain he must be in. His expression remained closed. A red stain was rising on his cheekbone, but at least the trickle of blood from his split lip had dried up. He looked a mess, but there was something else. Another hidden pain, deep within. She was the queen of hiding her emotions, so she recognized it when someone else tried it. He brushed the whole thing off as if nothing happened, almost as if the punishment was justified. Why would anyone think they warranted a beating? A frown furrowed her forehead.

'Thanks for the offer, Jenna.' He wouldn't meet her eyes. 'But trust me, I'll ask if I need help, so stop worrying.' She stared at him, daring him to look at her. Bloody hell he was stubborn. But before she could say anything an eager face appeared over the side of the ute. A lolling tongue and an unstoppable thumping tail greeted them.

Dan's face split with a smile and he leaned over to pat the dog's head affectionately.

'This is Blue.'

'Hiya, Blue.' Jenna patted the dog's head as she and Lynne climbed in. Dan had chucked a couple of unrolled swags in the tray to give them some comfort and Jenna pummelled her duffle bag into submission, so she could lean it behind her back. Blue lay down next to her, wet nose on her lap, looking up with unabashed longing into her face. She felt the dog's delight.

'He seems to like you.' Dan frowned. 'He's not normally that friendly with strangers.'

'Most dogs like me,' Jenna replied, a little uncomfortable when Dan's dark gaze remained fixed on her.

'I'm sure they do,' he answered cryptically, before turning and folding his long legs into the driver's seat.

Dan was just settling into the car seat when Shauna began to coo at him, telling him how brave he'd been to stand up to a man twice his size. Jenna zoned out of their conversation.

With the rush of the cooling air and the rocking motion of the car soothing her, she was able to relax for the first time in days. An uncertain kind of peace infused her.

'I can't wait to see this cattle station,' said Lynne. 'I know it's not one of the biggest out here, but it's still bigger than any farm I've ever worked on before.'

'Yes, me too.'

'I'm keen to do some proper cattle mustering. You know, learn some new skills.' Lynne's face became animated as she talked. 'I've never worked up north before, have you?'

'No I haven't, but I'm looking forward to it, like you.' Jenna stroked Blue's ears. The dog's contentment was coming through to her in reassuring waves.

'Yeah, I'm not sure how I'm going to handle the heat, though. I'm worried I might turn into a little puddle of sweat and disappear,' Lynne joked. 'And sure as eggs it's gonna make Shauna even grumpier than she already is.'

'Really?' Jenna raised a quizzical eyebrow and Lynne giggled. 'Have you and Shauna worked together before?' she asked, interest getting the better of her.

'Yep, we've been mates for a year or so now. We met on a sheep farm in central New South Wales. Being the only two girls on the place we kinda had to become friends.'

Jenna nodded in agreement. Women in these kinds of jobs were often few and far between.

'I know Shauna can be a bit loud and domineering when you first meet her, but she's not all that bad when you get to know her.' Lynne's voice held a touch of defensiveness, so Jenna left her comment alone. 'What's your story, then?'

The breath caught in Jenna's throat. Her peaceful bubble disappeared just as quickly as it'd formed.

'Oh, I don't have a story.' She cast an eye sideways at Lynne.

'Come on, everyone has a juicy story or two to tell, even if it's just about why you seem to like your own company so much.' Lynne was sitting forward, her eager eyes pinned on Jenna. When she didn't answer straight away, Lynne continued, 'You can tell me, I'm good with secrets. What brings you all the way to the top end of WA then?'

Jenna closed her eyes for a brief second. All the fatigue and stress of the last couple of days rose up in her chest. Lynne's questions were innocent enough, but she couldn't seem to quell her irritation.

'I'm just like you, I want to learn some new skills mustering top-end cattle. Stuff like that.' Jenna directed her gaze out over the red sand hills as they flashed by.

'You strike me as a bit of a loner. Do you always travel on your own?' Lynne didn't seem to want to take the hint. The dog moved beneath Jenna's hand. 'But don't get me wrong, I admire you for it. I don't think I'd like to travel up here without Shauna.'

Jenna clamped her jaw together tightly. Lynne was right of course. So, why couldn't she feel anything but annoyed?

'Tell me, where else have you worked, then?' asked Lynne, still chirpy.

Jenna wanted to spit out the words and tell Lynne she'd worked on over ten farms in the past few years, always moving on, never making any true friends and never earning the respect of her employers. She wanted to tell her she was a loner out of necessity, not because she liked it that way. Blue raised his head from where it'd been resting in Jenna's lap. The dog's eyes were sharp and brittle, fixed on Lynne. A low growl emanated from deep within his chest. Jenna laid a quick hand on top of Blue's head and he settled back down.

Then she gave Lynne the same line she gave everyone else. The one with the grain of truth at its heart. 'Oh, you know, I've worked here and there. Mostly sheep farms, like you. At the moment, I'm just trying to get as far away from the man who … who broke my heart. That's all.'

'Oh no, I'm sor—'

The ute came to a sudden stop, cutting Lynne off mid-sentence.

'Welcome to Shiralee Station,' Dan yelled out the window. They both turned around to peer over the top of the cabin. To the left stood a large weather-worn square of wood on which was scrawled:

Shiralee Station

Owners: Ted & Maggie Dawson

Manager: Bernie Kingsly

In front of them was the main gateway to the station, three swaying bits of wood propped up by rickety sticks on each side. Perhaps the things she'd heard about this station were true. Down on its luck and in need of a new manager, rumour had it. This was exactly the kind of place Jenna could hide in.

'Only another three hours,' Dan yelled.

The ute took off again in a spray of dust, leaving Jenna and Lynne to clutch the sides to avoid being rocketed out the back. The dog took it all in his stride, head stuck out the side and tongue hanging out.

'Wow, that's a long way to drive if you run out of milk or ciggies!' said Lynne. They both grinned at each other in shared joy at the vast isolation.

They sat in companionable silence. Jenna took the time to watch the heat haze rise from the surrounding shale hills and was overcome by the scenery. This was the edge of the Great Sandy Desert. The magnificence flowed right through to her bones.

A flock of little corellas circled and zigzagged above, calling and cackling to each other in their loud raucous voices. Jenna giggled in response, as if they'd told her some funny feathery joke.

Lynne gave her a confused look from under her hat. 'They're just birds,' she said. Jenna quietened down, but she could feel her spirits lifting higher and higher the further they got into the desert.

With her back towards the vehicle, she could make out a snatch of conversation or a giggle from Shauna every now and then. Once she heard Dan's deep rustic laugh and something in her stomach tightened at the sound. She chose to ignore the response. It would do her no good, anyway. She wasn't interested in him.

* * *

By late afternoon Jenna stood beside the single window of her room in the staff quarters, eyes searching the flat endless country beyond. It was hard to believe she was here on Shiralee Station, in the outback. Hearing people talk about this place was nothing to experiencing it. It was breathtaking. It was beautiful.

She gave her room an appraising look. A single bed took up the space along one wall, the bare mattress not quite hiding the sagging springs underneath. The only other bit of furniture was a small table with a single drawer. There wasn't even a cupboard or wardrobe to hang her clothes. She'd have to make do with neat piles of clothes on the floor at the end of the bed.

Opening her clenched fists, she drew in a deep, calming breath. This cattle station was one of the most isolated places in Australia.

How long will it take him to find me this time?

A familiar panic fluttered in her stomach. Perhaps he wouldn't be able to find her out here—perhaps she'd run so far he wouldn't be able to track her. She'd moved towns twice in as many months, was it enough to lose him? She hadn't seen a hint of Liam for months now. But somehow, she doubted it. Somehow, he always managed to turn up again.

Memories took hold and her eyes filled with reflexive tears as she thought about her father, Joe, the one person she'd truly loved; murdered. Joe was her adoptive dad, but he'd meant more to her than if he'd been her true father. He'd cared for her, nurtured her, loved her and raised her as his own. She didn't remember her biological father and didn't want to know him.

Her fear turned into something much uglier. Anger. Revenge. Shuddering, her hands balled into fists, fingernails scoring into her flesh. One day she would make Liam pay for what he'd done. On her life she made this vow, with only the desert to bear as her witness.

CHAPTER TWO

'Come and I'll introduce you to the rest of the boys,' Dan called down the long corridor of the staff quarters. His voice broke into Jenna's dark contemplation. She dragged on her boots and buried the exhaustion threatening to overwhelm her. Casting one longing glance at the bed, she followed the sound of the other girls' footsteps into the hallway.

The *boys* were slouching in the shade of the machinery shed.

'Thought you might like to meet our new station hands,' Dan drawled.

'What happened to you? Been up to no-good at the pub again?' A rotund man stared at Dan's battered face. 'Chasing some more skirt?' A malicious gleam lit his eyes. 'Keep that up and old Wazza will ban you from the pub for good.'

The grin left Dan's face and the muscles in his jaw bulged as he ground his teeth together.

'You know me, Coshy, always a sucker for a pretty face.' Dan sounded cheery, but the set of his jaw remained rigid.

The fat man's gaze shifted to the three women and he gave them all a welcoming grin. But the smile never really made it to his eyes and Jenna got the uncomfortable feeling she was being watched by some kind of local venomous snake.

'This guy, who's so good at stating the bleeding obvious is Tony Coshyian. Coshy for short,' Dan introduced. 'He's the station mechanic.'

Coshy looked at them from under the wide brim of his liberally stained hat. He flicked the end of a leather stock whip with one hand, his dirt encrusted fingernails stained a dark red by the unforgiving soil. His other hand lay across his protruding belly, cradling a half-smoked cigarette.

'Not more bloody newbies. Bernie's going to love this,' Coshy muttered as he brushed an ever-present fly away from his face. Jenna flashed Coshy a quick half-smile when Dan introduced her but kept her features blank. For no reason other than gut instinct, Jenna knew she wouldn't get on well with this man. There was an air of unfulfilled entitlement beneath his easy façade of affability. She'd gotten used to listening to her gut, and her gut told her Coshy was dangerous.

'Hi, I'm Shauna.' The large woman stuck her hand out for him to shake. Jenna had to stifle a laugh as Coshy took an involuntary step backwards when she got right up in his face. He gave his fingers a quick wipe on his blue stained flannelette shirt—which was just as dirty as his hand—to return her grasp. Lynne followed, holding out her hand, but with a little less aggression and more of her toothy warm smile.

Next in line, sitting unobtrusive and relaxed on the ground, was a whip-thin man whose chocolate brown skin looked smooth and inviting.

He gave each girl a boyish, shy smile, and said, 'Hiya, missus.'

'This is Eddie *The Moon* Magic. We all just call him Moon, on account of his howling at the moon some nights.' Dan gave Moon a genuine smile as he walked by. Jenna would bet her last pair of Blundstones he was a lot older than his baby-faced looks conveyed. There was wisdom in his ageless gaze.

The last man in line held himself motionless and upright. A freshly rolled smoke dangled between two nicotine stained fingers. His face was lined with sun and laughter. Jenna liked him straightaway.

'Meet Lex Davies. He's got lots of nicknames, but he won't let us use any of them,' Dan laughed.

Lex removed his hat and smiled. 'G'day, ladies. Good to meet you all.' The once brown hat looked like it'd survived a hundred stampeding horses thundering their hooves over it. Battered and dusty, with holes here and there, it fitted on Lex's head seamlessly. He was tall and thin, legs somewhat akimbo from too many long hours spent in the saddle. This must be the leading-hand she'd mistaken Dan for back at the pub.

Lex's gaze shifted from the women towards Dan.

'How bad are you hurt, mate?' he demanded. 'Has Cookie had a look at your face yet?' There was no recrimination in Lex's words, and no question of blame, just genuine concern for Dan's wellbeing.

'Yes, Cookie's already seen me.' Dan tilted his chin up in a hint of defiance. But under Lex's calm gaze his shoulders dropped, and a ghost of a smile began to play over his damaged face. 'It's damn near impossible to keep a secret from that woman anyway.' Lex just nodded and waited. 'Nothing's broken, just bruises that'll heal in a few days. Don't worry, I'll be fine to carry out my full workload.'

'That's good.' The expression on Lex's face didn't change as he held Dan with a steady gaze, but Jenna understood a silent conversation was going on between the two men. Dan's chin lowered when he could no longer meet Lex's eye. Dan's version of an apology?

'You'd better take them to meet Bernie.' Lex's voice held a warning as he caught Dan again with his direct gaze. 'He didn't have a good night last night.'

'Right. Thanks.' Dan turned on his heel. 'Come on, let's go and meet the boss.'

'What does he mean, *he didn't have a good night*?' queried Lynne as she hurried to keep up with Dan.

He drew in a sharp breath and slowed. 'I guess you may as well know, you'll find out soon enough anyway.'

'Know what?' chimed in Shauna, eager not to be left out of the conversation.

'Bernie's a decent sort of bloke, most of the time,' Dan said with a hint of protectiveness, 'but every now and then he's known to go off the rails a little.'

'Off the rails? What does that mean exactly?' asked Jenna, now also intrigued.

'His wife left him a couple of years ago. Said she couldn't cope with this isolation anymore. So she just up and went, and took the kids with her. Bernie's never been the same since. Every now and then he sinks so low he consoles himself with the booze.'

'He's a drunk?' said Shauna bluntly.

'That's a fairly harsh way of putting it.' Dan's voice was quiet. 'But yes, that's it in a nutshell. It doesn't happen too often, most of the time he does an okay job of managing this place.'

'So, everyone just puts up with him?' Shauna's undiplomatic questions were beginning to irritate Jenna. 'Why doesn't the owner just sack him and get someone better in?'

'A few of us have been wondering the same thing lately,' Dan admitted. 'Bernie is a friend of Ted, the owner, so maybe he's giving him some leeway, we don't really know. What we do know is this place is slowly but surely going downhill, and none of us can do a damn thing about it.'

'That's sad,' muttered Jenna.

'Yes, it is.' Dan glanced back at her. 'This station has huge potential, if only it were properly managed.'

They continued in silence as he led them towards what would once have been an imposing homestead. Snaking away from the left-hand side of the shed was a maze of large yards bounded by tall, rough-hewn wooden railings. Set back even further to the left sat the stable and more wide paddocks. Jenna slowed and stared at the horse silhouettes in the dying evening light.

'Do you want to meet some of the horses?' Dan must've noticed her searching gaze and she hesitated, embarrassed.

'Only if we have time. Won't Bernie be expecting us?'

'Bernie can wait.' Dan changed direction. She ignored the dark frown Shauna sent her behind Dan's back. 'We keep up to fifty horses here on the station, so we can rotate them. Some get spelled in the outer paddocks, while we work the others.'

They entered the yards, overhung by large old peppermint trees, offering shade and protection within their drooping leaves. Instead of stopping to look at the horses eyeing them with curious gazes, Dan led them through a murky entry to the large stables. Down the length of the left-hand side were six or seven individual stalls.

'This is where we keep the *special horses*. These horses are either in need of some TLC, or belong to one of the staff. The rest of them just get the run of the yards.'

'Who have you got in here today?' Lynne strolled towards the closest stall, where two pricked ears pointed at her from out of the gloom.

'That's Winemaster's Pardon, the boss' stallion.'

'He's a beauty.' Shauna sidled closer and reached out her hand. The ears laid back on the black head and the eyes rolled in their sockets. Shauna withdrew her hand in hasty retreat.

'He might be a beauty but that's about all the good he's ever gonna do this station,' snorted Dan. 'Personally, I don't know why the boss insists on keeping him, no one else can ride him and he's useless at stock work.'

Jenna hung back from the group, checking the rest of the horses in the stables. She was drawn to the stall at the end of the line.

'Hello there. Who're you?' She breathed gently into the gelding's nostrils. 'You're gorgeous.' He swung his large, square head around and gave her a curious stare. His colour was a glorious rich, dark chestnut. She glimpsed his hindquarters, which looked like they'd been spattered with white paint.

'An appaloosa,' she said aloud.

'That's Chainsaw.' Dan sauntered over to where she was examining the horse. 'I wouldn't go too close, he's not that pleasant either. Actually, he's worse than the stallion. He belongs to Lex.'

'Chainsaw. It's an interesting name.' Jenna's eyes never left the gelding.

'He used to be a rodeo horse. A bucking bronco, you know the type. He's really only half Appaloosa, his sire was an Australian Stock horse.'

'Not just good-looking but intelligent too,' said Jenna softly.

'He was a good bucker as well. He won Lex a pretty penny in his day. But that tends to make him an unreliable stock horse now. Lex is trying to wean him into mustering. It'd be a shame to have to get rid of such a beautiful horse in his prime.' Dan leant against the stall, looking at Jenna as he spoke. 'One thing you can say about him though, he's a big-hearted horse.'

'Like Phar Lap,' murmured Jenna, letting the horse nuzzle at her cupped hand.

'Yeah, kinda.'

'I'd like to ride him if Lex will let me.'

Shauna's patronising snort said it all.

'It can't hurt to ask Lex,' said Dan, still leaning his tall frame up against the wood, considering Jenna with a thoughtful gaze. She turned from her contemplation of the horse to find those intriguing amber eyes fixed on her. Butterflies erupted in her stomach at the intensity of his gaze. Even with the bruise turning his cheek a nasty shade of purple, Jenna recognized how handsome Dan was. In some ways the bruising gave him even more of an appealing, rugged look.

She'd almost forgotten what it was like to be attracted to a man.

Turning her head to watch the horse, she tried to block out the disturbing awareness of him. She couldn't allow herself to get close to anyone on this station. It was too dangerous. Somehow, she'd have to learn to work side-by-side with Dan without letting this magnetism get the better of her.

'Would you ask him for me?' She kept her gaze centred on the horse.

'If you like.'

Her initial instincts told her Dan was easy-going and approachable, never taking anything, or anyone, too seriously. But the way he'd just looked right into her—almost through to her soul—there was a deeper sense of self-awareness within him.

'Thanks.' She shouldn't care what lurked beneath the surface of Dan's character. And starting right now, she was going to make it her purpose *not* to care.

* * *

Bernie's gaze travelled the length of each of them from top to toe disdainfully, as if he were studying cattle. Disappointment was evident on his round face. Dan cringed inwardly. Lex had been right, Bernie wasn't in a good mood. The women all stood in a line with hands by their sides as if being inspected by a military drill sergeant.

'What the frigging hell have you brought me this time?' Bernie rounded on Dan, his pug-like features screwed into a frown. Dan had the height advantage but this was his boss, so he took a step backwards. A sharp stab of pain sliced through his ribs as he moved and he fought to keep his features blank.

'Not only are they newbies, but they're *girls* as well.'

'They're the only ones who answered the ad. You know it's hard to get workers up here.' He flashed them all an apologetic smile over the top of Bernie's head, praying they played along with his charade. 'Lynne and Shauna both have experience working on farms, and Jenna's not new to being a jillaroo either.' Dan threw an expectant glance towards Jenna, but just as she opened her mouth to elaborate, Bernie cut in.

'Well she doesn't look like she'd stick to the ground in a small gust of wind.'

Thankfully Jenna had the forethought to say nothing. He wanted to open his mouth and retort but gritted his teeth and balled his fists by his sides instead. He needed this job. Needed it badly. Not many other stations would hire a man with his background. He was lucky Shiralee was so short of hands. But it still cut deep when he had to listen to Bernie's bullying tactics and say nothing in return.

Bernie was obviously hung-over from his binge last night. God, please let the women make allowances for Bernie's behaviour. Please. It was a lesson they needed to learn if they wanted to keep their jobs. The cost of holding his tongue became a physical pain in his guts, while he stood and listened to Bernie harangue the three jillaroos.

'How is she going to drench a frigging steer,' he said, finger pointing at Jenna. 'Let alone pull one to the ground. And this one.' His finger moved towards Shauna. 'Well she's just plain fat! I'm not even sure she'll be able to get on a horse.' Shauna's eyes narrowed dangerously and she opened her mouth to speak, but Lynne laid a quiet hand on her arm. Shooting daggers at Bernie, she bit her lip and kept quiet. Thank God for Lynne. He was going to owe these women big-time, once Bernie had finished with them.

'We'll have to find an extra strong horse for her.' Bernie's eyes had taken on a sullen, sunken quality. 'I'll give you all a three-week trial,' he announced. 'And if I deem any of you unfit to do the work, you're gone. Outta here. Do you understand?'

'Yes, sir,' they all replied, sullen but civil.

'Harding has promised to send me over two of his ringers in time for the first muster,' Bernie continued. 'They're not doing so well over there this season. Their cattle numbers are down, so he can spare a few men to help us.'

Bernie turned towards Dan as he spoke, and as if seeing him for the first time his frown deepened.

'What the hell happened to you, boy?' He leaned in for a closer look. 'Been fighting again, huh?' Bernie shook his head. 'You know I don't take kindly to men who can't control themselves. Or drink too much. Don't let me see you like this again, Dan, or you'll be out on your ear, do you hear me?'

The irony of Bernie's statement didn't escape Dan, but he nodded his head, not trusting himself to say anything.

Bernie stalked back inside, banging the fly-screen door behind him, and they all let out a collective sigh.

'Sorry,' Dan apologized as soon as Bernie was out of earshot. 'You caught him on a bad day.'

25

'I can't wait to see him on a good day,' Jenna spat, glaring at the blank screen door. He had to hide a smile. 'Oh, he makes me so mad.' It seemed Bernie might be the first person to have broken though that barrier of self-control. It was the first time he'd seen her show any true emotion all day. She pushed past him in her hurry to get off the veranda and her close proximity set off a tingle of awareness. Same as when she'd helped him after the fight.

He strode along the veranda after her. She was just another station hand, he needed to remember that. And she'd already made it abundantly clear she wasn't interested in him. Why on earth would he want to waste another thought on a woman who wasn't keen to share her secrets?

'He's got a bloody cheek.' Shauna huffed like a disgruntled chicken. 'Calling me fat. How dare he!'

'We just try and stay out of his way when he's had a bender like this.' Dan shrugged, releasing some of the tension from his shoulders and took the steps off the veranda two at a time. 'I'm sure you'll all pass the three-week trial with no trouble.' Marching out in front, he tried to put Jenna out of his mind. Treat her like any other newbie. 'Come on I'll give you a tour of the place and then it'll be dinner time, so you can meet Cookie. She'll love having you three around, she gets a bit lonesome here with only men for company.'

'Cookie's a woman?' asked Lynne in her cheery voice.

Out of the three, she seemed to have been least affected by Bernie's bad mood. Like a ray of sunshine, she was always happy and willing to help. She'd do well on the station. Dan was glad to have her around.

'It's good to know us girls won't be outnumbered by you boys.'

'Yeah, Cookie's been here for longer than most of us. God knows why she stays, but she's the rock that keeps this place together. Watch out though, she's not one to take anyone's crap, even if you are a girl.'

'What's a ringer?' asked Shauna, butting into the conversation. 'Bernie said something about sending over some ringers.'

Dan hid his amusement at Shauna's ignorance. 'You're a ringer, Shauna, and so are Lynne and Jenna. Well, you will be once you get your horse skills up to par.'

'I am?'

Shauna's honest surprise was almost Dan's undoing and he coughed to hide a laugh. This girl had a steep learning curve ahead of her. Not for the first time, Dan wondered why she was here. Station life wouldn't sit well with her overinflated ego. He'd just have to wait and see. Maybe she was a hard worker, or maybe she'd be good with the horses, who knew. He tried not to allow his initial judgement telling him she was going to be trouble—probably lazy and a pain in the arse as well—to affect his manner towards her. If she kept up this immature behaviour, though, she was going to make it difficult. He was going to have to put a stop to her overtly flirty advances. A small shiver slithered down his back. She didn't interest him in the slightest.

Making sure his face was impassive, he replied, 'Yes, a ringer is just another word for a stockman. Someone who works with horses and cattle.'

'Oh, cool.' For once Shauna didn't have a lot to say as she digested Dan's words.

Lynne's voice floated to him from behind. 'So, just how big is this station?' Lynne was such a different kettle of fish to Shauna. Why she was hanging around with someone like her, he'd never know.

'It's about two thousand, two hundred and fifty square kilometres,' he replied, continuing his ground-eating strides towards the staff quarters.

'Wow, that's pretty impressive,' replied Lynne in awe.

'Come on, Lynne, stop gushing. It's not that big,' Shauna said scornfully.

Out of the corner of his eye, Dan caught Jenna's slight form pacing along behind him, lithe and petite, listening intently to their conversation. *Focus Dan.*

Lynne gave Shauna a look of wry disbelief. 'Even though it's on the small side for an outback station, it's still ten times the size of the last farm we worked, Shauna. Surely even you have to agree that is big.' For once Shauna didn't reply, so Lynne fired off another question at Dan. 'How many head of cattle?'

'We usually run an average of twelve thousand cattle, but if you ask me we're overstocked at the moment.'

'Why do you say that?'

'We didn't have such a good wet season this year, and although it may look as if there's plenty of green feed right now, it won't take long for all those cattle to eat it down to nothing. I know that none of you have worked a northern cattle station before, so you're in for a surprise when you find out just how hot, dry and dusty this place can get in a very short space of time.'

'Well, that's the exact reason I'm here, for the experience of it. All I can say is, bring it on!' Lynne gave him one of her wide infectious smiles as she strode along beside him with her long legs. Quick as a snake, Shauna appeared on the other side of Dan, shooting Lynne a look of dislike.

'Oh, Jesus,' he moaned under his breath.

* * *

This time as she entered the staff quarters Jenna looked a little closer. The kitchen floor was lined with faded linoleum and the cupboard doors were all in need of a good coat of paint. But it was spotlessly clean. Someone cared for this old building.

She trailed slowly through the kitchen and entered the main dining area. Here the plaster was cracked and peeling, an aged mottled orange colour. But still clean and dust free. There was something written on the walls. She moved in for a better look. The walls were covered in graffiti, signatures and names, dates and sayings, of all the people who'd drifted through this building in the last eighty years. 'Wow,' she breathed in wonder. It was fascinating. The walls were an artefact, charting the history of the property. Jenna studied the scribbles, letting her eyes roam over the scrawled handwriting, trying to get a sense of people's lives through their stories.

A loud thump from Lynne's bedroom down the hall brought Jenna back from her musing. Was Lynne moving furniture? They all had the luxury of a room to themselves. The building was large enough to have housed at least eighteen people and this, more than anything, spoke of the sad state of affairs affecting this station. If it'd been up to its full potential then all of these rooms should've been full, the place humming with noise and bodies and life. But, sadly this wasn't the case. Most likely due to Bernie's incompetence.

Drifting down the long corridor, Jenna looked into her very own bedroom. Paradise. She needed to unpack, make the place feel like home.

She'd got down to arranging the last neat pile of clothing at the bottom of her bed when Lynne's voice drifted up the corridor. 'Jenna, where are you? Dinner's on the table.' Standing for a moment at the end of the bed she took a long time straightening her shirt. Forcing one foot in front of the other she headed towards the kitchen.

Everyone else was already at the table, devouring plates piled high with food. She plonked herself down and took a cautious look at her meal.

Dan finally looked up from his plate and grunted, 'Not hungry, huh?'

Her stomach rumbled. Yes, she was hungry, but she couldn't eat the food in front of her. It was some kind of beef stew and bile rose in her throat at the sight.

'I might just make myself a sandwich.'

'Cookie will be mad if she thinks you don't like her food.' He stopped eating long enough to give her a roguish grin.

'Oh no, it's not that,' she protested just as the front door banged and Cookie marched in.

'What'll I be mad about?'

From the first time Dan had introduced them this afternoon, Jenna liked Cookie. She liked to watch her big arms wobble when she stirred a pot of food, and she liked her open-mouthed rumbling laugh. But Cookie was a red-head and she had the fiery temper to match.

'Jenna doesn't like your food, Cookie,' Coshy spoke up, watching Jenna with delight as she felt her face turn red.

'What's wrong with my food?'

'I ah … Well, it's just that …' Jenna stammered and stumbled getting more and more agitated as everyone stared at her.

'It's not your cooking … It's just, I don't eat meat.' Everyone stopped eating, forks suspended half way to their mouths.

'Ha. You're bloody joking, aren't you?' Cookie's loud laughter broke the deafening silence. 'You do know you're working on a cattle station, don't you?' she asked, through her bubbling mirth.

'Yes, I know that. But it's okay.' Jenna's throat was suddenly thick and it became hard to swallow. They didn't understand, no one ever understood. 'I'll make do, I always have.'

Coshy looked at her in exasperation, a piece of half-chewed food poking through the gaps in his teeth. 'How can you *make do*? That's what we eat out here, frigging meat, meat and more meat!'

'And I'm certainly not going to cook any special meals just for you,' said Cookie, wiping her eyes from her laughter.

'I don't expect you to,' Jenna retorted. Now the backs of her eyes were burning. Shit. The very last thing she needed today was to cry in front of these people. 'I told you, I'll get by.' The words came out with more force than she intended, but anger was replacing embarrassment.

'It's no wonder you're so scrawny,' bellowed Coshy as he patted his own big stomach.

'Do you mind if I ask why you're a vego?' Lynne's voice cut through the sounds of muttering.

'Because I don't believe we're entitled to eat another living being, that's all.' Too late, Jenna realized how belligerent her tone sounded.

'Just asking.' Lynne's indignant frown said it all. 'No need to get so defensive.'

'Sorry,' Jenna apologized. She'd allowed her temper to get the better of her. Again. For the second time today. 'You're right, I shouldn't get so hung up about it, I've heard it all before.' Jenna tried to make her smile seem repentant.

Dan still watched her, his fork hovering just above his plate. 'So, if you don't believe in killing things, then what are you doing working on a cattle station?' His voice was soft, but she heard the touch of irony in it.

She wasn't sure how to answer that question. It was her own personal stumbling block, and she found it hard to keep the justifications right, even in her own head. She was aware she probably looked like an enigma, but she didn't feel like explaining herself right now. She was tired. No, more than tired. Exhausted. It was all she could do just to remain standing.

Holding the tears at bay, she shrugged her shoulders with a nonchalance she didn't feel. Looking directly at Dan, she forced herself to hold firm. For some reason, she knew out of everyone here, Dan would be the one to comprehend the reasons behind her reticence to talk. It was written in the understanding that hovered at the back of his gaze and the interested humour in the curve of his lips. As their gazes locked, her stomach did the same flip it'd done earlier today.

Dan eventually broke the deadlock by saying, 'We need to talk about more pressing things. Our first muster is in a few days. It's already half way through April, so we're running a week or two behind the season as it is.'

Relief flittered through her. Relief and gratitude.

Jenna headed into the kitchen to make herself a sandwich, keeping one ear on the conversation. Cookie followed her, muttering good-naturedly under her breath about vegetarians being a pain in the arse.

An hour later, Jenna tried to get comfy on the sagging bed with the too-thin mattress. The first night in a new place was never easy. Her body would adjust to the surroundings soon enough. But tonight, bone tired as she was, sleep was still eluding her. Scrubbing a hand across weary eyes she lifted the covers and got quietly out of bed. Maybe a glass of milk might help.

She padded silently on bare feet up the corridor and was surprised to see a light on in the living room. The thought it might be Coshy made her pause. She didn't want to have anything more to do with that man again tonight if she could help it.

Tiptoeing stealthily into the kitchen, she reached up into the top cupboard for a glass. Her hand stopped, hovering half way as the low drone of voices reached her. It wasn't Coshy, it was Cookie and Lex.

'What're we going to do about him, Lex?'

'I don't know.' Lex sounded weary. 'Every time I think he might be learning, he goes and does something stupid again.'

'He's a good man. He'll come around, you'll see. Besides, who else is there to replace you?' Cookie's voice held a teasing note. Behind the teasing, Jenna was sure there was something akin to tenderness as well.

'Don't make light of this,' Lex growled in reply.

'You always knew it'd take time to get rid of that chip on his shoulder. He spent time in jail, Lex. That's a hard thing to get over. The fact he wasn't guilty is something a lot of people tend to overlook. It's a stigma not easily eliminated from people's minds.'

Jenna nearly dropped the glass. Dan had spent time in jail? What for? The idea seemed almost preposterous. Dan wasn't a criminal. Was he?

'I know, I know,' Lex sighed. 'But he'll step up to the plate sooner or later. He has to.'

Jenna stole back to her bedroom without her much needed glass of milk. Dan had spent time in jail. It was a shock revelation she needed time to digest.

It did give her insight into why he'd brushed off the pounding he'd taken in the fight earlier today. If he'd spent time in jail, then he'd probably witnessed a lot of that kind of violence. Probably been subjected to it himself. But it didn't explain why he seemed to think he deserved the punishment. As if he needed to atone for something. Snuggling back down into her lumpy mattress, Jenna pondered that question until she finally fell into a deep slumber.

CHAPTER THREE

Jenna glanced around at the others who stood in the early-morning dark, silhouetted in the single spotlight pointed at the horse yards. They were waiting for the call to mount up. It was the day of the first muster. Tiny wisps of steam escaped from warm mouths and the only noise was from the horses, which moved around, nervous and agitated. The bridle jingled a tune as her horse chomped on his bit. Jenna hugged her arms around her body and stamped her feet into her boots as the sky began to turn from pale violet to the stronger orange light of day. Cold air seeped in through the tiny gaps in her old duffle jacket, making the hairs on her arms stand up to attention like tiny soldiers.

The two new ringers from the neighbouring station, Pat and Ulrich, had joined them last night in the staff quarters.

Dan introduced them at the dinner table. 'This is Patrick Brown, Pat for short,' he said, pointing towards the shorter of the two.

'Pleased to meet you,' Pat said, holding out his hand. He had dark hair and dark eyes, watching her from a sun-lined face. Jenna judged him to be the older of the two, perhaps in his late thirties, obviously the one in charge.

'Hi, I'm Jenna. Glad you could join us.' Pat nodded his head in reply.

'And this is Ulrich Hensler,' said Dan with a grin. As Jenna reached her hand out the tall man removed his hat and held it in front of his chest in awkward formality. Long blond hair fell to his shoulders, surrounding chiselled features and arresting blue eyes.

'Ulrich is from Germany. He's on work experience for a year.'

Jenna shook his hand, but when she tried to pull it back, Ulrich didn't seem to want to release it again.

'Jenna, that's an unusual name.' His accent was unmistakable.

'Not really.' Jenna twisted her hand politely out of his grasp just as Lynne and Moon ambled up behind her. She stepped away to let Dan do the next introductions and sidled towards the table. Glancing back, she saw Lynne's eyes light up as she took in the symmetrical beauty of Ulrich's face. Jenna dropped her gaze when she noticed the German's eyes following her.

This morning, Pat and Ulrich kept to themselves, huddled with their horses in a corner of the yard.

'Everybody mount up,' Bernie called at last.

Jenna swept into her saddle. The yard came alive with yells and whoops of glee as everyone else followed suit. Gathering up the lead rope of her spare horse, she followed Lex at a quick trot into the soft morning light.

Bernie stared down from his vantage point, standing on the middle rung of the horse-yard fence. He wasn't accompanying them on the muster, but he still liked to preside over the leave-taking. Today Bernie was a man full of stern efficiency, a complete reversal from the day she'd first met him. His face had lost the ugly sneering quality, replaced by a sadness, hinted at in the lines around his eyes.

The Land Cruiser sputtered to life as Coshy put it into gear and took off, wheels churning in the soft dust. The vehicle was piled high with all the gear they'd need for the next ten to fourteen days. It'd taken them close to a whole day to pack all the food rations, petrol, swags, cooking utensils, ropes, spare tack, feed for the horses and a motorbike on a trailer attached behind the car.

Coshy was allocated the job of driving Cookie and setting up base camp near the old stock yards and he wasn't particularly happy about it. At least Coshy would be able to fire up the motorbike once at camp to help the other station hands yard the cattle.

'Look at the dogs, aren't they funny!' Shauna said with a loud laugh.

Jenna surveyed the vehicle as it roared along parallel to them, three heeler cattle dogs, as well as Dan's little kelpie dog, Blue, perched precariously in the trailer with the motorbike.

'Why are they coming, Dan?' Shauna asked.

'The heelers will help flush the cattle from their hiding places out in the desert.'

'The heelers?' queried Shauna. 'Oh, you mean the really ugly ones.' That comment brought a few laughs from those listening. Jenna had to agree. The blue heelers were blunt and squat and full of muscle, like an indomitable wrestler hoping to crush his opponent. Ugly was a good word for them.

'I wouldn't say that too loud near Lex,' laughed Dan. 'He loves his heelers.'

Jenna was riding Chainsaw. The last thing Jenna had wanted was to make a spectacle of herself when she'd asked if she could ride the horse, but that's exactly what'd happened three days ago in the saddle yard.

Quite a few people had gathered, drifting in one by one. Coshy was leaning over the top wooden rung of the saddling yard, the gaps in his teeth more evident with his mouth set to a sneer. It puzzled her as to why he'd taken such a dislike to her. He wasn't enthralled with women station hands in general, he'd made that abundantly clear over the past few days. But he seemed to keep a special spite for her hidden behind his ready smile. Why was he so threatened by her?

Moon also lingered towards the back of the shed, watching from between the shadows of the railings. Lynne and Shauna hung over one corner, cheering her on at the top of their voices.

Dan was nowhere in sight.

Chainsaw's chestnut coat glowed golden-red in the orange heat of late afternoon. He stood facing her, head up and ears pricked in recognition. She opened her mind to him. Some might call what she could do an empathy with animals. Some might even call her a horse-whisperer. But it was much more than that. Her gift went deeper than mere empathy. It worked mainly with horses and dogs, but sometimes there were other animals who would listen to her.

It was also her deepest secret. The only other person who'd understood what she could do was her father. And then Liam.

There was an aura of unease underlying the intense smells of dust and sweat coming from Chainsaw. She let calmness leach from her mind, laying it like a warm blanket over his disquiet.

Putting a hand on the side of Chainsaw's neck she revelled in the strength of the solid wall of muscle, his hair warm and damp with sweat. With a quick, practiced movement she had the bridle over his ears and he accepted the bit in his mouth with a quick shake of his head.

Lex warned her more than once this horse didn't like the restrictions of a saddle and her audience would be expecting some kind of reaction. She caught the big chestnut's deep brown eye as she pulled the girth tight. It wouldn't do to make this look too easy, so he gave a loud snort, his hind legs flying into the air as he danced and cavorted around, putting on a show.

Lex took two long strides out of his corner before she could raise her hand to stop him. He was nervous now, perhaps regretting giving his permission for her to ride the buckjumper.

With one fluid movement, Jenna was up, sitting immobile in the deep stock saddle, her hands resting evenly on the high pommel. A powerful surge of joy at the sheer beauty of being on the magnificent horse's back sent a shiver right through her. Oh, how she longed to hunch over his withers, grab a handful of dark mane and fly swift and sure over the dusty, red sand-dunes.

Chainsaw set off at a fast walk around the saddling yard, giving a few half-hearted little bucks and pig-roots before settling down and acting like the perfect horse.

She'd ridden him every day since then and now she was off on her first muster. A spare horse bumped along beside her left foot, keeping nice a pace with Chainsaw.

The cold of the morning soon gave way to the heat of a desert spring day. The warm coat she'd needed only an hour ago was tied over the pommel of her saddle and tiny beads of sweat formed beneath the brim of her hat. She was still getting attuned to the huge fluctuations of temperature out here. It could get down to near freezing at night, and then up to a scorching forty-degrees Celsius by the middle of the day.

The horses moved along in an easy jog, eating up the miles, conversation amongst the team as sparse as the scattered desert oak trees. The ever-present flies covered everyone's back like hundreds of plump sultanas. They crawled into Jenna's eyes and up her nose. Her horse was also tormented and constantly flicked his tail in irritation. It was easy and peaceful out here in the desert. The only sounds, those of the horse's hooves hitting the red dirt with muffled thuds, and a quiet giggle every now and then from where Shauna and Lynne had their heads together.

Pat and Ulrich rode together at the back of the team. Ulrich made an effort to catch Jenna's gaze whenever she looked back. She resisted the urge to roll her eyes.

Dan rode through the scrub parallel to her and she gave him a surreptitious glance from beneath the brim of her hat. His face had almost recovered from his beating, only a slight dark smudge under his eye highlighted the last of the swelling. The bruising on his ribs had looked pretty nasty when she'd inspected him outside the pub. But he seemed to be sitting in the saddle with ease, so he couldn't be in too much pain anymore; either that or he was very good at hiding it.

He was fluid and skilful when he rode. Never jerked or annoyed the horse, just let it get on with the job. Dan's horse, Domino, was a beautiful big brown bay with a quiet no-nonsense attitude. He wasn't flashy, but he was quick, reliable and intelligent.

Dan and Domino made a great team. She enjoyed watching him ride.

The thought brought her up sharp. The last thing she should be doing was indulging herself with some childish fantasy over Dan. Just because he could ride a horse didn't mean she could swoon all over him. And just because Dan was good to his horse didn't mean he was a good person either. He'd spent time in jail. She needed to keep her distance. *Especially* if he had criminal connections. It was just one more thing to add to her list of reasons to stay away from Dan. She touched the familiar lump of the ring beneath her shirt as she thought about Dan.

Whether it was a subconscious move or not, Chainsaw began to glide slowly closer to Dan's horse, while her mind mulled over the possible reasons Dan might've spent time in jail. Her gaze was drawn to his hands curled around the reins, hovering just above the horse's neck. He had long, tanned fingers, bruised and cut from hard work, but also gentle and forgiving on the animals. Hands that were capable of inflicting violence and mayhem, such as the brawl at the pub, but also sensitive and appealing.

How would those hands feel brushing against the soft skin on her throat? Trailing over the dip of her collarbone, and then lower, down the curve of her breast. Her own hands tightened on the reins at the sudden rush of heat that soared through her. Dan's fingers undoing the top button of her shirt ...

Dan turned his head and caught her staring.

Heat rose in her cheeks and she swore under her breath. Not only was she thinking like some horny teenager, she was blushing like one too.

But she couldn't look away, not even to hide her discomfort. Surprisingly, it was Shauna who came to her rescue as she thundered up behind Jenna, her horse in an awkward canter and nearly careened into Chainsaw, breaking their connection.

'Watch where you're going, will ya,' Shauna yelled as she dug her heels in the white mare they called Flea and took off towards Dan, never once looking back or apologizing.

Much sooner than she'd thought possible, the first camp appeared over a rise in the dunes. There was a helicopter, nestled onto a large red expanse of dirt, already tied down in case the wind decided to pick up later in the day. Bernie employed a contractor to help with the musters. The areas were often too large to cover on horseback alone. They'd all been introduced to Jacko, the baby-faced pilot back at the station.

The Land Cruiser was parked in a flat area under a clump of Mallee trees, and as they rode forward rustic wooden yards sketched themselves out of the shadows from beneath a few straggling river gums.

'Give us a few ticks guys and I'll have the billy on for you.' Cookie held up a packet of black tea leaves and Jenna let out a sigh. Billy tea always tasted so good. Lex instructed them to take off their horses' tack, give them a quick rub down and then hobble them.

'Why do we need to hobble them?' Jenna spoke before she could stop herself.

'Sorry, Jenna, if we don't, the brumbies might come and steal them.' Lex's tone was measured, as if expecting an argument.

And she *was* just about to argue when Shauna interrupted. 'Brumbies … cool! Are there lots out here? Will we get to see some?'

'I'll bet my last ten dollars you do,' chimed in Pat.

'How do you know?' Shauna sounded unconvinced.

'Because me and a few of the other jackaroos over at Hardings like to do a brumby run every season, if the boss lets us.' The topic made Jenna's blood run cold and she shuddered with dislike.

'Do you ever catch any and break them in?' Lynne was oblivious to Jenna's distress.

'Yep every now and then if we get some really good ones, we'll tame a couple of them.'

'What happens to the rest of the brumbies, if they only take a few?' Shauna's lack of knowledge was starting to irritate Jenna. But more than Shauna's ignorance, the idea of where the horses ended up was making her stomach churn.

'They go for dog food mainly, they're a pest out here you know,' Lex interrupted in a matter of fact tone.

Jenna couldn't look at anyone for fear they'd see the white-hot anger boiling inside her. How dare they! How could they do that to those beautiful animals? She turned away, so she wouldn't have to hear more of the conversation. When she put the hobbles on Chainsaw's front legs, she left the chains as long as she could, to give him as much freedom as possible. He lipped gently at the back pocket of her jeans in resignation.

* * *

A cloud of fine orange dust hovered in the air, accompanied by the faint cracking of leather stock whips and whistles, mixed with the barking of excited dogs. Dan urged Domino into a gallop beside a fence made of hessian. They'd built the hessian blind to help guide the cattle towards the waiting yards.

Off to his right, he caught the flash of chestnut followed by another flash of Jenna's blue shirt as she thundered through the scrub after a stray cow. He took off at a tangent, hoping to turn the cow back towards the run before it was too late.

'Turn her, turn her!' Dan cried. 'If we lose her the rest of the mob might follow.'

Jenna urged Chainsaw into a full gallop, the horse's hide rippling in the shadows of the trees, Domino matching him stride for stride. The tired cow slowed, and Chainsaw's shoulder bumped it gently, forcing her around in a half circle until she was heading back towards the open end of the blind.

'Great job,' he shouted, and Jenna gifted him with a happy smile. But there was no time for him to say more, as a large mob of cattle appeared behind them. They looked unsure and desperate, but as soon as they saw the heifer he and Jenna had just pushed into the hessian run they surged ahead to follow her.

Pat and Ulrich appeared down the left flank of the large mob, Pat with his whip cracking, keeping the cows headed towards the gaping funnel of the hessian. They'd been a godsend really. Thankfully, Harding's station was understocked this year. Dan wasn't sure how they would've coped without the two borrowed ringers. Bernie needed to pull his finger out and hire more station hands.

Not that the three women weren't doing an excellent job. Jenna especially, seemed to be taking to mustering like she'd been born to it. He reined Domino in next to her.

'How's the first day going?'

'Amazing.' Her smile was one of exhilarated satisfaction. 'I love it.' There were smudges of dust down her left cheek and her shoulders drooped with exhaustion.

It'd been a long day. They'd started out in the pale, cold dawn, but the quiet morning soon turned into a frantic race against moments in time and the restless cattle. His gelding enjoyed the breathless energy of the chase and Dan's heart pounded right along with his horse's.

Jenna's words came to him. And with a jolt of surprise he realized he loved this job too. Who would've thought that three years ago when he'd applied for a station hand position on some far-away farm that his life would change so much? For the better. Mostly. At first, it'd been to get as far away as possible from Tamworth and his old life. From the stares and whispers and innuendo. But now, he felt … grounded, productive, in control of his own destiny once more. In some ways, he owed Bernie a debt of gratitude. For giving him a chance when no one else would.

'I never realized what a battle of wills it is when you're mustering cattle.' Jenna held the reins in one hand and batted a pesky fly with the other. 'They definitely have a mind of their own. But that's all part of the fun.' He'd noticed she habitually touched something hidden below the opening of her shirt. He caught a flash of a necklace, with a large pendant hanging on it. It might have even been a ring now that he thought about it. Interesting.

'I'm glad you're enjoying it.' Just then, his dog, Blue, hopped up and lay with tongue lolling out, across the pommel of Dan's saddle.

Jenna laughed at the sight. 'He's done that to me a few times today too,' she said. 'And then after he's had a rest, he's off again.'

'Yep, it's a long day for everyone out here, human and animal,' Dan agreed. 'That was the last of the mobs for today. Shall we go over to the yards and see what Lex is up to?'

'Sure.'

He motioned for her to precede him, and Domino tucked his nose in behind the appaloosa's tail. Jenna was so petite, she looked like a child sitting on top of the large horse. He was glad he hadn't allowed her size to prejudice him when they'd first met, because she was much tougher than she looked. And a hard-worker too. He tried to keep his gaze locked onto her straight back but it was inevitably pulled downwards to land on her softly rolling hips as they pitched up and down with the horse's gait. Slim hips and taut legs from all that riding. She filled out her pair of jeans nicely.

He shook his head and muttered under his breath. There he was, doing it again. Thinking about her as something more than just a co-worker. How many times today had he caught himself actively looking for her through the trees to make sure she was okay? But it was more than that. His gaze was drawn to her. Bugger. He needed to get over this self-absorption, or whatever it was, and just bloody well get on with his job.

Lex walked over as they both unsaddled their tired horses and rubbed them down.

'Come over to the yards when you've finished here.'

'Will do,' Dan replied as Lynne and Shauna arrived back at camp.

'You two can come as well,' Lex said in his gravelly voice.

Dan hid his inward groan.

'I'll show you what happens to the cattle after we muster them.'

Shauna was really starting to grate on him. She was the loudest, most annoying person Dan had ever met. Lynne was okay, but with Shauna constantly by her side, it was hard to discriminate between the two sometimes.

He and Jenna strolled over to the yards, and she stood up on the first rung, peering over the high wooden fence with interest. The two other jillaroos arrived right behind them.

'Do you want a hand?' Jenna called to Lex over the fence, surprising Dan yet again. This woman was up for everything `. Dan had seen it all before, but never tired of watching Lex work. He was calm, controlled and never let a flighty mob ruffle him.

'If you like.' Lex tipped his chin towards her in acknowledgement. 'You other girls can watch what we do and then you can have a try, too,' he said as his fastidious fingers rolled a cigarette.

Dan respected Lex. A small, unspoken part of him understood he probably viewed Lex as a bit of a father-figure. A replacement for his own absent father.

'I know you've worked livestock before, Jenna, but these outback cattle are very different from anything you're used to.' His smoke now fashioned exactly to his liking, Lex tucked it into the band on his hat and waded into the throng of cattle. Dan stepped up to the fence and rested his arms over the top to get a better view.

'They're feisty and hard to manage. Don't get on the wrong side of them or you could find yourself flat on your back in the middle of an angry mob.' Lex gave her a quick glance to make sure she understood.

Jenna nodded. 'You make it sound so easy.'

'You'll catch on pretty quick,' he assured her. But as soon as Lex started to wade through the cows, whistling up a blue heeler to aid him, the mood of the cows changed, becoming anxious, turning from him like flocking birds with no set direction. The young calves who tried to stay close to their mothers' swinging udders added their desperate bawling to the ever-increasing din. Dan grinned, this was when things got interesting. Like Lex said, if you took your eyes off them for even a second, they could become dangerous. But Jenna remained as unruffled as Lex. She walked calmly through the mob and manned the race gate, standing on the second rail and leaning over the top of the fence so she could fling it open to let through a designated cow, and then slam it shut again to stop any unwanted ones slipping through. She did a great job. The cows seemed to be almost well-behaved. She didn't send a single cow the wrong way.

Eventually Lex called for Shauna to come and have a go, relieving Jenna.

'Go and grab a cuppa,' Lex yelled to her. 'You deserve it.'

'Okay,' she replied. But she didn't head straight toward the kitchen tent. Instead she walked slowly around the outskirts of the yard, trailing gentle fingers over any protruding part of an animal, be it a wet nose or a hairy rump.

She drew up with a start when she realized Dan was watching her. Her blues eyes were sad, filled with unshed tears and he remembered she didn't eat meat. Perhaps she regretted helping to send these animals to slaughter. It was a dilemma he'd dealt with easily, humans needed to eat after all. He hoped she could come to terms with it as well. His heart was hardened against the harsh reality of life a long time ago.

'You okay?'

She just nodded.

'Come on, let's get that cuppa.'

'Sounds good.' Her face went blank, the emotions no longer showing. Keeping her feelings hidden.

They both took a proffered metal cup from Cookie and stood blowing on their tea.

'It really does taste better out here,' she said. 'Tea is the remedy for everything in the bush.'

'Yep.' He liked listening to her talk. Liked the way she slurped noisily from her cup. Liked her so much he decided to warn her.

'Maybe you shouldn't go back over to the yards for the rest of the afternoon,' he said coolly.

'Why's that?'

'Because Lex will be branding the calves soon.'

'Oh.' Her face paled visibly. Perhaps not quite so good at hiding her emotions after all.

'No, you're right, I think I've done enough today.' She turned towards Cookie, face still pale. 'Do you need a hand with that. I'm good at cutting up veggies and stirring the soup.'

'That'd be great, luv. I can always do with another hand. And these blighters never stop to offer me one.' She waved a beefy arm in Dan's direction and he gave her one of his best smiles in return. Then he put his cup down on the trestle table and forced his tired legs back over to the yards. No rest for him yet. Lex would need his help.

* * *

Blank staring eyes gazed, unseeing towards the ground, mouth open and twisted in a grin filled with pain and tragedy. The pale-yellow moonlight glinted softly off his bald pallet, grey straggling hairs wafting in the slight breeze. In a futile effort she tore at the rope around his neck, breaking her fingernails. But she couldn't untie it, his weight too much for her. Great sobs rose unnoticed from her throat, echoing through the dead night and cascading down the tree trunks to fall unheard on the rough dirt.

'Wake up, Jenna, wake up.' A soft voice sounded close to her ear. Struggling out of her dream, her eyelids flew open to see the familiar mounds of people sleeping, scattered in a haphazard fashion around the low burning campfire. Dan leaned over her.

Lex's face hovered disembodied over Dan's left shoulder, his frown anxious.

Rubbing her face between the palms of her hands she assured both of them, 'I'm fine.' Looking up at them with more strength than she felt, she said, 'I'm really sorry, I didn't mean to wake you. I hope I didn't wake anyone else.' Searching among the jumble of bodies, it seemed no one else was stirring. Her fingers sought out the comforting weight of her mother's ring around her neck and touched it for a fleeting second.

'That's quite all right, I was just checking on the cattle anyway.' Lex could often be found keeping watch as he whiled away his sleepless hours in the small of the night. He stood up and moved off in his unhurried way.

Once they were alone, Dan leaned forward, resting a hand on her shoulder. 'That must've been some bad dream you were having. You were sobbing out loud like your heart was breaking.'

Jenna couldn't look him in the eye. The contact made her aware of just how close he was. She'd been doing so well at avoiding him and now here he was, touching her, bringing all her senses to full alert.

'Sorry,' was all she could think to say. 'It won't happen again.'

He shrugged but seemed reluctant to leave her side, his touch still feather-light on her shoulder. She couldn't make out his features in the dark, backlit as he was by the dying campfire. In profile, his t-shirt stretched across the muscles of his shoulders, giving the impression of masculine energy. He looked at her with unasked questions in his eyes. But she couldn't tell him. She couldn't trust anyone, especially not a man who stirred her emotions as much as Dan did.

'I really am okay, honest. I just have bad dreams sometimes, they don't mean anything.' She tried to raise a cheerful smile, but all she could manage was a small shrug. He remained motionless, his hand still on her shoulder, the darkness a shadow over his face.

It was his unwavering touch that was her final undoing. It seemed to offer shelter and sympathy, things she'd been sorely lacking in recent times. She wasn't used to human contact; it'd been scarce since her father died. A tiny chink in her armour broke at his touch and that was all her pent-up emotions needed.

A big fat tear escaped, tracing a wet trail down her cheek. His left hand came up to grab her by the other shoulder.

'You're not okay, are you?' Another traitorous tear rolled, hot and heavy down her cheek and tiny shudders coursed through her.

Before she knew just how it happened, strong arms surrounded her, his warm chest held firm against her cheekbone.

She couldn't stop it now, the dam burst and she cried like a baby, sobbing soundlessly as the tears streamed down her face. He never said a word, just settled himself more comfortably on the ground and held her, waiting out the tempest.

She hadn't allowed herself to cry like this since the day her father had been killed. After that she'd taught herself to ignore the rabid grief, keep it locked away in a steel trap inside her head. She couldn't afford the luxury of crying when Liam was after her every minute of every day. Why now? And why in the arms of the one man she was trying to avoid at all costs?

Well if she was going to let herself collapse into a puddle of tears, then she may as well do it in Dan's well-built arms. She could hear the slow thudding of his heart in her ear as it pressed against his chest. His fingers brushed across the bare skin of her neck as he re-positioned his hand. The light touch sent a frisson of sensation down her spine, bringing with it an unmistakable flare of heat. Her pulse reacted by becoming erratic and her breathing was suddenly shallow, her sobs now abating. Her body became acutely aware of his male physicality, so close all she had to do was tip her head up just a little …

Shit. This'll never do.

She sat upright, her arms stiffening within his embrace. Scrubbing the back of her hand across the drying tears on her face she drew in a deep, steadying breath.

'I'm better now.'

Also straightening his back, he regarded her with a measured gaze. 'Do you want to talk about it?'

The question hung between them for endless seconds before she answered, 'Not tonight. Maybe some other time.' He didn't probe further, for which she was grateful, but he also seemed reluctant to let her go.

'Thanks for … that. I'm not usually one for crying.' Her apology sounded lame even to her own ears. 'Please go back to bed, so we can both get some sleep.'

His eyes grazed her face as if weighing her words. At last he disentangled his arms and stood up to leave.

'As you wish.' He walked on soundless feet to his side of the smoking fire and climbed back into his swag.

She lay down. Her reaction to Dan gave her much food for thought. From all of Coshy's lewd insinuations, it seemed Dan liked the girls; had the reputation of flitting from one girl to the next, never settling on any one for too long. Fear of commitment, if she dared to guess. Ever since the time she'd first met him at the pub, he'd shown her nothing but friendship. But tonight, she'd felt something more, an eagerness in his embrace, more than just the affable courtesy of letting a friend cry on his shoulder. As if her vulnerability had spoken to an equal vulnerability within him.

The idea of Dan was an intriguing one. He was a good man. He worked hard, he was solid and dependable, he was kind to his horse. But he was also a bad man. He'd spent time in jail, and he was a fighter and a womaniser. Which was the true Dan?

But Dan wasn't really bad. Not when she considered him next to Liam. A shudder ran through her. Liam was evil incarnate. His face would remain etched into her brain. Even though his features had been wreathed in shadow that night he'd killed Joe, her father, she'd documented every harsh line of his hooked nose, every bristling hair of his goatee beard and the dark hues of the dragon tattoo that curled menacingly around his thick neck.

His words came back to her. 'If you'd just agreed to keep paying me the money, then all would still be sweet,' Liam had said to Joe. 'But I can't have you doing stupid things. Like threatening to go to the cops.' Jenna couldn't believe how matter-of-fact he'd sounded, his tone completely normal, as if menacing people was an everyday occurrence. Her father had only groaned in reply as he lay on the ground where they'd dropped him. She willed him to sit up. To fight these men. Tell them they'd made a huge mistake. That they'd got it all wrong. To go away and leave them alone.

'Did you really think you could keep your precious little princess,' Liam gestured expansively towards Jenna, 'a secret forever? It's time Alexander knew about her.'

She didn't have any secrets, and neither did Joe. Did he? What money was he talking about? And who was Alexander?

Her father was in no fit state to argue with these thugs. They must've hit him over the head. He moved slightly, but only managed a feeble lift of his arm.

Then she remembered how the two other thugs had dragged her father up to stand between them while Liam adjusted the rope. Her father was semi-conscious and slumped against them, a lock of limp grey hair falling over his face. They slipped the rope noose over his head and the two of them hauled mightily on the other end.

Jenna had screamed and screamed and screamed as her father's feet dangled off the ground.

Her hand went to her throat in a reflex motion. A lump formed in the pit of her stomach. *Shit*. The dream always did this to her. Left her with a residue of pain and anguish. Of memories. It was going to be a long night.

CHAPTER FOUR

Jenna stifled a yawn and almost dropped the lead rein of the horse beside her. They'd been riding for hours now and she was finding it harder and harder to concentrate on guiding Miya over the uneven ground. Miya was Jenna's second horse, the one she rode when she was giving Chainsaw a spell. She was a little dun coloured mare, very pretty with her black markings and light-coloured face, and a veteran of many a bush muster. They'd been up even earlier than normal moving camp. That coupled with the nightmares of her father made her bone-weary.

At last they rode over the top of a low sand dune and saw their second camp in the distance. The back-drop was a row of red shale-covered hills rising like teeth out of the soft gums of the dusty earth. These unsteady hills would mark the boundary of the area they were to muster. No cattle would venture into the unwelcome desolation of the hills, and no horse would be able to follow without going lame.

As soon as they entered the camp, Coshy pointed at two large drums he'd filled with water from the bore.

'You can water your horses over there.' He waved an arm at them, and then added, 'And some of you could do with a wash yourselves. You bloody well pong!' He held his nose and looked at the three women, all of whom hadn't had a proper wash in days. Jenna knew she was a bit on the smelly side, but she couldn't yet come to terms with the *bush shower*, a plastic bag of bore water, hung from the nearest tree.

Cookie was an old-hand at the bush shower and stripped down inside the meagre cover provided by the hessian walls, offering glimpses of her ample sagging breasts in a manner that defied anyone to say a word. The men all found a convenient reason to stay well out of the vicinity whenever she showered. The other women were not yet sure if they'd be afforded the same courtesy.

An hour later, Jenna was scouting the best spot to situate the bush shower when an ear-piercing scream shattered the suffocating heat. It sounded like Shauna. Last time Jenna had seen her she was heading out towards the bush dunny, a roll of toilet paper grasped in her hand. Jenna flung down the heap of hessian and took off towards the top of the nearest dune.

Another scream rent the air, but this was not Shauna, this was much deeper and more guttural; the sound of an enraged animal. Jenna knew what kind of animal made that roar and she ran even harder. She topped the dune and there was Shauna a little way in front of her, standing absolutely still, like a rabbit caught in the glare of oncoming car headlights.

In front of Shauna stood a horse. It was dark brown and huge. Dirty, with tangled mane and tail, his whither looming high above Shauna's head. This wasn't one of their tame stock horses.

Shauna had got her wish to see a brumby. Much closer than she'd ever imagined. This horse was a wild stallion and he wasn't happy. Shauna must've stumbled across him as he'd been sizing up the area, contemplating a raid to steal some of their domestic horses. Now he saw Shauna as a threat to both himself and his herd.

'Don't move, Shauna. Just stand still,' Jenna called.

The stallion pawed the ground and gave another challenging scream. The dust rose thick and choking around him as he wheeled and stamped, defying her.

Jenna crooned quietly to the horse, 'It's all right, we aren't going to hurt you.' But this horse wasn't listening to her, instead he took a few propping steps towards Shauna, nostrils flared. It was no good, she'd have to get closer to him. Physical contact always helped her make a connection. She weighed up her options. Maybe Shauna was in such a state of shock she wouldn't notice what Jenna was doing.

Walking towards the infuriated horse, she gave a low whistle. The stallion's ears—which had been plastered flat and menacing against his head—flicked up and forwards. Jenna advanced with slow steps until she was level with Shauna.

Never taking her gaze from the stallion, she muttered out of the side of her mouth, 'You should go now!' Shauna took off, scrabbling on all fours back up the hill, her red hat sliding sideways and covering most of her face.

Jenna continued her deliberate advance, not afraid of the huge animal who could kill her with one blow of a well-aimed hoof. As he watched her, his body language changed, the tense corded muscles in his neck relaxed, curiosity replaced anger in his eyes. Finally, she took the last step and laid a gentle hand on his shoulder and he dropped his head to meet hers. He whickered a greeting.

'What do you think you're up to?' Jenna crooned. 'You'd better get out of here, or those men over there are going to come and hunt you down and take your mares.'

The stallion snorted in contempt. She ran her hand over his coat, covered with a fine film of red dust. He was the epitome of a stallion in his prime, arrogant and wilful, all hardened muscle and strong sinew and Jenna revelled for a few seconds in the sheer wildness of him. He would never be cowed by anyone, and he'd fight to the death to protect his herd. For a second, Jenna wished her life could be so straightforward.

'Go on, get out of here before anyone else sees you. And don't come back,' she added, smacking him on the shoulder. He wheeled in the dust, cantering off in the direction of his herd, waiting in a small copse of trees. She could just make out a flash of a chestnut hide and the swish of a black tail as he led them out of sight.

Maybe she could go with them.

She was so caught up in her own thoughts she never heard Dan approaching.

* * *

'Jenna, what are you doing?' He kept his voice quiet, so as not to startle her. She whipped around to face him. Traces of guilt hovered in the lines around her mouth, but she quickly schooled her features into that blank face he was becoming used to. What did she have to be guilty about? The more he got to know her, the more secrets she seemed to be keeping. But he was determined to get to the bottom of this one. What the hell did she think she was doing, letting a wild animal get so close to her. She could've been badly hurt. Brumby stallions were notoriously unpredictable.

'Dan! I didn't hear you coming, you scared me.' She almost sounded accusing.

'You didn't answer my question.' He kept his features as impassive as hers, not wanting to show how concerned he really was. He wouldn't let her know how his blood had run cold when he'd crested the top of the dune to see her mere inches from the wild brumby. And then it'd looked like she'd reached up and patted the horse in a deliberate move and his heart had gone into overdrive, a huge hit of adrenaline jolting through him. But he hadn't made a noise for fear he might spook the horse. It'd taken every shred of willpower to stand where he was, as she remained within striking distance of those vicious teeth.

Now she was looking up at him with those piercing blue eyes and he could almost see her mind racing. A frown appeared on her forehead.

'How … how long have you been there?' She stumbled a little over her words.

'Long enough.'

There was rebelliousness in the tilt of her chin as she stared up at him.

He held her gaze for just a fraction longer than necessary, hoping to coerce a confession out of her. Instead a spark—a flash of something—lit behind her guarded eyes, and he felt an echo blaze through him. It hinted at a powerful magnetism, a connection he couldn't ignore. The impact made him want to take a step backwards, but she was the first to wrench her eyes away.

Grinding his teeth, he lowered his gaze. *She's not for you. Not your type.* He liked his relationships brief and simple, with no commitments and no heartbreak. It was easier that way. Jenna would want more than just a one-night stand from him. And to be fair, she *deserved* more than one night of lust. Plus, they worked together. He wasn't going to ruin their working relationship. It'd make things awkward. Or perhaps drive her away. The station needed as many hands as it could get right now. If only he could ignore the way her soft skin had felt under his fingers, and how small and vulnerable she'd been in his arms as she cried.

He focused on the ridge-line behind her, dragging his thoughts away from the memory of their intimacy last night.

He took a measured step backwards and spoke, a little sharper than he intended, 'Don't you know how dangerous a brumby stallion can be?'

Tiny beads of sweat formed on her brow as she bit her lip. She wouldn't meet his eyes for many beats of his heart. Then her shoulders hunched into a stubborn line.

'Of course I do.' Her voice held an icy warning. 'And that's why I was scaring him away.'

He quirked his lips in a sceptical grimace. So, she wasn't going to give him an explanation. No ordinary person could walk straight up to a brumby like that and get away with it. There was something else going on.

'It looked more to me like you were *letting* him get away!'

'I don't know what you mean.' She spun on her heel and turned her back on him, but not before he caught her blue eyes flashing with defiance. It was obvious she was lying, but about what exactly? 'I was just trying to help Shauna, and I was damn lucky that horse was as scared of me as I was of him. Are you implying I should've tried to catch him? On my own?' She stomped back through the growing dusk towards the camp. Putting on such a good show she almost had him believing her as he followed a few steps behind. 'He just ran away from me, there wasn't much I could do about it,' she said with a tone of finality.

'Right,' he muttered. His guts still told him she was lying, but there was no point in continuing the argument. Anger at her unwillingness to tell him the truth turned into anger at himself for caring. Caring about her wellbeing. He clumped along behind her the rest of the way back to camp with a clenched jaw.

But there was one more question that'd been bugging him all day. He drew in a few calming breaths and said, 'Jenna, I just wanted to make sure you were really all right, you know … after last night.'

Her shoulders slumped, and he knew he'd hit a nerve. The only other time he'd seen a woman weep as hard as Jenna did last night was the day he'd come home from school to find his mother lying on the floor. She was moaning and howling uncontrollably, and Dan had been frightened beyond belief. That was the day his father had left them. Dan was ten years old. But from that day onwards he became the self-proclaimed head of the family. Who else was going to look after his brothers and mother? A part of him wanted to reach out to Jenna, to help her in a way he hadn't been able to help his mother that day, so long ago. He grabbed her elbow, turning her so he could see her face.

'You sounded so—'

'Like I said before, Dan, I have bad dreams.' She didn't let him finish. 'I've learned to live with it. I barely even remember them in the morning.' She glanced quickly at him, eyes steely. 'I'll make sure not to wake you next time.'

'That's not what I meant,' he growled as Jenna propelled herself forwards again. But it was too late to pursue the topic as they stepped into the campsite. There was a buzz of conversation, the camp astir like a hornet's nest. Shauna was telling everyone about her encounter with the brumby. Lynne, Cookie, Pat and Ulrich were gathered around her with Lex leaning on a tree nearby listening and Moon still hurrying in from the outskirts.

Dan and Jenna arrived in time to hear Shauna say, 'And then he bloody well took off over the dunes.' There was a triumphant look on her face. 'He won't be coming back anytime soon.'

'Strewth, Shauna, that was so brave of you.' Lynne ogled her friend with awe. 'I would've been terrified. And I certainly wouldn't have been brave enough to go right up to the bloody thing and yell to scare it away.' she continued, eyes alight with glee.

'Nah, I wasn't scared at all,' Shauna retorted, looking sideways as Dan stopped beside her.

Jenna made an unladylike sound but didn't say a word. Dan didn't feel like calling Shauna out on her tale, either. Really, what was the point?

'Did you guys see the brumbies too?' Lynne asked Dan. 'Or did Shauna scare them off before you arrived?'

'Jenna saw everything, and she told me what happened,' he replied, not taking his level gaze away from Shauna's face. Her grin fell imperceptibly. Dan turned to ask Lex a question, but as he did so he noticed the hard, glittering stare Shauna threw Jenna's way as she strode off. Shauna didn't like being crossed, it seemed. It made him determined to keep a closer eye on her interactions with Jenna from now on.

'Tell me more,' Lynne interjected. 'What exactly did the stallion look like? I've heard brumbies can be pretty mangy looking. Was he all dirty and disgusting?'

Moon glanced over at Lex, his conspiratorial look echoing Lex's disbelieving grimace. At least they seemed to have guessed some of the lies Shauna was spinning. He knew Lex wouldn't be fooled that easily.

'Maybe we should organize a quick brumby run, Ulrich.' Pat nudged the young jackaroo, who gazed at him hesitantly. Poor kid, probably didn't even know what a brumby run was. Much less appreciated where the animals were going to end up afterwards. Ulrich stared after Jenna's retreating back and Dan hid a grin. Not only was he clueless, but lovesick as well.

'You can do that on your own time, not on ours,' Lex replied brusquely as he headed back towards the campfire and dinner. Dan was grateful to Lex. He could never agree to sending those poor animals off to become pet food, it seemed like such a waste, even if they were a pest out here.

The horses were kept well hobbled and a guard was posted for the next four nights they were at camp number two. Jenna argued with Lex that the brumbies wouldn't be back after their scare, but he wouldn't have it any other way. He didn't want to lose even one horse to the wild band.

Jenna was right—the brumbies never returned. And somehow Dan wasn't surprised.

* * *

It took all Jenna's self-control not to go tell Shauna what a lying cow she was. She couldn't let her temper get the better of her, not with Dan already suspicious of her behaviour towards the brumby. It'd attract more attention, which she didn't need. But goddamnit, Shauna rankled her so much.

Taking a deep, steadying breath, Jenna laid her hand on the smooth bark of the nearest snappy gum, using it as an anchor to stop herself heading back into the camp. She'd stay here, on the outskirts until her anger cooled. She grabbed the ring around her neck and gave the chain a few annoyed tugs.

It wasn't just Shauna who was making her head reel, however. Her righteous rage was mixed with a good dose of something else. Was it confusion? Or remorse? All because of the way Dan treated her. Because of the compassion he showed her, even in the face of her cold rejection. It made her so distracted that for a few seconds of madness, she'd actually entertained the idea of telling him everything. He'd seen her go up to the stallion, but there was no way he'd ever figure out exactly what she'd done. Her gift was something that just couldn't be explained. And it was better left that way. The less people who knew about what she could do the better.

But it was more than the sharp insight she'd seen in his eyes today putting her off-balance. It was the residue from being held in his arms last night. It'd been so long since anyone had even cared about her state of mind, let alone shown empathy. There'd been no one since her father died. Up until last night.

The memories of her nightmare still hovered around the edges of her mind, waiting to slide like an insidious snake back in an unguarded moment. Jenna placed her spine against the sun-warm bark and slid down until her bottom hit the ground. Resting her head on her arms she tried to quiet her heavy breathing and the clamouring emotions in her chest. The memories became louder in her head and against her will she was taken back to the fateful night her dad had died.

Liam's words echoed in her head. 'She's my ticket back in with Alexander. He wants his daughter back and I'm going to be the one to give her to him.'

She could still hardly believe what she'd heard. Alexander was her biological father. It shocked her beyond belief to find out those two incomprehensible truths. Liam, the murderer, knew where her biological father was, and her father wanted her back. But she knew without being told, there was going to be no happy families at the end of her story. If Alexander was prepared to send a hired gunman, a killer, a madman and his team of thugs to find her, then he wasn't a person Jenna wanted to know. Her mother had abandoned her as a baby, left her with kind-hearted Joe, who'd eventually adopted her. And now it was becoming clearer, exactly who and what her mother had been running from.

What does he want with me, she asked herself for the umpteenth time. She was no closer to finding out, and it seemed to be critically important. Liam and his mob of gangsters were prepared to kill for this man. Jenna worried her bottom lip with her teeth, deep in thought. Perhaps when she got back to the station she might ask Cookie if she could borrow her iPad to search the internet. Her last couple of searches had turned up nothing, but maybe this time she might get lucky. She screwed her hand into a fist and smacked it into the ground. Alexander was the key to her whole life and he was a goddamn ghost.

Liam's gibe haunted her almost as much as not being able to find Alexander. 'And don't think the cops are going to help you either,' he'd said. 'Some of me best mates are cops.'

Those words still sent chills skidding down her spine. At first, she hadn't believed him. Her faith in the law to protect innocent victims of crime was naively unshakable. How could Liam's reach possibly be that long? Or that strong?

She'd found out early the morning after her father died, after she'd escaped Liam's clutches. Arriving at the local police station, she spewed out her garbled story about a group of thugs murdering her father. At first the local Sergeant had been conciliatory and full of sympathy, dispatching a car to check out her story, while he got her statement. But as Jenna sat in the small interview room, sniffling into her cup of tea, a Constable in the next room received a phone call. Then he started to cast sideways glances in her direction through the doorway. Suspicious glances. And her instinct told her something was wrong.

A few minutes later the Constable interrupted the Sergeant's chat with Jenna, flashing a sheet of paper quickly as he spoke. Jenna caught a glimpse of the paperwork. It was an arrest warrant in her name. She was wanted by the police for questioning over a hit and run incident in the next town over.

Then she believed Liam.

Both police officers left the room to talk in hushed tones. That's when Jenna had snuck out while her dogs raised a ruckus at the main entrance.

If the police took her into custody, even on phoney charges, it wasn't beyond any stretch of her imagination that Liam would somehow get her released to him. Or to someone on his payroll. She'd never trust the cops again.

So she went on the run, finally stopping at a town in the next state. But it only took him three weeks to find her. She'd happened to see Liam walking down the main street of the town when she went in to buy supplies and ducked into an alleyway just in the nick of time.

After that she became more careful, changing her name from Emily and using her middle name, Jenna, instead. She'd also reverted to her mother's maiden name, which ironically, was Smith. It seemed to work for a while. She'd been safe at the next place for nearly six months. Then she heard someone was asking about her around town and knew Liam had returned. After that she'd only stayed two months in most places. Three months tops.

Now, two years later, with her back to the trunk of a tree out in the middle of the desert, she was still no closer to an answer as to how to escape Liam's dogged pursuit. Funny, but she was almost happy out here, in the isolation. Enjoying the hard work and the beautiful scenery. Almost forgotten about her predicament for a while, if that were indeed possible.

CHAPTER FIVE

The screen door slammed, and the kitchen was filled with a swearing whirlwind. Dan looked up from where he was sitting at the large table.

'The old bastard fired me. I can't fucking believe it!' Shauna banged her fist down on the bench, making a stack of plates rattle. Lynne's face was aghast, the spoon half-way to her mouth spilled its contents, unnoticed on the stove.

It looked like Bernie had told Shauna the news. She wasn't taking it well. He shouldn't have expected anything less.

'What … How … Why? He can't do that.' Lynne was lost for words.

'Well he can, and he did!' Shauna thumped around the kitchen bench, her face streaky red with anger. 'I can't fucking believe it,' she said for a second time. 'He called me up to that big bloody house cool as you like and told me I'd failed my three-week probation and to go and pack my bags, that I was going home.'

A flash of guilt lit up Dan's insides. This wasn't his fault. Not really. She brought it on herself.

'Did he say why? Surely he must've had a good reason.' Shock was stamped all over Lynne's face.

'Of course I asked him why. I stood up to that dickhead and demanded he give me a good reason for firing me.'

Shauna stood hands on hips and legs akimbo. 'But he wouldn't answer me.' Shauna's face became even redder with the memory.

Dan glanced over to where Jenna stood at the other end of the table, knives and forks in one hand. She looked shocked also. Flicking him a questioning glance, she went back to quietly laying the cutlery on the table.

'Someone must've said something to him. Something that turned him against me.' Shauna's seething gaze flew around the room—and settled on Jenna. 'It was you, wasn't it?' she spat as she advanced towards Jenna. 'You've always hated me right from the start. You lied to Bernie, didn't you? You made up bloody lies to get rid of me!'

Dan tensed at Shauna's words. Of course she'd try and blame someone else for her failings. It was just one more reason why she didn't belong on this station.

'What? No! I never did anything like that, Shauna.' Jenna was so flabbergasted she seemed almost lost for words.

'Yes you did.' Shauna jabbed a fat finger right in the middle of Jenna's chest, pushing her backwards.

Dan stood up. This had gone far enough. 'Now hold on there, Shau—'

Jenna spoke over the top of him. 'I'd never betray anyone like that, and you know I wouldn't, Shauna.' Jenna stood her ground. Good on her. He liked the way her blue eyes flashed, determined not to let the large woman get the better of her. 'Yes, it's true we're not the best of friends,' she agreed. 'But I'd never dob on you, or anyone else for that matter. Why would I do such a thing when this station needs all of us to keep it going right now?'

'Oh, you're such a little-miss-perfect, little-miss-golden-girl who can do no wrong. I know what kind of a conniving manipulating bitch you really are. You smile at all the boys to get them to come to your beck and call. Everybody loves you, don't they? And you just can't stand it when someone like me is a threat. So you run and tattle to the boss to get rid of me.'

Dan clenched his fists, ready to step in and physically protect Jenna if need be. Jenna swayed backwards at Shauna's spiteful words, her eyes going wide with disbelief. The woman's anger was overriding her sense of truth.

This time he made his voice deep and commanding. 'Okay, Shauna, that's enough. Get your—'

Without warning, Shauna lunged forward and caught hold of Jenna's long plait, dragging her head down towards the table. Lynne screamed and ran to pull Shauna off Jenna and the three of them fell in a tangle of arms and legs and bared teeth on the floor.

Dan took two long strides, reached into the fray and dragged Shauna back to her feet by the scruff of her neck.

He held her at arm's length while she kicked and screamed abuse at Jenna, using all his strength to keep her from attacking her.

'If you don't stop, I'm going to throw you to the ground and hog-tie you,' he threatened through clenched teeth. That seemed to get through to her. She stopped trying to break free from his hold.

'Are you both okay?' Dan scanned Jenna and Lynne for any injuries as they picked themselves up. Jenna's hair was messed up, strands sticking out at all angles and her shirt was wrenched up around her midriff. But otherwise they both looked fine. He shoved Shauna away from him with distaste. 'Go and pack your bags, I'm driving you back to town. Today.' Shauna glowered at him, pure hatred sparking in her eyes. She moved her glare back to Jenna. Dan stepped between them. 'Right now, Shauna!' Dan would never lay a finger on a woman, his mum had brought him up to respect them, but he'd do whatever it took to protect Jenna. Shauna stamped her foot like a child having a tantrum.

'Fine, I can't wait to get out of here then,' she sneered. 'Come on, Lynne, let's get our bags packed and leave.' Shauna was halfway down the corridor before she realized Lynne wasn't following her. 'Well come on, don't just stand there like a bloody goose.'

'I think I'll stay for a while, Shauna. I like it here.' Lynne sidled closer to Dan.

'What?' Rage flared bright in Shauna's eyes, but Lynne said nothing more. Good on Lynne. Finally, she was prepared to stand on her own two feet. She fitted in well with the small team at Shiralee. It would've been a shame to lose her.

'Well fuck you, Lynne. Fuck you all!' Shauna stormed into her bedroom, where loud thumps and bangs ricocheted back down the hallway.

'You sure you're not hurt?' Dan questioned Jenna again.

'Just a little shaken up,' she admitted. 'But otherwise I'm fine. Thanks to you. And Lynne, for getting her off my back.' She smiled at Lynne, and Lynne smiled weakly back at her, but her hands trembled and Dan knew she was pretty shaken up by the whole thing too.

'Jenna, you should probably make yourself scarce for a while. At least until she's gone,' he said gently.

Her pale face made her freckles stand out across her nose. He wanted to reach over and brush the strands of hair away from her face. Wash the surprised hurt out of her eyes. But he needed to get her out of striking distance, just in case Shauna decided to turn into a feral fighting machine again. 'I'll get her out of here as soon as possible. Half an hour at the most. Then you can come back.'

'Right. I might go and clean some saddles,' she said.

'Good idea.'

Shooting an encouraging look towards Lynne, Jenna went out through the doorway and let the screen door bang behind her. Dan released a small sigh of relief.

'Lynne, you should be someplace else as well when I pack her into the car.'

'I completely agree,' Lynne nodded. 'I'll go help Cookie in the food store.' She followed Jenna out of the door.

The sun was getting low on the horizon and it'd be dusk soon. It was going to be a long drive back to Smokey Creek tonight. But there was no way he was going to leave Shauna here until morning. It was better to get that failed jillaroo off the station as soon as possible. The thought of the four-hour drive cramped in the car with Shauna didn't please him. Hopefully she wouldn't speak to him. But if she did, he wasn't above telling her a few home truths. If he had to tell her he was the reason she'd been fired, then he would.

He went to pack himself a small bag for the overnight trip.

* * *

Dust motes hung suspended in the air, captured by the dying rays of the afternoon sun. Jenna blew a soft breath through her lips just to watch the dust dance and spin through space. In the half hour she'd been hiding down in the tack shed she hadn't managed to clean even one saddle.

She was disappointed and more than a little confused at Shauna's reaction. She and Shauna would never be the best of mates. Shauna's jealousy got in the way of that. She was also very annoying, especially when she opened her mouth to ask stupid questions without thinking first. But they'd been getting along well, given the circumstances. Shauna's horse skills did require a bit of fine-tuning. Was she being fired because of a lack of proficiency?

Suddenly, the air in the shed went still. The horse in the stable next to her laid his ears back on his head. Trouble was coming. Jenna turned around to face the large open door of the stables to see Shauna sneaking up on her. The large woman launched herself at Jenna, lunging with surprising agility for her size. Jenna only just managed to sidestep in time, receiving a glancing blow.

'What the hell are you doing?' Jenna asked, astounded.

Shauna recovered from her headlong run and rounded on her. 'I wanted to give you a parting gift before I left,' she snarled, circling her with slow, deliberate strides.

'Come on, Shauna. What do you think you're going to gain from this?' It was more than simple jealousy Shauna was harbouring. Hate gleamed bright and sharp in the woman's eyes.

'I want to smash that smug little grin off your face once and for all.' Again, Shauna made a grab at Jenna, raking her throat with long fingernails. And again, Jenna sidestepped, but this time she felt a trickle of blood run down her collarbone.

'Shauna, for the last time, I didn't say anything to Bernie. I don't want to see you sent packing. Bernie must've made some kind of mistake. Maybe if we all went to talk to him again?' Jenna was trying to stay cool, logical, determined her anger wouldn't get the better of her today.

Shauna was pacing like a cat stalking its prey. Then she lunged at her again. Jenna sidestepped for the third time but began to tire of all this evasion. Her brows lowered, and she narrowed her eyes.

'Please leave me alone, Shauna, you'll only make this worse for yourself. At least leave with some of your dignity still intact.'

Shauna lunged at her again, this time colliding into Jenna before she could step out of the way, nearly sending her sprawling to the ground. It took all her skill to remain on her feet, and as she turned to face her attacker, her anger ramped up, her vow to keep control of her temper fading quickly. The woman was shallow, small-minded and petty. Jenna had done nothing to deserve this treatment. She took a quick look around to see if anyone else was here. But the stables were empty.

Blue barked from where he was tied up at his kennel. He wanted to come and help her, but he couldn't get free. She really was on her own. That was okay, she could handle Shauna.

'Don't make me hurt you,' Jenna growled. 'I'm very good at defending myself.' Her threat wasn't made lightly. Jenna made sure in the past two years that she could indeed follow through on her boast. She'd taken numerous self-defence courses, some kung fu and even kickboxing.

Shauna gave a scoffing laugh. 'You couldn't hurt me if you tried, you little whore. I'm twice the woman you'll ever be.' Shauna displayed her beefy arms and protruding belly, as if they were some kind of lethal weapon. Then a vicious light entered her eyes.

'I know you're keen on Dan, you little bitch.' Jenna didn't answer. Whatever it was she felt for Dan, she'd never admit anything to this woman.

'Well, this might put a little dampener on your aspirations. I did it with him last night! He invited me to his room after we had a few beers out on the verandah, and oh Jesus, he was so hot. Such a sweet body. It's the greatest sex I've ever had.' Shauna's face screwed up in an ugly caricature, as she thrust her hips in a lewd imitation of how she and Dan had done it together.

Jenna doubted Dan would ever stoop so low, but that didn't stop her simmering anger from turning into a boiling rage.

'He told me it was the best night of his life,' Shauna continued. 'He said he liked his women big and round, and that a puny little scrap of nothing like you would never be able to satisfy him.'

The rage slowly consumed the logical parts of Jenna's mind. Her anger grew to an uncontrollable level. It was a kind of rage she'd never felt before. The kind that blocked out all other rational thought, hummed in her ears and fizzed in her veins.

Shauna continued to taunt her with words, lashing out with her hands and feet whenever she saw an opening, until finally Jenna's wrath devoured her completely.

A low howl emanated through the shed as all the dogs on the property let forth an eerie wail. The horses started to whinny in their stalls, adding their voices to the growing cacophony. Shauna and Jenna paid them no heed; they only had eyes for each other.

'I'll get you,' yelled Shauna as she hurtled at Jenna again. But this time Jenna didn't get out of the way. The dogs barked, a harsh frantic sound, and the horses in the shed kicked at the doors to their stalls.

When Shauna touched Jenna, she reacted with the lightning speed of a sprung steel trap, hitting, punching, kicking. In the blink of an eye Shauna lay on the ground at Jenna's feet—knocked out cold—a trickle of blood oozing from her nose, her face pushed into the straw.

The barking and thumping hooves stopped, leaving only deafening silence.

Jenna looked down at Shauna lying vulnerable on the ground and recoiled with dismay. The boiling rage she'd felt only moments ago was gone, turned into shameful concern.

Jenna crouched down next to her. Oh shit, what had she done?

Lex strode into the silence, parting the sun-kissed dust motes like he was wading through water. With one glance he took in the scene and knelt beside Jenna, reaching around her to check Shauna's pulse.

'Oh God, is her heart still beating?' Jenna asked in a whisper. Shauna moaned at Lex's touch and Jenna had never been so glad to hear a noise issue from her mouth as in that moment. She released the breath she hadn't even realized she was holding.

'I don't think I want to know what happened.' Lex looked up at her with a measured gaze. 'But you'd better get out of here until she's gone.' Jenna stared into Lex's concerned face, gratitude and shame warring equally. Gratitude won. She stood up.

'Is she going to be all right?' She still hesitated, unsure.

'I'll look after her, you just get out of here.' The lines of his face eased into a grim smile of understanding. Shauna groaned again and started to stir, her eyelids fluttering open.

'I don't think she'll tell anyone the truth, so you should keep your mouth shut too. I'll come and talk to you later. Go on, get!'

Jenna turned and fled.

* * *

Nobody else seemed to have heard what happened in the shed that evening, but Jenna remained withdrawn and remote for the whole of the next day. Both Moon and Lynne commented about the strange hullabaloo the animals had kicked up just before sunset, but Jenna only nodded and agreed with them.

Jenna was down at the stables, shoeing a horse when the dinner gong banged. She was nearly finished, so she ignored it. Her father had taught her to be a farrier. She loved the job. It brought him back to her in the soothing gentle rasp of the file on hooves and the tap of a nail into a shoe.

Over the belting of her hammer, she heard the scrunch of boots on the dusty gravel. Probably soft-hearted Lynne, who would've worried Jenna didn't hear the bell.

But it wasn't Lynne who rounded the edge of the steel shed. It was Dan. She dropped the horse's hoof in surprise.

She backed away, lowering her gaze, unsure of what Shauna had told him.

'What did you do to her?' He stood very close as he demanded an answer. The shock of his unexpected proximity made her skin tingle in response. She crossed her arms over her chest to shut down the sudden quickening of her pulse. Her gaze remained averted, anywhere so she didn't have to look at Dan's face. She focussed on his strong hands hanging by his side. Competent hands. *Sensual hands*, a traitorous voice whispered inside her head.

'She … um … She tried to …' Jenna didn't know what to say. The emotion of the last few days welled up, making her throat ache. She hadn't meant to hurt Shauna, but she'd also not deserved her nasty spite either. Tormented by guilt and indecision, she took a step backwards. The last thing she wanted to do was cry. Not in front of Dan. Not again.

'I didn't mean it like that,' he said as he followed her. 'I meant how could a little slip of a girl like you do that to someone as large and brutal as Shauna?'

Was that admiration in his voice? She lifted her head and looked at him from beneath lowered eyelashes.

'I can't believe you fought her on your own. Why didn't you call for help? I would've been there in a second.'

'Thanks, Dan.' She was sure he'd been about to admonish her. Instead his eyes glowed as he looked down at her. Lifting her chin, she added, 'But I'm pretty good at protecting myself. I've been doing it for a while now.'

'Yes, I'm beginning to see that,' he replied. 'But I want you to understand, you don't always have to fight your own battles. People will help if you ask.'

'I know, Dan, and if I *really* need help, I promise you'll be the first person I come to.'

Dan's sarcastic grunt told her he didn't believe her. Then without warning, he reached out long tan fingers and gently traced the deep scratch on Jenna's neck.

'You might be able to defend yourself, but she managed to hurt you as well.'

Jenna's skin burned like fire along the trail where Dan's fingers had touched. Her breath caught in her lungs. He didn't move, and his continued presence set her stomach quivering. She almost lost her self-control then, wanting to give in to the longing and step in towards him, to feel his body up against hers. Instead she stiffened. She had no business letting herself react that way, not when the absolute last thing she needed was romance in her life.

Seeing her back away, his gaze hardened. He turned to stride out of the stables, but Jenna needed to ask one more question. Something which'd been smouldering at the back of her mind all day.

'Dan, why did Bernie really get rid of Shauna?'

Stopping in his tracks, Dan half-turned back towards her. 'Bernie may be a little incompetent, but he's not stupid. It doesn't take someone with huge intelligence to see Shauna wasn't cut out to work here. She just wasn't gelling properly with the rest of the team.'

'Okay. If you're sure that's all it was.' Jenna tried to sound indifferent but even to her own ears she sounded more than a little unconvinced.

Dan gave a heavy sigh before he turned around to face her fully, his gaze penetrating.

'Why do you ask?'

'No reason.'

'What did she say to you? Don't you dare feel guilty about anything to do with Shauna leaving.' Eyebrows lowered in a frown, he took a few steps towards her. Shrugging, she made no reply. Muttering under his breath, Dan crossed the remaining distance between them.

'Look, if you really have to know, I'll tell you.' He paused for a moment, as if not sure how to continue. 'As long as you promise to keep this between us,' he said.

She nodded in silent agreement.

'I was the one who convinced Bernie he shouldn't pass Shauna on the three-week trial.'

'Why?' Jenna barely breathed the word. She was shocked to hear him admit this. Shocked, but not completely surprised. 'She was a little lazy I will admit, but she wasn't that bad, was she?'

Dan shifted his feet. 'She was passable, I suppose. Her laziness and not being a team player were part of the reasons we didn't keep her on, but not the main one.' Again, he paused before continuing, and Jenna could see it was costing him to tell her the truth. 'She tried to get into my bed the other night.'

So it was true after all. Her chest tightened painfully. She had absolutely no reason to be distressed, she had no claim on Dan. Yet the news still struck her like a physical blow.

'Oh, I see.' Jenna was astonished at how mild her voice was.

'But I didn't sleep with her. I told her to get out,' he added hurriedly. 'That isn't what made me ask Bernie to get rid of her.' He tilted his body towards her, as if it actually mattered to him what she thought. 'The final straw was when, the following morning, she had the audacity to try and blackmail me by saying she'd tell Lex and Bernie I forced her into my bed. She was going to make me look like some kind of lecherous rapist. Just because I rejected her.'

Dan might be many things to many women, but she was sure he was no rapist.

'I didn't tell Bernie the exact circumstances as to why I didn't want her to stay. But I did tell him she was spreading lies which had the potential to break apart the team. Someone like that can't be trusted, either on the station, or out on the muster. And Bernie agreed with me.'

'Thanks, Dan. Don't worry, I won't tell a soul.' She nodded gravely.

'Much appreciated. I probably owe you some kind of explanation anyway, after the way she tried to take your head off yesterday.' There was a self-deprecating curl to his lip that made her want to reach out and trace the line of his mouth.

She clasped her hands behind her back.

His smile brightened and he turned the full wattage of his charm on her. 'Besides, we might be able to replace Shauna sooner than we thought. Bernie heard a rumour a bloke with a good reputation is looking for some work. We might see him as soon as tomorrow.'

CHAPTER SIX

'Which of you ladies is going to explain how I tell the back end of a horse from the front end?'

Lynne and Jenna stared open-mouthed at the new guy and Dan hid a laugh at their disbelief before he slapped Mark on the back and winked at them. 'Don't have kittens' girls, Mark's pulling your leg. He's an old hand, and we're lucky to have caught him between jobs. He'll be a great help to this station.'

Mark smiled, his forehead creasing with mirth. 'No really, I mean it. I'd love to be shown around, and I couldn't think of a nicer pair of station hands to do the showing.' He took each woman by the arm and whirled them around, walking towards the stables.

Dan gave a grunt of surprise and shot a look at Lex. Lex gave him a thoughtful wink and then bent to the task of rolling a smoke. Moon also seemed unfazed by Mark's audacity and ambled off to the machinery shed, following in Coshy's wake. With a shrug, Dan followed a few paces behind the other three, listening to their conversation.

'Talk about a smoothie,' said Lynne laughing, bending her neck to catch Jenna's eye from behind Mark's back. 'What's your last name then, Mark?'

'O'Brien. But my friends just call me Mob.'

'Well I could think of all sorts of connotations to put to that name,' chuckled Lynne.

Dan took the opportunity to sketch out Mark's personality as he followed along. Would he fit in with the team? He was thin, with somewhat bowed legs, and he stalked along like a man with a purpose. His hair was short, almost army regulation short, and his teeth were white and straight. He came highly recommended. Lynne seemed to like him, she was certainly hogging all the conversation. Dan's eyes flickered to Jenna's swaying hips as she strolled along next to Mark. What would she make of him? He was easy to talk to, with a witty personality. Would she like that kind of thing? It was hard to imagine she wouldn't.

'I suppose Bernie will allocate you a horse,' Lynne said.

'Nah, I've got my own horse being trucked over.'

Dan remembered Bernie mentioning something about a horse arriving today as well.

'Wow, your own horse, that's a bit of a luxury. What's his name?' Jenna asked.

Dan gave a wry smirk. Trust her to be more interested in the horse than the man.

'No Name,' Mark replied with an impish smile.

'What do you mean, no name? Is that his name, or doesn't he have a name?' Jenna asked, confused.

'That's his name,' Mark replied. 'I got him as a yearling colt and I could never decide on just the right name, so I kept calling him No Name until it stuck. Haven't you heard the song?' Mark's deep voice reverberated in the air as he sang,

'I've been through the desert on a horse with no name,

It felt good to be out of the rain,

In the desert you can remember your name.

Cause there ain't no one for to give you no pain –'

Dan laughed in surprise. Of course he'd heard that song. The guy certainly had style, Dan had to give him that much.

'So, I'm not the only person with a horse with no name,' quipped Mark. Jenna gave him a hard stare that made Dan think she wasn't completely happy with his naming method and Dan was suddenly absurdly pleased she'd found something she didn't like about him. 'I think I'm going to enjoy working here,' Mark announced, flashing them both another wicked grin.

Dan strode forward so he was walking alongside the others. 'We're really glad to have you, Mark. Aren't we?' Dan asked the girls. They both nodded. The three of them were still walking arm in arm and Dan wanted to tell him to let go. Especially of Jenna's arm. But that was just stupid. Mark was only being friendly, he meant nothing by it. Dan had no business feeling protective of Jenna. She could look after herself. She'd showed as much in her fight with Shauna. But he couldn't quell the displeasure lurking like a stone behind his ribs.

'Let's get you up to speed as soon as possible, Mark. The next muster is only a few days away.' Mark's grin disappeared at Dan's businesslike tone. 'If you'll come with me, I'll show you where you can stable No Name.'

'Righto then.' Mark dropped the women's arms and repositioned his hat more firmly on his head.

Dan felt a small tug of remorse. His reaction had been petty. The guy had a big personality and just because he was completely at ease around women didn't mean Dan should be jealous of him. He was determined he was going to start liking Mark, as of right now.

Later that day, a big four-wheel drive truck pulled into the station, towing a large horse trailer behind it. Everyone showed up to see what all the fuss was about as Mark led No Name down the ramp, checking him over to make sure he'd survived the day-long trip unscathed.

He was a large, rangy horse and although the word ugly popped into Dan's head it wasn't strictly true. He was jet black underneath the blanket of dust, but there was no other identifying mark on him. No white blaze or splash of colour above a hoof to identify him. Just one solid block of black. A fitting compliment to the man.

Dan would be interested to see how Mark and his horse worked as a team. He must be a good horse for Mark to go to the expense of paying for him to be moved to each new job he took on.

Jenna approached the big black's head and curled her arm up under his cheekbone. The horse leaned into her, almost as if he were telling her a story as he breathed in and out. She certainly had a way with animals. He was reminded of the day she chased the brumby stallion away. She hadn't been in the least bit scared. Had trusted the horse wouldn't hurt her.

Dan narrowed his eyes. There was something different about this woman. If only he could figure out what it was.

* * *

'I'm so glad you stayed, Lynne.' Jenna and Lynne were sitting on the verandah, digesting the rather large meal Cookie had made in honour of Mark joining the team.

'So am I,' answered Lynne. 'It was definitely a spur of the moment decision not to go along with Shauna.' She turned towards Jenna and they clinked their glasses together. Then she extended her long legs and rested booted feet on the middle rung of the railing. 'And I must admit, I'm glad Mark is here to take her place. He's growing on me already.' They clinked their glasses together again. 'Sometimes I wonder why I ever picked up with her. I guess it was just habit that kept me with her. I got used to being bossed around. It actually feels good to be standing on my own two feet again.'

'Hear, hear!' They clinked their glasses for a third time, to independence and freedom.

'It was good timing Mark was here to meet Ted as well,' Lynne commented. 'All us *newbies* got to meet him at the same time.'

'Hmm. What did you think of him? Ted, I mean?'

Ted Dawson was the owner of Shiralee Station. He'd arrived—to everyone's great surprise—in a flurry of dust in a shiny black helicopter just after they'd finished showing Mark around. Bernie had run down to the staff quarters in a fluster and ushered them up towards the main house to meet him. It was obvious this visit was unusual.

Ted was tall, solidly built, with a head of well-groomed black hair and wings of grey at his temples. Some might even consider him ruggedly handsome. He wore spotless white moleskins, a black starched shirt and polished Blundstone boots. There was an air of entitlement around him. This was no struggling land owner. Did Ted realize Bernie was running this once magnificent station into the ground with his self-absorbed ambivalence?

'Do you reckon Ted knows about Bernie's drinking binges?' Lynne asked.

'I'm not sure,' replied Jenna. 'But it must be obvious to Ted, if he has any farming knowledge at all, that this place is on a downhill slide.'

'Amen to that,' said Lynne.

A small black nose poked out from beneath Jenna's chair and a sleepy face gave her an inquisitive look.

Lynne laughed at the curious puppy and said, 'Your dog thinks we're both as mad as cut snakes.'

'Maybe he's right,' giggled Jenna.

'He's very cute, but why did you call him Dune?'

'It's short for Sand Dune,' Jenna replied, a little self-consciously. 'You know, the colour of sand dunes, all reddy-brown, yellowy-tan, cinnamony, speckled—' She tried to describe the ever-changing colour that encompassed both sand dunes and the pup, but failed dismally.

'You've taken on a handful. These half-breed dingos have a reputation for being mean and hard to tame.'

'I don't think I'll have too much trouble with him,' Jenna said.

Dune had four pert little white feet, and a white patch splashed across his chest. His blunt little muzzle was dark, and his light brown eyes were outlined in black. The dark spots on top of his head highlighted his wiggling eyebrows and gave him a comical look when his head tilted to the side to catch a whispered word from Jenna. She rubbed his ear and he rolled over on the floor exposing a soft pink belly, begging to be tickled.

Jenna adopted Dune the day after they got back from their first muster. One of the female working dogs had been *got at* by a wild dingo. Lucky for the pups, the dog was a mongrel, half kelpie, half something else. So Bernie wasn't as angry as if she'd been a pure-bred blue heeler.

People would pay a pretty penny to buy a dog with wild dingo blood coursing through it. The pure-bred dingo line was fast dying out as it interbred with man's introduced dogs, but it still had a big reputation, especially out here.

Bernie managed to sell all five other pups for much more than they were worth, as they'd never make great working dogs. Dune was the runt of the litter. Bernie ordered Dan to go and drown the wretch when no one would take him. As soon as Jenna heard this, she'd raced over to the main house, tapped at the door and told Bernie she'd buy the pup. She promised him all the hard-earned money she'd accrue over the next month and then took the pup from an astounded Dan's arms.

'You're one crazy girl,' he muttered as he followed her back across the bare dirt towards the stables. 'I guess I'd better give you a hand to build him a kennel. Do you want to house him next to Blue?' Jenna nodded her appreciation, still amazed at acquiring such friends as these.

Dune didn't often spend the night in his new kennel. Jenna would smuggle him into her room after lights out and he would lie at the bottom of her bed and groan and twitch with puppy-dreams all night. It made her heart blissful to have him lying there.

* * *

Mob didn't have long to get accustomed to the farm, as they were back out riding their second muster within two days of his arrival. The new area consisted of sparsely covered open country that rolled away in endless waves towards the shimmering horizon. There weren't many clumps of Mallee offering shelter for the cattle, which meant they were easier to find.

The team gathered together a large herd of cattle throughout the morning and now the station hands all arranged themselves around the slow-moving bunch. Pat and Ulrich positioned themselves on either side to flank them and keep them heading straight. Lex, Moon and Mark were further out to catch any strays who wandered away from the pack. Jenna and Lynne pushed the cows forward from the back. Dan was out front, leading. No one got too close to the cattle, and no one tried to hurry them.

No Name's smooth gait brought Mob alongside Jenna and he looked down from atop his large horse, flashing her a wicked grin.

'How's the weather down there?'

Jenna pretended to glare back up at him. But Miya, the little mare she was riding today, flattened her ears, and quick as a striking snake, aimed a nip at No Name's shoulder. The black horse showed more manners than Mob by backing off and letting the mare jog in front of him with a sassy flick of her tail.

'Yes,' murmured Jenna to her horse. 'We sure showed him!'

'Hey, Rowdy, keep that horse moving up with the rest of the bunch.' She turned around in the saddle to see Mob give his best roguish grin.

She groaned. He'd just christened her with a nickname. Raising an eyebrow, she turned back around and ignored him. It was Mob's subtle way of expressing his affection to the people he was beginning to call friends. She grinned secretly to herself.

As soon as he arrived, Mob started to come up with nicknames for them all. The same day he arrived at the station, he started slipping the name 'Simmo' into the conversation when he was referring to Dan. Dan just grimaced every time the nickname was used; it wasn't the first time he'd heard that one.

Mob soon came up with one for Lynne as well.

'Hey, Sunshine, toss that spare blanket up here.' Mob looked straight at Lynne from atop the Land Cruiser he was helping them to pack.

She glared up at him. 'What did you call me?'

'Come on, Lynne, it's kind of cute,' Jenna chuckled.

'I'm not sure about that.' But from then on Lynne responded to the nickname with a quick smile, particularly if it came from Mob.

Mob let Coshy and Cookie's nicknames stand. He also left Lex alone. All it took was one sideways glance from Lex at Mob's first attempts to call him something different to put Mark back in his place.

And now even Jenna had one.

She settled back into the comfortable rhythm of Miya's rolling walk, looking over at Mob and his big black horse riding back out on the right-hand flank. He chose to ride in one of those deep western saddles that looked more like an armchair. Jenna did have to admit they were very comfortable. Mob's sunny disposition carried through into his riding technique and both man and horse were a happy duo.

Busy watching the two working together, Jenna didn't notice Dan sidling closer on Domino.

'Enjoying the view?'

Jenna's reverie was broken, and she looked at him mystified. If she hadn't known better, Dan almost sounded resentful. His brown eyes were dark and unreadable, his hands clenched into tight fists on the reins.

'What view are you referring to, Dan?'

He didn't answer, instead turning Domino sharply to ride off between the shrubs. What was that snide comment all about? Since his arrival, Mob settled himself into their team in record time. His friendly banter and humorous persona endeared him to everyone. Except Coshy, who seemed to make it his occupation to dislike most people he met.

She had to admit, she liked Mob. She liked his open honesty and the way he was so easy to be around. She was glad he'd joined the team. Of course, if she were being honest, Mob was a lot safer to talk to. He didn't engender any raw, unwanted emotions the way Dan did.

She assumed Dan liked Mob too, they both had similar work ethics. Maybe she'd been wrong, maybe there was an underlying current she'd failed to pick up on. Her gaze followed Dan's retreating back as he threaded his way through the scrub.

The afternoon wore on in a similar fashion to the morning, only this time the herds of cattle were smaller, wandering in dribs and drabs into the yard.

With nothing else to occupy her mind as she plodded along behind yet another small group of bumping red hides,

Jenna found her thoughts drifting back in time. Thinking about her father, Joe. He'd never made any secrets about being her adoptive father. But the details of her mother's life were few and far between. Mainly because Joe knew very little himself. He'd offered her mother a place to live for a while when he'd found her with a very young child living on the streets of his small town. Joe was like that, always taking in strays. After only three months her mother disappeared, leaving a note to say the kid was better off with him. That was it. That was all she knew. She never came back and never contacted them again.

'Here, this is yours,' Joe had said one day when they were sitting in the kitchen. The offhand way in which he spoke had her senses on immediate alert.

'What is it?' she'd asked as he handed her a ring. Silver with a pink stone set in the middle, and two diamonds on either side. The stone was round and polished, the surface like silk to the touch. On top of the domed face a twelve-pointed star radiated from within, moving and shifting with her eye as she rotated it, almost as if the stone contained a living presence deep inside. 'It's beautiful.'

'Yes,' her father agreed. 'I've kept it safe for you.' The muscles in her stomach spasmed. Had her mother left it for her? She had so many questions. Questions about why her mother abandoned her. Anything that was a link with her mother brought mixed emotions.

'Why are you giving it to me now?'

'I've been waiting for the right time, I guess.' She cast him an impatient glance, indicating for him to continue with a raised eyebrow. 'I believe it could possibly be a star sapphire. It's vintage and set in white gold. It's worth a pretty penny. I had it valued in town, the guy in the shop wanted to buy it from me on the spot. He offered me fifteen thousand dollars.'

'Wow … that's amazing.' But it wasn't quite the information she was searching for. 'So it was my mother's?'

'Yes. I'm sorry I can't answer more of your questions.' He laid a comforting hand on her arm. 'Your mother never told me much about anything.'

A lump formed suddenly in Jenna's throat.

'She left this in an envelope with a note. Asked me to give it to you when you were old enough to look after it.'

Placing the ring with great care on her finger—it fitted perfectly—she reached out and put her arms around his large shoulders.

'It's not your fault,' she said. 'She should've told you more.' A lot more. But that wasn't going to help her now. In her eyes, Joe was her father and always would be. He'd raised her as his own and she loved him unconditionally. From that day on she'd kept the ring close.

Miya gave a gentle snort, blowing the dust from her nose, startling Jenna. She re-focused her gaze and blinked a couple of times to bring herself back to the present. They were nearing the campsite and Jenna could almost taste the hot, sweet mug of billy tea that'd help wash the grit out of her mouth. Thoughts of her ring were forgotten with the anticipation of getting out of the saddle and being able to stretch her weary legs.

CHAPTER SEVEN

Dan stood in the shadow of the doorway. He'd come to bed the dogs down for the night, but now here was Jenna standing behind the horse shed, her eyes transfixed somewhere in the distance. He hesitated, not wanting to break her solitude. She was watching the muted sunset over the flat vista of Shiralee Station. There wasn't a cloud in the sky and with the sun now below the horizon, the colours in the atmosphere melted together like burnt toffee. A single star appeared as a bright pinprick in front of her. The scene before him was stunning. She was stunning. Something flickered in his chest. A feeling of … What? A need to touch her. To reach out a hand and feel her warm skin beneath his fingers.

Before he knew it, he stepped onto the beaten earth outside the shed, stopping behind her, only an inch or two separating them. So close he could feel the heat from her body through the fabric of his shirt.

He leaned forwards, placing his hand on the railing next to hers. She acknowledged his presence with a quick flick of her gaze before returning to concentrate on the scene before her. For once, she didn't move away from him, recoil to a safer distance.

'Desert sunsets are like nothing else, aren't they?'

'They sure are,' she breathed. 'I could get used to watching this every night.'

He'd been here almost three years now, and every night there was something new to enthrall him when the sun bronzed the sky. They stood together in silence, watching the night close in.

'Did you make a wish?' Dan pointed at the evening star close on the horizon.

'Yes, I did,' she admitted with a half-embarrassed smile. 'I don't normally.' There was a softness surrounding her this evening. Her well-constructed barriers were somehow not quite so formidable.

'What did you wish for?' The question was meant to be light-hearted, but when she hung her head, he suddenly wanted to take back his casual comment. It was obvious she'd wished for something important. He hadn't meant to be flippant.

'Forget I asked,' he said. 'You don't have to tell me.'

She lifted her head and stared at him. He kept the silence, hoping she'd fill it. Into the stillness a small sound came from above, an imperceptible squeak that teetered on the edges of hearing. Jenna tilted her head back and he did the same, just in time to see a tiny winged shape hurtle dark against the starry sky.

'Wow, a bat!' she said, joyfully. He dropped his gaze and his view was filled with the pale skin of Jenna's exposed neck as she stretched to see the flying animals. A traitorous urge made him want to taste her skin with his lips. He wanted her, the need like a sharp pain in his chest and he was surprised with the depth of his desire.

Friends. Work colleagues. But the mantra he used to remind himself to keep his distance didn't seem to work tonight.

There was no use denying his physical attraction to her. But was it just simple desire? And what did she feel for him in return? He'd been around the block enough times to recognize chemistry when it simmered between two people, and he'd seen definite desire flare in those intense eyes of hers. But she might not take kindly to him reaching down and claiming her mouth. With any other woman, he wouldn't have worried about their reaction. He would've followed his natural instincts and kissed her, to hell with the consequences. Most girls were quick to fall for his charms. Not Jenna. She wasn't the take-it-or-leave-it type of women he was usually attracted to. There was nothing lightweight or trivial about her. For the first time in his life, he found himself hungering for something more. Special. Fulfilling.

No, if this—whatever this might be—was going to happen then she'd have to be the first one to make the move.

'That's so cool.' Open delight played over her face. 'I haven't seen any of those little guys since I left home.'

'Home, huh. You're from the country then?' Eyes still locked on the tiny flying mammals, she didn't answer, so he pushed a little harder. 'I've worked with you for over six weeks now, and I still don't know anything about you. I know the middle names of all of Lynne's three brothers and how much sugar her mother has in her cup of tea, but the only thing I know about you is you suffer from bad dreams.' He raised an eyebrow, defying her to answer his question. For a second, he thought he might've overstepped the mark.

Then a smile played over her lips. 'I come from a normal middle-class family, in a normal, middle-class country town. Nothing interesting about me at all.'

Somehow, he doubted that, but he let it slide. It was a night for taking chances, so hardly daring to breathe, he moved his hand slowly along the railing until it rested up against hers.

She didn't pull her hand away.

'How about you? Where are you from?' she asked.

As he considered his answer he let his thumb draw tiny circles on the back of her hand, expecting at any moment she'd tug away. But for reasons he couldn't fathom, she surrendered to the intimacy of the small movement.

Another high-pitched squeak joined the first, and the air parted for two bats catching insects high above.

'I'm from Tamworth originally,' he said.

'The country music capital of Australia? I've always wanted to visit there,' she said, her blue eyes sparkling with uncharacteristic eagerness.

Angling his body more towards her, he brought his face to within inches of hers. 'Well I'd love to show you around one day.'

She stayed immobile and his heart pounded heavily, awareness of her fizzing through every nerve. He swallowed hard. Another bat joined the group above their heads. This one flittered down to within a few feet of them. It made more noise than the others and it caught Jenna's attention.

Her upturned face was right below his. Instead of turning his chin up to the sky, he kept his gaze locked onto hers. Her glance slipped from the bat to catch him full in the eyes. He couldn't look away. Her breath was coming in husky, shallow gasps. On impulse he brushed a trailing strand of hair away from her mouth and tucked it behind her ear. Her skin was warm and tempting to the touch.

More bats joined the melee above, making the atmosphere seem to shift and ripple with their wings.

The intense heat in her eyes held him, and he sensed she was confused, swept away by a myriad of sensations. Would she kiss him? God, he wanted to take her mouth, to hold her hard up against him. In that moment he was ensnared, unable to move, his breath all but stopped. Inexorably, she closed the gap, he could feel the heat from her mouth as she exhaled through her lips.

The bats came closer, but he paid them no heed.

A small plunging body swished overhead, just about raking them with tiny hooked wings, so close he could feel the puff of wind as it flew by. Dan looked up in surprise.

The spell was broken. Jenna backed away. *Damn it!*

She looked up at the circling bats, as if unsure whether to thank or curse them.

'Jenna—' What could he say to salvage this now?

The stillness was shattered by the sound of booted feet. Moon rounded the side of the shed and skidded to a stumbling halt in front of them.

'Dan, the Stallion is gone.' Moon's normal slow lilt was deep and rasping.

'What do you mean, gone?' Dan barked, irritated at being interrupted. The tingle was still warm on his fingertips where he'd touched her face and he wanted Moon to go away so he could have another chance.

'I went back to check him, I already checked on him about two hours ago,' Moon babbled, almost incoherent. 'The stable door was wide open. It's not my fault, Dan.' Moon cringed and looked ready to weep, knowing Bernie would fire him if he thought he had anything to do with it.

'Are you saying Winemaster is lost?' Dan's mind shifted gear painfully.

'I don't know, Dan.' Moon stood quiet and patient, black eyes imploring. 'What're we going to do?'

* * *

The whole station was humming with bright lights and shouting. Lex organized Dan and Lynne to go up the main driveway in the Land Cruiser to see if the stallion had taken the easy route and trotted up the road. Lex and Coshy revved up the motorbikes and headed down the largest track formed by a fire-break, their headlights dancing crazily off the trees. Moon employed his native tracking skills, to see if he could decipher the maze of hoof marks scattering the holding yards, and Lex ordered Jenna and Mark to help him out. Bernie was doing nothing constructive, just lots of yelling and cursing and waving his arms around, telling everyone Winemaster was a bloody priceless horse and they'd better bloody well find him, or jobs were on the line.

Moon was down on hands and knees sorting through the dust at the edge of the fence-line near the stables, with Mob following behind, trailing his horse and pointing a very large torch in the direction Moon indicated.

Jenna pretended to still be struggling with the task of saddling Chainsaw, when Mark called out for her to hurry up.

Chainsaw actually stood saddled and ready, with Dan's dog, Blue and the dingo pup, Dune, both panting at her feet. A herd of red kangaroos waited just outside the fence line. Her hand went across her chest in an absentminded gesture, feeling for the ring nestled against her breastbone.

When Mark was asked about it afterwards, he said both he and Moon had looked around at the sound of galloping hooves just in time to see three dark shapes streaking through the blackness; Chainsaw, as he cleared the fence and took off at a dead run into the scrub, and two smaller shapes that ducked under the fence and dashed off to join the thundering horse. He couldn't be sure, but he thought he'd seen the flash of bouncing hides jumping in front of the trio.

Jenna's respect for kangaroos grew as she and Chainsaw did their best to follow the bounding forms through the scrub. They could move damned fast when they wanted to. They were sometimes referred to as the *flying big reds* and now she understood why. She let Chainsaw have his head, trusting him to find the best way over the sandy terrain, and trusting her escorts to pick the safest route in the dark.

They were headed east, to a series of rocky gorges that twisted their way into the low-slung shale hills. The hills could be seen from Shiralee Station, hovering on the edge of the horizon like the spikes on the back of one of the little native thorny devil lizards. Jenna already knew Winemaster was headed in that direction. He was a stallion, with only one thing on his mind. Mares. He was going after the wild brumby's mares.

At a more reasonable pace it would've been over an hour-long ride, but she hoped to cover the distance in well under half that time.

Her mind was awhirl with confusion. How could she have let Dan get that close to her? Thank God for those tiny, mischievous bats who'd dived down in response to her churning emotions and broken the spell of sheer stupidity. She would've let him kiss her.

Better to think about other things. She knew it'd been Coshy who let the stallion out. It was in the impressions the other horses gave her. There was no doubt in her mind who it was. Why would he do something like that? Was it intentional? Or had he left the gate open by mistake? Winemaster was a valuable horse. Perhaps Coshy had plans to steal him. But that seemed unlikely. Maybe he was looking to hurt Bernie. With the amount of spite Coshy harboured for just about everyone on the station, including Bernie, Jenna wouldn't put it past him. Coshy was taking part in the search as if nothing was amiss, not even giving a hint he was the one to blame, or that he knew where the horse was.

The problem was, should Jenna confront him about it? Because it'd be more than likely he'd deny it outright. And then there'd be a scene. And then she'd have to tell everyone how she knew about Coshy. And that wouldn't work. Because Coshy would completely deny it. It'd be her word against his.

The whole situation had her going crazy with what-ifs, and maybes.

The question of whether Liam could have anything to do with it flashed through her mind. But she dispelled the idea as quickly as it came. She'd only been here for a little over a month, he couldn't have tracked her down that fast. This time she'd made a determined effort to flee as far as possible from her last place of residence. And there was no connection between Liam and Coshy. Was there?

Liam. Now she'd let her mind wander to the memory, he wouldn't leave. Her mind revisited the time she'd read the letter Joe had written.

On the night Liam and his thugs killed her father, she'd managed to escape when a pack of dogs had chased her three tormentors away. She'd scrambled back to the homestead, tears streaming down her face. The only thing she knew for sure was she had to get out of there. Fast. Shoving a few random clothes into an old duffle bag, she'd grabbed the small stash of money she kept in the shoebox on top of her wardrobe and her dad's .22 rifle from the old laundry airing cupboard. She stopped in the kitchen to quickly stuff some muesli bars and apples into her bag and her gaze alighted on the small desk tucked into the corner of the messy dining room. On impulse she'd gone over to the desk.

That was when she'd found the letter.

It was lying open on the desk. She'd seen her name at the top. It was unfinished. He'd been sitting at the desk, writing something, when the front door had suddenly exploded inwards with a huge crash and Liam as his thugs had broken in. He'd never got to finish it. She snatched the letter up to read later as she fled her family home.

It hadn't been until late the next evening, after she'd found out the police weren't' going to help her and she'd hunkered down in a remote hay shed, she took the letter out again. The rain beat a soft tattoo on the tin roof of the shed, and she made a nest deep in the Lucerne to find warmth from the growing cold of the encroaching night.

Why hadn't he just told her what she needed to know? With trembling fingers, she opened it, smoothing out the wrinkles from where she'd shoved it into her bag.

There's something I need to tell you, but I don't know where to start.

The hairs on the back of her neck rose up as she read his words.

You know how much I love you. You are my heart and soul, my everything. I've always thought of you as my flesh and blood, my one true daughter. But I'm sad to say I lied to you when I said I didn't know anything about your biological father. There is a reason why I've kept the truth of your parentage from you, Jenna.

She stopped reading at that point, tears glazing her eyes. She could see him now, sitting at his desk, gripping the pen tightly. Dashing the unshed tears from her eyes, she kept reading. Soon the light would be gone.

I just wanted to protect you, Jenna. That's why I started paying off that thug, Liam. He threatened to tell your father where you were. He asked me for money to keep your location a secret, and I'm sorry to say, I paid him. I needed time to think, to try and come up with a better solution. And to be honest, I thought—or maybe I hoped—Liam would just take the money and go away. But of course he didn't.

She kept reading, his words filling the page with the tale of how he'd paid Liam, larger and larger amounts of money to keep her safe. A strange foreboding squeezed her lungs tight.

I should have told you about your real father right from the start. Your mother did tell me that Alexander was dangerous. That she was running away from a monster. You need to stay away from him. He is …

The letter finished abruptly. Jenna's knuckles turned white with the strain of not crumpling the paper in her fist. That's as far as Joe got, before Liam broke in. He hadn't time to tell her why she should fear Alexander. Joe always denied any knowledge of her true father. Jenna was shocked by his deception.

The mystery gnawed at the edges of her mind as Chainsaw slowed to a weary trot. He was white with foam when they reached the cover of a copse of trees just below the first rise of the hills. She thanked him with respect for his great heart and swift legs.

A male big red and two small female roos were waiting as Jenna dismounted. When Jenna stood next to the male leader, she discovered just how big he was. He reared up on his hind legs supported by his thick tail and looked down his whiskered nose at her. There were jagged scars running across his huge, muscled chest, reminders of the battles he'd fought and won to keep the mob under his charge. He was at least a head taller than Jenna, and as she glanced over at his powerful hind legs and large, deadly claws, she was very glad he was on her side.

Not for the first time, she wished she could've let Mob and Moon in on her plan, but there was no way she could tell them how she knew where the stallion was without giving herself away. Or at least making them highly suspicious. It was the exact same reason she couldn't tell anyone about Coshy. She would spin some tall story about stumbling across the horse's tracks which lead her straight to him.

An urgent whinny sounded from somewhere ahead. Winemaster had found the brumby mares. She'd arrived in the nick of time. A scream of fury answered the black horse's call. The brumby stallion knew Winemaster was coming. Bloody stupid males. Why did they always have to fight over their women?

Jenna flung herself onto Chainsaw's back and he was off, galloping over the sloping ground, following a dip in the hills which soon opened out into a shallow valley. Straight towards the frenzied animal screams.

It only took a minute before they were upon the two infuriated stallions. Winemaster's shiny black hide reflected the eerie light of the moon, but the brumby was just a flash of teeth or a dark hoof in the moonlight. Even though Winemaster was following his primal urges—he desperately wanted those mares hidden safely further down the valley—he was a pampered spoilt station horse, who'd never had to fight for anything in his life. This brumby was going to kill him if she couldn't stop the fight.

She gave a loud whistle just as Chainsaw came to a jolting stop a little way from the incensed horses. Vaulting from his back, Jenna ran towards the melee. Dust churned up by the fight hung like a cloud in the night, shimmering in the moonlight. Both horses ignored her whistle and continued to scream and strike at each other, shattering the night with their duel to the death.

'Stop this,' she exhorted, sending out a mental order at the same time. Winemaster reared, but then backed away, still baring his teeth. The brumby completely ignored her and used the black horse's hesitation to his advantage, rushing in with snapping teeth, landing a blow on his shoulder.

'I command you to stop this,' she roared, nearly as incensed as the horses now. Winemaster was going to get hurt. And then what would Bernie say? She was within a few steps of the horses and she charged in between them, ignoring her own safety. The brumby propped sharply on his front legs and threw his head into the air, eyes wild. For a split second she thought he wasn't going to listen to her. At least Winemaster obeyed, even if she could feel he was still humming with lustful ardour and fury. She laid her calming aura over him, expanding the field to take in the brumby as well. Finally, the brumby dropped his head and his ears flickered forwards.

'Thank you,' she said. The brumby still showed the whites of his eyes, not completely convinced. 'Yes, I'm taking him back. Just give me a second.' The horse snorted contemptuously. 'No, he won't be back to bother you, so you can just put the idea of a re-match out of your head.'

Turning on her heel, she stretched out her hand to Winemaster. 'Bloody men,' she muttered under her breath. Winemaster lowered his head and gave an apologetic grunt. His gaze still rested on the milling shadows away down the valley. The mares. 'Yeah, whatever. I don't care if you never get any. These aren't your girls and you'll just have to deal with it.'

Jenna grabbed the horse's mane and leaped onto his back. She needed to get him away from the brumby before he changed his mind. Urging him into a fast trot, she whistled Chainsaw to follow them back down the valley. Winemaster favoured his left foreleg as he moved. Damn. Double damn. The brumby had injured him after all. Jenna leaned over his whither to see what damage had been done. That's when Winemaster tripped and went down, sending her sprawling to the ground.

Pain seared through her as she hit the unforgiving earth and she screamed in agony, hearing her shoulder crunch as it broke her fall. Darkness closed over her as she lay on the ground, unable to move or even think, knowing only indescribable pain.

As she lay with her eyes closed, pain coursing from her shoulder down the whole left-hand side of her body, her mind refused to contemplate her options. Clamping her teeth shut, she forced down the stupid urge to cry. It wouldn't help her situation.

Out of the dark, Chainsaw appeared, dropping his nose to nuzzle her. Dune and Blue also materialized at her side, whining with worry. Winemaster remained nearby but wouldn't come too close. He wasn't hurt, but embarrassment leaked from him.

'Can you get me home?' she grunted though gritted teeth. Chainsaw slowly got down onto his forelegs beside her and she managed to grab a handful of mane in her good hand and heave her leg over the saddle, crying out in pain as she did so. It was almost unbearable. God, she hoped she didn't pass out. How stupid was she, thinking she could come out here on her own? The chestnut got to his feet and started the slow journey back to the homestead.

CHAPTER EIGHT

The only thing keeping her on top of Chainsaw's back was the horse himself. He'd managed to hold her safe in the saddle by moving to stay underneath her when she swayed dangerously sideways, and he'd kept his walk low and easy.

Winemaster jogged alongside, like a chastised child. In the small part of her brain not in an utter fog of pain, she acknowledged his warm muscular shoulder as it rose and fell in harmony with Chainsaw's rhythm. His presence, pressed hard against her left leg kept her foot planted in the stirrup. The horse knew he'd failed her. He was doing the best he could to make up for it.

Dune and Blue panted along at the horse's fetlocks, their eyes sharp and bright.

At last she saw an outline of the high railing fence, lit by spotlights, but it seemed to swirl and disappear before her eyes as she fought to stay conscious.

Shouts breached her stupor-filled brain, breaking through the throbbing that'd become her world. She lifted her head long enough to see people running towards her from several different directions. Knowing she didn't have the strength to dismount from Chainsaw on her own, she waited, shoulders hunched, left arm cradled against her chest.

'Jenna, oh my God!' Dan got to her first. Gentle hands reached up and grabbed her by the waist, supporting underneath her good elbow.

'Let's get you down from there,' he muttered. Jenna clamped her mouth shut, willing herself not to cry out. A small gasp of pain managed to escape her steely resolve as the jolt from landing on the ground sent shock waves through her.

Her legs wouldn't hold her weight and she crumpled into Dan's body. He lifted her into his arms as if she weighed nothing, and started across the horse yards, yelling instructions as he went.

'It's okay, guys,' she heard him say, 'I'll look after her now. Good dogs.' He acknowledged her faithful partners, who still trotted, sentinel-like at his feet. She could hear other voices answering from far away, and every now and then a worried face would drift into view, but it was all otherworldly.

The only thing Jenna could concentrate on was Dan's face, hovering so close to hers. Concern was etched into the lines at the corners of his eyes and there was a firm, unfamiliar set to his mouth. His hat was missing and his disobedient curls fell down over his ears, brushing gently against her cheek. Through the pain that muddled her brain, she suddenly felt a very strong sensation. It took a few seconds for her to recognize the emotion, but in the end she knew being carried in Dan's strong arms, being embraced against his warm chest, made her feel safe. It was an unexpected and disturbing revelation.

* * *

'I've brought your breakfast … and a visitor.' Dan rapped on the door, the gentle sound at complete odds with the tension running through his knotted shoulders.

'Come in, Dan.' Her voice sounded light and normal. That was a good start. He carried the tray of food in, putting it on the makeshift bedside table. Dune padded in behind him, jumping onto the bed next to her and rolling onto his back for a tummy scratch. She looked different this morning, her long hair left to fall loose around her shoulders. It framed her face, made her look younger and somehow more vulnerable.

'Sorry, Dune wouldn't leave me alone. Kept looking at me with those beseeching eyes of his. And every time I tried to catch him to tie him up, he'd just dodge out of the way.' The dog hadn't left his side all morning. Every time he turned around, the dog had been there. And every time he saw Dune he'd been reminded of Jenna. Reminded of how he'd made her scream in pain. He could still hear the sound in his head, reverberating through him like a physical kick in the guts.

Her shoulder had been dislocated in the fall. She also had some impressive bruising down the left-hand side of her body, but it was the dislocation causing the pain. His mouth twisted in wry humour. The sad thing was, he was the best person to re-set it, thanks to his stint in jail. His cell-mate, Chokko, had a tendency to dislocate his shoulder, particularly if he was involved in one of the many courtyard scuffles with the other inmates. Chokko told him the ligaments were forever weakened as a result of a motorbike accident. So, Dan had gotten very good at helping him re-locate it after every fight.

He hadn't wanted to do it to Jenna, because he knew how much it'd hurt. And he really didn't want to hurt her. But Jenna pleaded with him, saying the last place she wanted to go was hospital. It went against all his better judgement, but in the end he gave in.

'I'm glad you let him in, Dan, thanks. He just wants to make sure I'm okay.' Jenna rubbed his pink spotted belly with her good arm, while he lolled his tongue out the side of his mouth in his best imitation of a smile.

'Cookie will kill me.' He shot the dog a quick glance and noted at the same time she seemed to be moving her damaged arm a little more freely now. At least he'd done a proper job on it first time round. Thank God he didn't have to attempt that twice. Hearing her scream like that once would stay with him for a lifetime. Twice might've damn near killed him.

'How're you feeling?' Dan didn't look at her, his gaze settling on the view outside the window instead.

'I'm much better now, thanks to you and Lex.'

Shaking his head, he strode across the room and sat down on the bed, shoving Dune out of the way. Her face was still pale. He had to fight the sudden urge to run his fingers down the smooth line of her jaw.

'You should've asked for help.' A frustrated frown lowered his brows. 'We've had this conversation before, Jenna. You don't need to do everything on your own.'

'I know,' she sighed. 'And I know I said I'd try. It's just that … Well it's easier sometimes, you know. Not getting anyone else involved.'

'Well, I'm going to keep reminding you, until you get it through your thick skull.' He tapped a finger lightly against her head. 'You could've been badly hurt out there on your own.'

She raised a dubious eyebrow at him and his scowl deepened. Bloody independent woman, what was he going to do with her? Her blue eyes sparkled and his gut tightened, reminding him of what they'd nearly done together last night.

Had it only been last night when he'd nearly kissed her? Why had he done that? Hadn't he already decided not to get involved? Lost in his own thoughts, he stared out of the window.

Reaching out, she laid a hand on his arm. The impression of her warm fingertips on his skin was as if she'd set a flame to his arm.

'Dan, have you got lots of younger siblings?' Her question took him totally by surprise. 'Because sometimes, you're very much like an annoying older brother. Always making sure I'm okay. Always offering your help. Even when it's not needed.' The statement was a soft reproach and he knew she was teasing him now, but it didn't stop the prickle of sensation that ran down his spine. She'd hit pretty close to the mark. About his tendency to act as the protector. He'd had no choice after their father left them, but to step up and look after his mother and two younger brothers. Who else was there to keep them safe?

'Always the good guy, aren't you, Dan?'

He flinched as if she'd pinched him. If only she knew the truth. The bed creaked as he turned to face her directly.

'No, I'm not, Jenna.'

'Yes, you are.' The quiet conviction with which she spoke squeezed at his heart. He wanted to tell her he was the exact opposite. He wasn't a good man, not by a long shot. The things he'd seen in jail. The things he had to do to survive in there. His tongue worked in his mouth, caught in his teeth, but refused to form the words.

Instead he took the easy way out. 'If you say so.' He was rewarded by the smile slowly reforming on her face, curling the corners of those sensuous lips up once again. Lips that he'd love to taste, to savour, to devour.

He was still aware of her hand resting on his arm and his eyes travelled unconsciously to it. There was something on the underside of her arm. He flipped it over, exposing the soft whiteness of her wrist.

'You have a tattoo!' He wondered why he should be so shocked. Most girls had some form of ink nowadays. She went to pull her hand out of his grasp.

'How come I never noticed that before?' He didn't let her go, trying to read the inscription on her skin. It was some kind of old-fashioned script.

'Because you never bothered to look.' This time she managed to free her hand and pulled it back into the safety of her body, automatically reaching up to touch the ring she wore around her neck. He'd need to ask her about that one day, too.

'What does *Be Brave* mean?' he asked, intrigued.

'Lots of things. And nothing really.' The shutters were back up in her face. 'I got it after my dad died.' Her strange half-strangled tone was not at all like the confident woman from a few moments ago.

'Sorry, I didn't mean to pry.'

'Doesn't matter,' she replied. Her words sounded light enough, but her eyes gave her away. Eyes that'd only seconds ago been a wonderful clear blue, had turned a stormy shade of dark indigo. He could've kicked himself. But it was too late, the moment was lost. Her secrets were once more shuttered behind that impenetrable façade of hers.

'I'll leave you to eat your breakfast in peace,' he said, heading for the door.

* * *

Jenna sat on a chair at the kitchen table and looked up into the sea of faces surveying her. They'd all gathered in the kitchen to hear her story. Even Bernie was standing there, impatient for her to start. She wasn't prepared for this and nervously picked at a stray cotton strand dangling from the sling holding her left arm. What to tell and what to leave out? How was she going to explain how she knew where to find the horse?

'I guess you all want to know how I found Winemaster?' She forced a light laugh. 'Well it wasn't me, it was the dogs. I just kind of followed them.'

A loud sarcastic hoot came from the back of the crowd, startling her. Everyone turned quelling gazes towards Coshy until he gave a self-conscious cough and hung his head. Of course it was Coshy. Jenna glared at him. How dare he mock her, when he was the one who let the damn horse out. But she'd already decided not to let on she knew, so she pursed her lips and continued, still glaring at Coshy.

'I tried to call Blue over to me so I could go and join Moon and Mob but he wouldn't come, and that's unusual for Blue.' She caught Dan's eye and he nodded. 'So I went over to investigate. He seemed to have picked up some kind of scent. And then I noticed some faint horse tracks leading away on the other side of the fence.'

'Why didn't you call for us to come and help you?' asked Mob, a slight coolness in his tone.

'Because I honestly didn't believe the tracks he'd found were Winemaster's.'

'Well you were obviously off somewhere in a hurry with that dodgy leap you took over the fence. I know you're a damn good rider, Jenna, but you should still be more careful.'

'What leap over the fence?' Bernie's ears pricked up at the mention of jumping fences. 'I hope you didn't put any of my stock horses at risk.'

'Give it a rest, Bernie,' growled Lex.

Jenna shot him a grateful glance as she said, 'So I followed the two dogs on Chainsaw, they seemed very excited about something and before I knew it I was well out into the desert.'

'Weren't you scared?' There was a mixture of admiration and trepidation in Lynne's eyes.

'Well, yes, when I lost sight of the lights of the station, I started to think I was being silly and I'd just decided to call the dogs back when I heard two horses ahead of me.'

'Of course you did,' echoed Coshy, but no one turned towards him this time, and Jenna ignored him as well.

'I found Winemaster and that brumby stallion in a full-on battle. Winemaster wanted to steal his mares, I think.'

'And nearly got himself killed, bloody horse,' Bernie muttered. 'It's going to cost me a bloody arm and a leg in vet fees.' Everyone ignored him.

'So how did you get hurt?' It was Lex who asked this question. 'I find it hard to believe a rider as good as you fell off.'

'It was stupid of me, but I tried to ride Winemaster home, and of course without a saddle or bridle ...'

'At least the stallion is back,' interrupted Bernie. 'But we still haven't answered the question as to how such a valuable horse got away in the first place. He damn well didn't take himself for an evening stroll, so who let him out?'

Bernie turned his dark, cynical gaze directly towards Jenna. 'It seems terribly convenient that you knew exactly where to find him.'

Jenna was shocked into speechlessness. There was complete silence around the room as everyone digested his comment.

'What're you insinuating, Bernie?' Lex was the first to speak the words they were all thinking.

'I have it from a good source, Jenna was seen lurking around the stables around the time Winemaster went missing.' Bernie stood up taller, eyebrows bristling.

'What?' Words deserted her as she took in the implication of Bernie's accusation. 'No, I wasn't—'

'I won't be made a fool of,' yelled Bernie. 'Whoever let that horse out better own up soon, or I'll take things further.' With that he stomped out of the door.

'What's he insinuating?' Jenna asked. 'I'd never do anything like that.' Tears suddenly threatened behind her eyes. She'd managed not to cry through the whole saga of having her shoulder reset, but the injustice of Bernie's groundless allegation hurt more than any physical pain. Coshy was intentionally trying to get her into trouble. The utter bastard. The words were on the tip of her tongue to tell everyone it was him.

Mob broke the tense silence. 'Rowdy, we all know you didn't let the stupid horse out.'

Everyone nodded their heads in agreement. But now Jenna scanned their faces, looking for a false smile, a false platitude. She found Dan's gaze fixed on her. Thoughtful and compassionate.

'Thanks, Mob,' she said, but her heart was still beating fast, her palms still sweaty.

Ulrich came up and looked at her with his liquid eyes brimming with passion as he held his hat in front of his chest. 'I believe you, Jenna. You love those horses, you would never do that.'

'Thanks, Ulrich.' Jenna tried to smile at him, but her mouth went all crooked. Such a charming kid. At least she was sure he was convinced of her innocence. She could do no wrong in his eyes. Which might not be such a bad thing. One more person on her side was always good.

Cookie flapped her large arms and gave her a pat on the good shoulder on the way back to the kitchen. 'Don't worry, girl, Bernie is just looking for a scapegoat. He'll get over it soon enough.'

Jenna raised a half-hearted smile at her support.

Moon and Dan banged out the door towards the stables and Coshy went to follow them, but not before he shot Jenna a sly grimace. What was she going to do about him? He obviously had it in for her, by trying to pin the blame on her. Was that his plan all along? His way of getting rid of her. Jesus, she'd underestimated him if it was. From now on she was going to keep an eagle eye on that bastard.

Perhaps it was time to start thinking of moving on. The last thing she needed was grief from some mean-spirited misogynist jackaroo. She was going to leave eventually anyway. But no, she'd bloody-well do it on her own terms, not let him dictate her life. Coshy was small fry compared to what Liam was capable of. She could handle him.

CHAPTER NINE

'Want to take a trip somewhere?' Dan's question seemed harmless, but it caught Jenna off guard.

'A trip? What, you mean like a holiday,' she asked.

Dan didn't turn around to speak to her, and his back gave away nothing. He sat hunched, his tall frame deceptively small beside the metallic hugeness of the tractor. Her eyes traced the outline of his neck and shoulders and she wanted to go up and untwist the knotted muscles of his back. Instead, she continued to wipe the dusty engine parts she'd been commissioned to clean. It was a good job for someone with a shoulder that was still only half-working. She had to admit it was getting better day by day, she'd ditched the sling yesterday, ignoring Dan's protests, but she was glad Bernie had delayed the next muster for a few days. The helicopter pilot wasn't available, some kind of engine problem, and because he was integral to helping them find and muster the cows, there wasn't much they could do but wait. It would've been a struggle for her to be out there tussling with cranky cows right now, not that she would've admitted it. To anyone.

'Bernie's just told me we can all have three days off. We haven't had more than two days off between the six of us since the start of mustering.' He kept his head lowered as he passed on the surprising news. Bernie had become even more rude and unpleasant, if that were possible, since Winemaster's escape. Nothing more was said about the matter, but he point-blank refused to talk to Jenna. Why he hadn't fired her was a mystery. The only reason she could think of was that Lex and Dan were both fighting for her. Most of the staff continued as if nothing untoward had happened, except for Coshy, who cast rancorous glances her way when he thought she wasn't looking.

'There's a place I've always wanted to visit.' Shirtsleeves rolled up to the elbow, Dan still seemed more interested in tightening the bolt than in their conversation. Jenna watched the muscles in his forearms flex and bulge as he strained to get the bolt tight. She wondered why he seemed suddenly so casual about the whole thing, almost indifferent.

'Lex told me about it. He said it's one of the most beautiful places on this earth.' From his tone he could just as easily have been talking about the dusty floor of the machinery shed, instead of a place of natural beauty.

'Sounds interesting.' She kept her reply non-committal. Two could play at this game.

'It's about four hours' drive from here, but I never seem to get my act together to go and see it. Now Bernie's given us some time off I thought maybe we could give it a go.' Finally, she twigged to his problem. He was afraid she'd say no. He was right to be cautious, there was every possibility she would turn him down.

'Does this place have a name?'

At last he turned his head to watch her, a bead of sweat swimming down his jaw line, his brown eyes unreadable. 'Yep, it's called the Bungle Bungle Ranges.'

She couldn't help but give a questioning giggle at the strange name.

'It's about four hundred kilometres north-east of here. Lex reckons he went there years and years ago, before many people even knew it existed. He keeps telling me I should go and see it now, before it gets ruined by the tourists.' He returned his concentration to the motor part before him, but Jenna's curiosity was piqued. Not that she was going to say yes. She needed more information first.

'Wow, quite intriguing.' She paused before asking her next question. 'Who else would be coming?' And that was the crux of the matter.

'I'm pretty sure Moon would come, he's always talking about seeing more of his dreamtime land.' His tone was back to his businesslike manner. 'And you could ask Lynne if you like. I'm sure we could borrow a Land Cruiser.' She could tell he was already ticking off the details of what they should take with them in his head.

'It does sound like a great idea.' Jenna was becoming excited by the plan, especially now she knew she wouldn't be traveling with Dan unaccompanied. That would've been a recipe for disaster. It'd be too dangerous for her to spend that much time alone with him.

Over the past few days she had to keep reminding herself she didn't want Dan. What would be the point of getting involved with him when she had to leave soon?

'So that's a yes then?' Dan asked.

'Yes. When do we leave?'

He gave her a warm smile and a tiny part of her heart twitched. What harm could a quick trip to the Bungles do?

* * *

The trip exhausted them all, as they watched the flashing scenery with its images of flat open deserts pass by. Jenna's eyes had the colours, red earth, brown grass and grey bitumen burned into her retinas. She pointed out objects of beauty or interest, a solitary huge boab tree standing fat and tall like a protector of the desert, or a set of low rolling hills running purple into the distance.

It was just the four of them, Dan, Moon, Lynne and herself. Mob declined to come with them, said he just wanted to take it easy for a while. Dan guided them expertly over the hundreds of kilometres of dirt tracks. Sometimes they'd hit sporadic pieces of bitumen, dropped there as if to lull them into a sense of inclusion, until it ran out as suddenly as it'd appeared, and they'd be racing along gravel again, spewing a comet trail of dust behind them.

They took turns to drive, only stopping once to refill with petrol and a scant meal washed down with a pot of billy tea.

Lynne was driving when Jenna suddenly saw what they were all waiting for. 'Oh God, there they are!' Her voice rose an octave. 'Look how beautiful the mountains are!' Dan's head sprang off his chest and he rubbed his eyes to get them working again. They came abreast a small rise in the road and Lynne stopped the car so they could all get out and admire the view.

Over the top of the haze of lush green spinifex grass floated a chain of mounded hills. They were all heaped together in a jumbled row as if a child had been making sandcastles with a rounded tea-cup. The mountain ranges didn't stand very high from the horizon, but even from this distance they could see the flaming colours, orange and red, variegated with black stripes, making them seem as if they were formed by some kind of demented, crouching tiger.

As they hopped back in the car and approached closer, the hues turned wilder and gaudier. The mountains became towering turrets of ancient castles, their unusual bands morphing through explosions of colour; auburn, red, crimson and purple as the sun set to the west. The shifting shadows accentuated the hills, showing gorges and steep cliffs plunging off into the heart of the range. Inside the car it was silent as they treasured the awe-inspiring sight in front of them.

They arrived at the Bungles just on dusk and had to set up camp in near-darkness. They'd have to wait until tomorrow to start exploring, but Jenna took a quick sortie around the campsite, while the others fussed over their swag placement. At the head of a large walking trail called the Piccaninny Gorge track, she found some large signs plastered with maps of the area as well as fact sheets about the Park. She flicked on the torch and used the yellow beam of light to read the placard that told about the many different activities and attractions on offer in the park. Humming to herself, she made her way back towards the flickering yellow glow of their campsite.

'I think we should walk up Piccaninny Gorge tomorrow,' Jenna said to Dan as she sat next to him.

'Shit, you scared me! Don't sneak up on me like that.' He nudged her with his elbow to soften his words. 'Where did you get off to? We were starting to get worried about you.'

'Just scouting out the place,' she replied.

'Well, while you were gallivanting around I've set your swag up next to mine, and I've organized the boys on the other side of the fire,' said Lynne in her best mothering tone.

'Thanks, Sunshine.' Jenna smiled, watching Lynne's eyes glinting in the firelight.

'Where did you say we should go again?' questioned Dan. 'Goblin Gorge?'

'No,' laughed Jenna. 'Picaninny Gorge. It seems like one of the longer walks, and it might get us right into the heart of the mountain range, away from most of the people.'

'But we've only got a couple of days,' Lynne mumbled around a mouthful of food.

'That's okay, we can walk up the gorge for a day, camp and then walk back again. It seems like there may still be some large pools of water remaining. We might even get a swim,' replied Jenna.

'Sounds like a plan to me.' At least Dan agreed with her. 'As soon as we've eaten, I'm rolling into my swag; all that driving has me beat.'

* * *

Stepping over water-rounded river rocks, feet sinking into deep thick sand, they wound their way up the gorge. Sometimes the towering walls closed in, almost shutting out the light. And then just as suddenly they would open out to a flat plain hundreds of meters across, allowing small white-trunked gum trees to poke up through the boulders and spinifex grass. Dan was amazed. He'd never seen anything like it before.

Following the creek line, they scrambled over large rocks, through tunnels of overhanging ledges, and stopped to admire every small nature-carved waterhole they came to. They all had a small swag slung over the top of a backpack in which they carried water and enough food for two days.

Compared to most of the other walkers who passed them, steaming ahead with earnest looks of intense awe on their faces, it seemed the foursome were traveling light. Lynne was walking in her tired old sneakers with a hole in the front, where her toe sometimes peeked out. He and Moon were wearing their brown leather Blundstone riding boots. His only compensation to the heat and humidity was the fact he'd changed from denim jeans to a pair of shorts, as had everyone else. They'd all put their swimwear on underneath their clothes, in case they came to a really good swimming hole and wanted to dive right in.

Bringing up the rear, Dan took the opportunity to observe Jenna's legs as they walked. They were pale after not having seen the sun for so long, but that didn't detract from her lean thighs and shapely calves. And those tight little shorts showed off her sexy arse much better than the jeans she normally wore. He was enjoying this little sojourn, and he congratulated himself on his great idea.

It was a welcome break to get away from the station. And he was glad to see even Jenna loosen up a little. She'd been tense and jumpy for the past few days, and he couldn't really blame her. Bernie still wasn't giving away who'd told him Jenna was the one to let Winemaster out. Dan knew without a shadow of a doubt she hadn't done it, as did Lex. But it was hard not to see the speculative glances some of the others cast her way when she wasn't looking. Dan clenched his fists at the memory. He wanted to yell at them all to mind their own business. Jenna had withdrawn back into herself, and she was now almost back to the person she'd been when she first arrived at the station. Cool and aloof. It must be hard for her, knowing there was someone out there telling fibs about her. In some ways he didn't blame her. But he wished ... What did he wish? That she'd trust him more? Open up to him more? Because, God knows she needed to talk to someone. Perhaps this short time away, with people she trusted might do her some good.

Towards lunchtime they stopped at a deep waterhole and plunged their tired feet into the cool water, soaking their spinifex cuts and blistered heels.

'Arghh, there's something tickling my toes,' Lynne screamed and hopped backwards out of the water.

'It's only the little rock-hole frogs,' said Jenna, laughing. 'Come and look at them, they're really cute.'

Dan stared into the waterhole. 'Look there are even little fish in here as well,' he said. Everyone crowded around so he could point out the tiny creatures.

In the late afternoon they walked across some bulky parallel spans of rock and came to a large waterhole suspended in the corner of two rock faces. The sign at the site called the spans of rock "The Fingers" and suggested a good campsite could be found by the side of the pool.

'This looks fantastic. What do you think guys?' Dan asked, wiping the sweat away from beneath the lowered brim of his hat.

'Yep, it'll do me,' Lynne agreed with gusto. 'Anything to be able to stop walking and just relax.'

'Great, let's set up camp.' Dan dropped his backpack and swag on the ground and Jenna did the same. She took off her hat and ran her hand through her hair.

'What do you think?' he asked softly, capturing her gaze with his. Her blue eyes sparkled, reflecting the sky.

'I love it.' She drew in a deep breath and blew it out through her nose. Then a wicked gleam came into her eyes and she punched him in the shoulder. 'Last one in is a rotten egg,' she shouted and sprinted towards the waterhole, dropping her clothes in a haphazard trail on the way, until she was down to her swimwear. Dan smiled. Yep, this trip had definitely been a good idea.

* * *

Cool water suspended her like a hammock. Jenna had almost forgotten what it felt like to be encased in silky, fresh, clean water. It was the closest thing to heaven she'd felt in a long while. Tiny ripples lapped against her cheek as she lay on her back, face upturned to a patch of blue sky.

The water swirled against her limbs and she knew someone else was swimming nearby. She popped her head up and opened her eyes to see who was approaching.

Dan's curls lay plastered and water-dark against his skull, making his smile seem even whiter against his tanned skin. She smiled back.

It was the first time she'd seen Dan without a shirt on, and it was doing strange things to her insides every time she caught a glimpse of all that olive skin stretched over hardened muscles. He was just as tantalizing as she'd imagined. It was sheer torture to have him so near and not be able to reach out and touch him.

Jesus, had he seen her staring? Tearing her gaze away from his wonderful torso, she said, 'Thank you so much for bringing us here.' How could she ever explain to Dan the serenity he'd given her by introducing her to this place? As if she'd escaped reality for a while. As if her other life, the one of hard physical labour combined with the constant worry about staying one step in front of Liam, had been put on hold for a fraction of time. But she had Dan to thank for bringing her here. And she was here with the three people she trusted the most in this world. She was determined to treasure these few days, because she may not get many chances to be this carefree again.

'I knew you'd like it,' he replied. 'How's your shoulder now?' Something dark flashed over his face as he mentioned her arm.

'Heaps better,' she said, rolling it around to show how she could move it freely now. 'Thanks to you. It only twinges now and then if I move it too quickly or lift something heavy.'

'You'll need to look after it. It might never be quite the same again,' he said, shrugging off her gratitude.

Before she could even open her mouth to reply, something tugged at her leg. She didn't have time to scream before she was pulled beneath the surface. The water wasn't deep and she managed to touch the bottom and come bouncing back up, laughing and coughing at the same time, trying to grab Lynne by the arm and pull her under as payback. Dan joined them, diving and gliding, pushing and skylarking in the tannin coloured water, until they were all breathless from laughing and had to lie on the sandy edge of the rock pool to catch their breath in the beating sunshine.

Moon grinned at them from further along the bank, where he sat with legs half immersed in the water, dark skin almost black in the lapping waves.

Dan and Lynne returned to the pool, delighting in the sheer decadence of being able to swim in a body of clean water. Jenna stayed nestled at the water's edge, in the shade of one of the sparse Livistonia palms that grew in this area. Moon moved closer to her, settling down a few feet away in the browning grass. They sat in companionable silence. His eyes almost closed, Moon seemed to be lulled into a heat-induced daze.

A flash of iridescence buzzed in front of Jenna. The blue flash returned and stopped to hover for a second at the water's edge. Lacework wings beat in perfect synchronisation, as the dragonfly stopped to ogle, twisting its head to get a better view with large grey eyes. Like a small puff of wind, the dragonfly alighted on her large toe, tickling with his hard exoskeleton legs. Jenna couldn't help but admire the beautiful azure-blue armour that covered his long tail, and his membranous wings.

She started to hum under her breath as she became absorbed in the wondrous creature, forgetting about Moon only a few feet away.

Another smaller helicopter-shaped insect blazed past, this one was more of a dull copper, but so fast it was hard for her sleepy eyes to follow him. It landed on the little toe of the same foot and turned to view her with ancient eyes. Soon three more zoomed in, materialising from the air to land on her feet, and one on her knee. Two of them were smaller and fire-engine red, and one blue, like the first. She hummed along with their gentle wing-rustling drone.

Suddenly she remembered Moon sitting next to her and snapped her head around. His dark eyes were wide and she knew he'd seen her playing with the insects. Damn. What did she say? Had he guessed? About her gift?

'I knew since I first met you,' he said, as if reading her mind. There was no falsehood in his simple statement. 'I see it in you when you talk to the horses and the dogs. The kangaroos, even they love you.'

Bugger. No one had discovered her gift before, this was an unfamiliar path, and she wasn't sure what to say.

'Please don't tell anyone else,' she implored, as she looked into Moon's ageless face. 'Don't tell them what I can do.' It was the first thing that came to her, but it was also the most important thing. Dan or Lynne could emerge from the water at any second.

After what seemed an eternity he answered, 'Tell them what?'

Relief flowed like syrup through her bones. 'Thanks, Moon.'

'I'm not sure why you keep such a wonderful thing hidden, but I will, if that's what you want.'

'It is. Maybe one day I can explain why no-one else can know.' She paused. 'But for now, it needs to be our secret.'

He nodded. The feeling of a noose tightening around her neck receded.

'Whatever you say, missus. It's all good to me.'

Jenna pretended to turn her gaze to the other two still swimming in the rock pool as the silence stretched around her and Moon again.

Damn. Damn. Double damn. Things were starting to get out of her control. Perhaps it really was time to move on from Shiralee. The thought was coming more often now. She should start listening to it.

CHAPTER TEN

'Mmm … smells good,' Jenna said, nose hovering in the steam rising from the blackened pot. 'Why does macaroni cheese always taste like the best gourmet food in the world when you're camping?'

'Because out here you know how lucky you are to be alive,' Dan said from his spot on the other side of the flames, giving her a quick wink.

After dinner all four of them leant up against the grey skeleton of a fallen tree trunk, sitting in an unbroken line of companionship.

'I have a bit of a detour I'd like to take on the way back tomorrow, if you're all happy with it,' Jenna said to no-one in particular. 'It'll take us out through a different gorge than the one we came up, and I'm hoping it'll open out into some really spectacular country at the other end.'

'As long as you don't get us lost.' Lynne's eyes were drowsy and half-closed in the heat of the fire.

'Sounds fine to me,' acknowledged Dan. Jenna was sitting on the far end of the log, Dan right next to her. They sat very close. She hadn't meant it to happen that way, but when he'd parked himself on the ground between herself and Lynne, she couldn't disagree without making a scene. Deciding to enjoy the simple closeness of him, she didn't let herself think too much about it. She laid her head back against the log to watch the infinitesimal slow dance of the stars as they wove across the sky. They were so clear and achingly bright, some forming clusters of pinpricks, while others stood proudly away from the main carpet of light.

Inhaling the still-warm air, it seemed to contain the essence of everything pure and soul-nourishing. Her heart filled with conviction that, at least for the space of one night, she was safe from Liam. Tonight, even her long hair was allowed to hang loose over her shoulders.

Maybe it was this glow of wellbeing that made her more receptive to the effect Dan had on her. Who knew? But every time he laughed or gestured, his thigh would brush against hers. Jenna delighted in the feel of him through the fabric of her shorts. She found herself not concentrating on the conversation anymore; waiting for his next touch. She fiddled with her ring, finding comfort in the feel of it as she let her mind wander.

Dan seemed oblivious to her exquisite discomfort. Until he made a deliberate move to lay the full length of his leg against hers and left it there. His eyes flicked onto her face for a split second as he continued with the flow of chitchat, seemingly unaffected. Every detail of his muscular leg pressed into hers, the firm weight searing through her nerves. Strange, but it was comforting to have the restrained strength of his contact down the length of her leg. The tiny little voice inside her head that told her to move away was easy to ignore.

Jenna couldn't say with any certainty how long they stayed connected—it felt like an eternity—when Lynne suddenly sat forward and emitted a face-shattering yawn. 'I know it's still early guys but I have to hit the swag. Sorry, I can't keep my eyes open any longer.'

'Night, Lynne,' they chorused as she shuffled, half-asleep over to the other side of the fire. They could hear her muffled rustles as she settled down in her swag, and a big sigh when her head hit the pillow.

On cue, Moon muttered, 'Me too. See you in the morning.' He was impossible to see, the dark night blanketing his skin as he walked to his swag.

Frozen by uncertainty, Jenna remained motionless. What to do now? There was no one else's conversation to provide an invisible barrier between them. Her safety net had been stripped away. Last time she'd been alone with Dan she'd nearly kissed him. Her face flushed and she was glad of the deep orange glow from the fire to drown the heat rising in her cheeks.

'Just us now, huh?' His voice broke through the night sounds of cicadas singing and the soft starlight.

'Hmm … I guess I should probably go to bed too.' She made a move to get up and found his hand on her wrist.

'Stay a little while longer.'

She hung suspended in mid-air, uncertain.

'I'm not going to bite, you know.' Stung by his comment she sat back down. 'We haven't had much of a chance to just sit and chat, you and me. There's a lot I still don't know about you. We never finished our conversation from the other night.'

'Dan,' she said, hoping to change the subject. 'I want to thank you again for taking us on this trip. This is the best time I've had since I started working here.' At least this was true and she knew he'd hear the absolute sincerity in her voice.

'Yep, this place is as beautiful as Lex said it'd be.' His voice was low and agreeable. 'We're quite similar, you and I. Don't look at me like that. I mean we appreciate the same things.' He grabbed her hand from where her fingers were restlessly tapping on her denim shorts. His warm fingers slotted between hers, making the perfect tangle of digits and her confusion increased until she had to close her eyes. But when they were closed it made the searing friction of his skin on hers almost unbearable, so she opened them again in a hurry.

She'd allowed herself the small reward of feeling his well-built leg laid down the length of hers because she'd succumbed to the peace and shelter of this night. Now it was time to halt whatever was happening between them. Before it had any more chance to build. It was time to take her hand and gently disentangle it from his.

But her hand remained where it was.

'I told you I come from Tamworth, but I still don't know where you were born,' he said.

Neither do I. Had she said that out loud? Oh God, he was curdling her brain. He pulled her hand towards his body and tucked it against his chest, where the faint thread of his heartbeat pulsed.

'It's time to remedy that. Tell me more about you.' His brown eyes sparkled in the firelight. He angled his body towards her, his face coming to within inches of hers.

Thinking became almost unmanageable, her awareness was so full of the man in front of her. Her body hummed with a slow, spreading heat.

Swallowing hard, she tried to focus her thoughts. 'Umm, there's really not a lot to tell.' She fought for words to distract her from the warmth flushing up her neck. 'I was born in a little town called Berridale, up in the NSW highlands.' She'd told this lie many times before and it should come easily now. But somehow with Dan it made her feel uncomfortable. Part of it was true; she'd grown up there. But she hadn't been born there. Problem was, she didn't know where she'd been born. It was just one more of the mysteries her mother took with her when she left. 'It was just me and my dad and a few sheep.'

'Mmm, interesting.' His deep voice sent shivers through her, molten liquid running through her veins. His gaze remained fire-bright and fixed on her face, the flare of craving in his eyes telling her he was no longer interested in where she spent her childhood.

Gradually, he pulled her towards him and she didn't resist. Her chest came to rest against his. She drew in one jagged breath. After that, she daren't breathe at all.

Like a butterfly landing, he kissed the corner of her mouth. She sighed and closed her eyes, letting herself fall for just a second. She'd wanted this kiss for so long now, her whole body was suddenly alive with anticipation. The touch of his lips on her face eradicated any lingering fears. Fear of letting go. Fear of trusting someone else. Fear of having to leave again. She'd managed to stay so strong up till now, so independent. But that was before she met Dan. The crushing uncertainty she'd felt only moments before evaporated into the night sky. She wanted to hold this perfect moment forever. Dan's lips rasped down the line of her jaw, searing her skin, making her stomach clench with want.

A low groan escaped her lips.

Had that been her who made that noise? It was the sound of someone enmeshed in a deep ocean of lust and want. She opened her eyes, her fingers uncurled and released their hold on Dan's broad shoulders.

Dan must've felt her tense beneath his shoulder, ready to push herself away, because he said, 'Oh no you don't.' Taking her chin in his hand, he pulled her body hard back against his. 'This time we're going to finish what we started,' he growled. Capturing her lips, his mouth trapped hers. It was warm and inviting and the desire funnelling through him caught her off guard. He tasted like fresh-mown hay, and coffee and strawberries. His skin was taut and supple beneath her hands as they ran up underneath the back of his shirt. She was melting into him, surrendering within the sanctuary of his solid chest.

Feeling the subtle shift within her, Dan's kiss became more demanding. He grasped the long hair at the back of her head and drew her in even closer.

She could feel the muscles of his back move like moulded iron as he held her suspended, tighter and tighter. Shutting her eyes, she gave in to the physical craving as her heart pumped crazily and her overheated blood rushed through her body.

Disentangling his fingers from her hair, Dan moved his hand to cradle the curve of her cheek, looking deep into her eyes. The intimacy of the gesture shook Jenna to the core. He cared for her. Deeply. It was there in his eyes. It'd never been this way with anyone else before. On the few occasions she'd allowed herself to be with a man, it'd only ever been a one-night fling, all over in the space of a few hours, with neither of their hearts any the worse for wear afterwards. She'd never allowed herself to become this caught up with anyone else. The possibilities were enormous. She might be safe and loved in the hands of this man. Her heart constricted.

It was this cruel thought that brought Jenna back to reality.

No matter how much she wanted—needed—to give in to Dan, she couldn't. There was no way she'd drag her friends into the private battle that was her living nightmare. No one else could get hurt. Not because of her.

Putting one hand between them, she gave a gentle but inexorable push on his chest, driving them apart. Her fingers felt his pounding heart through the fabric of his shirt. Then she took her hand away and drew backwards, making herself watch his dark eyes, the pupils still large with yearning, a question mark on his lips.

'Why are you pushing me away?'

She didn't answer. She was hollow and empty.

'Why won't you trust me, Jenna?'

Because life had taught her she could only rely on herself. No one else. That was her harsh reality and she was better off remembering it.

* * *

They packed up their meagre camp early, so they could start the trek back to the car. Jenna tried to catch Dan's eye a few times during their packing, but he pretended to be busy so he didn't have to return her gaze. The others didn't notice the tension between them.

He wasn't sulking, he didn't do that. He just didn't want to talk to Jenna this morning. Or hear her lame explanations. She knew what kind of women he liked to hang out with, so why would she risk her character with him? In her mind, he only wanted a quick fling, nothing more. And normally that's all he asked from a woman. Just not this time. This time he wanted more. Hell, he wanted all of her, if she'd let him have it. But she'd pushed him away and he never got the chance to tell her how he really felt. And that was the way he was going to leave it. It was better that way. For both of them.

If only his younger brother, Patrick, hadn't stolen that car and then the cash from the local twenty-four-hour convenience store. Maybe Dan's life would be different. Now he had to live with the stigma of a criminal record hanging over his head. He'd never be able to wipe the taint of his time in jail from his life, even if he knew he was innocent. But Patrick was barely fifteen. Young enough to do stupid things, but old enough to go to juvenile detention. Dan couldn't allow that. He already knew how his mother had folded in on herself—became more withdrawn and shrunken—all the other times Patrick had flouted the law. To have her youngest son behind bars would've killed her. So Dan took the rap, said he'd been the one to steal the car and burgle the store. At least his brother had the sense to wear a balaclava, so it was easy for Dan to say it was him. There was no digital proof to say otherwise. It was no big deal. He'd lived through the ordeal, done the two years and was out now, completely fine. *Wasn't he?*

He had his mate, Damien, to thank for finally getting him out of jail. He and Damien were best mates at school, and Damien went on to become a cop. But he'd only recently been commissioned into the force when Dan first went to jail. After two years, Damien had come and asked him point-blank if he'd stolen the car. At first Dan refused to answer, but in the end he agreed that he hadn't but he would never tell Damo who had. There was no way he'd implicate his little brother. There'd be no point. Damo had gone away again, but soon after, an appeal to shorten Dan's sentence was launched and Dan was set free two years earlier than his original sentence. Damo admitted he'd helped with the appeal, but never went into details, telling Dan that he didn't owe him anything but his continued friendship.

'Lead on, Jones,' gestured Lynne, sweeping her hand down in a mock bow for Jenna. 'We shall follow our intrepid leader to the ends of the earth.' Lynne seemed oblivious to what'd occurred between him and Jenna last night.

'Thanks.' Jenna gave her friend a reassuring pat on the shoulder as she passed by. Lynne's face split into one of her infectious wide grins, which on any normal day would've picked his mood up as well, just not today.

Jenna led them around the back of a thick clump of bushes behind their campsite. River rocks covered the ground like flat brown bubbles, coaxing them back towards the river they'd followed up the canyon. But she ignored the well-worn trail and headed off over a low rise, where three smaller gorges all ran off on errands of their own choosing. They made towards the left-hand one and as they dove into it the steep sides blocked the early morning sun, dropping the temperature to a much more manageable level. He followed along at the rear of the group, hat pulled down low, hands in his pockets.

They walked quickly and soon the rock faces dipped lower and before he knew it they'd emerged out of the canyon into a sea of spinifex. There was the horizon, with the multi-hued sky a vivid blue, running like water colour into the edge of his vision. An obvious trail marched in front of them, enticing them out into the open country. Large spires, much taller than him, reared up like a smattering of red pointy teeth from the ground; termite mounds housing colonies of invisible millions, standing to attention throughout the clearing.

'At least you haven't got us lost,' declared Lynne. 'This trail looks like it's well used.'

'Worried, were you?'

'Not at all, dear friend.' Lynne took off with long strides, Moon following right behind.

Jenna stopped and waited in the middle of the trail. Damn, he really didn't want to talk to her right now. Just the sight of her standing there made him tense. She looked so fresh and clean, as if this trip had washed years of worry from her face. The denim shorts showed off her pale legs to good advantage, highlighting the curves hinted at beneath. He wondered if women understood just how good they looked in cut-off shorts. No, he corrected himself, it was Jenna who looked good in them. So good he wanted to go up and cradle her bum in his hands and pull her up against his chest—hard. He wanted to make her groan with pleasure the way she had last night.

That was a mistake. Thinking about kissing Jenna last night was causing blood to rush to places he'd rather it didn't.

'Dan?'

'Yep,' he said, hoping he sounded nonchalant.

'Could we please talk about last night?'

Here it came, the excuses and the lies. At least it put an end to the burgeoning bulge in his pants.

'If you want to.' He kept his gaze on the distant horizon, determined to avoid looking at her. 'I don't have a lot to say. I'm fine. I can pretend nothing happened, if that makes it better for you.' He rammed his fists deeper into his pockets and said nothing more.

'Really?' He heard her curse under her breath. 'Well it doesn't make it better.' Her voice held a sudden raspiness that made him glance up. 'I don't want … what happened last night to affect our friendship.' She halted, as if searching for the right words.

'I'm assuming when you refer to *what happened*, you mean when you pulled away from me, shut me down. Shut us down, as if you couldn't bear to be near me.' He was stunned to hear the anger in his own voice and he saw her flinch at his harsh words. That should've made him happy, after all he'd wanted her to feel as bad as he did. But for some reason shame rose in his throat.

'That's not how it was,' she protested.

'Then what happened? Why did you pull away? Why did you …' His words trickled away before he could say, *why did you reject me*? And that was the crux of the matter. He was angry because she'd rejected him. Maybe she hadn't felt the white-hot heat flowing between them as they kissed. Maybe it'd only been in his imagination. How could he have misjudged her feelings so poorly? He was sure their desire had been mutual.

She twined her fingers together nervously. 'I pulled away from you because I'm not ready for another relationship so soon.'

There was that vulnerability in her eyes again, hinting at secrets buried deep. Something she was hiding. The need to protect those close to him kicked into overdrive. But he had no idea what she needed protection *from*. She was already one of the gutsiest and most determined women he knew. She wanted to be brave—that's what the tattoo on her wrist declared—but exactly what that meant, he was yet to find out. His anger dwindled away.

'So soon after what?' He moved in closer to see her face more clearly.

'Before I came to work up here the only man I ever loved left me.' There was a strange twist to her features. 'He went away and left me on my own, and I'm still recovering. I came up here to get away. To get over it.'

That was her secret, a broken heart?

'Your bad dream the other night. Was it to do with the guy who left you?' he asked as the pieces started to fall into place.

'Kind of,' she agreed. 'I'm just not ready for another relationship. There's not enough left of me to get involved with anyone yet. I need more time. That's why I pulled away, Dan, it wouldn't be fair on either of us. Do you understand what I'm trying to say?'

At last she was saying something he *could* understand. He could live with the idea of a broken heart. They healed over time. Didn't they? And at least it meant it wasn't him she was shunning, it was the whole male species she wanted to avoid. What she needed was a friend right now. Someone she could lean on and confide in. Friends, nothing more, nothing less. If only he could control his raging libido whenever she came near, then everything would be fine. He'd just have to practice, by pretending that her nearness didn't make all of the tiny hairs on his body stand to attention. Starting right now.

'Why couldn't you just have said that last night?' If she had, he wouldn't have spent the whole night tormenting himself, replaying the scene of her rebuff over and over again in his head. He'd been so mad at her last night, wondering why she refused to let down her guard, even for a second, when he thought he'd made it obvious his feelings were genuine. It was clear she had major trust issues, but now at least he had an inkling as to why.

'It all happened so quickly. I didn't have time to say anything. Can you forgive me?'

'I'll think about it.' His mouth quirked upwards, so she'd know she was off the hook. 'But you owe me big time for this, you know.'

'Do I?'

'Yes. You owe me all the details we didn't get into last night, about your life.'

'Ask away then,' she said, a small sigh escaping her lips.

* * *

Jenna had lain awake and tussled with the idea of not explaining herself to Dan after he kissed her. It would've made her eventual leaving of the station a whole lot easier. Except for a small, but very insistent, voice that told her maybe it *was* okay to have a few friends. For sanity's sake. She could make no sense of the inexplicable way Dan affected her senses, but it forced her to admit she'd come to respect him. It was okay to have a friend she trusted and respected, as long as she didn't let him get too close. And it was the same with her other friends, Lynne, Moon, Lex, Mob and Cookie. Wasn't it human nature to want companionship? She'd just have to put up with the extra pain she caused when she left, hoping the guilt wouldn't overwhelm her. At the moment, it was enough to know she'd accepted their friendship. She'd worry about what-ifs later.

But she couldn't tell him the real reason why she'd rejected him. What she'd actually lost. Who she was running from. So she'd made up a lie. Well, part of it was the truth, her father would never be returning from the grave, and he had been the only person she'd ever loved. But it'd been harder than she expected. Her words got tangled together when she'd tried to explain. Dan wasn't a man who played at being anything other than himself. He was genuine and dependable. How would he react if he ever found out she'd been deceitful? Had spun him half-truths and twisted lies.

'We should see if we can catch up with the others, look how far ahead they are.' Dan's voice brought her back to reality. It was true. Moon and Lynne were now like tiny ants moving through the grassy mounds. Grateful for the distraction, she started forward with a lurch and they both picked up their pace, their boots crunching in symphony on the red stones.

Two hours later they emerged into the carpark, hot, sweaty and elated. The walk back had been a hard slog, but the beautiful countryside made it all worthwhile. Jenna was keen to get to the car. Her injured shoulder ached from carrying the backpack for so long, and she was desperate to get it off and then hopefully give it a quick surreptitious massage while no one was looking. She was the first to notice a group of four or five people gathered around their Land Cruiser.

'What's going on,' she said, walking a little faster towards their car. Dan caught up with her and pushed past.

'Is everything alright here?' he enquired of an elderly gentleman who was bent down looking at their front tyre.

'Oh hello, laddie. Are you the owner of this car?' He was spry, thin and wiry, with an intelligent glint in his eye.

'Yes, why?' Moon and Lynne caught up and they all gathered around the car with serious looks on their faces.

'Well my wife, Beryl, and I,' the gentleman gestured to a grey-haired woman standing at the front of the 4WD, 'were just minding our own business, unpacking our caravan.' He pointed a bony finger towards an enormous caravan and 4WD nestled in the corner of the large gravel carpark. 'And, Beryl, said to me there was a shady looking character hanging around your car over here. So I shouted at him and he took off into the bush.' The old guy gave a proud smile, almost as if he expected a pat on the head. The other people gathered around the car murmured their agreement.

'Yep, I saw him too,' said a good-looking guy with tattoos up both arms. 'I looked up when Donald here yelled, and he definitely took off like a jack rabbit once he knew he'd been spotted. Me and my mates were just about to head off and walk up the Piccaninny Gorge trail.' Tattoo Guy glanced around at his other two friends and they nodded in agreement. 'Mike chased him into the bush, but he was too quick. We think he might've had a motorbike, because we heard one start up not long after.' Tattoo Guy gave a happy grin, as if he too had achieved something wonderful.

'Oh, thanks,' Dan replied, looking nonplussed. 'But why would someone be meddling with our car?'

'Well I'm not exactly sure, laddie, but it looks like he's slashed your tyre.'

'What?' Dan bent down to look at the tyre and Jenna sidled in next to him. Yep, the tyre had three deep cuts in it and was completely flat. 'Bloody hell.' Dan stood up and swiped his hat off his head. 'Why would someone do that?'

'I dunno,' replied Tattoo Guy. 'But I think you're lucky we scared him off, because he was about to do the same to your other front tyre. Hope you've got a reliable spare in the back.'

Jenna's blood ran cold. They only carried one spare. What would they do if they had two flats? Or three? They would've been stranded here, for hours or even days, until someone could bring another spare out to them. Which wasn't the end of the world, they had enough food and supplies to keep them going. But why would someone want to delay them like that?

'Wow, well I guess we owe you a debt of thanks,' replied Dan, his brows knitted together in a thoughtful frown.

'Anytime, laddie,' said Donald as he and Beryl turned to make their way back over to their caravan. 'Just glad we could help.'

All four of the Shiralee team exchanged loaded glances.

'I don't suppose any of you could tell us what this guy looked like,' Dan asked.

'Nah, sorry, he was too far away,' replied Tattoo Guy. 'He was wearing all dark clothing, and had a cap pulled down over his head. He might've even had a scarf wrapped around his face. It was hard to tell.' His other mates muttered they hadn't got a good look either.

'Sorry, laddie, my eyesight ain't what it used to be.' Donald gave a hearty shrug.

'Thanks anyway,' Dan said to their retreating backs.

'I guess we'd better get the spare out,' said Moon, dropping his pack on the ground in resignation.

'This is all a little odd,' Lynne said to Jenna as they watched the two men unhook the spare tyre from the back door of the car.

'Hmm.' Jenna was too preoccupied to give any more of an answer. Surely this couldn't have anything to do with Liam. It must be a coincidence.

But if it was, then was it the same coincidence that led to Coshy letting the stallion out and then trying to blame it on her? And Coshy rode a motorbike.

CHAPTER ELEVEN

It was hard to shake the glow around the four of them, even once they were back into the mundane world of station life. Jenna's mind drifted back to the feeling of lying in the warm, silky water of the rock pool. The trip had changed them all in a subtle way, binding them a little closer together.

The night after they returned from the Bungle Bungles, Cookie shot a dark look at them across the dining table. 'What did you four get up to when you went up north? You're all walking around with stupid smiles on your faces, as if you've got some kind of secret you're keeping from the rest of us.' Her expression said she was only half joking.

'We aren't keeping secrets from you, Cookie,' laughed Jenna. 'You know how it is when you go on holiday, it's always hard to come back to reality.'

'I guess so.' Cookie's response was half-hearted.

'And it really was so beautiful and so special up there, Cookie, you should've come with us.' Lynne couldn't help but gush.

'Yeah, yeah, I've heard it all before.' Cookie dismissed Lynne's enthusiasm with a wave of her plump hand. 'I can't see me being interested in looking at yet another pile of rocks. I'd much rather stay here and read a good book than gallivant around bushwalking all day.' The look on Cookie's face said it all.

The following day, the station was buzzing with the anticipation of getting ready for the next muster of the season, and everyone was moving a little faster than usual. Cookie practically ran to the kitchen on some errand, and Lex's rolling gait covered more ground than usual on his way to check the saddles one more time before they were loaded. This time they'd be trucking the horses and people out to their first camp, as it was too far for the horses to go on foot.

'Hey, when are you going to fill me in on all the gory details of your holiday?' Mob stood in front of Jenna, blocking her path. He laid a hand on her shoulder, surprising her with his contact.

'How about tonight at dinner?' asked Jenna, a little breathless from carrying the large box of food to the Land Cruiser for Cookie.

'Okay,' Mob said in his affable way. 'Do you promise?'

'I promise.'

As she went to move around Mob he stopped her. 'Hey, Jenna. I missed you while you were gone.' His keen gaze locked onto hers as he spoke.

'I missed you too,' she said automatically. It wasn't until later when she thought about his comment that she became troubled. What exactly had he meant by it?

She was so busy, she almost forgot about their problem with the tyres. Dan spoke to Lex about it as soon as they arrived home, Jenna and Lynne hovering nearby. Lex rolled a smoke in his unhurried way as he considered the issue.

'It's odd,' he replied eventually. 'But it's not unheard of for some hooligan dickheads to go around slashing tyres as some kind of sick joke. It's happened before.'

'That's true,' Dan acknowledged. 'I remember Wazza from the Pub said it happened a year or so ago in town. A whole line of cars had their tyres slashed.'

'Yep, probably some young kids who weren't brought up right with nothing better to do,' said Lex.

Dan nodded, but his brown eyes were troubled as he walked away.

Jenna wasn't convinced either. The old guy at the carpark, Donald, had said it was a man who ran away, not a young kid. And he was on his own, not with a group of hooligans egging each other on. And why had he taken so much trouble to disguise himself? Something just didn't feel right to Jenna. But she couldn't put her finger on what it was, so she said nothing more.

* * *

Dan watched the desert scrub fly by the window. One hand gripped the handle above his head to stop himself from being bounced out of the car seat. The road was incredibly rugged, if indeed it could be called a road at all. Jenna, Lynne and Mob occupied the back seat and even Mob's inane comments had evaporated after hours of being flung around inside the car.

'Almost there,' Coshy said. Dan's sigh turned into a loud grunt as the car flew over yet another large sand hump. Dan decided Coshy's driving was almost as unpleasant as his personality.

'There it is!' He couldn't keep the relief out of his voice as he pointed towards a low stand of Mallee trees.

The Land Cruiser came to a shuddering halt. Dan jumped out of the passenger seat at the same time all three people in the back piled out of the car, landing in a laughing heap on the red earth. Jenna, still giggling, looked up at him from the bottom of the pile. It was one of those rare moments when she let a genuine smile touch her face. Such a dazzling smile, it lit up her eyes with humour and made his heart swell. He reached down towards her as Mob and Lynne helped each other struggle up from the tangle of bodies.

She grabbed his hand, allowing him to haul her up onto her feet. A surge of heat flowed through him at her touch. He could feel every detail of her hand, the firm pressure of her smaller palm as it flexed in his. Images from the night they'd kissed flooded in. The way her eyes flashed as if they contained the very flames of the campfire. The way her indulgent lips tasted on his. Suggestive, teasing, intense, setting off an equally intense desire deep inside him. The way her hair felt running through his fingers, silken and fragrant.

For a second he was unable to control his visceral reaction to her as he watched the beating of blood through the vein in her throat. That pulse beat faster under his gaze.

Friends, that's all they were.

She was the one to break the deadlock, stepping away from him as she said, 'Thanks, Dan.'

He kept his face frozen, hoping none of his inner turmoil showed. 'Let's get these yards built,' he said, making his voice extra loud so the people exiting from the second Land Cruiser pulling up behind them could hear as well. 'Lex should be here with the horses in a couple of hours and we need somewhere to keep them penned up.' If she just wanted a friend then he'd make damned sure that's all he was. He was cool efficiency and steely control once more.

Dan helped Pat and Ulrich, putting together the metal fencing for the yards that'd house the cattle. The heat was oppressive. Even in the mottled shade of the Mallee trees, he could feel the bite of the sun. Their shirts were wet with sweat within minutes.

As he bent down to pick up a hammer, he caught site of Jenna helping to put up the hessian blinds. He'd given her a job that required less heavy lifting. A concession to her injured shoulder. Not that he would ever tell her, otherwise she'd probably demand she take over what he was doing instead.

What would she say when she found out he'd spent two years in prison? The question had been playing on his conscience for a while. He'd found himself wanting to tell her the other day in the Bungles, when she'd confided in him about her lost love. The words had been on the tip of his tongue. But he knew without a doubt the knowledge would push her away from him for good. That well-constructed wall would go up with a clang, never to come down again. Nevertheless, he wanted her to know the truth about him. It hung like a great weight on his shoulders, a huge impediment to their ... Their what? Their relationship? That seemed like a word fraught with too many possibilities. Their friendship?

Stop this. Shaking his head to dislodge the gloomy thoughts, he slammed his body weight against the hot steel fencing, pushing hard so Pat could bolt the two pieces together. Work was what he needed. Work so physically arduous he wouldn't have time to think about her. The muscles in his arms strained against the heavy steel of the fencing and a sharp pain shot through his shoulder. He pushed harder. Pain was good. Physical pain he could understand.

The daylight was fading as Dan stood near the dinner table later that evening, stomach rumbling. He'd definitely earned his food today. Jenna ambled over, giving her shoulder a surreptitious rub. It was obviously still causing her pain. She hung her head over the pot of Cookie's vegetable soup.

'Mmm, that smells great.'

'Yes it does,' he agreed and was rewarded with a smile. Most of the rest of the team were also milling around, waiting for dinner.

'Where are Pat and Ulrich?' Jenna asked, only half-interested.

'I think Pat said something about going to show Ulrich how to shoot like a man.' Dan gave a mirthless laugh. 'They've gone to cull some roos.'

'What?' Jenna's head flew up. 'Where? Which way did they go?'

Shit, he should've thought. She wouldn't like that idea. Any thought of killing animals always got her all worked up.

'Why do you wanna know? Are you going to join them?' Cookie asked, mistaking Jenna's worry for interest.

'Please, just tell me where they've gone,' she pleaded.

Before he could stop her, Cookie said, 'I think they went north, back through the fence and onto Harding's property. I'm pretty sure that's what Pat said.' But Cookie was now talking to Jenna's retreating back.

Dan strode after her, but she was too quick for him. She didn't bother to saddle up Chainsaw, just throwing on a bridle and leaping onto him bareback. Then they cantered out of the camp going as fast as the terrain would allow. Leaving Dan to stare, dumbfounded, after her.

* * *

It was pitch black in camp, everyone else in their swags long ago. Dan hoped the rising sickle moon would lend enough light for Jenna to find her way home. He'd been worried sick. Both he and Lex waited by the fire. Should he be out there searching for her?

Pat and Ulrich returned to camp with a strange tale about Jenna descending on them like a demon from hell after they'd shot and killed a roo. Pat seemed only slightly bemused by the whole thing, but Ulrich was more than a little upset. She'd then demanded they go back to camp and leave her alone. What was she doing out there, with a dead kangaroo?

Finally, they heard the jangle of a bridle and knew she'd returned. Lex went to bring her over, while Dan waited by the fire. His anger built with every second he sat there. How dare she do this to him. To them. It was irresponsible and stupid.

'Jenna. Are you alright? You're not hurt, are you?' Dan half-raised himself from his seated position as she entered the fire's glow.

'I'm good, Dan,' she replied. He lowered himself back down and waited for them both to take a seat.

Jenna sat on the dirt cross legged, but wouldn't look at him, while Lex took the log on the opposite side of the fire. There was silence for several long seconds.

Jenna was the first to crack. 'Sorry. I guess you heard what happened.'

'We heard those other blokes' version, yeah.' Lex's rasping voice issued from out of the darkness. 'I'm more interested in your version, though.'

Jenna finally looked up and stole a glance in Dan's direction, biting her bottom lip. Quickly she lowered her gaze again. She was scared of what he'd say. Good. She should be scared. Now he knew she was safe, his concern had morphed into an anger so powerful he didn't trust himself to speak.

Lex broke the impasse. 'When you took off like a bat out of hell, we were all worried about you.'

'I'm sorry, Lex, but I didn't have time to tell anyone where I was going.' She continued to stare at the ground, unable to look either of them in the eye.

'Sorry, Jenna, but it's not good enough,' said Lex. 'Harding's men had permission to leave the camp. You didn't. We didn't know where you were, or if you were coming back.' Even Dan was surprised by Lex's curt reply. He must be nearly as mad as Dan if he was going to call Jenna out. He was normally so calm and sure.

Obviously stung by his words, Jenna raised her head. Different emotions played over her face. Was she trying to work out what lies they'd believe? Would she tell them the truth? Dan still didn't trust himself to speak.

'I'm sorry.' It sounded like the simple truth. 'I guess I didn't take the time to think it through properly first.'

'That much was obvious,' Lex growled. 'At least when Ulrich and Pat came back they told us where you'd gone.' Pausing for a second, Lex seemed to be struggling with his next words. 'This can't ever happen again, Jenna. I'm deeply disappointed in you.'

Jenna grimaced, as if Lex had dealt her a physical blow. Even though she deserved it, Dan's anger softened and died.

'There are some people who think you should be punished for this.' Lex let the sentiment hang in the air for a few moments. 'But I don't agree with them. Not this time at least.'

'You mean Coshy?' she accused.

'Never mind. Now I've said my piece, I'm off to bed.' Just like that, Lex's tone was no longer authoritative, reverting to the fair-minded man they were used to. Jenna stared after him as he rose from his log and stamped off to find his swag under the stars.

Now Lex had gone, Dan finally found the capacity for speech. 'Are you going to tell me what happened out there?' he asked softly.

She jumped at the sound of his voice, as if she'd forgotten he was there. Then she drew in a deep, reluctant breath. 'Didn't Pat already tell you?'

'Yes, he told us his side of a rather strange story, but I wanted to hear it from you. Why did you do that Jenna? You know you put yourself in danger, what if they'd shot you by mistake?'

'People who kill animals for sport are pathetic.' She spat the words. 'That was a living, breathing animal before those bloody Neanderthal arseholes took his life away. They're nothing but murderers. At least I stopped them before they killed anything else.' Firelight flared in her eyes as she raised her chin and glared at him. What she was saying was crazy. Surely she realized that?

As he gazed at her, the vision of those lips close to his, warm breath caressing his own slammed into his memory. He wanted to scrunch his eyes shut, as if that might block out the image. It didn't work. He couldn't let her affect him. Not now.

Dan drew in a deep breath. 'I know you like animals, have an affinity with them, even. But, Jenna, we work on a station, this kind of thing goes on all the time. Surely you have to see Pat was just showing Ulrich some of the skills he'll need if he wants to become a good jackaroo.' He was right, of course he was right. It was the way it was. The way it would always be.

'What skills? How to kill and maim helpless animals!'

'Jenna, that's what we do out here,' he said incredulously. 'We're all about the raising of animals so they can be slaughtered for human consumption.' He couldn't help the hint of tenderness sliding into his tone. He felt bad for her, he really did. She had some kind of strong connection with animals. A connection even he couldn't guess at. But how could she care so much for animals yet be prepared to work on a station and bring them to their ultimate death? It was an elemental stumbling block she'd have to get over. Either that, or she'd eventually leave.

'I know all that, Dan, and I'm trying to sort myself out. Believe me, I am.' She couldn't hide the sadness from her tone. They were both silent, the quiet filled by the crackle of the campfire.

'Do you agree with Pat, that killing roos for sport is right?' Her question surprised him.

Gazing into the fire, he finally said, 'No, I don't condone Pat's urge to kill for no other reason than the thrill of it.' He turned and laid a hand on her arm to reinforce his words. 'But that doesn't mean I think I have the right to stop him from doing it, either.'

She nodded her head. 'I'm sorry I put you and everyone else in a bad position tonight.'

'Well at least you accept you were unprofessional, which reflects on the team. And you definitely owe Pat and Ulrich an apology, Jenna.'

'Yes, I'll apologize first thing in the morning.' Her words sounded contrite, but something about the gleam in her eye told him she wasn't as sorry as she made out.

With a sigh, he said, 'Right then, I'm off to bed. See you in the morning, Jenna.' She flinched again, like she had when Lex voiced his anger, but he couldn't call back the coldness from his voice now. Much as he hated to admit it, he wasn't sure how he felt about her. She was the most intriguing woman he'd ever met. She was becoming a tangled web inside his mind, one he was frightened he might never be able to tease free of.

She remained seated, staring into the fire for a long time after he went to bed, disenchantment evident in her hunched shoulders. It shouldn't have to hurt this much to watch her struggle with her internal demons. And yet it did.

* * *

Jenna stifled a yawn, finding it hard to keep her concentration on the job. She was horse tailer—the person who went and retrieved the stock horses from where they'd wandered overnight—and the horses all jogged behind her in a line through the early morning light. It'd been a night full of restless thoughts and self-recriminations. She wasn't looking forward to facing anyone this morning. It was still early, people just starting to rise and ready themselves for the new day. For now, she was alone as she yarded the horses. Dismounting, she threaded through the throng of horses, keeping her voice low and soothing.

Chainsaw warned her he was coming, even before she heard the tread of heavy booted feet behind her. She hunched into Chainsaw's side, pretending to check him for saddle sores.

'So, the saviour of the world has returned.' Coshy was the absolute last person she wanted to see this morning.

With no real hope he'd follow her instruction, she said with a sigh, 'Leave it alone will you, Coshy.'

He sniggered and she could imagine him taking his arrogant stance behind her, feet firmly planted in the dust, hips shoved forward, hands in pockets with a supercilious smirk on his unshaven face.

'What did you think you were up to, galloping off into the night? You stupid girl.' She didn't endorse his question with a reply. Keeping her back towards him, she moved off through the horses to check the rest for any physical hurt after their night in the bush. It was the first time Coshy had ever confronted her face-to-face. A small shiver of trepidation slid down her spine.

'Do you think you can personally save all the roos from everyone with a gun in this country?' He followed her through the horses, stalking her like a malicious tiger. She could feel the anticipation oozing off him. 'Roos are just brainless animals that deserve to die anyway.'

Her shoulder muscles went rigid and Domino snorted down her back, sensing her growing anger. Coshy was intentionally taunting her, but she couldn't stop her anger building. This wasn't like Coshy. He was one to do things deviously, not out in the open. Why had the method of his personal vendetta against her changed this morning?

'You're even more brainless than those useless animals, if you think they're worth saving.'

A spasm of fury twisted through her guts and she whirled around to face him. Glaring up into his pasty blue eyes she saw his grinning mouth full of missing teeth and felt physically repulsed.

'Leave. Me. Alone.' Jenna enunciated every word. His grin got larger and he took a step closer, so she could smell exactly how unwashed he was. Coshy was a good head taller than her, but she was too riled up now to back down and she stood her ground as he towered over her.

'Why should I leave you alone? Don't you like hearing the truth? Poor little weak and vulnerable, Jenna, always brown-nosing to Lex or hiding behind Dan's skirts.'

The horses in the yard started to stamp and wicker with unease. Domino laid his ears flat and showed the whites of his eyes.

'You're a bad influence out here, you and your daft tree-hugging ideals.'

'Oh really?' Jenna ground out from between gritted teeth as she balled her fists tight and watched him with suspicion. Coshy moved in so his face hovered mere inches from hers. She wanted to tell him she knew it was him who'd let Winemaster out. Just to see the conceited grin slip from his face. Let him know she had a secret she could hold over him. She opened her mouth to speak, but he talked over the top of her.

'You need to watch out. Some people out here don't like you.' Pure hostility dripped from Coshy's tone. She brought her clenched fists up in front of her chest in anticipation. Trepidation turned to cold fear. It was almost as if he knew something she didn't.

'Is that a threat?' she shot back.

Just then, Domino let out an ear-splitting whinny and lashed out with one of his front hooves, narrowly missing Coshy's shoulder, making him duck for cover.

'What the—' The alarm on Coshy's face was priceless and if Jenna hadn't been so furious she would've burst out laughing.

Lynne's voice broke through the sound of the man's blubbering shock. 'Coshy, Cookie needs you to set up the tables for breakfast.' Coshy continued to glower at Jenna until Lynne came up and tapped him on the shoulder.

'Bloody women,' he muttered, and finally turned away, stomping back towards the camp.

'What was all that about?' Lynne asked nervously.

'Nothing. Nothing I can't handle, anyway.' Jenna flashed a brazen smile at her.

'I'm not sure you should take him on, Jenna. I don't think he cares you're a woman. He can be right nasty when the mood takes him.'

Jenna sniffed in derision. 'I'm not afraid of him.' But that wasn't strictly true anymore. That dark flicker of something evil in Coshy's eyes *had* made her afraid. It also made her wonder if he really did have something to do with the tyre slashing incident.

If Coshy was prepared to challenge her out in the open, something had changed to make him feel even more arrogant than normal. What was it?

Lynne changed the subject. 'So, you gave us all quite a fright last night. You have to tell me what happened. You could have gotten lost in the dark or something.'

Jenna went on with her thorough check of every animal in the yard, giving short yes or no answers to Lynne's barrage of questions.

With Lynne still heckling her, Jenna made her slow way back into camp towards breakfast, keeping her head down, trying to judge the other's reaction to her presence.

Cookie gave her a familiar warm smile from behind the breakfast table as she approached. At least Cookie didn't seem to have any issues with her night-time escapades.

Pat and Ulrich were standing at the table, their backs toward her, loading their plates with bacon and toast. Straightening her shoulders, Jenna walked towards them.

'Good morning, Pat. Morning, Ulrich.' Acknowledging each man with a nod she said, 'I owe you both an apology'.

Pat returned her level gaze without saying anything, but Ulrich fumbled with his plate like an eager puppy.

'That's all right, Jenna, we understand that you felt—'

'Let her apologize, Ulrich.' Pat's gruff voice bulldozed over the top of Ulrich and he ground to a stuttering halt.

Jenna drew a deep breath. 'I'm sorry I said those things to you last night. I shouldn't have called you an arsehole.' She had to fight the sudden urge to ball her hands into fists, hiding them behind her back instead. 'I was angry at you for killing the kangaroo, but that's no justification for hurling abuse at you both.' She hesitated, knowing she should add they were welcome to go and shoot wherever they wanted, and she wouldn't interfere again. But try as she might, she couldn't make the words come. Instead she said, 'Everyone has their beliefs and values in life and I acknowledge you have just as much right to yours as I do. I hope our altercation last night doesn't affect our working relationship. Will you accept my apology?' She stood tall, her gaze direct but polite.

'Well, I guess in your own way you're probably right,' Pat admitted. 'We all have different standards in life. But I do question how you think you're going to hold onto your high and mighty morals out here, in this country.' He raised a speculative eyebrow and then took his overflowing plate of food to find a log to sit on.

Ulrich's long blond hair fell around his shoulders as he gave her one of his best, winning smiles. 'I thought a lot about what you said last night.'

'I'm glad you did, Ulrich.' Jenna kept her tone neutral.

'I'd like to talk to you some more about it. Kangaroos are pests out here and I've seen the damage they can do with my own eyes.' He ducked his tall frame lower so the planes of his high cheek-bones were mere inches from her face, intruding into the circle of her personal space. He was a sweet boy, and very attractive, but his blue-eyed innocence wasn't for her. She tried to edge away from him without being obvious.

'Why don't you come and tell me more while we eat?' Grabbing hold of her arm with his free hand, his striking blue eyes lit up with fervour.

She followed him with reluctant feet, catching Dan's eye as he passed on his way to gather breakfast. He gave her a nod. Nothing more. No smile to tell her she was forgiven, no quick word of camaraderie. She was no longer hungry. Although she followed Ulrich, her movements were mechanical, her mind racing with the implications of Dan's cold rejection. Would things ever be the same between them again? And did she want them to be?

And now with Coshy's declaration, things were coming to a head. Her instincts were screaming at her. She needed to move on. Whatever Coshy had against her, she didn't have the time or the patience to stand up to him. If she called him out, then her own life would be put under the spotlight, and questions would be asked. Questions she was never going to answer.

She made her decision. It was time to go. As soon as they got back from this muster, she was leaving.

CHAPTER TWELVE

Dan stood at the edge of the camp, blowing on his mug of billy tea. The growing heat of the morning crowded the air, and every time Dan breathed in a warm lungful he could smell the red dust mixed with a hint of moist fresh plant sap from the grasses he'd crushed underfoot.

Jenna broke away from the rest of the team, who were finishing up their breakfast, and started towards him. Her petite shape weaved through the tall spinifex, her shirt illustrating the outline of the smooth rounded curve of her breasts.

Much to his annoyance, the thud of his heart became loud in his ears. He was unsure if he was ready to do this. She thought he was still mad at her. And he was. Well, he should be. But there was no real reason for him to keep up his air of injured pride. Except perhaps for some sort of self-preservation.

It was more than just a physical attraction that set an ache in his groin, although the mere sight of her hips swaying through the grass made the front of his jeans grow uncomfortably tight. He'd kissed many women in his time, but never had he experienced that depth of desire. He'd not been ready for his own gut-wrenching reaction to their kiss back at the Bungle Bungles. Ever since then, he'd been careful to hide his reaction to her, hoping he could somehow smother these foolish emotions and pack them away into a safe corner of his mind. They'd do him no good, she only wanted to be friends. And he was a changed man because of his time in prison—less deserving. It wouldn't be right to start something he couldn't finish.

She also carried a steaming mug of tea and she held it with intense concentration, negotiating the rough terrain without spilling the contents. The soft line of her mouth was full and luscious. And strangely vulnerable. His insides contracted. Yes, it was probably time to get over the cool aloofness he'd worn for the past two days, since the night of the roo shooting. If he wasn't to have this woman heart and soul, then at least her friendship was some consolation. *Wasn't it?*

'Hey, Dan,' she said, an unasked question in the tilt of her head and the tremble in her smile.

'Hey, Jenna,' he answered cryptically. She cleared the last few feet of spinifex and stood next to him. He gazed at her fine fingers wrapped around the tin mug, small and elfin. And capable of making his skin flame whenever she touched him. *Concentrate.*

'Sorry, I hope I haven't interrupted your peace and quiet.'

'Nah, it's fine,' he replied. He looked down on her from beneath the shade of his Akubra and she held his gaze for long drawn-out seconds. He gave in and smiled at her. Her eyes softened and she smiled back. A smile of relief and joy. His chest expanded along with her smile. Then she looked away over the rolling sand hills and they stood in companionable silence. She'd got her answer and things were good between them. He just couldn't stay mad at her.

'What about you? Are you here trying to stay out of Coshy's way?' He knew the question would set her on edge. She might think no-one else noticed their altercation the other morning. But he wasn't the only one who'd seen what happened.

'No, why would you say that?' Her eyes flicked to his face and then back to the view.

'You don't have to pretend with me, Rowdy. I know something nasty is going on between you two. And don't blame Lynne either,' he said as he saw the grim set of her jaw change. 'It's pretty obvious.' He saw a play of emotions run across her face, wondering if she'd admit to any of it.

'It's no secret Coshy and I will never be the best of mates,' she replied, and he gave a loud laugh. She hadn't told him anything he didn't already know. 'But there is certainly nothing more sinister going on, if that's what you're implying.'

He'd seen their confrontation from behind one of the trucks, after emerging from his swag. Not close enough to hear what'd been said, he nevertheless saw Jenna's fists come up in front of her as if she'd been in a boxing ring. Knowing he was too far away to stop anything if Coshy hit her, he still took two strides towards the duo anyway, before he caught sight of Lynne bearing down on them. As Lynne broke their stand-off, he couldn't help the swell of pride for this woman, who was courageous enough to take on Coshy. Brave and naïvely independent. Why she'd not called out for help was beyond him.

He shrugged his shoulders. 'I've said this before, and I'll say it again. I want you to know I have your back. We all do.' He stepped around, so he filled all of her view. 'You should watch out for Coshy, he can be an untrustworthy piece of shit sometimes.'

'Thanks for the warning, Dan, but I can look after myself.'

He'd heard those words before. She wouldn't return his gaze, but let her eyes remain levelled out over the saltbush towards the horizon. Brave and courageous she might be. But she was also stubborn and pig-headed. Beautifully stubborn and fiercely pig-headed.

The words tattooed on the inside of her wrist said it all. She wanted to be brave, no matter the consequences. He wanted to reach out and take her in his arms. Tell her it was okay, she could trust him, he would protect her.

'Wow, it's flat out there, isn't it?' she said, changing the subject.

Dan's eyes roved over the perpetual desert, watching it roll away from them in waves. The sky was a perfect powder blue. 'Yep, it goes on forever out that way.'

'I think I might be getting addicted to the desert,' she joked.

'Hmm, well you'll just have to stay for a while then,' he replied.

For some strange reason her face closed up and she threw the dregs of her tea on a salt bush. What had he said wrong?

Half an hour later the helicopter from Harding's stood waiting with its rotors swinging in the small clearing. Pat and Ulrich were leaving. Harding needed them back to start with their own, much smaller mustering season. Pat stood with Lex, shaking his hand and laughing at some remark he made. Dan had already said his goodbyes and was standing back, waiting for them to leave. But where had Ulrich gone? There was Jenna with her arms full of pots, packing them away after breakfast.

Then out of the blue, Ulrich rounded the front of the Land Cruiser and stalked towards her. Even Dan had to admit the guy was good-looking, with those flaxen locks flowing over his shoulders and his striking features. Terribly likeable, but not the sharpest tool in the shed.

Ulrich's gaze zeroed in on Jenna and Dan suddenly realized what he was up to. A grin spread over his face. This was going to be interesting. He sidled closer, so he could hear their conversation.

'Ulrich, aren't you supposed to be getting on the helicopter?' Jenna asked with a restrained sigh.

'They won't leave without me. I wanted to talk to you, alone. But you're a hard woman to track down.' He stepped in close, leaning down to bring his face within inches of hers. She took a step backwards and Dan felt a pinch of relief. Ulrich was completely enamoured with Jenna. And who could blame him. But she obviously found his enthusiastic charm a little overwhelming. 'We never got to finish our discussion about shooting animals for sport,' Ulrich continued.

'No, we didn't. Sorry about that. It'll have to wait for another day.' She raised her shoulders with mock dejection as she made to move off, the pots and pans clanging together.

'I also never got to say how much I respect you for your stand, Jenna.' She stopped mid-stride. 'And ... I also wanted to say that ... that I'd like to get to know you better.'

Way to go, kid, Dan thought. At least he was laying his cards on the table. Dan found he was mildly curious as to how Jenna would react, but there was no burning jealousy grinding through his gut. Which told him more than any words could convey, how little of a threat Ulrich was.

'Thanks, Ulrich, that's ah ... nice to hear.' She took a number of small steps backwards, and then glanced around and saw Dan standing behind Ulrich, snooping. Her face reddened, and she shot him a fierce glare he supposed was meant to warn him off. No chance, he was having way too much fun.

'I meant as a friend of course.'

'Of course,' she replied faintly, still backing away.

'I'd like to be able to discuss this with you some more. Do you think that might be possible?' The eagerness in his voice made Dan want to cringe. He almost felt sorry for the kid. Almost.

'Well, our two properties may be next to each other, but we're still a long, long way apart you know, Ulrich,' she hedged.

'That distance is nothing out here,' he said, waving a casual hand, his gaze never shifting from her face.

'Ah ... Well, you know I don't get a lot of time off' she replied.

The smile on Ulrich's perfect features fell slightly. Then he said, 'We can work something out, I know it,' and took two long strides and disappeared around behind the car. 'I'll see you soon, Jenna,' he called as he left.

Jenna's eyes speared into Dan. 'Don't you dare say a word,' she stage-whispered, then turned on her heels and stomped away. Dan snapped his mouth shut with a click, but he couldn't hide the grin.

* * *

Leaning against the verandah post, Jenna contemplated the soft darkness that hung like a seamless veil outside the yellow pool of light from the spotlight above the steps. All the station hands were partaking in a celebratory dinner after returning from the muster, everyone glad to be back enjoying the comforts of home. She'd needed to escape from the noise inside for just a moment to contemplate the past few days. This would be her last night here. She needed to leave tomorrow.

Dune sat at her feet, ecstatic to have her home once more. He'd showered her with licks and wriggles when she first arrived and now he wouldn't leave her side. His joy rubbed off on her and she couldn't help but let the warmth of his love infuse her.

Her memory flew back to yesterday morning, when she and Dan had stood on the edge of the camp and he'd forgiven her for her indiscretion with Harding's men. She'd felt such a warm flood of gratifying contentment the second he smiled at her, it'd nearly overtaken the burning desire melting her bones from the touch of his strong muscled bicep against her shoulder. Somehow it was easier to breathe when Dan wasn't angry at her. But what did that really matter now? She was leaving and would never see him again. The warm, peaceful feeling fled.

And then there was Ulrich. He was so sweet and eager. Just not her type. He hadn't taken her subtle hints that she wasn't interested. She'd miss him too, but not nearly in the same way. Actually, she'd miss everyone here.

The silence of the night was broken by the squeak of the fly screen door. Jenna turned her head and smiled warmly at Mob as he half-stumbled out onto the verandah, beer sloshing dangerously in one hand.

'Hey, you. Whatcha doin' out here on your own?' He draped an affectionate arm around her shoulders and leaned drunkenly on her.

Jenna didn't mind the affection. Mob was harmless, and she welcomed his friendly closeness. Dune moved over to let Mob stand next to her, his tail thumping on the wooden verandah.

'I'm escaping from you men,' she teased. 'There's just too much testosterone in there sometimes.'

'Oh come on, you girls wouldn't have it any other way. You like us guys.'

'I like some of you more than others,' she laughed.

'Am I the some or the other?' he asked, suddenly serious.

'Well let me see, Mark O'Brien.' She stood away and pretended to look him up and down. 'I guess you'd be one of the ones I like.' It was the simple truth and they both knew it. He was a nice guy. Sociable, funny, engaging and always happy. Another person to miss.

'I like you too, Rowdy.' His next reaction took her by complete surprise. He caught her chin in his free hand, pulled her towards him and leant in and kissed her on the lips.

Startled, she pulled her mouth away, but left his arm around her shoulder and gazed at him steadily. She'd felt nothing, apart from the gentle weight of his warm lips as they pressed against hers. There was no sizzle of anticipation as he kissed her, no liquid fire scorching through her veins. Mob didn't provoke even the tiniest desire to flare within her. He wasn't the person Jenna very much wanted to be kissing tonight. Dune pushed in between the two of them and stared up at her with worried eyes, ready to tell Mob to get away. She soothed his fears, told him his help was appreciated, but not needed. With a snort the dog went back to lie down on her other side.

'What do you think you're doing, Mark?'

Uncertainty swirled in his drunken eyes. 'Expressing how much I like you?' But already he knew he'd done the wrong thing. Something thunked on the wooden verandah and they both turned in unison to witness the look of surprised hurt on Dan's face. He was poised halfway through the door but turned and disappeared back into the noise and light as soon as they saw him.

'Damn.' Jenna bit her lip.

Mistaking her distress, Mob said, 'I'm really sorry, Jenna, I thought—' His drunken vagueness was beginning to lift as he struggled to say the right thing.

'It's okay, Mob, don't worry. That was as much my fault as it was yours,' she said. 'I really do like you, Mob. You're one of my best mates out here, but my feelings don't go beyond that.' She hugged him in closer for an instant and then let him go, taking a few steps away so she could lean against the side of the building. How could she have misjudged Mob's feelings towards her so badly? What she'd seen as harmless fun and flirting, he'd obviously taken more seriously. She'd missed the signs on this one.

'Thanks for not getting mad at me, Jenna. Most girls I know would've snotted me for that kind of mistake.' He mimicked someone punching him in the face. 'Do you really forgive me?'

'Of course I do, Mob. Now let's drop the subject, shall we? I won't tell anyone if you don't.'

He sighed with relief. 'I'm fine with that,' he agreed. 'But do you think Simmo saw us?'

Jenna's shoulders sagged. 'Yep, he saw us all right.'

'I hope he doesn't go and blab to everyone inside.'

'I doubt he'll do that,' Jenna replied, hanging her head with barely disguised misery. He'd definitely seen them.

What the hell was happening this week? First Ulrich and now Mob. It was all too much male attention. Attention she hadn't initiated, but now had to deal with, nonetheless.

Mob studied her. 'Are you sure you aren't sweet on Dan?'

'Mob!' Her offended reply was punctuated by her hands settling on her hips.

He raised his palms up in mock surrender. 'Forget I even mentioned it.' Then, taking her by the hand he pulled her behind him as he went back inside. 'Come on let's join the party shall we.' Her obedient body followed, but her mind was absorbed by the tangled emotions rolling around in her head.

A longing welled up inside her, a longing for what could never be. For friendships inevitably broken, for happiness and compassion never to be hers for the taking. A desperate need for her days on the run to end flooded through her and her throat closed up with an unbearable ache. Why did she suddenly feel like this now?

It had become hard to breathe again.

* * *

The next day found Jenna offering to help make lunch with Cookie. She even said she'd stay to help clean up afterwards.

Anything to keep away from Dan and the questions in his eyes.

The whole time she went through the motions of dragging food out of the fridge and laying the table with cutlery, it felt like a great lethargic beast sat on her shoulders, pulling her pretence of a smile down at the corners, even while she struggled to keep it glued to her face. Dan thought she'd kissed Mob. It was better to leave it that way. Now she was going, it would hurt him less if he thought she didn't care.

Her plan seemed to work, as all through lunch while they sat at the table and ate, Dan fixed her more than once with a dark frown but he didn't dare ask her what he wanted to know front of the rest of the team.

Her plan failed in the end, however, when Dan managed to corner her as she stood at the kitchen bench washing the last of the dishes after lunch.

'So, are you going to tell me what all that was about last night?' His voice was rough, resentful. Jenna scanned the kitchen, looking for someone, anyone, to come to her salvation. 'Don't go looking for Cookie, she's off sorting out the food store.' Dan was standing very close, his hand resting against the bench, his arm creating a barrier to escape. Jenna bit her bottom lip.

This wasn't going to end well, she had no lie ready on the tip of her tongue. And his proximity was sending her already jangled nerves into overdrive.

'What's going on between you and Mob, Jenna?' Twisting her sudsy hands together, her gaze remained locked on the sink in front of her. 'Jenna. Look at me. This isn't just about you and Mob last night, is it? Something else has changed. What is it? Is it Coshy?' He reached out and took her chin in his hand, tilting her head up so he could look directly into her eyes. The breath hissed in over her teeth at his unexpected contact. Although she knew he was angry with her, his touch remained gentle, tender almost. Each one of his long fingers seemed to burn a brand into the skin along her jawline.

She lifted her eyes and stared into his. There were flecks of green hidden within the darker brown depths that she'd never noticed before. For countless seconds she was lost in his beautiful amber irises, so compassionate, so courageous, so sensual.

If she gave him an explanation, he'd probably forgive her. Again. If she told him why she had to leave, he'd want to protect her. All it'd take was one word from her and he'd gather her into his arms. He could shelter her. God, it'd feel so good.

'Jenna, please let me in, just this once.'

Her mouth moved but no words came out.

'Dan, where are you?' Coshy's harsh voice broke their reverie. Dan closed his eyes. When he opened them again, anger slashed through them and he whirled to face Coshy.

'What the hell do you want?' His voice was almost a snarl. Coshy slammed through the fly screen door like a seething black cloud and stood in front of Dan.

'Bernie just ordered us to go and check bore fifty-three, it's jammed or something.' Bits of spittle flew from Coshy's mouth as he spoke. 'And don't bloody well look at me like that, I don't like this anymore than you do. Let's just get it over with, so we can be home in time for dinner.' He spun around on his heel and headed for the door. 'Lex wants us to take Lynne with us, to increase her skill levels or some such drivel.'

'All right,' Dan said with a loud sigh, swiping a hand through his hair. 'I'll be out in a second.'

'No, not in a second. Now!' Coshy stood belligerently and waited in the middle of the room. 'I'm not going to hang around waiting while you have a tete-a-tete with your shitty little girlfriend.'

'Mind your tongue, Coshy. And you bloody well will wait until I'm ready to go.' Dan's face flamed red and he took a few steps towards Coshy, leaving Jenna's escape route unblocked. She didn't hear the rest of the loud argument as she stared at the open exit, trying to decide.

She slipped past unnoticed by the quarrelling men, and it wasn't until she reached the back door that Dan caught sight of her.

'See you when you get back tonight.' She tried to make her voice sound normal, and then made a quick dash for the food stores, where she could hear Cookie singing. It was for the best. He'd find out tonight upon his return that she was gone. By then there'd be nothing he could do to stop her.

Two hours later, Jenna walked slowly up the well-worn route from the stables to the staff quarters. As she made her way up the path for the last time, she observed every tree and fence and building, carving them into her memory for later. Everything was packed and ready to go, a note explaining her absence tucked into her jeans pocket would be placed on her bed before she left. The brumbies would be waiting for her just before sunset. They'd carry her out to the nearest main road and she would hitch a ride from there. She was as ready as she'd ever be to go.

Suddenly both Chainsaw and Winemaster's voices sounded in whinnies of recognition. She squinted into the sunlight. The white Land Cruiser sped into view and came slithering to a dusty halt just outside the main house.

Her heart pounded loud. Dan was back early from fixing the bore. Despair clamoured with delight as she wondered if his reappearance would interfere with her departure.

Coshy tumbled out of the car almost before it stopped moving and he stumped up the stairs into the main house.

What were they doing home so early? The back of Jenna's neck prickled with foreboding.

Dan exited from the driver's seat, his head hung low as if with fatigue. He turned on his heel and straightened his back as he marched towards the stables, where Lex was sorting out the stock feed. This was getting stranger by the minute. And where was Lynne? She tried to catch a glimpse of Dan's face, but the brim of his hat concealed his features. She turned back towards the stables, abandoning her course for the staff quarters. She had to know what was going on.

She reached the stables at the same time Dan did. Unable to control her curiosity, she asked, 'Dan, what's going on? Why are you home so soon?' He continued to walk into the shadow of the stables, his back to her. 'And where's Lynne?'

He stopped walking so suddenly she almost bumped him. Turning around to face her she could finally see what he'd been hiding. His face was stripped bare, shock imprinted in every line.

'What is it, Dan? What's wrong?' Her voice rose an octave as fear took hold.

'Lynne's gone,' he said, his voice dull and lifeless. 'She went missing from the bore site, and there's absolutely no sign of her.' Jenna's knees wanted to buckle underneath her and she reached out to steady herself on the wall of the stable.

No! Please don't let this be happening.

CHAPTER THIRTEEN

It was well after midnight and everyone else had collapsed into bed. All the arrangements to start a full-scale search for Lynne at first light were in place. There was no point searching for her in the dark, they might miss an important sign, or worse, inadvertently cover her tracks with their own. People would be coming in from neighbouring properties, and helicopters would also be arriving in the morning. Dan and Lex had been on the phone for hours organising the search and rescue event.

Jenna was the last to leave the kitchen, walking down the long corridor to her bedroom when she'd passed Dan's open door. He sat on the end of his bed, unmoving and unseeing, pain and exhaustion etched into his face. Jenna knew what Dan was thinking. He was responsible for losing Lynne. Lex trusted him to take Coshy and Lynne out to do a job, and he'd failed. He'd told Lex that Coshy asked Lynne to go and get him a tool from the Land Cruiser. The car was only a hundred or so meters away from where they were working on the bore. Admittedly, it was behind a large clump of Mallee, parked to make the most of the scant shade. They'd both got distracted, lining up a tricky bit of piping and it was fifteen minutes later when Dan remembered Lynne hadn't come back with the tool. She didn't answer his calls and when he walked over to the car, there was no sign of her. He couldn't understand where she'd gone, and the desperation was eating away at him.

She knew exactly how he felt. But in her case, her feelings were warranted. It wasn't his fault Lynne was missing. It was hers. And hers alone. Liam had Lynne. And Coshy probably had something to do with it. It was the only possibility. Coshy had to be working with Liam and his thugs. He wasn't smart enough to pull something like this off on his own. How could she not have seen it before now? She should've listened to that tiny voice telling her there was more to Coshy's shenanigans than met the eye. Even though she wanted to shout and rage at him, she'd held her tongue. She still had no proof. And he'd remained in Dan's sight the whole time. He must've tipped Liam off as to where they'd be somehow. She might be able to convince Dan that Coshy had something to do with Lynne going missing. But it'd take too long, time was of the essence now. A sickening fear had been turning her stomach inside out ever since she'd heard Dan say those fateful words. She could hardly hold it together, but she needed to remain composed and come up with a rescue plan.

Liam had taken Lynne. And soon she'd know where he was keeping her, when her faithful friends, the kangaroos reported in.

She knew what needed to be done. She just couldn't let anyone else realize what she was up to. Particularly Dan.

Still, it wrenched her heart to see him sitting there, shouldering all the responsibility of letting one of his team-mates down in such a disastrous way. She had to do something. A need to soothe his hurt took over and she found herself walking towards Dan, her hands reaching out before she could stop herself.

'Dan, you mustn't blame yourself, it's not your fault,' she whispered. His head hung so low she could only guess at the expression haunting his features. Kneeling down on the hard wooden floor in front of him, she used one hand to tilt his head up until she could look straight into his eyes.

How could she make him understand none of this was his fault without giving away her role in it all? Icy fingers of remorse trickled down her spine. For a few seconds she even considered telling him everything. Maybe they could work together to get Lynne back. *Don't be stupid*. The possibility of one, or both of her friends getting hurt was too high. She would handle this alone. It was her only choice.

* * *

'Lynne's a survivor, she has loads of common sense. She probably just wandered away and got lost, and right now she's hunkering down, waiting for one of us to turn up and rescue her,' Jenna said.

Her words made sense and Dan wanted to believe them. It'd be the logical thing for Lynne to do, and of course they'd find her tomorrow. If only he could lift this weight which'd settled in the middle of his chest the minute he discovered Lynne missing.

'Dan, please!' Something in her plea broke through his fog of self-damnation. He raised his head just enough to catch her eye.

'God, I hope you're right, Jenna.'

'I can hear the *but* behind your words, Dan.' She could read him too well.

'But … I have a bad feeling about this whole thing. No one has ever gone missing from the station before. I don't understand. Why would she just wander away from the bore? It isn't like Lynne to do something like this.' He tore his gaze away, going over everything for the hundredth time in his head. And for the hundredth time he came up with the same uneasy feeling clawing at his guts, telling him that laid-back, ever-smiling Lynne was somehow in more trouble than he liked to imagine.

'I agree, it's very strange. It's not in Lynne's nature to do something so irresponsible.' Jenna's voice pulled him back to the present.

'If only I'd kept her close by, instead of letting Coshy send her back to the car. Bloody Coshy, he's so lazy. He should've gone to get that tool himself, not sent her. Or I should've gone instead.' He'd already lamented this dozens of times today to Lex, but it did nothing to ease his guilt, even now. 'Where could she have gone? She can't have gotten too far on foot in the few hours she was missing. Why did she leave? What was she thinking?' He knew he was going over and over the same questions time and again. That feeling of unease was still there, roiling in the pit of his stomach. 'What if she didn't just wander away?' His voice sounded more like a guttural growl, even to his own ears. 'What if she was … abducted or something?'

'Abducted? Out in the middle of the desert?' Her eyes widened with shock at his suggestion.

'I know, I'm probably over-reacting. But I have this horrible feeling there might be something else going on here.'

Her hand rested gently on his knee, the warmth of her fingers leaching through the fabric of his jeans. She smelled faintly of dish soap and spices from her kitchen duty. The smell wound up his nose, captivating his senses. He could see wisps of hair escaping from her plait, silhouetted against the light from the door, framing her pale face. In the shadowy light she suddenly seemed very young and very exposed, kneeling there before him.

Jenna shifted her weight and turned to sit on the bed next to him, her shoulder leaning against his. The human touch felt good. He hadn't realized how tense he was, wound tighter than an iron spring. With her simple gesture, a profound sense of comfort washed through him. As usual, whenever she was close she set off a purely physical reaction in him. A desire to hold her. To have her body entwined with his. How his body could still react to her like this was a mystery to him. But perhaps it mightn't be such a bad thing. It might shift his focus away from the tragedy of Lynne's disappearance. To have something else to concentrate on, even for just a few moments, was a welcome relief.

'Dan, I know I've already said it, but this really isn't your fault. You have to stop blaming yourself. You'll be no good to anyone in the morning. And we're going to need you more than ever to help us bring Lynne home safe and sound.' Her voice remained low, but took on a quiet ring of authority. 'You need to stop worrying and get some sleep tonight.' Jenna smiled and laid her hand over his.

'I hear the sense in your words, but I don't think I can sleep knowing Lynne might be lying there, hurt and desperate.'

Letting out a heartfelt sigh, Jenna said, 'I know, I feel the same way.' She started to stroke his knuckles absentmindedly and though Dan knew she wasn't doing it on purpose, he couldn't deny the sensual fizz through his veins as her fingers caressed every rise and fall on the back of his hand. 'But I have a feeling Lynne will be all right, Dan.' She tilted her head towards him. 'Call it a premonition or whatever you like, but I know we'll find her soon.'

'I wish I had your faith, Jenna …' Dan was only half concentrating on what she was saying. He liked the feel of her hands on him. No other woman had been able to affect him quite like she did. Her touch brought out such a mixture of emotions. Lust, serenity, pleasure, all blended into one. Her fingers stopped moving and he snapped back to reality as he guessed she was waiting for him to finish his sentence. 'You're right about one thing. We have to keep hoping. If we don't have hope, then what do we have?'

Nodding her head in agreement her fingers started up their stroking again, her voice taking on a faraway edge as she said, 'It's not just a hope, Dan. I know I'll find her, and when I do she *will* be okay. I'd never let one of my friends get hurt like this. I'll make sure she gets home in one piece, safe and sound.'

Hang on. What had she just said? It almost sounded as if she thought she was going to rescue Lynne on her own. Cold beads of sweat broke out on his brow.

'What exactly do you mean by *I will find her*?' His mind skittered back to the night she'd set out to rescue the stallion on her own. He knew she was one determined, independent woman, they were two of the many qualities he admired about her. But she couldn't possibly be considering the same scenario again. Could she?

'I meant *us. We* will find her, together. It'll take all of us, but I know we can do it.' He stared at her and she stared back. Finally, he dropped his gaze. He'd misunderstood her, that was all. He was seeing problems where they didn't exist. The dreadfulness of the afternoon was starting to take its toll. Shaking his head to clear it of the weary exhaustion, he ran a shaky hand over his eyes. Taking off his Akubra he let it fall with a loud plunk onto the wooden floor beside the bed.

* * *

'Thank you, Jenna.' Dan sighed heavily and fell backwards onto the bed, stretching his arms to rest above his head.

Releasing the breath that'd stilled in her chest, she exhaled gradually. He believed her. She was a dirty, deceitful little liar, but he believed her. The only way she'd gotten away with it was to stick as close to the truth as she dared, but it still felt like she'd betrayed him terribly. She was capable of lying to the one man who'd offered her his help, who wanted to protect her if only she'd let him. Her heart constricted. Now it was her turn to feel the burning flame of guilt and shame.

'Thank me for what?' Her tone was heavy as she turned to look at him over her shoulder.

'For being you, I guess. Whenever you're around everything seems a little lighter somehow.'

'Really?'

The bed creaked, and Dan moved, lifting a hand, running it through his hair. 'Jenna, can we clear something up right now, before it comes between us?'

Her heart skipped a beat. 'What do you mean?'

'I have a confession to make. When I saw you kissing Mob, I just wanted to … '

She let out a noiseless grunt of relief. 'Dan, if you'd stayed on the verandah for just a few more seconds, instead of storming off, you would've heard when I told Mob he was an idiot and he'd only ever be a good friend to me.' She swivelled on the bed, watching him weighing up her words. 'Mob knew he was in the wrong, and I should've told you the truth about what happened straight away. I guess I sort of chickened out.' She lifted her hands in a plea for forgiveness.

'It was such a kick in the guts to see you and Mob. It took me by surprise. I'm not normally the jealous kind.' The bed creaked again as he moved his arm. He laid his hand in the small of her back. The contact made her acutely aware they were alone on his bed. In the dark. And he was only inches away from her. 'Come here.' He tugged on the rear of the waistband of her jeans and she fell backwards onto the bed beside him, her head pillowed on his left bicep.

He smelled good, even though he'd been out sweating all day in the hot desert sun. She liked the dusty, honey-warm musky smell that was Dan. This wasn't supposed to happen, she was allowing herself to cross the boundaries she'd put up with such care over the last few days. If her evening had gone according to plan she'd be long gone into the desert by now, not lying cradled in Dan's arms.

She couldn't let all of the reasons she'd gone over and over for staying away from Dan just dissolve with one touch from him. *Surely, I couldn't be that weak*? It was just that every time she was with him, thoughts of Liam and the horror of her last two years on the run disappeared. Like they'd never happened. Like he was a rock for her to cling to in an endless, tossing ocean.

'You want to know something else, Jenna?'

'Hmm.' She didn't trust herself to speak. Lying next to him, her fingers itched to run up underneath his shirt, to feel the warm buzz of the hairs on his chest beneath her fingers. The effort of not touching him tested her self-control to the limit.

'I missed having you out there with me this afternoon.' That statement had her attention, jerking her focus away from her wandering hands. 'When Lynne went missing, you were the first person I wanted to tell. Because I knew you wouldn't judge me.' He paused, staring straight up at the ceiling and she could feel him holding his breath. 'I like talking to you, Jenna. You're not like any other woman I've met before. I'm even starting to appreciate some of those strange things that happen when you're around.' He looked at her sideways and she was glad it was dark, so he couldn't see the sudden blush suffusing her face. She was stunned by his revelation. 'And when we kissed … All I could think about was wanting more. Wanting you.'

The flush on her cheeks deepened. The memory of the taste of him on her lips came flooding back, sending a rising heat through the rest of her body. He raised himself up onto one elbow and hovered above her, gazing down into her face. She nearly forgot to breathe.

'Jenna, I want to tell you something else.' His face lingered tantalisingly, only inches above hers, his nearness muffling the warning bells going off in her head. Her gaze traced the outline of his sensuous lips before it returned to float—like a moth to a flame—into the intensifying golden wells that were the depths of his eyes.

'Hmm.' Again, it was the only sound she trusted herself with.

'I think—' He faltered for a millisecond. 'I like you, Jenna. A lot.' Pausing again, uncertainty swirled in his face as he searched for the words to go on. 'I know you only want to be friends. But I more than just like you. I think ... I may be falling for you.'

In the silence, Jenna could hear the fierce beating of her own heart. So fierce it drowned out all other thought and emotion. This time she really did forget to breathe.

Her body went rigid and her mind went blank. Closing her eyes, she tried to block out the sight of Dan's face, open and unguarded, waiting patiently for a reply. She tried to sort through the numerous emotions flittering across her brain. There was apprehension, mixed with confusion as well as intense desire. But the feeling was that of ... Truth. His admission was echoed by her own sense of rightness. This thing between them was right.

But it was forbidden to her. She wasn't allowed to have these feelings until she broke free of Liam. She couldn't say the words he wanted to hear; the answer he deserved. If Liam ever found out about him. It would be Dan's death knell.

'Oh, Dan ...' It was her turn to hesitate. 'I'm flattered you trusted me enough to say that, but ...' This was like crossing a raging river with only unstable stones to keep her feet safe. If she lost her footing, then both of them would be dragged into the depths and they could be lost to one another forever. 'You're an extraordinary man and I can honestly say I like you a lot, too.' She shrugged, helpless. 'But I'm not sure I'm the right woman for you.'

Instead of withdrawing his face, he remained hovering over her, a deep scowl settling on his brow. 'You're *definitely* the right woman for me.' Dan's voice was hoarse. 'I've never felt like this about anyone else before.'

Jenna puckered her lips with unhappiness as she studied him. What did she say to that? Then to her surprise, Dan smiled down at her, his teeth white in the night-dark room.

'It's all right, Jenna, truly it is. I expected your answer. I knew what your reaction would be. You're not prepared to let anyone past that indefatigable wall you have surrounding you. But I've been watching and taking notes, and I can see small chinks appearing, even if you won't admit it. I'm quite happy to keep chipping away until I eventually break through. I'm a patient man.'

She blinked. He gave another satisfied Cheshire-cat grin that stunned her to silence. He wasn't angry with her? How could that be? Her throat worked as she swallowed hard, the skin on her forearms prickling into goose bumps.

'What're you saying, Dan?' How could he be so damned understanding when she'd just rejected him? Again.

'You'll come around,' he said, voice dropping to a husky whisper. His face descended the final few inches, his lips closing the gap until they rested, warm and inviting on hers. His mouth lingered, meeting hers with sensual need, letting her appreciate his growing desire. The tentative slide of his tongue into her mouth sent a stab of sensation racing through her body. Her lips parted of their own accord, and her tongue darted into his warm and waiting mouth, tracing the edge of his hard, white teeth. Dan's hand swept underneath her neck, lifting her head off the bed, the urgency of his kiss deepening.

She could feel the wonderful solidity of his muscled chest as he lay on top of her. The pounding of his strong beating heart intensifying with each deepening kiss. Settling his hips further onto hers, they seemed to fit together like two pieces of a puzzle.

Reaching up a hand, she flipped open the buttons of his shirt, one by one. Then she ran her hand inside the fabric and the heat from his skin made her palm tingle with awareness. Breaking their kiss, she used her lips to softly explore the muscles of his chest, his nipples hardening to her touch as she brushed over them. His skin tasted like warm citrus. Then she slipped her hand around his waist and followed the hardened physique of his back and shoulder blades, up towards the curve of his neck. Digging her nails into the softer flesh near his collar bone she dragged his mouth back down towards hers.

As her tongue twined with his, he groaned softly and there was no way she could miss what he wanted, not with his erection beneath his jeans pressed hard into her stomach. She ran her hands down over his back and gripped his buttocks, wanting him closer. Dan started to make slow circles against her body. She trembled as a firestorm of need travelled through her, his hot grinding motion causing an eruption of heat between her legs.

If Dan chose to make love to her right here and now, she'd let him. No. More than *let* him. She wanted him to. Her decision might cause heartbreak later, but she'd deal with those consequences when they arose. A strange sensation started in her chest, as if something inside had grown wings and was battering on her ribcage, demanding to be let out. It was an indescribable feeling, one she couldn't lay a name to.

Dan's heart hammered in his chest, echoing her own as he crushed down against her breasts. His normally calm fingers now fumbled with her shirt buttons. Tugging at the ends of her shirt, he got it un-tucked from her jeans, laying her stomach bare. His persuasive fingers traced around the bare skin at the top of her jeans, making her belly twitch at his touch.

Brushing her abdomen with his palm, he made burning circles on her skin, moving slowly upwards. Each callus on his work-hardened hand rasped against her soft skin. But they were Dan's hands; tough, hardworking hands, that still managed to convey how much he treasured her. Twisting her fists in the fabric of the bedclothes as his fingers found their way upwards until they finally threaded beneath the fabric of her bra, she let out a low groan. Her breath started to come in uneven gasps. Unable to control herself anymore, she closed her eyes and arched her back towards his touch.

A loud thump sounded from the room next door and Coshy gave a grunting snort as footsteps made their way towards the kitchen. They both froze. A switch flicked on and the light filtered into Dan's bedroom. The moment was broken into a thousand shards, splintered into dancing shadows along with the rays of light. Jenna pulled her shirt together to cover her semi-naked torso. With a deep sigh Dan lifted himself off Jenna, picked her up and stood her on her feet.

'Sorry.' It was just a whisper as she fled noiselessly to her room.

CHAPTER FOURTEEN

The sound of snorting horses surrounded her, pounding hooves drumming a muted tattoo in the sand beneath flying feet. Scattered along the peripheries of her vision she caught the flicker of red-grey hides as a smattering of kangaroos kept pace with the herd of brumbies. Dawn had come and gone and now the sun was climbing, beating down on the fast-moving bunch. Chestnut mane whipped up into her face as she clung to Chainsaw's back, his sweaty sides foaming beneath her thighs. A brief thought of Dune—tied up back at the station—flittered through her mind. He would be desperate and longing for her. But she couldn't bring her dog today. Liam would surely kill him on sight. A tight lump formed in the back of her throat. She'd miss her dog terribly.

Jenna had left Shiralee in the dead of the night, soon after she talked to Dan. The herd of brumbies joined them half-way to their destination, when she'd stopped at bore number thirty-nine for a rest and a drink. She needed to get moving, otherwise the search and rescue mission would catch up with her.

A line of mountains rose from the horizon, cutting a dark red swathe through the blue sky. The shale mountain range was close to the bore where Lynne had gone missing. The kangaroos told her it was this range where Lynne could be found. Dan and Lex had organized people and vehicles to help search the crests and rocky valleys with a fine-tooth comb. But Jenna intended to get there before everyone else, so she could free Lynne and be gone with Liam before they were any the wiser. Because she knew that's what he wanted. There could be no other reason he would abduct her friend. She would swap herself, become his hostage in exchange for Lynne's freedom.

A low drone filled the air behind her and she turned to see a small helicopter flying high and fast over the desert toward her, the sun glinting off the metal. It was approaching too fast, there was no time to hide. She flattened herself against Chainsaw's back to make herself less visible and hoped they wouldn't notice a small band of running brumbies. The helicopter buzzed away to the left, continuing on its trajectory towards the mountains. Regaining her seat, she watched as the helicopter disappeared over the rise of the first foothills.

Maybe Dan was in that helicopter. No, that was stupid. That was pure wishful thinking. And even if he was, it didn't matter because she wouldn't be seeing him ever again. All morning she'd managed to keep a lid on the emotions threatening to overwhelm her whenever she thought about Dan. The way he'd kissed her last night made her stomach go weak with heat just remembering. And then he'd said he was falling in love with her. The idea ripped big holes in her already shattered heart. She'd have treasured the possibility of allowing herself to fall for him.

Chainsaw slowed, breaking her thoughts. She'd need to get down and walk soon as the ground was becoming rocky and unmanageable for the horses.

'Well, Chainsaw, where do we go from here?' Her question was rhetorical. Jumping down from Chainsaw's back, she noticed the incline had already steepened, making her breath come faster and deeper.

Swinging her injured shoulder in careful loops, she tried to relax the ache that'd descended after the long ride. Stopping to unzip the pack strapped securely to her back, she removed a bottle of water and took a couple of large gulps.

Liam knew about her gift, so she had to believe he'd count on her using her connection with the animals to help her find him. He'd take Lynne someplace hard for other humans to find, but accessible for someone with her special talents.

It was a game of cat and mouse both of them were playing, with the rules being made up as they went along.

A female roo appeared at Jenna's side, her rusty grey fur tickled Jenna's arm as she reared upright, her sturdy tail propping her erect. A picture of a steep canyon with a solitary tree standing against soaring terracotta cliffs appeared in Jenna's mind. Then the roo shook her ears as if laughing and Jenna sent her a silent thank you.

Now she had a picture of the place she needed to be, her heart beat a little faster. Thoughts whirled around her head. What would happen once she handed herself over to Liam? Even the mere idea of being close to Liam had her automatic flight response taking over, threatening to send her plunging back down the slope. Just run away. The impulse had become so ingrained. To run and keep running.

Please let Lynne be unharmed. Please let her not be making this sacrifice in vain. Without a backward glance she turned her mind to climbing higher, determined to get there as fast as possible.

It was soon obvious the horses could no longer continue over the ever-steepening, rocky incline. They stumbled and tripped, sometimes sliding backwards a few meters on the unstable ground, until Jenna halted and took a few jumping steps back down the slanting hillside to stand next to her beloved Chainsaw. His sides heaved with exertion, but his gaze remained indomitable.

She reached her arm over the crest of his neck and buried her face in his warm dusty mane for a few priceless seconds. Thanking him for his help, she extended her thoughts to the stallion and his mares who had run beside them. They'd go and wait at the base of the last hill, in the shallow valley that offered shade and a little protection. The kangaroos continued the journey up the mountain with her.

Chest heaving and lungs burning, she made it at last to the edge of a high cliff-face rising up in front of her, where the entrance to a dark crevice ran backwards at an angle from the slope. It appeared to head right into the heart of the mountain. The crack was just wide enough for her to squeeze through and then it opened up so she could touch each wall if she held her arms outstretched.

The kangaroos wouldn't fit through the small cleft in the rock. The alpha male made sure she knew the small herd would stay and guard the opening.

Accompanied by nothing other than her fading shadow, she worked herself into the crevice and made her way with care over the uneven floor of the fissure. Soon the light from the opening faded, until it was utterly dark. The only way she knew she was even moving forward was by the touch of her hand trailing along the rock-face. Why hadn't she thought to bring a torch with her?

The sheer darkness weighed heavily upon her and her steps soon slowed, becoming hesitant.

What if this was a trap? What if Liam pounced on her from within the dark and she never got to rescue Lynne after all? Her mind's eye wouldn't stop reeling off scenarios in her head that made her twitch and jump at every rock she stumbled into.

It was no use trying to occupy her mind with plans for rescuing Lynne and then escape, because it wasn't going to happen. Jenna would be giving herself up peacefully, so Lynne may live.

Giving herself up to what end, she wasn't sure. It seemed Liam was going to hand her over to her biological father, Alexander. But she'd witnessed Liam brutally murdering her real father. And although he had corrupt police in his pocket and a bogus arrest warrant out in her name, he must still be worried about the possibility she might testify against him one day. Once he had her in his grasp and handed her over to his boss, surely he must have some kind of guarantee from Alexander she'd never have a chance to run to the police and tell her tale. Which didn't bode well for her.

But what could Alexander possibly want with her? Liam hinted that Alexander was rich and powerful and hated to be crossed. By anyone. He'd also hinted Alexander was still hunting her mother as well. Did he want them back so they could play happy families together? The guy was completely deranged if he thought that was going to happen.

No one else is going to die on my behalf again. The thought echoed in her brain and kept her feet moving forwards, one foot in front of the other. She repeated the words over and over. Her mantra to push herself forward.

She couldn't say how long she paced down the fault line in the rocks, but as she rounded a slight bend a splinter of light appeared ahead, dazzling sunshine beckoning her forward.

She was here. Her fate was no longer in her hands.

* * *

The light in the small canyon seemed overly harsh after the gloom of the crevice and it took Jenna's eyes a few minutes to adjust. Neither Liam nor Lynne were in sight, but the back of the canyon plunged deeper into the mountain. They must be in there somewhere. She passed the lone tree and continued into the darkening cave. This time the cleft didn't narrow as much and a high rock ceiling towered overhead. The air cooled as she went deeper into the cave.

A flicker of movement caught her eye as she rounded a sharp bend and, too late, she flinched and tried to duck. A hand reached out and grabbed her by the throat, the grip so tight no scream could get past his iron grasp.

'So, you managed to find us after all.' It was a man called Brad. She remembered him from the night her father died. He was one of Liam's two thugs, the one who'd thrown the rope over the tree and hung her father by the neck. He stood before her, solid and stocky, biceps bulging as he held her without effort. Jenna licked her lips and tried to swallow past the restriction of his fingers. Her clammy hands slipped as she grappled with his strong forearms. Forearms crawling with tattoos. Ugly tattoos, of knives dripping with blood and naked women, sprawled up his elbow. Fear crowded her brain, pushing all coherent thought away and she began to claw ineffectively at the tattoos swimming before her eyes.

'I wasn't sure you'd come. But Liam said you would, and he's always right.'

Gasping for air, she was desperate to regain some kind of rationality.

'For a stupid girl, you show some kind of guts walking in here alone and empty handed.' His hold loosened. Anger swirled, fast and furious, replacing the fear in her chest. She wanted to smash that smug grin right off his bearded face.

'Let me go, arsehole.' Her words emerged past the constraining fingers.

'Whoa, feisty huh? I like it when they're feisty. Bit different to last time I saw you, hey?' His grip tightened again, and he brought her closer, so they were practically nose to nose. His smarmy grin showed off a row of crooked teeth. He licked his lips slowly and deliberately. Rage rose like bile in her throat.

She saw red; blazing red fury burned its way through her veins. This bastard helped Liam to kill her father.

Her right hand flew up and struck out with all the force she could muster. Using her nails like claws she dragged them over his face. The feeling as they bit into the flesh of his cheek was perversely satisfying. She raised her knee at the same time, hitting the soft flesh between his legs with a substantial thud.

'You fucking bitch,' he gasped between gritted teeth, releasing her as he bent over in pain. Taking a step backwards Jenna surveyed the man in front of her with a mixture of disgust and gratification. The desire to do him more harm, to exact some of her own revenge pulsed though her and she began to line him up, so she could aim another kick, this time at his head.

'Brad, what's going on out there?'

She froze at the sound of that voice. Liam. She'd know his voice anywhere.

The next thing she knew, she was flat on her back on the hot, dusty ground. Brad stood over her, still cupping his wounded genitals in one hand.

'When I said I like 'em feisty, I didn't mean quite like that, you little whore,' he growled. A trickle of blood ran down his chin where she'd scratched his face. He reached his tongue out and licked it off his jawline, the smarmy grin back in place once more.

'Brad, don't you be messing with my property. Send her in here. Right away.'

The big, hairy man hesitated. He swore under his breath. 'Righto, boss.' He landed a quick, sharp kick into her ribs then stepped back slowly, still grinning. She doubled over in agony, lying curled up in the dirt. The whole left side of her body throbbed, stabs of pain snaking their way down her legs. It was the same side that'd copped a beating when she'd fallen from the stallion.

'Get going, whore.'

She levered herself slowly off the ground, her left hand clutched around her ribcage. Forcing her back straight, she took slow, deliberate steps into the cavern, head held high.

She didn't need to go very far to find what she was looking for. Flickering light drew her onwards until she rounded another sharp bend to see a large cavern lit by a lantern in the middle.

Lynne was there, standing right in front of her, but slumped at an awkward angle. It took a second for Jenna to realize she was unconscious and tied to some kind of wooden stake rammed into the rocky earth. Jenna rushed forward and was within a few steps of her friend, when a booming voice halted her in her tracks.

'Don't touch her.'

Jenna stopped but scrutinized Lynne to make sure she could see the rise and fall of her chest. She was alive. And hopefully unharmed. Thank God.

She peered around the drooping form of her friend. Where was he?

'I'm glad you could join me, Jenna.'

The hairs on the back of her neck stood up. The revulsion at being so close to the man who killed her father made her gag.

She forced her words out through numb lips. 'What kind of game are you playing, Liam?'

Taking a small step to the side, so Lynne was no longer blocking her view, she cast her gaze around the dim cave. There he was, standing atop a large outcropping of rock. His black leathers kept him camouflaged against the dark cavern walls. Only the pale skin of his face stood out, ghostly white in the dark, floating like a vestige of his missing humanity.

'I presume you haven't brought any of your pack of furry friends with you this time? Because if you have ...' He let the threat hang in the air between them.

She ignored him. 'I need to know Lynne is unharmed.'

'Yeah, yeah. She's ... shall we say, very relaxed. I gave her something to help her sleep, while we have our little chat.' Jenna gave an ironic snort. 'She'll wake up in a few hours with a nasty headache, but no other lasting effects.'

'I assume you want me instead of Lynne?'

'You assume right.' His jarring voice made her want to grind her teeth. Last time she'd seen him, terror had completely controlled her. She'd watched him kill her father. After two years, the terror was still there, waiting to rake its way up her throat and turn her into a blubbering fool. But now there was something more as well. A hard-won determination. A fortitude that hadn't been there before. She was resolved to stand up to him this time. He was just some filthy little low-life thug. This time she wasn't going to show her fear.

'How's Lynne to be returned to the station? How are they supposed to find her in here?'

'That's all been taken care of. I've set up a signal fire and a flare that'll go off an hour or so after we leave.'

'Why should I trust you? You're just as likely to leave her here to die.'

He gave a cruel laugh. 'I guess that's fair enough. But you'll just have to trust me. I promise I won't harm her—unless you force my hand. She hasn't seen our faces, so she can't identify us. I don't hurt innocent by-standers if I can help it. Not usually.'

'Oh really?' Her face contorted in a sneer. 'My father was innocent, but you felt no compunction to show him any mercy.'

His face hardened faintly in the dim light. 'Your father was a sad victim of his own pride. He was going to turn me over to the cops, when all he had to do was keep paying my little bit of revenue. If he had, he might still be alive today.'

Jenna didn't believe him for a second. Liam was a cold-hearted bastard. He wouldn't show anyone mercy if it didn't serve one of his own twisted agendas.

'What was your blood-money for?' she demanded.

'What, didn't step-daddy-dearest tell you?' His open-mouthed laugh echoed off the walls of the cavern. 'Your dad was paying because he thought it'd stop me turning you over to Alexander. But I was biding my time, enjoying my little windfall. I was always going to take you to Alexander. It just turned out sooner, rather than later, when your wonderful father stopped the money.'

She'd never met him, but God she hated Alexander.

'Get over here, so I can have a better look at you.' Jenna hesitated. 'Now!' She jumped at the menace in his tone. She really had no choice. Whatever it took to save Lynne.

Sidestepping around her friend's inert body, she surveyed the rest of the cave as she approached Liam's rock pedestal. Although the light cast strange shadows across the cave's gloomy walls, it seemed the grotto was a dead end. No way out, except back the way they'd come in.

As she approached, a rare smile lit up Liam's face. The snarling dragon tattoo glared at her from beneath his left ear. 'That's right, all you have to do is obey me and your lady friend over there will stay healthy and alive.' There was glint of something metal in his hand. Was it a knife? A small shiver of trepidation ran down her spine. She had no doubt he'd use it on her if she gave him any excuse. Standing ten feet or so in front of Liam, she looked up at him warily.

'I don't understand. Alexander is my biological father. That's all. He has no other claim over me. My real father is dead. Because of you. What in hell could Alexander possibly want from me? Why have you been pursuing me for so long? What do you want from me?' Her last words came out on a sob.

'Didn't your sad excuse for a step-father enlighten you? I assumed he must have guessed at least some of it, with all the hints I gave him. After all, I was blackmailing him for months. He must've known who I was.' He cocked an eyebrow at her, the jut of his chin making his goatee beard appear to point at her.

'So all he told you was Alexander was your true father? Is that all?' He gave a vicious laugh. 'That's so sad. You see, *Jenna*,' he snarled the last word, as if it hurt to say her name. 'You and I are more alike than you know. Even though the idea makes me sick to my stomach.' He made a disgusting sound in the back of his throat and then spat loudly onto the rock floor.

Through the hum of Liam's speech Jenna thought she caught another sound; the very faint echo of a dog barking. Dune. It could only mean that he'd escaped and followed her here. She hoped Liam hadn't heard the sound as well. Silently, she entreated Dune not to follow her into the cavern. But she wasn't sure he got the message, he was still too far away for it to be clear.

'You and I are entirely different in every perceivable way,' she said. A wicked smile lit up his face, the grin spreading his beard, so it bristled with vindictive humour. She hated that little black beard. 'I don't have any idea what you're babbling on about and I don't care either,' she snapped, only half listening, trying to make her conversation a little louder to cover the sound of Dune barking.

'Well, that's where you're wrong.' He held his hands up in front of his face in an expansive motion. 'We have the same life-force running through both of us.' She only half-heard him. Dune's barking had stopped.

'Life-force? What are you saying?'

Liam snorted in disgust. 'Much as I hate to admit it, you and I have the same blood running through our veins.'

Her mind was spinning. What was he saying? Her body went weak, her legs turning to jelly underneath her.

'I can't believe your step-father took this secret to his grave.' Liam sounded incredulous. 'When I say we have the same blood running through us, I mean that literally.'

'We're not the same.' She said the words only because to hear them out loud might make them true. The words echoed around and around in her head in desperate denial.

'We have the same father, you and I. We're half-brother and sister.' The note of triumph in his voice only managed to make her feel lightheaded. 'Our *father* has been searching for you a long, long time. He's a controlling bastard. An arrogant, self-centred, dominating bastard. I've heard him called a narcissist more than a few times.' Liam gave a snort of contempt. 'But he's a rich controlling bastard, and he's free with his money if it means he gets what he wants. And he wants his wife and his daughter back by his side. Where you belong. No matter what it takes. No matter how long it takes.' Liam gave an evil giggle of glee. 'Along with his only son as well, of course.'

Her legs failed her and she landed in a crumpled heap on the dry dusty floor.

'No, it's not true,' she whispered. 'You're not my brother. He can't ...' She let her words trail off, disbelief giving way to detachment. She couldn't be Liam's half-sister. It couldn't possibly be true. There was no way on earth she could be related to this ... Barbarian. This spawn of evil. Could she? None of it made any sense. And what kind of man would spend half his life searching for a runaway wife and a missing daughter? A very sick and twisted kind of man, that's who. A psychopath. She shuddered violently.

For the first time in her life, Jenna wanted to die.

When she looked up again, Liam was standing beside her. She hadn't even seen him dismount his rocky dais. The knife glinted in his hand.

'Get up, we're outta here, Sis.' He reached down as if to grab her arm and haul her up from the floor.

'Don't you dare touch me!' The words were pure venom dripping from her lips. 'I'll come with you, but don't you touch me again.'

His arm dropped back by his side and he glared at her through narrowed eyes. On autopilot, she stood up on shaky legs and followed his leather-clad form towards the entrance. Her gaze settled on Lynne's body, still tied to the stake in front of them. The sight of her friend bound and unconscious brought some clarity back. It didn't matter that she might be Liam's half-sister and he was dragging her off to meet some demon-spawned father who was going to ... what? Keep her locked up like a slave by the sounds of it. It was Lynne who mattered now. She had to make sure Lynne was safe. That's why she'd come here in the first place, wasn't it?

'Release her from that damned pole,' she demanded.

Liam gave a delighted laugh. 'How selfless of you, thinking of your friend even in the midst of your own loss.'

'What exactly do you mean by *her loss*?' The deep voice echoed around the cave making Jenna pause in shock.

* * *

'Whatever you're about to lose, Jenna, I'm going to make damn sure it doesn't happen,' Dan said, barely able to control his rage. Whoever this dickhead was, he wasn't about to let him get away with anymore bullshit.

He stepped out from his hiding place in a shadow at the side of the cavern. Jenna stared at him like she'd seen a ghost.

For a split second he drank in her presence, checking her over with a quick glance to make sure she was okay.

'Fuck! Brad, get in here now!' Liam's voice was commanding, yet unafraid. But he should be afraid. Very afraid. Because Dan wanted to kill the son of a bitch.

'Brad's not coming,' replied Dan in the calmest voice he could muster. 'He wasn't feeling very well, so I gave him the rest of the afternoon off.'

'Dan! What—How—You have to get out of here.' Jenna's voice was panicked and screechy as she stood slightly behind this Liam fellow, still staring at him.

Dan pulled a gun from the back of his jeans and then delved into his pocket and proceeded to empty a handful of bullets onto the ground, where they gave a metallic ping as they hit the rocks.

'Oh, sorry, I forgot to tell you. I borrowed Brad's gun, along with his spare bullets. Just in case you got any fancy ideas.' The only sign Liam had heard him was a slight narrowing of his eyes. This character was familiar with guns and violence. He obviously thought he still had the upper hand. Well, that was about to change. Dan was about to wipe that smug grimace right off his ugly face.

'Thanks for your concern, Jenna, but I'm not leaving without you.' He kept his gaze riveted on Liam. 'Mob, go get Lynne.' Dan spoke in a low tone, not wanting to spook the gangster too much.

'Mob's here too?' Jenna mouthed the words, but still looked too stunned to move as she watched Mob emerge from another hidden shadow just behind Dan. Mob headed towards where Lynne was tied to the stake. Dan had been impressed with Mob over the past few hours. A kind of steely determination had replaced his normally jovial personality as soon as he found out what Dan intended. He was just as desperate to rescue Jenna and Lynne as Dan was.

'Oh God.' A groan of terror left Jenna's lips. 'Dan, please just go away, I have everything under control.'

What did she mean by that? Everything under control? That thug was just about to lead her away to God knew where. From the little he could decipher, Jenna was offering herself up as a hostage in exchange for Lynne. Why she was prepared to make that kind of sacrifice was definitely one of the ten million questions that needed an answer, but now wasn't the time.

'I won't be responsible for more people's blood on my hands. Please, Dan,' she entreated. 'Please, won't you just go away?'

Dan didn't answer, instead he walked toward them, slow but unwavering. He wasn't leaving either of the women here.

'What do you think you're doing?' Liam spoke to Dan as if he'd just found a squashed bug on the bottom of his shoe.

Mob never batted an eyelid as he continued towards Lynne, and Dan didn't stop his slow stalking, both of them unafraid of Liam's threat.

'I said stop what you're doing, right now!' Liam didn't raise his voice, but as he spoke he raised up a sharp-edged dagger. Pinpricks of light danced off the blade as the polished surface shone in the weak lamplight. He pointed the dagger directly at Mark. 'Don't touch her.'

Dan moved, and was between Mob and the razor-sharp knife in the blink of an eye. He raised the gun and pointed it directly at Liam. This guy was a little bit simple or something. How did he think he could overpower two of them, especially as Dan had a gun? Did he think he was bulletproof?

'Don't underestimate me, Liam. I know how to use this thing.' Dan's voice was quiet. Deceptively so. 'I'll tell the police it was self-defence.'

Liam's snort was loud and full of incredulity. 'I'm not sure if you're brave or just plain stupid. I don't care what the cops think. Those pigs will never be able to pin anything on me. I'm untouchable. But you're not.' Now it was Liam's voice that became deceptively quiet. 'The police don't look too kindly on ex-cons shooting a civilian.'

What the ... How the hell did he know Dan had spent time in jail? This whole thing was getting more out-of-hand by the second.

Jenna started to sidle closer behind Liam's back. He willed her to stop what she was doing. Liam seemed to have all his focus on the two men in front of him, but she'd be stupid to believe he'd forgotten about her.

'He must be something special, if he's willing to point a gun at me to help you.' Liam's black eyes narrowed with speculation.

'No, he's nobody. I never asked for, or wanted anybody's help.' The desperation in her voice was marked. She twitched her head two or three times, indicating Dan should go. That he should leave. But Dan didn't move a muscle, staying in front of Liam with the gun pointed at him.

'Dan, I have a plan. Everything was going fine. Please leave Lynne where she is and turn around and go,' Jenna implored him. 'Lynne will be safe, I promise.' As she spoke, she sidled even closer to Liam. What was she planning to do? Take him from behind? He wanted to yell at her to stop. She was now so close to Liam that if Dan tried to use the gun he might hit her instead.

Dan glanced quickly over his shoulder to where Mob was now by Lynne's side, his fingers working at the knots in the rope holding her up.

'Lynne will be safe, will she?' Dan's gaze flicked to Jenna then back to Liam and his knife, trying to tell her to back off with his eyes. 'But what about you? Are you going to be safe?'

Her mouth tried to form an answer but no words would come.

'Yeah, that's what I thought,' he replied.

Mob muttered, 'I've got her,' to Dan's back.

'Jenna, let's go.' Dan still sheltered Mob and Lynne behind him, but he reached an arm out towards her.

'Stay exactly where you are, Jenna, or I'll kill them all.' Liam's command went through her like a whiplash and she stopped, uncertain.

'I'm the one with the gun here. There's nothing he can do that won't end up with him lying, bleeding on the ground,' scoffed Dan. 'Get Lynne out of here, Mob.'

'What about you two?' Mob wasn't happy with Dan's command

'Just stick to the plan, Mob, I'll look after Jenna, you make sure Lynne's safe.'

'This is all fucked up!' Mob swore.

'I know, Mob, but I promise I'll get her out of here.'

Out of the corner of his eye, Dan saw Mob lift Lynne gently and drape her inert form over his shoulder. Then he started backing towards the entrance, watching Liam through judicious eyes.

'You can have the fucking slut. It's not her I want anyway.' Liam's shout made Mob flinch but he didn't stop his backwards retreat. 'I'll let you live if you just go away and leave Jenna with me.'

Dan wanted to laugh. It almost sounded like Liam was trying to negotiate. 'How about I let *you* live, as long as *you* just back away and leave her with *me*.'

Liam didn't reply. Then he turned, and quick as a snake, grabbed Jenna by the neck and held the knife to her throat. She gasped, helpless. Her mouth moved, but nothing came out. Shit, that was exactly what he was trying to avoid. What did Jenna think she was up to? An evil grin split Liam's face and Jenna jerked in his hold. Liam now had Jenna between himself and the gun. Using her as a shield.

What should he do? He took a step to the side, still pointing the gun at Liam's head. But both of them knew he wouldn't use it. Not if there was a chance he'd hit Jenna. He wasn't a great marksman, not by any stretch of the imagination.

Liam frog-marched Jenna closer. There was a wild look in her eyes.

'Jenna?'

Jenna's eyes bulged with horror, but she still didn't speak. Dan could do nothing. Not for her. Not for him. They were too close. He went to take a step backwards, to keep Liam in his sights. His ankle rolled as his foot landed awkwardly on a rock. Dan stumbled. That was all Liam needed.

As if it happened in slow motion, Dan watched Liam raise the dagger high above his head and drive it down towards Dan's chest. He tried to duck. But he was too slow, and the dagger stabbed into him. The echo of the gun going off shattered his eardrums. Jenna uttered a soundless scream beside him as Liam stepped back to admire his handiwork. The bullet missed Liam, going wide, lodging in the back wall of the cave. Dan lay on the ground, the dagger embedded in his flesh, his blood pumping crimson red onto the dusty earth.

CHAPTER FIFTEEN

Jenna knelt on the cold floor of the cave as Liam bent down to retrieve the gun from Dan's useless hand. Fear, horror, despair raged through her. She was completely helpless. As if she'd been transported back to that night, two years ago, when she'd watched her father die.

But this time she wasn't helpless. This time her hands and feet weren't tied. She was free to move if she wanted to. Free to use her hard-won fortitude. Free to change the outcome.

She wasn't going to let him kill Dan.

She hadn't come completely unarmed. God knows why she'd brought it, some fool notion made her slip it into her back pocket before she left the station. It was only small, a farrier's tool she used to bang old nails out of horseshoes. A spike of metal with a sharp point.

Liam's back was turned to her, as he worked the gun free from Dan's hand. This was her chance. He'd only taken his focus off her for a second. But it was all she needed.

She surged to her feet, the spike in her hand before she even knew how it got there. Then she lunged at Liam, her unexpected weight sending him sprawling on the ground, the spike driven deep into his back.

A scream ripped from his throat and his whole body went rigid. The gun skidded across the ground, coming to a stop when it finally hit the wall, nearly ten feet away. Jenna scrambled off his back, her gaze flicking between Liam and the gun.

Dan still lay on the ground, bleeding. She hesitated. Liam rolled over and started to get to his knees, swearing at the top of his voice. He spotted the gun. She was closer. They both knew he wouldn't make it in time. Whatever it took, she'd drive him away from here. She'd even kill him if the opportunity arose. She ran for the gun. Behind her was the sound of booted feet. Oh God, was he going for the gun too? Not daring to look behind, she put on a desperate spurt of speed and grabbed the weapon off the floor, using the wall to stop her headlong flight. Then she spun around, gun raised— just in time to see Liam disappear around the bend in the cave. Should she chase him? She took a few stumbling steps forward. The gun shook almost uncontrollably in her hands. Then Dan groaned.

Dan, she couldn't leave Dan.

Standing dazed and drained of all strength, she heard Liam screaming. 'I'll kill you both for this! I'll hunt you to the ends of the earth, just so I can tear you limb from limb!'

* * *

'Wow, I'm glad I'm on your side.' Dan had to force the words out through clenched teeth. She jumped, as if she'd forgotten he was there. 'You're a regular Indiana Jones.'

'Oh shit, Dan, I can't believe he stabbed you. Are you alright?' Her voice was shaky. Jenna knelt down beside him on the ground to examine him. The knife still protruded from his chest. It was imbedded just below his right collarbone, in the soft hollow of his shoulder. Blood trickled slowly, but at least it wasn't gushing.

It hurt like hell and for once, he was at a loss at to what to do next. But at least Jenna was safe. When he'd first stuck his head around the pillar of rock and seen her slim form standing in front of Liam, vulnerable and completely at his mercy, flashes of red blinded his vision. Anger and a sense of purpose welled up in a volcano of emotion. He would protect her no matter what. Even give his life for her.

'I think we should leave the knife in, at least until we can get somewhere safer with more light where I can have a good look at it. If I take it out now you could bleed to death before I can stop it.'

He nodded his head, thankful at least she seemed to be thinking clearly.

'I think you're right. We need to get out of here. Fast.' That bastard had disappeared, but there was no telling when he might reappear and he didn't like his chances of fighting the man with a blade sticking out of his chest.

'Hang on, I might have something we can use to bandage it.' She flung her backpack onto the ground next to him and pulled out a spare shirt. Proceeding to rip long strips from the bottom, she wadded it with care around the protruding knife. She was trying to be as gentle as possible, but more than once he had to close his eyes and grit his teeth as she scrabbled with the bandages.

'I'm so sorry, Dan.' The anguished edge filling her tone made him utter a silent curse. She was doing her best, she shouldn't be blaming herself. He knew better than to let an armed man get that close. There'd been a few times back in jail where he'd been forced to defend himself, and he'd always come out on top. The gun gave him a misconceived idea of having the upper hand. He'd be ready for it next time. He wasn't letting that snivelling weasel of a man threaten Jenna again.

'It's okay, I know you're just getting some of your own back,' he said, referring to when he'd set her shoulder.

'How can you joke about it, especially at a time like this?'

Yeah, it probably was a bad time to be making jokes. Jenna lurched to one side and sat down with a heavy thump beside him, her hands shaking. Tears shone bright and unshed in her pale blue eyes. His stomach contracted into a knot.

'Shit. Jenna, are you all right?' She turned her face up to him in mute reply. 'What's the matter? You're not hurt too?' He hadn't seen any injuries on her, but he also hadn't bothered to ask. What if Liam had hurt her somehow before they'd arrived? The blood pounded hot in his temples at the idea.

'No, no.' Her answer was a hasty reassurance. 'It's just that …' She hesitated for a second, as if the words wouldn't come, and then they tumbled out in a torrent. 'It's just that I thought you were dead. When Liam stabbed you, I thought you were going to die. I don't know what I'd do if you were to die, Dan.' Her last words came out as half sobs.

'I'm not dead, Jenna.' He aimed a soft smile at her and lifted his good hand to stroke the side of her face. She was worried about him. No, it was more than just worry. She was terrified of losing him. He could see it in her eyes.

'I know, Dan, I'm sorry,' she apologized, sucking in a few steadying breaths to regain her composure.

It seemed she did care for him after all. That hard veneer had finally cracked open. As he knew it would one day. Maybe he should've engineered a madman to come and stab him before now, if that's what it took to get Jenna to admit her feelings for him.

'How bad have you hurt him? How long do we have before he comes after us?'

'I don't know. It was just a nail spike I drove into his back, it's probably not too bad.' Her face conveyed her bewilderment at what she'd done.

'Okay.' He made his tone as soothing as possible. 'We can talk about this later, first we need to find somewhere safe.'

He struggled to fold his long legs underneath him and lever up to a standing position. Every breath he took sent a stabbing fire down through his ribcage. He fought the pain and managed to stay standing, swaying on his feet. Jenna jumped up from the ground and took hold of his good arm, draping it around her shoulder for support, tucking the gun into the back of her jeans at the same time.

'Can you walk?'

'Of course I can.' That had to be the truth, otherwise they were both in a lot of trouble.

Jenna stopped dead when she saw Brad tied up and stuffed behind an outcropping of rock. He was still out cold from where Dan had hit him over the head with a rock. The man got what he deserved, and he'd have more than a few reminders of his exchange with Mob and himself.

'What about him?' The dislike was more than evident in Jenna's tone.

'Leave him. The police can deal with him later,' Dan replied.

'But what if Liam comes back and unties him?'

He didn't like that prospect any more than she did.

'There's nothing we can do at the moment.' It grated, but with him injured, Dan was helpless to do any more. 'We'll have to leave him, and hope Liam is too busy getting the hell away from here to worry about him. That bastard doesn't strike me as the type who'd come back to rescue a mate. He's more worried about his own skin. And we have a gun.' Which was true. But Dan still didn't like leaving loose ends. It was just one more reason they'd need to guard their backs until they could get out of here.

'I guess so,' she replied. But the frown on Jenna's face suggested her mind had already gone down the same path as his.

The trip back through the fissure in the rock was made easier by the aid of the torch he'd brought along. He couldn't imagine how he and Mob would've coped walking through here in pitch darkness without it. But Jenna had done it. On her own. Tough and dauntless, prepared to give up her life to save her friend. He was still humbled by the sacrifice she'd been prepared to make.

Small sounds were magnified in the crevice, the brush of their boots against the sand, the rasping of his breath as he struggled to stay upright. He knew the sound was upsetting Jenna, but there was little he could do to shut it down. It was taking all his energy just to stay upright, even with her as a crutch.

At last they emerged out the other side into the bright light of the desert. Mad, delighted barking welcomed them into the sunshine.

'Sorry, Jenna, I tied Dune to that salt bush. I didn't want him to follow us in.' He knew how she loved that dog.

'That's fine.' She helped to lower him onto a rock and then rushed over to Dune to untie him. He made it hard for her as he jumped and licked and wriggled, making Dan laugh despite the dull agony eating into his shoulder. 'He's not supposed to be here, I tied him up in his kennel before I left. I don't know how he got free, but he must've followed me.'

'It was Dune that led us to you.' Now he'd stopped moving it was easier to catch his breath and he even had the strength to lay his good hand on top of Dune's head as the young dog rushed over to greet him. 'Mob and I would've walked right past this place on our way down the mountain to try and find you, if he hadn't barked to alert us.'

'You did the right thing.' She walked over to join him, settling her neat bum on the rock beside him. There were a few seconds of silence and then her brow wrinkled charmingly. 'Hang on. On your way down the mountain?

How could you be heading down the mountain without going up it first?'

'Aha!' He waggled an eyebrow in her direction. 'I know you better than you think I do. I figured you'd do something like this.'

'Really. Well, Mr Top Secret Spy, good for you, but we still need to get out of here and find somewhere safer, soon.'

She stood up to survey the hillside and he followed the shape of her pert backside with his eyes, nicely revealed by the tight blue jeans. He couldn't believe that his libido was still responding to her seductive curves, even with a knife jammed in him.

Still grimacing at the absurdity, he said, 'I might know a place we could go.'

Jenna looked back up the hill at him, startled. 'Where?'

'Just a short way around this hillside is a low saddle which leads to a kind of pass through to the other side of this mountain range. That's the way Mark and I came in.' He started to clamber to his feet and she rushed to help him. 'We landed the helicopter on a flat outcropping on the other side and made our way through to here.'

'What are you talking about?'

She was beautiful even when she was tetchy.

'Don't you remember a helicopter flying right over the top of you and that mob of brumbies?'

Her step slowed, and she looked up through narrowed eyes at him. 'You were in that helicopter? I was sure no one saw me. How did you know where I was going?'

He laughed again. 'The Top Secret Spy is always one step ahead, Jenna.' He gave her a sly smile. 'But right now, I can tell you there should be a bag of provisions dumped at the helicopter landing site, and I'm hoping there'll be first aid supplies in there. I need to get onto the two-way and let Mob know we're okay.'

Their going was made slower by the fact they had to traverse sideways along the shale-filled, unsteady slope. Jenna did her best to help him stay upright, but soon his breathing became laboured again and it took all his concentration just to put one foot in front of the other.

The helicopter was indeed gone when they came upon the small, flattened area. Dan could imagine Mob's internal struggle to make the decision to tell the pilot to fly off without them. It would've cost him dearly to leave. But he was the ultimate team player, and in the end he would've followed Dan's command to make sure Lynne was returned home safe and sound. They wouldn't have all fitted into the small mustering helicopter anyway. It was just large enough to fit three people, and even that was a tight squeeze.

Once they found the bag, Jenna made him drink some water. It was tepid, but it tasted better than any ice-cold beer he'd ever drunk. Then she dug the two-way out of the black duffle bag, and he radioed Mob to tell him they'd got out. Mob's voice crackled over the two-way as he told them they were still on their way back to the station, as it was nearly half an hour away by helicopter. Dan told him that he and Jenna would find a safe place to hide until Mob could send the pilot back to pick them up.

'And I'm calling in the cops,' Mob said.

'No!'

Dan jumped at Jenna's loud protestation.

'Why not? We have to, Jenna. The bastard and his side-kick abducted Lynne. And he was about to take off with you. They're criminals who need to go to jail.'

'Please … I'll explain later. But please, don't call them just yet. Give me a few hours,' she pleaded.

'I don't understand,' said Mob. 'Simmo, what's going on with her?' he questioned over the radio.

'I don't know,' Dan replied, slowly scrutinising Jenna's worried face for answers. She seemed to be more scared of the cops than she was of Liam. But why? 'It'll take the cops a couple of hours to get here anyway,' he said thoughtfully. Police were thin on the ground out here. There weren't any police stationed in Smokey Creek, it was too small. The closest station was in Halls Creek, a four-hour drive away. People in these isolated towns were used to solving their own problems a lot of the time. 'Okay, we'll play it by Jenna's rules for a while. But we will have to call them in eventually.'

She nodded sullenly, not looking him in the eye. This woman had so many secrets it was making his head spin. 'I'll call you back soon, Mob. Can you keep this under your hat until then?'

'Bloody hell,' Mob swore. 'Okay, I won't do anything till I hear back from you guys. And I'll tell Lynne to say she doesn't remember what happened, which is pretty close to the truth, anyway. Over and out,' Mob replied, but they could both hear the reluctance in his voice.

'We need to move,' she said, squinting back up the slope warily, as if Liam was going to come hurtling down on top of them at any second.

'Down there.' He pointed down the slope to a patch of bright green, which stood out amongst the dull olive and ochre of the surrounding desert. 'There's a waterhole down there. Lex and I found it once while we were out on a muster.'

'Okay, sounds good. Let's get you down there,' she urged.

Sweat was running freely down the sides of his face and he was struggling to see straight. The torment from the knife and blood loss, combined with walking for an hour through the sweltering afternoon heat of the desert was taking its toll on his body. He just hoped he didn't collapse on top of Jenna before they got to the oasis.

CHAPTER SIXTEEN

'It'll need stitches,' she said, staring at the deep wound in Dan's shoulder. Kneeling over him, she peered at the fresh blood seeping lazily down his olive skin. Her stomach lurched, and she backed away.

He lay on the ground in the midst of dark emerald-green grasses, cradling him in their fronds. Dappled shade offered by a white-barked snappy gum rained down. Dune whined, worried by Jenna's anxiety.

'It's alright,' she soothed, glancing back at the dog so he could see her eyes. 'He's fine.' Was she convincing Dune or herself? She sent him an image of Liam and asked if he wouldn't mind searching the perimeter while she was occupied with Dan, to make sure they hadn't been followed. He trotted off with tail in the air, glad to be useful.

Head propped against a large tussock, Dan searched her face from a few inches away. 'Can you stitch it for me, Jenna?'

'What? No. Won't that hurt?' There were many things she was prepared to do working on a top-end station but stitching up Dan's shoulder definitely wasn't on her list. Grimacing, she looked away.

'I'm feeling much better now, the drugs are really kicking in. Look.' He demonstrated by rolling his injured shoulder a few times, making the red blood ooze liberally.

'Don't be an idiot, Dan,' she snapped, laying a hand on his shoulder to quell the movement. 'I know those pain-killers you took are strong, but they're not a local anaesthetic. It's still going to hurt.' Despite all his protestations, she was more than a little sceptical about the whole thing.

'Jenna, you need to do this for me.' Seriousness replaced the attempt at light-heartedness in his voice. 'We don't know what to expect from that crazy man out there. And if you don't want to involve the police then we need to keep moving, so we don't really have a choice.'

She nodded her head in unhappy agreement.

'All the medical supplies should be in that bag, including sterile wipes and needles.' He indicated the black bag they'd picked up at the helicopter site. She still hovered over him hesitantly.

He took her chin and held it steady in his hand, forcing her to meet his gaze. 'I'll talk you through it, I've sewed up a few injured horse legs before. Then we'll be even when it comes to inflicting pain on each other.'

'Oh, stop being an idiot,' she said, frowning down at him.

'That's twice you've called me an idiot.' He gave her a roguish smile.

'Maybe it's because you are one at this particular moment.' She sighed heavily and went to rummage in the bag, her mind skimming back over what Dan had done when they first arrived at the waterhole.

Once they'd reached the relative safety of the oasis, she'd laid Dan down and pulled out the first aid kit. It was well stocked. She'd found the strongest pain-killers in the pack and helped Dan sit up so he could swallow them. Then, just as she'd gone to have a further search through the bag, he'd surprised her by reaching over and pulling the dagger out in one swift movement. She'd gasped with shock and rushed to cover the wound with a clean bandage as he sat doubled over, fists clenched until his knuckles turned white.

'Better to do it quick and clean,' he'd panted through his agony.

'And how do you know that wasn't the only thing stopping you from bleeding to death?' she'd retorted in her most teacher-like voice, pushing the bandage hard over the wound.

Now she found herself, curved needle in hand, poised over Dan's naked torso, not really sure what to do next. The desert heat was intense, even in the shade of the snappy gum and a trickle of perspiration ran from her temple, leaving a wet trail down the side of her face.

'I hope it's just like sewing up a loose hem, because that's all I know how to do.'

'You'll be fine,' he encouraged. 'Anyway, I have a great topic I'm sure will distract us both from what you're doing.'

'I don't think I need any more distraction,' she replied in a tight tone, swiping a hand over her brow. That part, at least was true. Being this close to him while he lay half-naked, his butterscotch skin gleaming with sweat, was almost more than she could handle. Her gaze kept wandering over the hard planes of his chest and then she found herself staring at the undulating muscles of his stomach.

'What's the topic then?' She glared at him.

'Why don't you tell me about this man who just tried to kill us both? Don't spare any of the details. You can also tell me why you don't want the cops involved, too. That ought to keep both our minds off what you need to do.'

The comment brought her back to the task at hand. She'd have to leave plumbing the depths of his perfect stomach muscles with her eyes for another day.

'I guess I owe you some kind of an explanation,' she admitted. 'Where shall I start?'

'How about at the very beginning.'

'That might take a while, and I don't know how long we've got.' She cast a worried glance back up into the low-lying hills.

'I'm hoping you hurt him pretty bad,' Dan said. 'And he also has no idea which way we went. I'll wager tracking is not high on his list of abilities.'

'Okay,' she replied unhappily.

The shrieking curse Liam uttered came back to her, and she shuddered. He'd said, 'You'll both die' and she knew without a shadow of a doubt he would be out hunting them as soon as he was able. At least they still had the gun. That gave them an advantage. If they could stay out of sight until nightfall, then they might have a chance to escape under the cover of darkness. But what then? Now that Dan and Mob knew about Liam they wanted to put him in the hands of the cops and let them sort it out. That was what most sane people would do. So how was she going to convince them it wouldn't work? Liam had corrupt cops in his pocket. She knew they couldn't be trusted, she'd found out the hard way. Even if that phoney warrant for her arrest wasn't still active, there was no way she was going to let the cops close enough, just in case. How was she going to convince them that her going back on the run was the best way to handle this?

'Jenna, are you okay?' His gentle prompt brought her back to the present. First things first, she'd sew up Dan's wound, so they could move on.

Her story was hard to tell, chiefly because she was afraid Dan wouldn't believe her. But the first time she pushed the needle into his skin and he sucked an involuntary breath in over his teeth, the words started to tumble out of her mouth.

'Part of the reason Liam's after me is because I'm a witness to a murder.' There was no other way but to come out and say it. 'I saw him murder my father. My step-father,' she amended as she gazed squarely into his face.

'What?' His amber eyes flooded with a mixture of sympathy and anger. 'I'm so sorry, Jenna.' He sat up, ignoring the needle still implanted in his skin and engulfed her with his good arm, holding her close against his undamaged side. In the silence his compassion flowed into her, filling her with strength.

'It's okay.' And somehow it was. She'd thought when she did finally tell her story, she'd be overcome with grief. But saying it out loud wasn't as bad as she imagined.

'You are a remarkable woman, Jenna.' She pulled away, so she could look into his face. 'I don't know how anyone could experience that kind of atrocity and not become twisted and bitter. But your spirit is so beautiful and resilient.'

She was taken aback. But then she began to wonder. Yes, she hated Liam and his henchmen with an intensity that scared her. But her core beliefs remained unchanged.

'It was a hideous day, I won't deny it, and it has defined my life ever since.'

'Now I really have a reason to hurt that arsehole.' There was a feral light in his eyes, the likes of which she hadn't seen before. 'Do you know why he … did that?'

'I think I'm starting to understand why. Dad was protecting me.'

'Against what?'

'My biological father,' she answered quietly.

'Oh, Jesus,' he replied just as quietly. 'It's just gets worse. So your half-brother murdered your step-father? Because of your real father?'

'He's not my *real* father,' Jenna hissed, 'Joe was my *real* father.'

'Sorry,' he said, holding up his hands in placation. 'That came out wrong.'

'It's not your fault,' she apologized. Hearing Dan put it that way had caused a rush of fury to swarm through her. But he wasn't the one to blame, he was just trying to understand this convoluted web of lies that was her life.

'I used to think Liam was some kind of hired thug. Hired by my father to bring me home. To what ends I'm not sure. But today, not only did I find out he's my half-brother, but it seems Alexander is some kind of rich-prick, power-hungry control freak who doesn't like to be on the losing end of anything. Once he decides he owns something—that it's his property—then he's entitled to do whatever he likes with it.'

'So, he wants you back to what ... to play some kind of delusional happy families?' Dan looked as confused as she felt.

'I think there's more to it than that,' she replied unhappily. 'I don't know a lot about my mother, but I do know she was running. Away from Alexander. And I'm sure it wasn't because he was some doting guy who cared about the state of her health. At first, I hated my mother for leaving me behind. Not that I didn't love Joe, but it's just that ... she was my mum. Why did she leave me? But now I'm older and I've had time to think about things—plus experiencing Liam's hatred first-hand—I've come up with some different scenarios as to why she left me. Let's just say, there must've been something dark or twisted, or both, going on to make her so scared that she'd dump her only daughter onto a practical stranger because she thought I'd be safer with him.' She finally stopped talking and drew a breath.

His eyes filled with compassion and he leaned forward as if about to say something. She held up a hand.

'Wait, there's more.' Now she started this, she may as well make a full disclosure. She'd just admitted to Dan how completely screwed up her life was, so she may as well finish making a total fool of herself. Here came the part where she revealed her innermost secret. She'd thought the last part of the conversation was hard, but now it came to telling him about her gift, the words stuck in her throat. Her tongue was glued to the roof of her mouth.

Drawing back, she sucked in a deep breath. 'How do I explain this?' she mumbled, more to herself than to him. 'I believe he may also want me for a … talent I have. Something I can do. I guess the easiest way to explain it is that I can understand certain animals.' She wanted to drop her gaze, so she wouldn't have to see the disdain she knew would be in his face. But something made her hold his stare. Defiant. Waiting. She could see his thoughts racing through the possibilities and implications. Searching her face for the truth of her statement.

'Okay, that's … interesting.'

Studying his eyes for a sign of condescension she found none. She'd been ready for almost any answer, preparing herself for laughter, or disbelief. She'd even steeled herself for utter rejection. He would've been within his rights to tell her she was crazy and walk away. But this cool acceptance caught her off guard.

'Did you hear what I said?'

'Yes,' he answered evenly. 'You can communicate with animals'.

Well, I wouldn't say communicate, exactly. But why don't you seem surprised?' She raised her brows at him, not quite able to believe he'd take this so calmly.

'Nothing much surprises me about you any more, Jenna Smith.' There was frank acceptance in his statement. 'Actually, it's a relief to have all of those odd little quirky things you get up to with animals now finally start to add up,' he teased lightly. 'Of course, I have millions of questions, like how does it work, is it all animals you understand, stuff like that. But no, I'm not really surprised. I always knew you were special, right from the very first time I laid eyes on you.'

She nearly dropped the needle. Then considered what he'd just said.

'From the first time you met me?'

'Yep.'

She thought she'd been the only one to feel that tingling awareness the day they'd met outside the Elsewhere Pub.

Another trickle of blood ran from the wound, reminding her of the task at hand and she returned to her grisly job.

'So, can you explain to me how this communication thing works? It's not like Dr Doolittle is it?'

'No, I'm not Dr Doolittle,' she laughed. Then went on to tell him her whole life story, from the time her dad adopted her when she was only a baby—too young to remember her mother—right up to the second Dan appeared in the cave to rescue her.

Every now and then he'd interrupt to ask a quick question. But for the most part, he allowed her to unburden herself from the past and from the lies she'd told him. In the end she ran out of words and silence ensued.

'Did you ever guess Liam might be your half-brother?'

Jenna shook her head in resignation. It was such a new and raw revelation. She hadn't had time to process it yet.

'Can he do what you can do?'

'Does he have a talent, do you mean? An empathy with animals? No, I don't think so.' She let out a frustrated sigh. 'You deserve some answers, Dan, but I know so little about this whole thing. I must admit, I've been almost ignoring my gift, hoping that if no one else found out then it wouldn't be a problem. But that's not good enough, is it?'

'No.'

He was right of course. The questions buzzed in her head, all demanding answers she didn't have.

Dan was also right about another thing, telling him her life story while stitching his wound did pass the time a lot faster than she'd expected. At least for her it did anyway. She was sure he still felt every tug of the needle and thread no matter how much she poured out her heart to him. At least he only needed six stitches to pull the edges of the injury together enough to stop the bleeding. She didn't think she could've handled watching Dan pretend to ignore how her hand shook and fumbled every time she went to make a stitch.

He held extremely still for her, considering what she was doing. The trust was there for her to see as he stared into her face while she talked and sewed.

At last she tied the thread off with a simple knot, watching him relax, the strain of holding motionless leaving him drained and weak. Laying his head back on the soft grass, he closed his eyes and let a sigh escape his lips.

'Thanks, Jenna. See it wasn't that bad, was it?'

He smiled but didn't open his eyes and all of a sudden she was undone. She was the one who should be thanking him, not the other way around. If it wasn't for Dan, her life would be forfeit to Liam by now. He'd risked his life for hers. Only one other person had ever done that; her father. And he'd loved her like no-one else could. And just now, Dan had accepted everything she said without batting an eyelid. Almost as if none of it really mattered. Her life was a complete and utter screw-up, but that didn't seem to frighten him.

Was it true, could Dan be in love with her? Back in the cave, when she'd thought he might've been killed by Liam's knife, she'd felt a tidal-wave of passion flood over her, and she'd wanted to shout out her true feelings for Dan.

Dare I admit I'm in love with him?

She fixed her gaze on him, drinking in every detail as he lay unmoving, just the rise and fall of his chest showing he still breathed.

It was the way he held himself, with such a quiet dignity. There was stillness in the way he got things done. He had a reserve of hidden strength. Strength of mind as well as body. And an earthiness, a bone-deep bond with the land that attracted her.

Tentatively at first, Jenna ran her fingers along the hard, muscular curve of his undamaged shoulder, damp with sweat. As her fingertips brushed his tanned skin his amber eyes flicked open. Her fingers tangled in his sun-bleached hair that curled down over his face. She watched his irises darken, the pupils dilating as she stared into their unfathomed depths.

Just to see that flash of desire when she touched him would almost be enough. She could leave it there, and perhaps never ask for more. But how could anyone be drawn into that good-natured, courageous soul and not want more? She was bereft of will to deny him anymore.

His hand reached up and caressed her jaw, pulling her closer, until she closed her eyes and their lips met.

'Dan.'

'Yes,' he murmured against her lips.

'I should've said this last night, but I was too scared.' She laid her face alongside his in the sweet-smelling grass.

'And now you're not scared anymore?' He turned to stare at her.

'No. I understand now, what will be will be, and I owe this to you as much as I owe it to myself.' She hesitated. *Breathe. You can do this.* 'I'm falling in love with you, too.'

A dazzling smile lit up his tired face and she knew what it felt to be saved as he reached for her again.

She manoeuvred her body, so she was lying on top of him, taking great care to stay well away from his injured shoulder. His delicious mouth curved upwards at the corners as she nestled herself onto his chest, using her elbows to prop herself up so she could stare down at him. Her whole body started to tingle beneath Dan's dark gaze, which was full of hungry need.

Dipping her head, she brushed her lips against his neck, tasting the salty sweat still gleaming on his skin. Inhaling his masculine scent, she used the sharp edges of her teeth to nip at the muscles in the curve of his neckline, feeling his pulse become erratic beneath her mouth. A hunger for connection with this man pushed her now, and his hands on her skin drew a searing need through her body. Desire flared and she knew she wanted to make love to Dan, here in the long grass of the desert.

As if reading her mind, he gave a low groan and before she knew what was happening he'd rolled her over so that now her back was cushioned by the downy grass, his mouth capturing hers, his tanned hands sliding around her rib cage. As he moved his hand down to the small of her back she caught a wince of pain. She'd forgotten about his wound in the rush of emotions.

'Wait. I forgot.' She pushed against his chest, worried. 'We shouldn't be doing this.'

'Yes, we should, Jenna. I'm fine.'

Then she remembered Liam. And Brad. She reached out to Dune. He was on the peripheries of her mind, a long way from the waterhole, but he'd picked up no scent of either of the two bad men. They were safe, for now.

'If you think I'm going to let you get away this time, Rowdy, then think again. This time we are going to finish what we started, and no one is going to interrupt us,' he growled against her cheek, running a series of kisses down to her earlobe.

His face remained serious as his deft fingers attacked her buttons and her shirt was soon discarded into a nearby tuft of tussock. Trailing kisses from her belly-button upwards, he found the edge of her bra. His hand worked its way around her back and unfastened the bra strap. Impatient now, she helped him by slipping each strap off her shoulders and then lay back down in the grass as he stared at her.

Wondering at her lack of self-consciousness, she found she wasn't the least bit shy under his gaze. Instead she drew the hand from his uninjured arm up to cup one of her breasts. His touch sent an intense awareness through her chest and down into her legs.

'God, you're beautiful, Jenna.' He ran his hand over her breasts, exploring his way down her belly. As his fingers worked their way back up he stopped at the top of one of the large yellow and purple bruises that still covered the side of her ribs. They were no longer sore to touch, but his fingers remained tender as they traced the outline. His brows knit together in consternation.

Now it was his turn to ask, 'Are you sure you're alright?'

'Never been better,' she laughed, giving some of his attitude back. 'Don't you dare stop now!'

His hand wavered then changed tack and instead she found him pulling at the elastic binding her hair into its usual single long braid, winding gentle fingers through the strands to free them. Lifting a lock of blond hair to his face, he inhaled through the silken tresses then let her hair fall back to spread over her bare shoulders.

Undressing him should've been easy; he was already minus his shirt. She thought she'd fumble with his big belt buckle, but it was surprisingly effortless to undo. However, the buttons on his jeans seemed to evade her every effort to open them. Dan took over and with one deft motion pulled them off, laying back on the grass next to her while she toyed with the image of his powerful thighs, made strong from so many hours astride a horse, tapering into long, well-built calves.

He lay there naked in front of her and she knew he was the most stunning man she'd ever seen. His olive skin highlighted his perfect physique, lean but well-muscled. She stood up and took off her own jeans. Settling down next to him, she gloried in the feel of their legs entwining together, skin on skin.

Rolling her over, he lay the length of his body onto hers. His weight on top of her in the warm desert grass felt so satisfying, so right. Her mouth met his with equal ferocity as he descended, pulling him until his chest crushed her breasts. Her nerve endings were alive with every touch. Feeling his lips drift down her neck and then down further, she drew in a gasping breath as they came to rest, hovering over her nipple. Gently he sucked, drawing it deeper into his mouth, the feeling so exquisite her fingernails dug into the skin on his back.

His arousal jutted against the hollow of her hip, and the thought of him inside her made her close her eyes from the pure force of desire. Heat coursed from her groin up through her belly and then rushed straight to her pounding heart. She needed him inside her, the desire was now almost more than she could bear. Pulling his lips away from her breast, his amber eyes locked with hers, asking the wordless question.

'Please, Dan …' Jenna wasn't even sure if she said the words aloud.

'Wait a second,' he gasped, voice hoarse. Then she saw him reach for his jeans and fumble around in the pocket until his fingers came up with a little foil packet. Jesus, thank God he'd remembered, her mind was turned completely to mush by the feelings he was arousing.

He lay back down on her and stared into her eyes. Then, as he surged into her, her body became pure awareness, driven by a need more powerful than coherent thought. Moving together, Jenna revelled in the sheer perfection of Dan's intimacy and her heart soared free for the first time in her life.

She was aware of his body, sliding over hers, creating waves of sensation so pure it was almost a physical torment. Her mind was overridden by the feeling and she became a corporeal creature, intent on gaining sweet release from the raging fire that now engulfed her. She hovered on the brink, blissful climax awaiting her as she lay poised on a knife's edge, savouring the moment. Then she heard Dan let out a growl from deep in his chest and she crashed down the heaving wave with him.

They shuddered together and lay panting, slick with sweat, until Dan rolled off her, to lie smiling up at the heavens.

Languor overtook them both as they stared into each other's eyes while the dappled sunlight played over their faces. It was a long while before either of their breathing came back to normal.

CHAPTER SEVENTEEN

Jenna stirred beside him and his torpid mind was slowly dragged back to reality. A rustle in the grass made him flinch and reach for the gun. Then a sand-coloured muzzle poked through the sheltering shrubs into their hideout, followed by a chestnut one a second later.

'Dune,' Jenna exclaimed. 'He brought Chainsaw.' She jumped up to give the big horse an ecstatic hug, ignoring her nakedness.

Dan let out a snort of relief. They'd probably been more than a little stupid. Making love while a crazy man prowled around in the desert somewhere, looking for them. But Jenna convinced him Dune had been keeping guard. The dog would let them know if anyone was nearby. And goddamn, it'd been worth it. He'd do it again in a heartbeat. Laying back in the grass, he luxuriated in the view of her uncovered body as she buried her hands in the horse's dusty mane. More snorts and thuds of hoofs on rock told him that the herd of brumbies were probably also here, taking a much-needed drink from the waterhole's drain further down the rocky gully.

He rolled his shoulder. It still throbbed but the pain was bearable now. It might need some more pain killers soon, but at least the wound was clean and covered. Jenna had done a great job. She should never have doubted her ability. It was a bad habit of hers he was determined to break.

Still languid from their lovemaking, he relaxed on the ground, allowing the aura of peace and intimacy to stay with him for a few moments more. He was surprised to find himself hardening again at the sight of Jenna standing naked and gorgeous in front of him. As she rubbed her hands on the horse's neck it made her pert breasts jiggle seductively, reminding him of how she'd moaned when he'd taken each nipple into his mouth. He wanted her again, right now, the need a piercing dagger to his soul. God, he was in trouble when it came to this woman. His feelings wouldn't be denied. The power of his love frightened him.

'We need to call Mob soon, before he decides to act on his own and send the pilot back, or call the cops. Or both.' He cleared his throat, trying to erase the huskiness from it. 'They'll be back at the station by now, and he must be worried sick. People will be asking all sorts of questions.' He didn't want to interrupt her reunion with the horse, or his entertaining view, but it was time to make a few decisions. Decisions she might not like.

Turning blue eyes on him, she smiled. A smile of open honesty. A smile that told him how much she trusted him. Trusted him to keep her safe. To keep her secret safe. The news she could talk to animals would take some more consideration. But in the end, it was just another part of her to accept without prejudice. And he knew he'd have to accept it, no matter how surprising or odd it was. If he wanted her in his life. And he did want her in his life.

'Before we talk to Mob though, we need to formulate some kind of plan.'

Her smile faded. 'Yes, we should let them know.' Her hand dropped away from the horse's mane as she considered her next words. An apprehensive frown flitted across her face.

'And I need to make sure Lynne is alright as well. To apologize to her.' The blue in her eyes darkened to grey. She was probably mad, or embarrassed, or both, that Lynne had been used by Liam. Perhaps worried Lynne wouldn't accept her apology. Not many people caused their friends to be kidnapped, drugged, tied up and put in mortal danger by a madman. But Lynne wasn't just anybody. She was a generous soul and Dan knew she'd be a lot quicker to forgive than Jenna might suspect.

Giving Chainsaw one last hug, she searched around for her clothes, pulling on her crumpled blue jeans and bra.

He levered himself up, grabbing his jeans out from a hollow in the grass. Before he put them on, however, he sauntered over to her, pulling her face up to his, kissing her with a fervour meant to make her understand just how much he would've liked to continue their lovemaking. The kiss she returned was hot, echoing his own hunger, and it was with a sigh of regret he let her go so he could find his shirt.

'What do you mean by formulate a plan? Surely the plan is to get out of here as quickly as possible, isn't it?' She was doing up the last button on her shirt, and her voice remained studious, devoid of any emotion.

'If that's what you want, then yes, that's the plan.' He had a slightly different idea, but if she chose not to follow his lead, then he wanted her to be sure he'd stick with her, no matter what.

'Isn't that our only option?'

'That's the question I've been mulling over.' He caught her gaze as he sat back down and tapped the grass next to him, indicating she should come and sit.

Nodding her head, she went over and laid a hand on Chainsaw's shoulder until he gave a quiet snort and moved off through the scrub.

Sitting close to Dan's side in the soft grass once more, she said, 'Just posting some more sentries. What other plans do you have?'

Here goes nothing. 'Well, as you know, at first I thought we should just call the police and let them do their thing. That is their job, after all, and they should be able to catch a bastard like Liam and put him in jail to rot.' Her eyes narrowed sharply, and he knew she was about to argue the point. 'But after I heard your entire story it's obvious the police may not be able to help us as I'd hoped. Even though that bogus arrest warrant has probably disappeared, it might be better not to even risk it. At least not until Liam is no longer a threat.' She was right, if there were dirty cops loyal to Liam, then it'd be futile to involve them, she'd always be looking over her shoulder, wondering. Even with witnesses like Mob and himself to back up her story, if the cops doubted her for even a second and took her into custody … He shuddered to think what might happen if Liam was allowed to get to her through his corrupt contacts in the force.

'Maybe it's time to stop running, Jenna. Maybe it's time to turn from being the hunted and become the hunter instead.'

Her head jerked up.

'Don't get me wrong, I'll go along with whatever you decide.' He grabbed hold of her hand, enclosing it to lend strength to the meaning of his words. 'But am I right in saying he'll never stop, now he has you in his sights?'

She nodded her head, catching her bottom lip between her teeth in an unconscious sign of her inner turmoil. Glancing at her face, his stomach gave an agonising twist. He needed to steel himself against the worry and indecision swirling in her eyes. He needed her to be safe and this was the best way he could see to do it.

'So unless we do something about him, we'll be running for the rest of our lives.' His grip on her hand tightened.

'Hang on, what do you mean, *we*?' Her blue eyes were wide and dark, brow furrowed.

'I mean that if you leave, I'm coming with you. If you go on the run, you won't be going on your own this time.'

'But I can't ask you to do that, Dan.' Was that tears shimmering in her eyes? 'I can't ask you to put your life on hold. For me.'

'No, you're not asking me to. But I'm telling you, that's what I'm doing. Do you really think I could love you this much and let you go? Let you run headlong into danger to deal with this violent bastard on your own, and keep on with my own life, safe and unchanged?'

She studied him for many seconds, the tears finally spilling over and running down her cheeks. 'I don't know what to say, Dan. I—'

'Don't say anything,' he whispered. 'You don't have to do this alone anymore, Jenna.'

She leaned suddenly into him, resting her head against his chest. He gathered her in with his good arm and let her absorb the truth of his certainty. He loved her. It was all that mattered. He would protect her with the last breath in his body.

Finally, she drew in a deep breath and lifted her head from his chest. 'So, you were saying you had another plan. How are you going to make it safe for us, so we don't have to keep running? Oh God, do you mean you want him dead?'

He laughed in surprise. 'Slow down there, girl. If you're asking, do I think we'd both be better off if he was dead, then yes I do.' That much was completely true. He'd love nothing more than to punch the shit out of that loathsome man until he was just a bleeding pulp on the ground.

'I'm not sure either of us is the murdering type, however, so I'd say that avenue is out for us. What I am saying is maybe we should turn the tables on him. Capture him instead.'

'What'll we do with him then?' There was a hitch in her voice which made him want to gather her up in his arms. Of course she didn't ever want to see Liam again, let alone come face to face with him. But that was exactly what he was asking her to do.

'When I agreed we shouldn't involve the cops, I wasn't telling the complete truth. I do know one cop we can trust.' It was now or never. Time to reveal his past. And hope like hell she didn't just up and walk away from him. 'He's a friend of mine and I know we can rely on him one-hundred percent. If we can capture Liam, we can get my friend to pull some strings and he should be able to take care of the rest. He's stationed in Karratha.'

'A friend who's a policeman? Are you sure?'

'We went to school together, and we remained friends ever since. It's kind of a long story, but you see—well I guess I've been keeping a secret from you too.'

'Really?' Curiosity hovered in her steady gaze. But there was something else there as well. Was it awareness?

'Yes. The reason I know we can trust him is that he helped to get me out of jail.'

'Oh.' The sound was small, insignificant, but it put Dan on edge. She reached up and touched the ring hidden beneath her shirt in a movement he was starting to recognize meant she was either unsure or embarrassed. She was hesitating. 'Umm … Actually, I already know. I overheard Lex and Cookie talking about you one night.' She cast him a crooked smile. 'But you're not guilty, right?' This time it was her turn to squeeze his hand. He was lost for words. She already knew. 'Please don't hate me for not letting on.'

'You're okay with me being a crim?' He couldn't hide his scepticism.

'If Lex says you're not guilty, then that's all the proof I need. And besides, that's not who you are, Dan. You're a good man. One I'd trust with my life.'

* * *

Jenna stared at Dan as they sat together in the grass. There seemed to be one rather large point he was overlooking.

'How are we going to capture Liam? He's not going to walk like an innocent lamb into our trap. And what about Brad? Even though we have Brad's gun, if Liam's gone back for him, it means there's two of them now.'

She leaned away from him. Liam could have more weapons stashed away somewhere, she wouldn't put it past him. Or even more of his thugs skulking around in the background, just waiting for his call. This was madness. What was he thinking? She wasn't ready to face Liam again, or his thugs. Perhaps running and hiding was the coward's way out, but it'd worked to keep her alive so far.

As if reading her body language, Dan stood up, pulling her along with him. 'The difference is, this time you won't be doing it alone.' Dan started pacing backwards and forwards through the long grass.

'What do you mean?'

'You have good friends, people who love you. Use their help. Don't you know others don't like to see you hurting?' She couldn't hide her gasp of disbelief. 'I know you believe you're shutting people out for their own good, Jenna, but it's too late this time.'

Backing away from him, she shook her head. He couldn't possibly know what he was asking. He grabbed her by the shoulders and pulled her into a tight embrace.

'Mob and Lynne are already involved, whether you like it or not. We all are, Jenna.'

'People have been hurt because of me.' Her voice small inside the warmth of his clasp. 'Lynne has been drugged and kidnapped and you're lucky to be alive. What if that knife had struck your heart like Liam intended?' Just the thought of todays near catastrophe brought back memories of her father's death mask; hanging in the tree, broken and lifeless. Panic threatened to take over. 'My father died because of me.'

'I'm so sorry about your father, Jenna. But I'm okay, and so is Lynne. I made the decision to come after you and I wouldn't have it any other way.' He gave her a little shake to make sure she understood the passion within his words. 'I'll make sure everyone else is aware of the risks and if they don't want to be mixed up in this then they don't have to be. Everyone is free to make their own decisions. And that's the way it should be, Jenna.' It was hard not to believe his words when she stood sheltered in his arms like this. He grabbed her wrist and turned it over so they could both see the words tattooed there. 'Isn't it time you fulfilled this wish? Be brave, Jenna, and let us help you.'

All her efforts to keep herself emotionally distant from Dan had failed. He'd scaled that wall and brought it tumbling down. But with that final act he'd also exposed all her weaknesses. Weaknesses that could be used to Liam's advantage. She could hear Dan's logic, but she was fighting against years of independence, which shouted loudly for her to reject him and just run. Run far and run fast.

Unsure and frustrated, a heavy weight settled inside her chest, making every thought a battle. She gritted her teeth and clenched her fists into balls as wave after wave of dark uncertainty threatened to overwhelm her.

'Stop protecting yourself and let other people in, Jenna.' His voice was quiet as he pulled her in towards him, his strong body resting against hers, his lips in her hair. Standing there, in his safe, enveloping grasp, the tension and resentment began to drain away. The instinct to run became less and the weight encircling her upper body like a vice relaxed slowly.

He kissed her forehead. 'I love you, Jenna.'

She reached up and tugged on her necklace, still unsure.

'Is that something special,' Dan asked. It took her a few seconds to realize he meant the ring.

'Yes, it's the only thing I have left of my mother's.' She pulled it out from inside her shirt to show to him.

'It's beautiful,' he said. His next words took her by surprise. 'What do you think she'd want you to do?'

'Oh … I don't know. I never really thought about it before.'

What would her mother make of her life over the past few years? She didn't know her mother, not really. She'd left when Jenna was only a year old. But she was pretty sure her mother would hate the idea of Jenna running and hiding from a sick bastard like Liam. Of following in her own footsteps. Her mother had the strength and the courage to defy Alexander by escaping from his clutches. Maybe that'd been her ultimate act of love. She'd done all she could to make sure Jenna was safe. Even if leaving her behind had felt like a betrayal to Jenna, in some twisted way it was her mother's way of saving her life. Perhaps it was now Jenna's turn to do the same. Stand up to him. Did it make her weak to let someone stand by her side when she faced her demons? She knew she could trust these people, and they truly cherished her for what she was. It was as if a ray of sunshine lanced through to her very soul, shattering the barricade of darkness inside her into a thousand pieces, leaving her feeling dazed but vital and … alive.

It was time.

'Okay, what's the plan?' she asked, her gaze still fixed on the words inked into her wrist.

* * *

The dust was still clearing after the Land Cruiser slammed to a stop as Mob strode across the desert towards Jenna and pulled her into a bear hug. Then Mob called out to Dan, 'Bloody hell, it's great to see you both.' He released Jenna and slapped Dan on the back making him wince in pain. Either he'd forgotten about Dan's wound, or was proving a point. Dan didn't really care, all that mattered was he was here. The plan was coming together. 'I was more than a tad worried after I left you in the cave with that lunatic,' Mob continued.

'I'll second that,' growled Lex, whose rolling swagger brought him into their campsite right behind Mob. Moon glided in from the semi-darkness behind him, his gleaming white smile telling them without words how pleased he was to see them.

'You don't know the half of it,' mumbled Dan.

A flying bolt of black and tan fur exploded out of the bush and landed at Dan's feet, nearly knocking him over in surprise.

'Blue, what're you doing here?' He knelt down and tried to contain the squirming ball of happiness.

'He wouldn't leave me alone.' Mob had the decency to look a little sheepish. 'It was almost as if he knew you were out here and he wasn't letting me out of his sight until I brought him along. I think if I hadn't let him into the car he might've damn well tried to bite me, or else he would've just hung on to the side bar with his teeth all the way over here.'

Dan laughed. It was the first time he'd laughed all day. It relieved some of the tightness in his shoulders.

'I know one thing for sure, he would never have bitten you. But the hanging off a moving car is a distinct possibility,' said Dan. Blue trotted over to greet Jenna, and she knelt down to receive his warm licks.

'It's okay, I'm glad he's here, Mob. Don't beat yourself up over it.'

'I wasn't,' Mark replied with one of his wisecrack grins.

Tipping Jenna's hat off her head as he strolled past, Mob asked, 'So, what have you two been up to out here while you were waiting for the cavalry to arrive?'

She gave Dan a helpless look, a red flush rising up her neck. He gave her a cheeky wink in return. Mob's question was harmless enough, after all he couldn't have known what they had gotten up to.

'Hiding from a lunatic. What did you think?' Dan said, rescuing Jenna from her flustered surprise.

'Hmmm.' There was a note of suspicion in Mob's voice as he watched their exchange and Jenna turned away to retrieve her tumbled hat. 'Maybe you can fill us in on the rest of the details later then, huh?'

'What about Coshy?' Dan decided a change of subject was in order. Jenna told them of her suspicions where it came to Coshy. That he was actually working with Liam.

'Yeah, I told him in no uncertain terms he wasn't wanted on this mission. I also told him he should clear out before we get back, or I was going to have a chat to Bernie about him.'

Dan grunted in reply. It was better than Coshy deserved. But they didn't have any proof he'd done the things Jenna was accusing him of, so the best idea was to send him away.

'Any word on that Brad character?' he asked. The helicopter pilot, Jacko, had agreed to fly back to the landing spot in the shale hills and check on Brad for them. To make sure he was still tied up tight and guard him until more help could arrive and they could pack him off to the police station. It wasn't the best of plans to send the pilot up there on his own, but he was the only one who could be spared, and he was more than keen to do the job. A bit of excitement to freshen up the stories he'd tell at the pub on the weekend.

'Ah, yeah. Jacko just called in half an hour ago. Brad's gone.'

'Shit.'

'Not the best news,' Mob agreed. 'The ropes were cut, so I think we can safely say he didn't get free on his own.'

'And no sign of either of them?' Dan asked through clenched teeth.

'Nah, I told Jacko to get out of there as fast as he could.'

'Good idea.' Dan was only half-listening. Now it meant there were two psychos out there. Who knew, they might both be hotfooting it out of here and they were all now embarking on some fruitless goose-chase. There'd been no sign of any vehicles parked nearby, but they couldn't walk all the way out of the desert. Had they hidden a car somewhere? Or was there a driver or an accomplice helping them?

Even though Dan believed they were probably both long-gone by now, Jenna was adamant Liam wouldn't be that easily cowed. Especially if he thought he'd been made to look a fool. He'd been so close to his quarry—her—that he wouldn't leave without a fight now. Which made his plan all that much easier to follow. Once the team was all present and ready, Jenna was going to send the word out. Send a few of her *scouts* to track the men. Jenna assured him it wouldn't take very long once she sent out the call. Dan shook his head. He was actually relying on animals, a herd of brumbies, to bring him back details of where two men were hiding. Their whole plan hinged on that information. It should be completely unbelievable. And yet, he'd hardly even needed any persuasion. The world was a strange and wonderous place sometimes.

'What about everyone else? Did they believe your story?' Dan asked, wondering if all the rescuers had been convinced by their cobbled-together story.

'I think so,' Mob mused. 'They were all very relieved to hear Lynne was safe, and they were happy to head off home with a good outcome, so no one questioned me about the details.' Mob's face hardened as he seemed to remember calling off the search. Mob agreed that if the police weren't to be involved, and if their plan to capture Liam was to work, then Lynne would need to say she'd just wandered away from the bore and got lost. Keep the abduction and drugging to herself. It was risky, but only they and Jacko knew the truth. And Jacko swore he wouldn't tell anyone. Dan hoped he'd keep his word.

'What about Bernie, how's he taking all this?'

'Pretty much as you'd imagine,' Mob replied. 'Not happy at all. Stomping around roaring at people. He thinks we've just come out here to collect you guys and bring you home. Doesn't suspect anything else is going on. He wasn't happy that a new jillaroo just wandered off. We're going to have to come up with a better story if Lynne is to keep her job. I think she's safe for tonight, though. He'll be drowning his sorrows in a bottle of rum by now.'

Dan grimaced at the thought of how drunk Bernie would get tonight. Not a pretty sight, but at least it'd keep him out of their hair for a while. 'We'll sort something out,' he said to Mob.

'Yeah, well, if she goes, I go.'

Dan looked at Mob in surprise. What did he mean by that?

'How's Lynne? Is she all right?' Jenna interrupted their conversation.

Dan glanced over at her and saw the questions in her eyes. Mob might not pick it up, but Dan knew how much his answer meant to her. In their quick exchange over the two-way, Lynne had accepted Jenna's apology in a heartbeat and told her not to worry about it again. But if he knew Jenna half as well as he thought he did, guilt would still be lurking at the back of her mind. She hated to be indebted to anyone.

'Yeah, yeah, that delusional friend of yours was right when he said he hadn't hurt her. She's still a little disorientated from whatever drug he used on her. She wanted desperately to come with us and she was bloody mad when I told her she couldn't.' As he said this, his hand unconsciously rubbed at his chin. 'She actually got a little violent.'

'What did she do to you?' Knowing Lynne, Dan had his suspicions.

'She punched me in the mouth.' His voice carried the echo of a bruised ego. 'But she didn't really hurt me.' Mob waved his hand glibly. 'Anyway, she realized I was right in the end.'

'But are you sure she's okay, Mob? I don't mean just physically, but … you know … mentally?'

'Who're you kidding, Rowdy?' Mob snorted in disgust. 'It'd take a hell of a lot more to keep our girl Lynne down. She's still the bouncy, bright, bubbly and oh-so-annoying person she's always been. I didn't call her Sunshine for nothing, so don't you worry about her.' He came over and gave Jenna another quick reassuring hug and for once Dan was thankful for his consideration.

The low drone of an engine reached their ears and Mob went to stand on top of a nearby tree stump to peer into the deepening twilight. Dan glanced over to the other side of the small clearing, where Lex and Moon were busy unpacking the equipment for the night's escapade. They were barely visible, screened behind some thick scrub and they'd not heard the approaching car.

'It's Pat and Ulrich,' Mob called over his shoulder.

Dan went over to Jenna, his arm grazing hers. He'd contacted the two men on the radio shortly after Mob agreed to their plan, and they'd been only too happy to join in the undertaking. *A bit of fun*, Pat had called it.

'They're still a way off, I'll see if I can intercept them and show them the way.' Mob walked off into the desert, towards the sound of the car.

'Dune, will you please go with him and make sure he doesn't get lost.' Jenna voiced her request out loud, and Dan suspected it was probably for his benefit, because by now he knew her communication with the animals was usually silent.

As soon as Mob disappeared, Dan furled her into his embrace, and they stood together in silence for long seconds. Everything looked as if it'd been painted with the dark grey smudging paintbrush of twilight, and he tilted his head to gaze at the emerging luminary stars. He wanted to capture this one perfect moment. Out here under the stars, with this woman he was so in love with. Wanted to be with her forever.

'Jenna, when we get out of here, I want you to know I intend to marry you.' The words came as just a whisper. But it was the complete truth. It may be the wrong time and the wrong place, but he was deadly serious about her.

She disentangled herself and peered up into his face. The look in her narrowed eyes said she thought he was joking. 'Is that so, Dan Simmonds?' she said with a sardonic grin.

How did he make her believe him? He dropped to one knee, taking her hand in his.

'I've thought about this a lot over the last couple of days, Jenna. Will you marry me?'

The grin fled from her face. Replaced by disbelief, then amazement and then a sense of purpose.

'You sure know how to pick your times. But if we get out of this, then yes, I will marry you.'

Dragging him back off his knees by his good arm, she couldn't hide the grin that cracked her face from ear to ear. Running her hands inside his unbuttoned shirt she wrapped her arms around his waist and pulled him in for a lengthy, delicious, unbelieving kiss. She was sweet and hot and he loved her like nothing else on this planet.

He couldn't quite believe it himself. In all his imaginings he never would've thought he'd ever propose out of the blue, in the middle of the desert with a madman on the run hunting them down. It was perfect.

He crushed her to him, never wanting to let her go. If he needed any more determination to make sure they both survived through this night, then this was it.

Something tickled at the back of his mind. His proposal wasn't perfect after all. He'd forgotten something. A ring.

'I've just thought of something.' She gazed up at him, cheeks still pink with delight.

'Wait here till Mob and Pat and Ulrich get back. There's something I need to do.' His fingers slipped from hers and he disappeared into the dusk, his trusty dog following close at his heels.

'Can I come with you?' Her voice drifted to him in the dimness.

'Not this time. I won't be long, stay close to Lex and Moon. I'll be back soon.' Five minutes, that's all he needed. To find something, anything that'd serve as a ring. To make their promise to each other complete.

* * *

Jenna touched her lips with her fingertip. Had it been real? Had he really proposed to her? And had she just said yes? The look on his face had been as vulnerable as she'd ever seen it, his whole-body trembling slightly, telling her like no words could how much it meant to him. She'd never dared dream before that anyone would put their unprotected heart out there for her to take as her own.

Her answer had burst from her lips. Her heart knew what she wanted, even if her head told her to slow down, think about things. But now she'd said yes, she would never renege on her promise.

A twig snapped behind her and she turned with a smile, anticipating Dan's return. A hand reached out of the dark and covered her mouth and nose with a wad of cloth, and another grabbed her around the waist. Opening her mouth to give a muffled scream, she breathed in sweet chemical fumes and knew nothing more.

CHAPTER EIGHTEEN

Something sharp stuck into her left side. It was bothersome enough to drag Jenna's consciousness away from her dream. She didn't want to leave her dream; it was a satisfyingly joyful vision that involved lots of kissing Dan beneath the desert sun.

There it was again, that infuriating jab in her ribs. Disappointment and frustration replaced the wonderful images of her and Dan, pulling her up towards awareness. Swift reality came. The earth was cold and dusty beneath her body.

She understood now, the source of the pain was a piece of stone wedged beneath her body. She was lying on the hard, unforgiving ground.

She tried to roll away from the stone and found her arms tied together in front. Moving her legs to sit up, she found they were also bound cruelly together.

Her eyes sprang open but everything around was dark and blurry. The sound of low voices drifted to her through the night air and she froze, listening.

One of the voices belonged to Liam.

And the other ... belonged to Coshy. She'd recognize that snake-like voice anywhere.

Realization hit her like a ton of bricks, and it helped to clear the last vestiges of drug-induced haze from her brain. He'd abducted her. Snatched her from the safety of their camp right under everyone's noses. In those few seconds of awareness before the drug had overwhelmed her, she knew it was Coshy who captured her. Coshy the deceiver! How could he have been so bold? They'd sorely misjudged him. He'd been true to his word after all. He was getting rid of her alright.

The bindings on her arms and legs were tight. Coshy spared her no compassion. Her limbs were already becoming numb and useless. She'd need to get the circulation going again, or her legs would be ineffectual if she managed to escape.

Instinctively, she opened her mind to sense any animals who might be close by. But instead of many warm, ephemeral minds, she met only a blank wall. She recoiled in shock. This had never happened. There was just desolate silence. She was on her own, as she'd never truly been alone before. Was this another of Liam's tricks?

She rolled onto her side towards the voices, taking in her surroundings as best she could. She was lying on rock-strewn ground, a great, dark boulder blotted out most of the night sky. Moonlight from a three-quarter moon shone down, its crisp light acting as a natural spotlight to underscore everything in hues of black and white. In front of her the ground sloped away in a large cleared space. At the furthest edge of the clearing she could make out the shadowy forms of Liam and Coshy, deep in discussion.

'I'm surprised you managed to get her. You did better than I expected.' Liam's tone reminded her of someone praising a well-trained pet.

'Cut the crap will ya and hand it over. I want to be well out of here as soon as I can.' Coshy's untidy hair bobbed as he peered into the desert. 'Come on, ya bastard. I did what ya wanted me to do, now give me what you promised, so I can get the fuck outta this place.' Coshy's voice rose to almost a shout.

'Settle down.' Any hint of praise had left Liam's tone now, replaced by distaste. 'Here, take it.' He beckoned Coshy forwards and held his hand up. 'You can't tell anyone where you got this. No one at all. Do you understand?'

'Yeah, yeah.' Coshy waved dismissively, eyes fixed on Liam's hand, not really listening, as something small and silver dropped into his palm.

'No!' Jenna's cry came unbidden. Coshy was holding her pink sapphire ring, she just knew it. She tried to see if it still hung around her neck. There was something there, but now she realized it wasn't her light chain, it was heavy and rough.

They both turned in surprise at her anguished shout. A greasy grin spread over Coshy's face and he walked towards her, clutching the ring in his palm.

'Serves you right, you little bitch,' he gloated. 'I warned you this would happen.' Holding the ring out in front of his face, so she could get a good look at it, he gave a menacing snigger. 'All I can say is, I hope you two have a great life together. You deserve each other. I don't know what Shauna's gonna make of it all, though,' he chuckled, making a great show of placing the ring in his shirt pocket, patting the rounded hump it made on his chest in satisfaction.

'No! You can't have it.' Her cry was more of a sob. She lay like a trussed chicken, powerless to do anything to stop him. She tried in vain once again to make contact with an animal, someone, anyone to come to her aid, but the invisible shield was still there, solid and immovable.

Hang on, had Coshy just mentioned Shauna? Surely, she'd imagined it. Shauna was long gone. Wasn't she?

'Yeah, whatever,' said Liam from behind him. Coshy turned to face her nemesis.

'You paid me, that's all I care about. Pity our other little plans didn't work, but you got her in the end,' Coshy boasted. He came back to leer at her again. 'When the stallion went missing. That was me. Did ya know that?' He gave her a maniacal grin. 'I was gonna grab you in all the confusion. But bloody meddling Lex wouldn't leave me alone, said we had to stay together or some such bullshit. Then I didn't know where'd you gone.'

Jenna's heart stuttered in her chest. 'You were the one who slashed our tyres up at the Bungles, weren't you?'

'Yep,' he crowed. 'See, you ain't as stupid as I thought.'

'Yes, Coshy and I have been mates for some time now,' Liam said, interrupting their conversation. 'Pity those old biddies interfered before he could let down all the tyres. We were gonna grab you that night, while you waited for the punctures to be fixed. But c'est la vie, we got you in the end. He helped me with Lynne as well, but you obviously figured that one out.' Liam indicated with a jutted chin towards a black lump on the edge of the clearing. 'It's time you left, Coshy.'

'Righto, don't get your knickers in a knot.' Coshy headed towards the dark lump, which morphed into his motorbike. 'I'm outta here.' He jumped onto his bike and gave a few quick downward thrusts with his foot to kick-start it. The machine sputtered a few times, but the engine didn't fire and Coshy swore.

'Oh dear, won't it start?' The emotionless edge to Liam's voice sent shivers up her spine. What was he up to? He walked towards Coshy, his eyes spearing into him, a hunter fixated on its prey. His movements were a little stiff and he cradled his left arm against his body. Was it because she'd stabbed him in the back? It obviously hadn't slowed him down enough.

Liam was now close enough to touch Coshy, and he reached out and grabbed him by the neck. Coshy made a strange, inhuman sound. The bike fell, forgotten onto its side in the tussocks. Before he could react, Liam held a wicked-looking knife to his throat.

'You stupid dickhead. Did you really think I was going to let you get away with that precious ring?' Even though Jenna had every reason to wish Coshy harm, she found herself willing him to move, to break free.

'You don't get that ring. It belongs to my father and he wants it back.'

In the moonlight she could see every muscle tensed. The veins on Coshy's neck stood out and his eyes were large and bulbous.

'Run! Run away!' Jenna's shout came out as a primal instinct, even though she knew she couldn't help him. She tried to struggle against her bonds, but they only seemed to tighten around her wrists when she moved. She couldn't just lie there and watch this nightmare unfold before her. Terrible memories of the night her father died flooded back. It was happening all over again. And again, she was powerless to stop it.

Liam made a sudden slicing motion.

Coshy's strangled screech became a liquid gurgling sound and then there was a loud thud. Coshy hit the ground. When Liam crouched down over the prostrate form she closed her eyes and screamed. Again and again she screamed. The same hysterical sound she'd made when Liam had killed her father. She screamed for someone to come and help her. She screamed all her rage and terror at what Liam had just done. At the loss of another human life. And she screamed because she knew she wanted to do the same to Liam. She wanted to kill him.

'Stop that fucking awful noise.' A heavy boot landed in her side as Liam kicked her and all the air left her body.

'You fucking murderer.' she managed to pant out through winded gasps. 'How many people have you killed, Liam? You sad, pathetic excuse for a man.' She wanted to spit in his face, claw at his eyes. How dare he make her witness yet another death. Bile rose in her throat.

He knelt down and held something up in front of Jenna's face, so close it took her a few seconds to focus properly. It was a switchblade knife, still dripping with Coshy's cherry-red blood. 'I prefer knives. They're so much more personal. Don't you think?' Her head whipped back in revulsion. Liam must have a whole stash of the lethal things. This one was even bigger and more barbaric looking than the one he'd left embedded in Dan's shoulder.

'And to answer your question, only one person's death will make me truly happy.' His eyes glittered hard and cold in the moonlight and she couldn't help but shrink back from the open hatred in his gaze. Hatred for her.

'But regretfully, it's Alexander's call. Oh, and now I've got your precious ring back, too. I'm surprised you mother left it for you. Did you know Alexander gave it to her? As a wedding present.'

She held her breath at the mention of her mother.

'This ring was part of your downfall. It's how I first found you. When your step-father had it valued in town he didn't realize. But I have my little spies everywhere, don't you know?' he twittered, sounding like a deranged school-girl. 'Alexander will be most pleased to get it back. He paid a lot of money for this ring, to give to your mother as a present. It's special. One of a kind. A token of his appreciation. And what kind of thanks did he get? She stole it from him. Just like she stole you from him. Bitch.'

Her head was ringing with all this information. 'What're you going to do with me now, Liam?'

'Ahh, my little sister, always the inquisitive one. You'll find out soon enough.'

'Stop calling me that,' she said between gritted teeth.

'What? Little sister?' He came back to tower over her prone body. 'Does it hurt to know who you are at last? Do you think perhaps that you're the white side of the coin and I am the black? Well it ain't that simple, Jenna.'

'It's not true. We can't be brother and sister.' Her denial sounded weak, even in her own ears.

'And yet we are. I remember very clearly the day your mother came to our house. I was only eight years old, but I remember how her long, black hair tumbled down her back. And the dimple in her cheek when she smiled. I'll never forget the look in our father's eyes whenever he saw her. Completely lovesick. It was disgusting. Serves him right for being such a sucker for a beautiful woman.'

'What happened to her?' The question left her lips before she could stop it. She hated that she was asking him these questions, but he was the only one who might be able to answer them. And she'd waited so long for the answers.

'You should've asked your pathetic adoptive father.' He scowled down at her. 'But then maybe it's to my advantage you're so under-prepared.' His scowl turned to a self-satisfied grin. 'Let's just say your mother had a change of heart when you were born. She didn't agree with our father's ... ah, shall we say, tough love. And at the first chance, she bolted, taking you with her.'

It was like a sword to the heart to finally hear something about her mother's life, even if the story was biased and lacking in details. But if her mother defied Liam and

Alexander, she must've done so for a good reason. It was as she'd guessed.

'Father changed after she left with you. Became more circumspect, turned inwards, but also became infinitely more dangerous.' There was a desperate edge to Liam's voice when he talked about his father. 'He never forgot about her. And as soon as I showed I was capable, he ordered me to find her. To find you. I haven't had any luck tracking her down. Yet. But I did find you.' Liam smoothed the edges of his black jacket, lost in thought. 'I was only blackmailing your father to make a bit of money on the side, biding my time really. I was always going to turn you over to Alexander in the end.' Why did she doubt the sincerity behind that sentiment? 'Who knows, maybe when I bring you in he'll be so grateful to have his wayward daughter back, he might finally appreciate me. I can't wait to see the look on his face when I surprise him.'

Shit, Liam was like a deranged puppy, desperate to please a father, who sounded for all intents and purposes, like a true psychopath. She'd heard enough to know she was dealing with a lunatic. A very dangerous lunatic.

Dragging in a ragged lungful of air she tried to compose herself. Where were the rest of her team and did they even know she was missing yet? She had no idea how long she'd been unconscious. Again, she battered at the mental shield, needing to get a message out to any animal that might be near.

Almost as if he knew what she was up to, Liam looked at her askance. 'Don't think you can break that screen either. It's impenetrable, so there's no use calling out to your furry friends. There'll be no pack of dogs to save you tonight.' He stroked his beard, perhaps remembering how she'd gotten away from him the first time. It seemed he came prepared this time.

Liam came over and knelt down next to her. She flinched backwards when he brought his knife up towards her, but she didn't feel the slice of metal through flesh as she'd expected. Instead he lifted something around her neck. A heavy leather cord. When she looked down, there was a dark grey blob of rock attached to the end.

'This was a present from Alexander. He told me if I ever caught up with you, it'd come in very useful. You see, that's one of the reasons he was so distraught at losing you. He knows about your … little talent. He wants to explore it if he gets the chance.'

Suddenly there was a loud crashing and a figure appeared from behind the large boulder. Brad. He carried what looked to be a sawn-off shotgun in front of his bulging belly. Even in the surreal glow of the moonlight she could trace the deep scratches running down the side of his face. Scratches she'd inflicted. She hoped they burned like fire. And she also hoped his head throbbed from where Dan hit him with the rock. Bastard.

'I can't see no sign of them yet, but we need to get out of here. It won't take 'em long to figure out where we are.' Brad shot her a look of cold animosity as he spoke to Liam.

'Yeah, yeah. Jude and Toady will be here with the other truck any minute now. You go and clean up that mess over there.' Liam pointed to the spot where Coshy's body was hidden by the tussocks. 'I'll get rid of his bike.'

Liam just mentioned two more men. Where had Liam conscripted them from? That'd make four men against the Shiralee seven. The numbers were still in their favour. But what if they were all armed like Brad, with guns? They hadn't factored lots of heavily armed felons into their plan. She had to warn them somehow.

'Righto, boss.' There was no flicker of emotion on Brad's face to show he was troubled by having to clean up a dead body. Probably done it numerous times before. The utter slime-ball. She hated Brad almost as much as she hated Liam.

'Liam, where are you?' A female voice carried over the dark desert sand.

'Over here.' Liam sounded irritated. 'What do ya want?'

'I've been sitting in that damn car almost all day long. How much longer is this going to take?'

Jenna's skin tingled all over. She recognized the woman's voice. And then a shape materialised out of the gloom and Jenna was one-hundred percent sure.

It was Shauna. What the bloody hell was she doing here?

As if Liam could feel her staring, he turned around and a feral grin lit up his face. 'Oh, by the way, Jenna, I've brought a friend with me. You might remember her. She certainly remembers you. She's been very … helpful. I might not have found you so easily without her. She really hates your guts, do you know that? She was telling the whole pub down in Kalgoorlie how much she hated you. How you'd cost her a job. It wasn't hard to put two and two together. I knew you were in Western Australia somewhere. It must've been fate I was in that pub at just the right time. Don't ya reckon?'

Jenna didn't know what to think. Anger warred with shock at the woman's duplicity.

'She helped introduce me to Coshy. Now there's a man with a huge chip on his shoulder. He was most keen to join my little band of merry men and '*fuck the lot of you up*', as he put it so succinctly.' Not only had Coshy betrayed her, but so had Shauna, leading Liam right to her front door.

'Hi, Jenna.' Ridicule dripped from Shauna's words. 'Bet you didn't think you were going to see me again.'

'What … Why?' The possibilities all tumbled around in Jenna's head and she couldn't formulate just one coherent question.

'Go get back in the car, Shauna. We ain't finished here yet,' Liam interrupted.

'Oh, but, babe, I'm so hungry. I just wanna get out of here,' Shauna whined.

Jenna had forgotten just how annoying the woman's voice was until right at this second. She'd called him babe. Did that mean … Oh God, where they sleeping together? The prospect was terrifying.

'Yeah, well, you wanted revenge on Jenna and all her cronies, and now you're gonna get it,' said Liam, his voice getting slowly louder.

'Can't we just load her into the car and get going?'

'No, we can't, you stupid woman. We're waiting for Jude and Toady to get here with the ute. Now get outta my face and get back in the fucking car.' Liam was shouting now, his face screwed into a mask of fury.

Shauna pouted, but didn't say any more. Liam started to walk towards Coshy's bike, Shauna following slowly in his wake. When he got to the bike, he picked it up and Shauna said, 'Where did that come from?' Liam ignored her, but Shauna peered around his bulk to get a better look at the bike. 'It looks like the one Coshy used to ride.' Then Shauna's head snapped up and she stared over to where Brad was walking backwards, dragging something heavy through the shrubs. 'Oh shit, Liam, did you kill Coshy?'

'Yep, and if you don't wanna be next then get your fucking arse back in the car,' Liam snarled.

'Oh no. Oh fuck. But Coshy helped you. I talked him into helping you. And you just—' She doubled over and was sick into a nearby saltbush.

Jenna felt a stab of satisfaction. Served Shauna right. She probably had no idea how violent and ruthless Liam was. Well, she was about to find out. The hard way. Jenna almost felt sorry for her. Almost.

Shauna cast one slightly pitiful glance back at Jenna before she made her slow way back to the car.

The two men continued with their gruesome tasks, leaving her lying on the ground, alone. Plans for escape raced through her head. She tried to wriggle away on her back, but it was a futile effort. Her hands and feet were bound so tight she'd lost all the feeling in her extremities.

The night was already starting to get icy. The cool air nipped at her bare arms. The cold would slow her circulation down even more, making her next to useless if she didn't do something soon. She cast around for something that might help her cut the ropes, a sharp rock or stick perhaps.

The unmistakable drone of a diesel engine drifted from around the side of the huge boulder. Shit, Jude and Toady were here already.

Liam's stocky form re-appeared at the sound of slamming car doors. 'Jude. You guys bloody well took your time.'

'Sorry, boss, all these bloody sand dunes look the same out here.' Jenna swivelled her head just in time to see a man's bald head bobbing in the moonlight as he ran into the clearing. Following hot on his heels was another man, stooped in a submissive posture. Probably Toady. Both men were carrying guns. She could see the shapes, hard and metallic in their hands. It was as she feared, Liam's gang each carried a gun.

Then another tall form materialised from between the dark tussocks, breathing hard, as if he too had just sprinted from the car. There must've been a third man in the truck with Jude and Toady. She couldn't make out his features in the dim light, but he did seem familiar somehow. Could he be the other thug who helped Liam that night they'd come to her farmhouse? She'd never found out his name, but she remembered he was tall and well-built, like this man, with short cropped hair and a massive square jaw. He was carrying what looked to be some kind of machete.

Jenna groaned. Now there were five of them and they were all carrying weapons. The Shiralee team would be no match for five hardened criminals. Six really, if you counted Shauna sitting in the other car somewhere out of sight. Jenna didn't think Shauna would be too much of an issue though.

'Get the girl in the back of the truck, I'll be with you in a minute.'

'Boss, there's something else we need to tell—'

'Tell me later,' Liam barked. 'We need to get out of here before that snivelling bunch of cowboys show up.'

'Well that's just it, boss. They're on their way, we saw them coming over that other dune over there.' He pointed to the horizon on the left. 'Just as we was getting out of the car. There's six of 'em and they're all on horses, that's why we didn't hear them coming.'

'Fuck!' Liam stopped in his tracks. 'If you bloody imbeciles had been here when you should've, we'd be outta here by now.' As he spoke he threw an angry punch at Jude's face, but Jude ducked just in time and stepped away from the smaller man.

'We did the best we could.' There was a dangerous edge to Jude's tone.

'We'll just have to get rid of the bastards then. Everyone spread out, find a place to hide. You know what to do. Don't start shooting until all them cowboys are visible. We don't want any of them getting away so they can tattle to the cops. We gotta kill them all.' The other men moved a little way off into the desert to hunker down behind a tussock or pile of boulders.

'What about her?' Jude pointed towards Jenna with the butt of his rifle.

'Leave her there, we don't have time to move her. She can be the bait.' Liam drew out his large switchblade and flicked it open. 'Remember, let 'em get real close before you open fire. Make sure they're all dead.' Then he melted around the back of the large boulder at the top of the clearing. The area was now silent and still. No one would ever guess there were five men hidden, waiting. There was no way the Shiralee team would be able to tell they were heading into a deadly ambush.

Jenna sent desperate images out, still hoping to somehow break through Liam's talisman shield. 'Go back. Don't come here!' She sent pictures of darkness and death to warn the horses, to try and force them to turn back.

But it was too late. Two lean four-legged forms leaped over the outlying tussocks that marked the edge of the clearing and raced towards her. The sound of thudding hooves followed.

Dan's tall figure was running hard, right behind the dogs.

Mob came from behind and vaulted from the back of a brumby mare half-way into the clearing, landing with a thump, raising swirling puffs of dust. He crouched, wary and watching, indicating that Dan keep coming.

'Dan, don't!' Jenna shouted. 'There's too many of them. They all have guns.' Both men ignored her.

'You untie her, I'll cover you while you get her away,' Mob called to Dan over his shoulder as he darted forwards. He was carrying a rifle, held high on his shoulder and knelt in the tussocks, aiming it at the large boulder at the back of the clearing. The one Liam was hiding behind. Where'd he get a gun? She felt sick. Where was everyone else? They had to get out of here. Now.

* * *

'Thank God you're all right, Jenna!' Adrenaline coursed through his body, the feeling euphoric. He scanned the surroundings in the dim light, searching for movement, or any other give-away. They were here somewhere, waiting for them. He needed to be quick.

'You shouldn't have come. They've all got guns, Dan. Get out of here. Please.'

He ignored her despairing pleas, his fingers working on the tight knots. With a frustrated grunt he pushed Dune out of the way, as the overjoyed dog tried to get as close as possible to Jenna. Blue hung in close proximity as well but did a better job of staying out of his way.

'Okay, you're free. Can get you up?' He lent her a hand as she struggled to stand, but she fell back into the dust with a crash before he could catch her. *Shit*. Her legs must be numb from the tight ropes. Bending down, he gathered her up in his arms, ignoring her protests. As he lifted her he felt the stitches in his shoulder pull and he couldn't hide the grunt of pain as agony speared through the wound. Gritting his teeth together, he kept going.

Her arms shook as she clung to his neck, her slight form trembling as she curled in against his chest. She was terrified and it was all his fault. She'd been right. What kind of delusion had he been under to think that any of this half-baked plan might work?

A gunshot ricocheted around the clearing and something zinged past Dan's ear. Fuck, someone was shooting at them. He landed on his knees in the dirt, cradling Jenna beneath him as he hunkered down on the edge of the tussocks. Another shot zipped over his head.

Then Mob's rifle sounded in reply. Once. Twice. The bullets stopped, and Dan took the silence as an excuse to start crawling towards the sheltering grass. Thank God for Pat turning up with a rifle stashed in the back of his car. Two guns might help even the odds a little. If only they knew exactly how many men they were up against.

'Move, Jenna,' he hissed, pushing her into a commando crawl in front of him. Just as they reached the grass, Lex thundered into the clearing astride Chainsaw. His eyes were fixed, staring straight ahead and it made the back of Dan's neck crawl. Lex had the pistol he'd stolen from the guy in the canyon, Brad, pointed at someone behind Dan.

'I wouldn't do that, if I were you.' Lex's voice was clear and intimidating across the sweep of the hill.

Dan chanced a glance over his shoulder and saw Liam had appeared from behind the rock, brandishing a large knife, a crazy grin splitting his features. Jesus, another knife. Dan's shoulder throbbed in memory of Liam's first blade. His gaze continued until he found Mob, his wiry frame strong and tall against the backdrop of moonlight and madness. His rifle was pointed at the silhouette of another man, black against the night sky, slightly to the left of Liam and further back in the desert. That must've been the guy shooting at them, he held a long-nosed rifle loosely in one hand. Dan weighed him up with one quick glance. Bald and muscular, a sinister air of *don't-fuck-with-me* surrounding him. Scary, but Dan had seen worse in jail; had fought worse. He wouldn't be silly enough to make a move while Mob had his rifle trained on him. That made one henchman. How many more? Was Brad here somewhere?

Dan's gaze flitted away from Mob to find the shape of Moon further around the clearing. He remained obscured from Liam and his thug and was working his cautious way around the outskirts of the clearing to come up behind them.

He could hear a further exchange going on between Lex and Liam in the background, but his concentration went to Jenna. She struggled to sit up in the tussocks that spread out at head-height above her. At least they were out of sight, but not out of range if anyone else decided to start shooting.

'There are five of them altogether,' she panted, seeming to struggle with something tied around her neck. 'Three of them have guns. And Shauna is here somewhere. Hiding in their car, I think.'

Shauna? What did she mean Shauna was here? That was impossible, she'd left weeks ago. He dropped the idea of Shauna and tried to weigh all the scenarios up in his head at once. Where were the rest of the men hiding?

'Help me get this off, will you?' She was still tugging at what looked to be some kind of rudimentary necklace.

'Let me,' he said, irritated. Why in hell was she worried about this when they were being shot at? It was a piece of leather, knotted at the back with some kind of rock tied in the middle. He gave an almighty tug and the thing snapped in his hands. Jenna let out and audible sound of relief. 'Thanks. It was blocking my ability. I can hear the animals again.'

Dan glanced backwards to see how the stand-off was going. A third man had materialised in the desert, right in front of Moon, and he was holding what looked to be a machete high in the air, his stance threatening and arrogant, his height lending more menace as he towered over Moon. *Shit. Shit.* At least this one didn't have a gun.

'Come on, Jenna, all Liam really wants is you. Once we get you away the others will have a better chance of getting away too.'

'No, you're wrong, Dan, he'll kill us all. This is a game to him now. He won't stop until we're all dead.'

His overwhelming urge was still to get Jenna to safety. But he could hear the truth in her words. Before he could utter a word, the loud blast of a gunshot made them both swivel around in shock. Another man—it was Brad—was now standing out in the tussocks to their right, aiming at Lex. He was holding a sawn-off shotgun and was reloading quickly.

Thank Christ it was only a single barrel and he was a bad shot. That made four now. Where was the fifth?

Brad ducked behind a smaller boulder as Lex swung his pistol around and fired back.

The big chestnut reared in a mix of defiance and terror. Lex hung on as best he could, but with one hand occupied wielding the pistol, it was obvious he was struggling. Then Brad fired for a second time around the side of the boulder. Chainsaw reared again, but this time Lex—already caught off-balance—tumbled off his back, landing with a sickening thud of finality on the ground. Dan willed him to sit up, but he didn't move. Had he been shot? There was no way of telling.

'Lex.' Jenna's scream of desperation pierced the night.

Without Lex on his back Chainsaw propped sideways and back, but then pranced to a stop, unwilling to leave his rider alone. Lex lay defenceless and unmoving. Shit, now Lex was down, Mob was the only one with a gun. Dan needed to get that pistol.

Mob daren't take his aim off the man with the rifle. But at least rifle guy and Liam were relatively close together, and from where Mob stood, he could keep them both pinned down fairly easily with one gun. Brad gave a snarling grimace and took a step towards the clearing, already re-loading his gun.

Suddenly there was a blood-curdling yell and Dan caught the flash of flowing blonde hair as someone launched himself onto the fat man.

It was Ulrich, lying in wait out of sight, until just the right moment. He landed on Brad's back, flailing wild punches towards the man's face, yanking on his long beard. Unable to sustain the weight of the enraged German, the pair hit the ground, rolling around together. Loud grunts and incoherent shouts sprang from the writhing duo, and the tussocks shook with the force of their fight.

Automatically, Dan went towards them, knowing, although Ulrich would fight with all his heart and soul, he didn't have any experience brawling with a hardened felon twice his weight and as tall as a giant. But he couldn't leave Jenna alone and unprotected. As he hesitated, Ulrich let out a scream of pain, and rolled over in the dirt. He struggled to sit up, clutching an arm to his side. Brad stood up, no longer holding the shotgun—he must have lost it in the struggle—but he went straight for Ulrich, determined to take the advantage.

Mob watched the struggle from the corner of his eyes, but never wavered from pointing his gun towards Liam and the other guy with the rifle. Moon still held the machete-waving thug at bay. At least they had those two covered. That decided it, Dan took several running steps in Ulrich's direction.

Without any warning, Pat appeared on the other side of the bearded henchman. Silent and wraith-like he stalked the man, a long metal pole raised in one hand. Pat would sort Brad out.

Dan's mind whirled. Everything was happening too fast to keep up. Two of his friends had now been injured in the space of only a few seconds and the rest of them were quickly putting themselves in harm's way. At least Mob was still doing his job. He had Liam and the bald guy with the gun at a standstill, neither of them willing to move. How long the stalemate lasted remained to be seen.

A scuffle to his left distracted him and he pivoted on his heel to see Moon attacking the man with the machete, parrying with his makeshift spear and then stepping back to deflect an ill-timed slash. The man might have an advantage of the extra reach his height afforded him, but it looked like he wasn't too skilful when it came to wielding a machete. Moon let out a deep bellow as he struck again.

The gun. He needed to get the gun, to even up the odds. It was still in the tussocks somewhere near Lex.

Liam! If I want to stop them, I have to stop Liam.

It seemed the identical thought had just occurred to Jenna as well, because she was now striding across the clearing towards Liam, Dune padding in her wake. He dropped the idea of the gun and raced to get in front of her. Protect her at all costs.

'Dan, don't. Leave him to me.' She kept her voice low, so only he'd hear. But he didn't stop trying to get in front of her. Blue followed him, a few paces behind.

'Toady, anytime now would be good,' Liam shouted above the sounds of the fighting men.

A fifth man slid from around a large pile of rocks near where Ulrich and Pat were struggling with Brad. He seemed hesitant for some reason, his posture a little stooped. He held a large semi-automatic pistol.

Both Dan and Jenna stopped dead in their tracks.

Unaware, Pat sent a cracking punch into Brad's jaw and he staggered backwards, dropping to the ground like a stone, unmoving. Pat gave a satisfied grunt and turned around to see Dan and Jenna trapped like deer in the headlights. Then he too stood still.

Liam fixed his gaze on Dan, watching him with disdain. His eyes narrowed, and he stood up straighter, his stupid goatee beard bristling like a spiky brush.

'Checkmate,' Liam said with a sadistic glee curling the corners of his mouth. 'Put the gun down, fuckface.' He motioned to Mob.

Mob lowered the rifle.

CHAPTER NINETEEN

Despair and doubt flooded Jenna's mind, robbing her of any strength.

Her friends were falling like leaves around her and she could think of nothing to save them. She'd warned Dan they didn't know enough about Liam's gang and now her dire predictions were coming true.

Mob lowered his rifle and Jude raised his, and was pointing it at Pat and Ulrich, while Toady kept her and Dan squarely in his sights.

Checkmate indeed.

Out of the corner of her eye, Jenna could see Pat had overcome Brad and was now kneeling, exhausted in the dirt next to his unconscious body. He was holding his head, blood seeping through his fingers, but his gaze remained sharp and measured as he fixed it on Liam. She could just make out Lex's boots poking from behind a clump of grass, still immobile and lifeless.

'Marco, stop fucking around with that black bastard and take him over and tie him up with the rest of them.' Moon threw down his spear in disgust and the guy called Marco—chest heaving with exertion—grabbed him by the arm and dragged him around the clearing towards Pat and Ulrich. Marco was breathing hard and walked with a substantial limp and she suspected given a few more minutes, Moon might have indeed overpowered him.

Liam flung a coil of rope towards Marco and watched as he started tying her friends together. Yet she still couldn't move a muscle. The situation before her was just too surreal. Dan and Mob both looked like they were chewing rocks, but neither of them dared move.

Liam's harsh laughter crackled through the black fabric of the night. 'You hick bunch of idiots are no match for me and my men.'

'Let them go, Liam.' It was senseless plea, but she had to say something.

'No, I don't think so. I want to watch your face as they die.' The goatee beard twitched on his face with malevolent mirth. She didn't doubt he'd do what he said. Dune sat hunkered at her feet, where she'd commanded he stay.

Once Marco was finished tying up Pat, Ulrich and Moon, he went over to where Dan and Mob were standing. He pushed Dan forward and laughed loudly as he stumbled and hit the dirt hard. 'Stay down there,' he snarled.

'Don't!' She took a step forward.

'Or what? You going to stop me?' Marco laughed. When she didn't answer he went over and did the same to Mob, then strung the two of them together like tethered pigs. Where was Blue? She was sure he'd been at Dan's feet, protecting him, just a few seconds ago. She could feel him, out in the cover of the tussocks. Good, at least he was safe.

Jude's gun was still trained on Dan, making sure Jenna complied. All of her six companions were now helpless. Jenna stared at Liam. A single tear escaped down her cheek.

'If I even hear one bark, or get one sniff of a dog hair, I'll shoot them all,' warned Liam.

'Liam, what's going on?' It was Shauna, calling out from somewhere in the desert, Jenna presumed near where the car was parked. 'What's all the shooting?'

'None of your fucking business. Get back in the car, or I'll shoot you too,' shouted Liam, never bothering to turn around and look at her. From where she stood, Jenna could just make out Shauna's pale face hovering in the distance. She didn't retreat, however, just stood there staring at the carnage going on around her. Jenna put her out of her mind. They'd get no help from Shauna.

'Put a noose round her neck,' Liam said to Marco.

Jenna started at the sound of his voice. Her legs were like jelly and her breath came in panicked little pants. No. They couldn't do this. They'd put a noose around her father's neck.

Dune growled, deep and low in his throat. She couldn't let him get hurt as well. She told him to back off. To go and find Blue and stay with him. She was surprised when for once, Dune did what she asked, slowly slinking backwards, away from her and Marco towards the safety of the tussocks, sharp teeth bared in the moonlight.

'Try anything and your boyfriend's dead meat,' snarled Marco as he came towards her.

Was she really going to stand meekly by and let him do this? One anguished glance towards Dan gave her answer. Another tear rolled down her cheek. Marco's hands were rough as they tied the thick rope around her neck, leaving her scarcely enough room to breathe. Her hand went instinctively to her throat to grab the rope. Then Marco walked back across the clearing, machete swinging from one hand and placed the other end of the rope into Liam's hands. The rope burned into her neck. Liam pulled her towards him, inch by inch, as if roping an unwilling steer.

'You were never going to win, you know.'

She could feel Liam's rank bitterness, as well as his twisted malicious glee humming through the line. She struggled against the bindings, against the hypnotic lethargy that was overtaking her body. There was a horrible pain in her head, almost as if she could feel Liam's mocking laughter inside her.

'This shouldn't hurt too much, my dear,' he crooned.

Liam had won.

He'd achieved his goal. He was rejoicing in her anguish. She had to fight him. But what else could she do? She heard someone sobbing and realized the sound was coming from her own mouth. She fell down in the dirt, not feeling the pain as her knees hit the rocky ground. Hot tears flooded down her cheeks now, distorting her vision, blotting out the stars. The coarse rope rasped her neck as Liam continued to draw her towards him. Unable to resist she was forced forwards, planting her hands in the red earth. On all fours now, he continued to reel her in, dragging her across the dark, dusty clearing. The sand rasped between her fingers, cold and gritty.

'Look, she really is just a dog.'

Jude gave a rude hoot at Liam's taunt. She closed her eyes. If he was going to kill her then he should just go ahead and do it. Get it over with. Liam stood right before her now, while she knelt in the dust beneath him. Close enough to touch him.

He'd won. There was nothing she could do to stop him. All her fears had come true. The friends who all wanted to help her would end up dead because of her. She'd never, ever recover from the guilt. He may as well kill her now.

Something faint stirred at the back of her mind. Like a small ray of light in the darkest of nights. The light got bigger, began to glow. Then she knew. They were coming. The desert was full of surprises. Liam was about to find out just how full of surprises it could be.

In one fluid moment she stood up and flung a handful of desert sand into Liam's eyes.

'What the—'

She lunged at him, grabbing the hand that held the switchblade knife in both of hers. They fell together into the tussocks. He was stronger than her. But she was fighting for her life. For Dan's life. For her friends' lives.

Gunshots rang out around her, but she focussed on the knife. It twisted between them, as if it had a life of its own. She was holding her breath, straining so hard. Fighting him.

He grunted and then yelled, 'You fucking bitch. I'm blind.'

He rolled over and nearly got on top of her. She arched her back, elbowed him in the face, never letting go of the knife. Kicked out with her legs. The noose still around her neck was hampering her. Then he did get on top of her, slammed his whole weight down to keep her pinned to the ground. The breath left her lungs and she gasped.

Liam went still as a statue, eyes wide and disbelieving. He rolled off her.

Vaguely, she realized the shooting had stopped.

That's when she heard the snarling of dogs. Lots of dogs. Dingos. With Dune and Blue in the lead.

'Jesus Christ!' Jenna jerked her head around to where Jude stood, rooted to the spot. 'What the fuck? Where did all the dogs come from?' He raised his gun, but they surrounded him. He'd never be able to shoot them all before they brought him down.

'What the bloody hell's happening?' Marco's voice echoed from out in the desert. Then he must've spotted the dingos, because his shout turned to a low groan. 'Oh God, not again.' He threw her a panic-stricken glance. Of course, he'd remember from the night her father was killed. The dogs had come then, too. They'd nearly ripped his arm to pieces before he could get away. 'I'm outta here,' he screeched. The racket of Marco crashing his way through the scrub echoed through the night.

'Wait for me,' Toady stammered, lowering his gun and running from the snapping jaws of the dogs.

That left Jude, staring dumbfounded as dingos stalked towards him through the desert, closing in.

'You chicken-shit bastards,' he yelled. He lowered his gun and held his hands up in surrender. 'Tell them I won't shoot if they leave me alone.' The sound of an engine gunning, wheels biting through sand as they spun, came from behind the large boulder. 'Wait for me.' Jude ran through the desert towards the disappearing car. The dogs let him go.

'Liam!' Shauna's strangled cry sounded from out in the dunes.

Jenna refocussed on Liam, lying unmoving on the ground in front of her. His eyes stared unseeing at the sky, one hand sprawled, palm upwards, as if reaching for something. The dragon tattoo snarled at her, as if come to life around his neck. The large switchblade knife protruded out of the centre of his chest. Nausea bubbled up in her throat. What had she done?

Was he dead?

Shauna screamed loudly again, but Jenna couldn't see where she was. The dingos had found her and brought her down. Jenna told them to hold her, but not to harm her.

Dan.

She ran to where he lay on the ground, trussed like a pig on a spit, the noose still dangling from her throat. His face was covered in dirt from when Marco had shoved him. His beautiful, wonderful, gorgeous face.

He looked up at her. 'You did it, babe.'

Great sobs rose in her chest.

* * *

'What a sorry bunch we are!' chortled Mob. 'It looks like we've all just come out of some kind of war zone.'

'And that's exactly how I feel,' grunted Pat, holding a thick wadded bandage to the side of his face.

'Bah, that was nothing.' Mob tried his best to joke the seriousness away. 'At least we're all still alive to tell the tale.' He waved his arms towards the circle of people scattered around the hastily built campfire.

Dawn was breaking, the skyline all pinks and mauves. Jenna's chest expanded, drawing in a large breath of dewy air. She'd never seen a sunrise so rich, with colours so penetrating. It heralded freedom. Life.

Quietly, she felt for the ring beneath her shirt. It was back where it belonged. Jenna had closed her eyes and felt around in Liam's pocket until she found it. There was no way she was losing her mother's ring, even if the idea of searching a dead body to find it filled her with loathing.

'Not that anyone will believe our tale,' Lex's deep voice issued from where he was lying down near the fire, his head propped up on a jacket clutching an ice pack to the back of his skull. 'I'm not sure I even believe it.' Thank God Lex hadn't been shot as she feared, but had hit his head when he fell and was knocked unconscious.

Crouching back down, she took up her position next to Ulrich but didn't dare pass comment. She didn't know what to say to this team of people. Didn't know how to voice her gratitude and deepest thanks to these men who'd risked their lives to help her. Instead, she concentrated on wrapping Ulrich's arm as gently as possible, while Dan held it straight between two splints of wood.

Ulrich's arm was broken in two places when he was crushed into the ground by Brad. But he didn't seem too fazed by the prospect of having it in a cast for the next eight weeks. And now the pain-killers were working their magic, he was more interested in debriefing everyone.

'Did you guys see how I jumped on that big bloke's back?' Ulrich's eyes glowed with unrestrained delight. 'And then I was yanking on his beard like crazy to try and get his attention.' He demonstrated the action one-handed, a happy grin on his face.

Jenna's breath caught in her lungs, a small smile playing over her face. So young and courageous.

'You were very brave, Ulrich …' How did she tell him just how much of a debt she owed him? 'Thank you from the bottom of my heart.' She looked up, glancing at them all in turn. 'I want to thank all of you. I don't know how I can ever repay you, any of you, for putting your live's at risk for me.' Her throat tightened so hard it hurt and tears welled in her eyes before she could stop them.

'Come on, Jenna, you don't need to gush like a bloody girl.' Mob strode across the campsite and gave her a quick pat on the back. 'We all know what you're trying to say and it's okay. That's just what we do here. Help out a mate. I'm sure you'll repay the favour someday.' She smiled up at him through her tears, grateful and humbled. 'And Ulrich had a great time, didn't you, mate? I bet you don't get too many chances for an all-in brawl like that back in Germany, now do you?'

'Nope,' Ulrich agreed. 'I'll never forget my trip to Australia because of you, Jenna.' He turned his baby blue eyes up to her and gave her one of his most endearing grins.

'Oh, I see, so it's Jenna you'll remember from your trip to Australia then?' Pat's gruff voice sounded from the other side of the fire.

'Well no, that's not exactly what I meant.' Ulrich was flustered now. 'Of course I'll remember you, Pat. You taught me what it means to be a jackaroo.'

Pat laughed. 'I was only kidding, mate. I don't think any one of us will easily forget what happened last night.' Pat gestured to the wad of material still covering the gash on the side of his face. 'Now, can I get someone to come and look at this hole in my head please?'

'Sorry, I was just getting to you.' Jenna gathered up the first aid kit and hurried over to where he was sitting. It turned out Brad had hit him with a rock before Pat finally managed to subdue him. Removing the covering she tried not to cringe at the large cut. She should be immune to the sight of blood by now. But it was hard when she knew all these men's injuries were her fault.

'It'll need stitches,' she acknowledged. 'But I'm not the one to do the stitching this time. I think you should leave it to the experts. After all, you don't want to scar this handsome face, do you?' she joked. 'I'll bandage it up tight; it's almost stopped bleeding anyway.' Rummaging around in the first aid kit, Jenna pulled out a couple of long bandages and a clean dressing and went to work.

'Thanks, luv.' He winked, and for once she let him get away with it. 'So, what exactly are we going to say to Bernie, or Harding, or the police?' He raised his voice, to include everyone in his question. 'And what the hell did Coshy have to do with all this?'

'And Shauna,' Lex added quietly. They all cast simultaneous glances over towards the desert casuarina behind their campfire. Shauna sat on the ground beneath it, trussed up like a Christmas turkey and glowering at them through her beady eyes. They'd had to gag her just to shut her up. She wouldn't stop screaming obscenities at them. Brad lay beside her. Tied up, but still unconscious. Pat had really done a job on him. They'd left Liam lying where he fell. Dan said it'd preserve the evidence, or something like that, for when the police got here.

The joking mood subsided.

'I wish Liam hadn't killed Coshy.' Jenna was surprised by her own words.

'No one deserves to die, especially the way he did.' Dan came up and put a comforting arm around her.

Ulrich stood up, his broken arm resting in the makeshift sling. 'Maybe he didn't deserve to die, but he still wasn't a very nice person.' He searched her face with open frankness. 'He was in league with Liam. As was Shauna. Thank the Lord their other plans to kidnap you failed. He was a greedy, conniving pig. All he wanted was your sapphire. He didn't care about anything or anyone else but himself.' The planes of Ulrich's face were hard, his blue eyes steely cold for once.

She went back to bandaging Pat's head, considering Ulrich's words. She shouldn't mourn Coshy's death. Nor Liam's for that matter. But it wasn't that easy. Guilt was a slippery thing at the best of times. It came back to haunt you when you were least expecting it.

She wanted to talk to Moon, he was the only person she hadn't made sure was alright after their ordeal. She'd been too busy making sure Dan was okay to say more than a few encouraging words to him. As soon as she had finished wrapping Pat's injury and taken another look at the large, egg-shaped bump on the back of Lex's head, she went to sit next to Moon on the far side of the fire.

'Hi, Moon.' She nestled herself down beside him on the damp earth. The rising sun was bringing the heat back into the desert and soon the cool morning would be replaced by the baking temperature of another day.

'It's good to see the sunrise again,' Moon replied, closing his eyes and tilting his head to catch the warm rays on his face.

'I hope Marco didn't hurt you last night. That he didn't …' She was unsure how to phrase her query.

'You are strong missus, I knew you'd defeat them.' At last he looked up and caught her gaze for a few seconds. Again, there were tears welling in the corners of her eyes. One thing was for sure, it was going to be an emotional roller coaster of a day.

* * *

Lex was last to be loaded onto the helicopter, beside Pat and Ulrich. Dan smiled to himself. Lex was still grumbling. He didn't believe his *small bump on the head* warranted a trip to hospital, but he'd been outnumbered. Dan was sure he'd still be protesting to anyone who'd listen in the helicopter about how *able-bodied* he was and how he didn't need any bloody doctor poking and prodding him.

Dan sighed under his breath. His shoulder ached. The medic had inspected it and declared Jenna had done a good job, he just needed to keep it clean and rested for a few days. Closing his eyes for a second, he sucked in a big lungful of air. God, he was tired. And there was still the long drive back to the station to contend with and more explanations when they got there.

His police mate, Damien, was still up at the crime scene, taking details, making measurements, counting bullets, carting away Brad and Shauna for questioning. And putting Liam and Coshy into body bags. He'd been one of the first cops to arrive, having somehow appropriated a police helicopter. Dan owed him big time for this. Sometimes it really was who you knew, not what you knew, that made a difference. Damien made sure he was present when all of the Shiralee team gave their statement, taking copious notes.

Finally, they were free to go, with the proviso there'd be more de-briefing to come. Lots more de-briefing. Dan wanted Damien's guarantee none of them would be charged over the shoot-out. That Jenna wouldn't be charged over Liam's death. His mate said he couldn't give him that. Even though it looked like a case of self-defence, the body had to be sent to autopsy, and there'd be months of extensive tests, questions research and investigation. But as long as Shauna told the truth—which was in her interest if she wanted a short jail term—then she'd corroborate their story. And Brad. Well, who knew what Brad would say when he eventually woke up? Damien said both he and Shauna might be able to cut deals for less jail time in exchange for information on the rest of Liam's little outfit. Damien would also have to corroborate the story about Liam killing Coshy. If it really was true, that Liam's gang abducted Jenna and attacked the rest of them when they tried to rescue her, then it should be straight forward and simple. But none of them were allowed to leave the station anytime soon.

Damien wasn't happy Dan and his team hadn't called the police in straight away. But the way Dan spun the story made it seem like they had no time, they had to act, or Jenna would've ended up dead. Damien shook his head and muttered over that for quite a while. But in the end, he'd let them go.

Dan scanned the camp, searching for Jenna. She had her back to him, tying Dune and Blue into the tray-back of the Land Cruiser. She turned a millisecond before he grabbed her and spun her into his arms.

'Come here,' he growled into her neck. He just needed to hold her, to make sure she was really okay. He was still in awe of this gorgeous woman.

'Someone will see us,' she warned.

'I don't care.' Smiling like a rogue, he lifted her higher into his arms, so her feet were off the ground. She was alive. He was alive. They'd survived together. She laughed, and the sound expanded in his heart. It was carefree and happy; the sound of liberty.

Then she sobered, as if remembering something. 'You'll hurt your shoulder.' A worried frown creased her beautiful face.

He watched the flecks of darker blue in her eyes shimmer in the sunlight. He wanted to kiss her, deeply, passionately. But not with everyone's gazes on them. It'd have to wait.

Lowering her down onto her feet, he took a step back. 'Nah, it's fine now. See.' He rolled it around several times and then tried to hide a flinch of pain. 'Well maybe it's not quite one hundred percent yet.' But it would be fine, soon. They'd all be fine. 'You did it, Jenna. You took Liam out of our lives.' He searched her gaze for an inkling of how she felt. She didn't baulk at his stare, but a torrent of emotions flitted across her face. Pride. Grief. Conviction. Remorse. All valid reactions.

'I'm not saying I'm happy another human being is dead,' he corrected in a hurry. 'What I am saying, is that I'm extremely proud of you. You're a fascinating and complicated woman, Jenna, and I'm very glad I'm in love with you.' He was rewarded with another of her genuine smiles.

'I'm not sure I know how I feel about Liam yet.' Her forehead wrinkled with distaste. 'It's all kind of hard to believe. I don't know if any of it has sunk in. It's a bit like a dream, you know?'

'Yeah, I know.' He looked down and stroked her hair.

'There's still Alexander.' Her voice was so quiet he almost didn't catch her words.

It was true, Alexander was still an unknown entity. Dan couldn't believe a father could be so cold, so calculating, so rapacious, when it came to his own daughter. Alexander couldn't have known what Liam was up to. If he had known the violent and vicious methods Liam was employing, surely he would've stopped him. But then again, perhaps that was where Liam learned his brutal ways in the first place.

'Something Liam said to me tonight, that Alexander was going to get a big surprise when he finally turned up with me in tow. It made me hope … perhaps he doesn't know where I am.'

'Neither of us can really be sure, Jenna. But from the little I've learnt about Liam, it seems to me he might've kept the fact he found you a secret. Liam had a huge ego. You were going to be his prize. His way to impress Alexander.'

'You think so?'

'I hope so.' The last thing they needed was to be looking over their shoulders for the rest of their lives.

'You never told me what you were up to when you left me alone last night.' Her tone lifted, became light and teasing, but the sentiment *left to be snatched by Coshy,* hung in the air between them.

'Oh, yeah, that.' He broke out in a cold sweat just thinking about it. 'It was just something stupid that seemed important at the time. Now, I can't believe I left you, even for one second. I should've known.' How many times had he said that to himself over the course of last night?

'No one was to know Coshy was involved,' she replied. 'It's no good worrying about things we can't change.' She gave Dan a pointed look. 'So, are you going to tell me what was so important you had to dash off into the night?'

Contemplating his answer, he kept his head down. Should he tell her the truth? What would she think of him if he did? *Damn it.* Without answering, he took her left hand in his and reached into his hip pocket with his other. Her hand was warm as he slipped the ring onto her slim finger. Shock replaced curiosity in her eyes as she stared at her hand.

He snuck a second glance at her face as the long seconds of silence became too much to bear. Tears filled her eyes and overflowed down her cheeks. He'd gone and upset her again. Bloody hell. Would he ever get this right?

'Don't cry, babe,' he said in a soothing voice. 'I'll get you a better one later, I promise.'

'No, no! I don't want another one. This is perfect.' She gazed at the ring, wonderment playing across her features. 'Did you make it?'

'Yes. That's where I went last night. I got this idiotic idea you needed an engagement ring straight away. Sorry it's not very good, but it's all I could come up with out here.' He was sorry the idea had even occurred to him and even sorrier he'd been thoughtless enough to follow through on the whim. She deserved better than a homemade ring. He'd made it from tightly wound tussock grass with a tiny, white flower nestled on top instead of a jewel. At the time he'd thought himself quite clever, now it just looked like a clumsy excuse for his love.

'It's the most amazing thing I've ever seen.' Jenna stared at the ring, taking in every detail.

'Sorry, the flower got a little squashed in my pocket,' he mumbled, still unsure if she really liked it.

'I can't believe you actually made it. How did you do it?' she asked, her eyes soft and glowing.

'It's made from a small key ring, with grass and flowers wound around it.' He stopped and shrugged his shoulders. 'Easy really.' He'd just wanted to make her happy.

'It is so beautiful. I'll cherish this for the rest of my life.'

'That might be harder than you think,' he said, gazing at her through hooded eyes. 'Odds are the flower will be dead by the end of the day.'

'I don't care, I'll keep it forever anyway.' Standing up on tiptoe she grabbed him by the nape of the neck, dragging his head down until she could reach his lips, and kissed him. She actually seemed to understand that ring stood for everything he treasured about her. He'd poured his heart and soul into making that ring.

'So, are you still going to marry me?' he asked, breaking their kiss.

CHAPTER TWENTY

The swish of dry grass against her fingertips was a stark contrast to the sanctuary coming from Dan's cool-skinned embrace. They walked together in silence out into the waiting desert night.

'This'll do nicely,' Dan grunted as he heaved the swag over his shoulder, so it landed with a soft thud on the ground.

A large snappy gum reared up in front of them, its trunk ghost-grey in the starlight. Dan unrolled the swag, butting it up against the tree trunk and then sat down on the mattress, using the trunk as a perfect backrest. Jenna curled up beside him on the swag, nestling underneath his arm.

It was wonderful to have his solid body next to her. Closing her eyes, she breathed long and slow.

'You feel so good,' Dan murmured into her hair.

'Hmm, so do you.' She kept her eyes closed.

'It's nice to get away from everyone for a while.'

Jenna placed her free hand on top of his thigh and ran it slowly upwards, revelling in the feel of his hard muscles beneath the fabric of his jeans.

Her hand trailed up over the top of the belt on his jeans and found the lighter material of his shirt. Her fingers worked their way over to the buttons and started undoing them, one by one, slow and unhurried.

Two days had passed since the war in the desert. And a lot had happened in that time. This was the first moment she and Dan had found to spend truly alone together.

'I still can't believe Mob and Lynne are together. I'm so happy for them,' she sighed. Her mind drifted back to when they'd all arrived back at the station. Lynne was waiting on the verandah for them and she'd run towards the approaching vehicles. Dan had to stamp on the brakes hard, to avoid hitting her.

Not even waiting for Mob to fully exit the passenger door, Lynne grabbed him in a huge bear hug. Wrapping her arms and legs around him, she threw her whole weight against him, making Mob stagger backwards under her weight. Then she did something even more surprising, she pulled Mark's head down and kissed him. A kiss full of passion, full of possession.

Jenna stared open-mouthed at the pair. Wow. She hadn't seen that one coming. But thinking about it, they did make a good couple together. It was great to see Lynne back in high spirits. The sight of her bound and drugged in the cave had shocked her to the core.

'Whoa,' was all Mob could say when he was allowed up for air.

'I'm so glad you're back,' Lynne answered with a smile, lowering her feet to the ground.

'Well I'm glad you're glad that I'm back.' He pulled her in for another long kiss. They'd been inseparable ever since. It was so cute.

Jenna's mind wandered to the dinner they'd eaten later that night. All of them sitting around the table in the staff quarters looking like so many walking wounded.

Cookie created a banquet to welcome them all back, safe and sound.

'I'm not sure they believe I can understand animals,' she said, voicing her doubts. 'Both Lex and Cookie gave me sceptical looks the other night when they thought I wasn't watching.'

Dan's laugh was loud in her ear. 'Well I'm not surprised, I must admit I'm still coming to terms with the idea myself.'

Jenna told them the whole story as they sat devouring Cookie's wonderful food. She told them everything, including the revelation about her gift. They all deserved to know after all they'd been through.

'Ulrich thought you were *awesome*,' Dan continued, giving her a wicked wink.

'Hmm. Yes, well he would, wouldn't he?' she giggled. But it was true, Ulrich had been intrigued and amazed by what she could do. And everyone else had been quite chilled about it, actually. The whole thing had been much easier than she anticipated. Perhaps that's what having true friends really meant. They approved of you, no matter what.

'Do you think Lex will accept Ted's offer?'

Dan stared down at her. 'Your mind is all over the place tonight, isn't it?'

'Yeah, sorry. There's just a lot to think about,' she apologized. She flicked the last of the buttons on his shirt undone and pushed the clothing aside, so she could run her fingers over the planes of his chest. 'But I haven't forgotten what we came out here to do,' she said playfully.

His arm tightened around her shoulders. 'I know,' he agreed. 'And yes, I do think Lex will become the new station manager. He's just not the hurrying kind of guy when it comes to making decisions. But we all know he'll be fabulous for the job.'

It was another surprise awaiting them after they returned from the desert. Last night, the owner of Shiralee Station, Ted, had landed his helicopter, catching them all unawares. Then he'd stomped into the staff quarters and called them all together for an impromptu meeting, Bernie trailing morosely behind him.

Ted started speaking once everyone stood around the table. 'As soon as I found out what was happening here, I commandeered the closest helicopter to get here as fast as possible.' Shooting Bernie a quick, but consequential glance, he continued, 'I know Bernie was trying to protect you all, but I tend to take it a little personally when problems big enough to involve the police happen on my property.'

No one spoke into the silence, not sure how much Ted knew, or what to reveal.

'And I can't wait to hear your story. But first I need to tell you all something. Bernie and I have had a long chat over the phone. And we both concede that Bernie needs to get himself cleaned up and healthy. He's agreed to move on. He's now no longer the station manager,' said Ted into the hushed room.

There were gasps of shock from all around the table as the import of his statement sank in. Jenna felt a sudden stab of pity for Bernie.

Bernie nodded. 'I'm sorry. This place deserves someone who can look after it … Well you all know what I mean.' Deep down, Bernie really cared about the station and the people who worked here, but his own personal demons had overridden all of his good intentions. With that, Bernie disappeared through the doorway to shocked mutters of farewell from the rest of the Shiralee team. Short and sweet, typical of the man.

'So, I'd like to offer the job to Lex.' Ted beamed at everyone. 'We all know how capable, hard-working and honest he is. He'll be perfect for bringing this station back to it's full potential.'

Lex was completely taken aback and didn't speak for many long seconds. 'Thank you for your faith, Ted, but … I'm not really one for all that organisation, you know all the paperwork and stuff. I'm more of the practical, hands-on type.'

'Take your time and think about it, Lex. There's no rush. We can talk about it some more later,' Ted had said and then he'd changed the subject, asking them to explain exactly what they'd been up to over the past few days.

Jenna shook her head and brought her thoughts back to the present. 'Yes, he'll be perfect for the job. We'll convince him of that. Shiralee needs him.'

'Hmm, just like *I* need *you*,' Dan said, kissing her earlobe.

Wriggling free of his arm, Jenna manoeuvred herself until she was sitting in his lap, facing him. He wrapped a strong arm around her waist. His other hand reached up her back to tangle in her long flowing hair at the nape of her neck.

'And I love you, no matter if you can talk to animals or not. I love you because you're you.'

Slowly but surely, he dragged her head down towards his upturned face until his warm mouth claimed hers. She parted her lips, so she could feel his tongue slide between them. He kissed her with a building urgency and her body became warm with longing. Tugging at the bottom of her sweater, Dan lifted her arms and in one swift movement had removed the jersey over her head. Jenna heard his sharp intake of breath as he gazed at her in the starlight.

'You really are the most beautiful woman I've ever laid eyes on.' He stroked his hand down over the mound of her breasts, lingering for a few seconds above her nipple, before tracing the line from her belly-button to the top of her jeans.

Jenna gave a half-groan at the exquisite caress of his fingers. She soon found the rest of her clothes had been discarded and were lying in a tangled mound along with Dan's. Lowering herself down onto Dan's body, she gloried in the feel of his thighs and chest against her bare skin, as Dan enfolded them both in the shelter of the swag. Resting there for what seemed like time without end, she stared into his dimly featured face, watching pinpricks of light reflect in his eyes from the cold starlight.

Unconditional love. This is what it feels like. How could she ever thank Dan enough for helping to liberate her from her self-imposed shackles, for showing her what a truly fearless life should feel like?

Wrapping both his arms over the small of her back, Dan pulled her tighter into his body, lifting his head so that he could kiss her neck. Sighing, she let the heat of her hunger for him flush through her veins as she discarded all conscious thought and allowed physical desire to take over.

They made love twice that night, cradled in the shadow of the tree above them and the earth below. The first time was even more urgent and rapid than their lovemaking at the oasis, full of need and necessity and overpowering emotions. But the second time, Dan took his time exploring her body, bringing her slowly back to an awakening yearning, until she had to cry out for him to take her before she burned up in an all-consuming fire. Dan came with her in a long, thrusting abandon that seemed to last an eternity.

Lying enfolded in his arms, Jenna cast her gaze skywards and found the familiar constellation of the Southern Cross. The two bright pointer stars drew her eyes onwards into the five-star group that formed a ragged diamond shape. How many times had she gazed up at this familiar set of stars? But this night of all nights, it was as if she were seeing them for the first time.

CHAPTER TWENTY-ONE

Dan walked slowly up the embankment, eyes fixed on the slim figure standing at the top. Turning her head, Jenna smiled as he came up behind her. He stood beside her and they gazed in silence out into the desert.

The sky was an aching blue, a stark contrast to the deep ochre-red of the earth. Against the blocks of red and blue, the olive-green spinifex tussocks floated, spiky and round. The intense colours were as much of a feeling deep inside as they were an ordinary shade for the eyes to see.

The first rains of the wet season had washed through in a thunderous cacophony and left everything shimmering and replenished. The brown, broken grass was now sending up effervescent green shoots and wildflowers were erupting in all their raw naked hues with the breaking of the dry.

Another season came and went within the blink of an eye. Time was nothing in this ancient landscape, and his life felt almost insignificant.

Dan loved it here. This was where he was meant to be, with Jenna by his side.

'Are you ready?' He scanned her familiar face and drank in every detail, her sky-blue eyes staring back at him. It was so easy to drown in the inspiring soul that lingered behind them. She was breathtakingly beautiful in a simple cream dress, thin straps highlighting her pale shoulders. He couldn't believe she was truly his.

'Yes.' She reached out and laid her hand on his chest. There was a slight tremble in her fingers and he saw the pulse in her neck from her wildly beating heart.

He knew how she felt. Just thinking of the people waiting for them at the bottom of the hill had his heart skittering, too.

Damien had driven down from Karratha, was going to spend the week here at the station. He might even learn to ride, he'd mumbled to Dan when he thought no one else could hear.

Damo came bearing good news. 'Shauna told us everything,' Damo said, as everyone gathered around him yesterday after he arrived. 'She pretty much gave away Liam's whole operation. She got five years for being an accessory to murder. But because she was so informative, the judge brought that down to two, with good behaviour.'

'Hmm,' Lex said, obviously not happy with the short jail term.

Damien went on with his story. 'It turned out Liam was pretty much small-time. Drug dealing and some gun-running. He was also linked to a local bikie gang over near Newcastle, on the east coast. The police raided a few properties over there and have disbanded anything that was left of his crew. They never found the other three guys who got away.'

Dan was holding Jenna's hand, and her fingers tightened around his at this news. So Jude, Toady and Marco were still out there somewhere. Hopefully they'd learned their lesson. Not to mess with the stock hands at Shiralee Station.

'Brad never told us anything. Clammed up tight as a gnat's arse,' Damo continued. 'Typical bikie code, never rat out a mate. But he got nine years for his part in the kidnapping and murder, so he probably got what was coming to him.'

Afterwards, there had been much more discussion about how this might affect all of them, but in the end it was sorted out. Jenna was never charged with Liam's death, it was determined self-defence. And the rest of them, while the technical term was *going armed to cause fear*, had been let off on a good behaviour bond. There was only one dark cloud to Damo's story. They couldn't find a link to anyone with the name Alexander. If Liam had been working for someone else, the guy was a ghost.

Dan's chest expanded as he thought about the other people who'd arrived yesterday. His mum and two brothers were also here. The first time they'd all been together in many years. His mum looked radiant as she pulled him into a hug. It made him realize how much he missed her. She told him she'd started seeing a new man, which was perhaps what helped her to look so joyful. But perhaps it also had something to do with him getting married. Patrick, younger by nearly four years, seemed to have matured, finally. Was actually holding down a steady job and not stressing his mum out as much. It made Dan wonder if perhaps his time in jail on his brother's behalf was worth it after all? If his brother turned out okay in the end. Grew up to be a good man. Then perhaps it was.

Jack, the middle child, had started up his own accounting business and was getting married himself at the end of the year. Jack hadn't become boring, as such, but he'd certainly *settled* in the past few years.

Is that what Dan was doing now? Settling?

Jenna grabbed his hand, breaking his thoughts. 'Come on, let's go. They'll all be waiting for us.'

Instead of following her, he pulled her back into his arms, cradling her face with one hand. 'I love you.' Running a hand over her bare shoulder and up the side of her neck, he lifted her chin and met her serious gaze. No, he wasn't just settling.

His love for her was the strongest force in his life now. And forever.

'I love you, too.' She ran her fingers up the back of his neck until they knotted in his hair and then pulled his head down towards her so that their lips hovered close together. That's all he wanted to hear. It would be enough for him. 'Kiss me,' she murmured.

His mouth devoured hers, his heartbeat quickening.

Eventually she pushed him away, her breath coming in gasps and said, 'Now can we go and get married?'

* * *

'Heya, Rowdy, there you are. Wow you look spectacular.' Mob's familiar cheery voice greeted them as they made their way back down the dune towards the main house. 'And you don't scrub up too bad either, Simmo.' Dan's hand tightened its grip on hers, but Jenna couldn't help but smile at Mob.

'I was sent out on a scouting mission to make sure you two hadn't vanished for good. We're all ready and waiting.' Mob's intelligent eyes searched their faces.

'We're still all go for this bloody wedding thing aren't we? Because I'm desperate to get out of this monkey suit and get back to my comfy blundies and jeans.' He smiled his usual crooked-toothed smile, but the creases at the corner of his brown eyes were tense.

'Yes, Mob, the wedding is still on,' she replied.

The tight lines around his brow relaxed. 'That's good. It would've been such a waste of all those damn flowers you had us picking. And all that food Cookie's been slaving in the kitchen over for days.'

'Thanks for the support, Mob,' Dan snorted.

'Anytime.' He slapped Dan on the back.

'Now, I think you should run along, Simmo. I believe you need to be there before the bride makes her entrance. Don't worry I'll make sure she gets there in one piece.' Draping his arm around Jenna's bare shoulders, Mob tucked her into his side, pushing Dan down the track in front of them. 'Go on, I've got her. We'll see you in a few minutes.'

Jenna watched Dan as he gave her one quick, meaningful glance and set off down the pathway, his long legs taking him down through the tussocks and out of ear shot quickly.

'You don't look half bad yourself, Mob. You should wear a suit more often. The brown colour highlights your eyes.' Jenna gave a girly giggle as he shot her a dark frown.

'Only for you, Rowdy. I don't wear suits for just anyone, you know.'

'Thanks, Mob. I know you don't.' Jenna squeezed him around the waist. 'I'm sure you'd wear fancy clothes for Lynne though, wouldn't you?'

'Maybe. As long as she asked real nice.' He tried to keep his features deadpan but failed as a large grin split the freckles on his face.

'Lynne's good for you, Mob. You two are good together. And I'm glad that two of my closest friends are happy.'

'Well thanks, Rowdy. And I guess I have to say ditto. I'm glad you and Simmo got it together. I wouldn't have let just any guy get his hands on you. He'd better take good care of you, or he'll have me to answer to.'

There was a moment of silence and Jenna contemplated the many good friends she had nowadays.

'So, now Dan's been offered the leading-hand job, I presume you'll both be staying here for the long haul.'

'Yeah, I guess so.' They hadn't had time yet to discuss the full implications of Dan's offer.

The owner, Ted had flown in early this morning, ostensibly so he could attend the wedding. But within minutes of landing, Lex was summoned up to the big house for a meeting. Returning with an unconcealed grin of pleasure, he'd broken the news to them all as they huddled—still half-dressed in preparation for the upcoming nuptials—in the kitchen area.

'Dan, where are you?' Lex hollered. When Dan trailed into the room, still buttoning his pants, Lex continued. 'Ted has a wedding present for you, but he thinks it'll be better coming from me.' Everyone held their breaths, waiting to hear what it might be. 'Ted is promoting you to leading-hand.' Lex beamed like a proud father as Dan opened and shut his mouth a couple of times. Mob and Moon started clapping.

'I knew it,' crowed Cookie the spirals in her hair jiggling up and down like miniature springboards as she waved her curling tongs in the air.

'Are you sure?' Dan heaved in a gulp of air. 'I'm not sure I'm up to—'

'Course you are,' Lex interrupted. 'We'll make a great team, you and I.'

And then everyone had gone back to getting ready for the wedding. The ramifications of Ted's offer would have to wait until later, but Jenna could see Dan was still shell-shocked. It would be okay. He just needed to have as much faith in himself as everyone else did.

'Looks like everyone is here and waiting for you.' Mob's voice brought her back to the present. Releasing his grip, he pointed at the group of people waiting before them.

They all stood in a semicircle at the outer edges of a small clearing in the desert. Dan waited inside the circle with a tall grey-haired man by his side. Flanking the humans, dotted in haphazard groups around the glade, Chainsaw and the other station horses were grazing on the new shooting grass. Everyone, including the horses, turned their heads to stare at them as they descended the last small incline.

All of a sudden, she felt self-conscious, and her sandalled feet scuffed the red sand as she hung back.

The clearing looked flawless and serene, suffused in the orange radiance of the setting sun and bejewelled with large bunches of wildflowers they'd all helped to pick. Jenna knew the spot was perfect because she'd chosen it herself, with a little help from Chainsaw and the brumbies.

She'd been drawn to the smallish hollow the previous afternoon, situated just over the first rise from the homestead boundary fence. There was no spinifex growing here and the clearing was framed between two desert oaks and two white snappy gums. She'd broken a couple of branches from the trees and used them as a broom to sweep the enclosure free from any twigs and leaves, picking up all the small rocks and hiking them over her shoulder.

Searching between the scratchy clumps of grass, Jenna located four largish rocks and rolled them into the clearing. Unerringly, she placed them at the points around the circle, indicating north, south, east and west. As she bent and straightened and felt the dust rub between her fingertips, her mind filled with clarity, bright and immense. This place was full of good energy, she could feel it soaking deep into her bones. At last she was learning to listen to what her feelings told her. Her heightened senses had always been there, but she'd chosen to ignore them until now. At least she could thank Liam for that one small thing, he'd awakened her spirit and conscious mind to the possibilities her gift gave her.

Noticing her hesitate, Lynne broke away from the group and came to take her by the arm. 'It's alright, Mob, I've got her from here.' Lynne shooed Mob away and started to fuss with Jenna's hair, tucking a few small native white flowers behind each ear. 'You look absolutely gorgeous, Jenna.' She stopped pulling on a wayward strand of Jenna's blonde hair and fixed her with a kind gaze. 'I don't think I've ever seen you in a dress,' she mused. 'It actually really suits you.'

'Do you think so?' She'd bought the dress online and it'd been delivered in the mail run a few weeks ago. It was a straight length of cream silk with thin straps to go over her shoulders. Jenna was surprised it'd fitted her so well when she'd tried it on and had been a little shocked at how grown-up and feminine it made her feel. She almost hadn't recognized the woman staring back at her from the mirror this morning.

'Come on, Jenna, don't get all shy on us now. It's a bit late for that. You look beautiful, and these flowers finish off your look completely.'

'Thanks, Lynne.' She wanted to say more. Much more. She wanted to tell Lynne how lucky she was to have her as a best friend. To thank her for her strength and courage and persistence in the face of her own dogged need for independence. Without that true friendship, and the friendship of all the others, Jenna knew she'd still be living a hunted life, devoid of any hope or light. Now she was about to marry the most gorgeous man with the most genuine soul she'd ever met, in front of the people closest to her heart. How could she convey all that to Lynne?

The taller woman took one look at Jenna's face and pulled her in for a trade-mark crushing bear hug.

'I love you too, silly. Now go on, go and marry that handsome man waiting for you over there.' Lynne grabbed Jenna by the shoulders and propelled her forwards into the clearing.

Jenna nodded to all of the people as she passed by them. Dan's mate, Damo was there, looking spiffy in his tuxedo. A bit overdressed for an outback wedding, but never mind.

Dan's mum, Cathy, and his two brothers, one with his fiancée, stood in line. It was so nice to finally meet his family. Now she could see where Dan got his curly hair from. And his courageous grin. Cathy asked if she would take her out riding sometime, it'd been a long while since she'd been on a horse. The idea frightened and thrilled Jenna all at the same time.

The spike of hurt that her dad, Joe, couldn't be here to see her get married flashed through her heart. Perhaps he was watching. From somewhere.

Sturdy Pat was there with tall, gangly Ulrich at his side, both of them beaming like idiots. It was good to see Ulrich had his cast removed and he swung his arm to show her how good-as-new it was. She returned their grins.

Lex's bare head looked strange without his ever-present hat as he stood next to Cookie in the line, but he gave her a solemn nod of his head as she passed. Cookie had taken the rare opportunity to go all out to dolly herself up, and she stood out like a bright bird of paradise amongst the dull desert tussocks. She'd donned a scarlet flowing dress that clashed mightily with her primped red hair. She looked absolutely wonderful.

Moon had oiled his black hair until it shone and put on his first ever suit and tie. The suit was borrowed from Mark, but it fitted him well, under the circumstances. The dark blue colour set off his white teeth to perfection.

Mob and Lynne were the last to join the group as they took their places at the end of the line next to Ted.

Jenna made her way into the centre of the circle where Dan stood waiting, Dune and Blue at his feet. He grabbed her hand and trapped it within his warm fingers and she felt the tingle of desire that flooded through her whenever he touched her.

She turned to smile at the older man standing in front of them. He'd arrived with Ted this morning in the helicopter.

When Ted found out Dan and Jenna planned to get married at the station, he'd let them know he wanted to contribute something towards the wedding. After lengthy discussions, Dan asked the owner over the phone if he might be able to arrange a special kind of celebrant for them. Dan and Jenna were having a very non-traditional wedding, which called for a special kind of priest to carry out the ceremonies. One that couldn't easily be found here in the middle of the outback.

When Jenna met the grey-haired man, all her fears evaporated. He was ideal. A kind of quiet empathy radiated from him and he seemed to have an immediate understanding of what the couple wanted from their nuptials.

The celebrant had a gentle soft face but his voice was strong and clear as it rang out over the desert hollow.

'Welcome, all of Daniel and Jenna's friends and family, who will bear witness with me to their handfasting ceremony. I am a Celtic Priest, but I've also been ordained to make this marriage legal and binding. I've already invoked the energies of the four elements, north, south, east and west, to create a sacred circle in which this couple will be joined as embodiments of God and Goddess.' The priest smiled at them as he brought their hands up and linked them together with a long twine of soft, silver rope. 'Let us take a few moments of quiet to allow our souls to believe why we're here tonight.'

Jenna took a deep lungful of air and calmed her beating heart, closing her eyes so she could open her ears to listen to the gentle acoustic music from the air around them. The small sounds of the impending evening became larger and more intense. The gentle noise of the horses lipping at the velvet grass. A cricket chirruped, sporadic at first, then with increasing bravado into a looming crescendo. Even the sound of the rising moon sending out her silent white light was deafening.

A faint rustle announced the presence of something moving through the spiky desert grass. Jenna knew who it was even before she heard a low gasp of astonishment from Cookie. When she opened her eyes, she saw Cookie covering her mouth with her hand, eyes round and wide staring at something outside the circle.

Materializing, wraith-like, out of the darkening desert were the dingoes. They too, had come to bear witness.

Then Jenna heard a quiet call from somewhere close by in the desert and knew that the mob of kangaroos were also here to pay their respects.

The priest never indicated he'd seen the animals, just continued in his patient way with the ceremony.

'Daniel, and Jenna, I bid you look into each other's eyes and say the vows you've prepared for today.'

She could feel Dan's utter devotion flowing through his fingers into her as she began to speak. 'Above us are the stars and below us is the earth.

'Like the stars, love should be a constant source of light, and like the earth, it should be a firm foundation from which to grow.

'You cannot possess me for I belong to myself.

'But while we both wish it, I give you that which is mine to give.

'I shall be a shield for your back, and you for mine.

'I pledge to you that it will be your eyes into which I smile every morning.

'My living and my dying are each equally in your care.

'This is my vow to you.'

Jenna felt surprising tears flowing down her face. As she looked deep into Dan's tawny eyes she felt the love overflowing, reaching out to carry her to dizzying heights as he spoke, returning his vows.

'Flames from our days dying embers will bronze the sky.

'I will give up forever for you to be my angel bestowed.

'You cannot command me for I am a free person.

'But while we both wish it, I give you that which is mine to give.

'I shall not slander you, nor you me.

'I shall be a shield for your back, and you for mine.

'I will share your pain and seek to ease it.

'The red earth and blue sky entwine as do our vows of love forever.

'This is my vow to you.'

There was complete silence as they held each other's gaze, lost together in a world of devotion and commitment. The priest moved forward and wrapped the cord around both of their hands six times before tying it off.

Then he stepped back and projected his voice. 'These promises you make by the sun and the moon, by fire and water, by day and night, by land and sea and sky are made in truth.

'If one drops the load, the other will pick it up.

'The union of one and one creates a new one.

'You will both work to keep the oath you pledge today in the knowledge that you have the support of your many loved ones. You may now place the ring on Jenna's finger,' he said.

Dan slipped the little home-made ring on her finger. She'd refused to get anything else, telling him it was the most perfect thing she'd ever seen, even if the little flower was now dead and brown. Her mother's ring sparkled in the sunlight on her other hand. She wore it proudly for everyone to see now.

'I now pronounce you husband and wife.'

Cheers erupted from all sides of the circle as Dan lowered his head and took her mouth in their first married kiss. Jenna's heart rocketed upwards, feeling like her chest would burst open. A sound of wild neighing blasted out of the surrounding dark desert. The stallion had brought his brumby herd to wish her well. She opened her mind, and for a few seconds ran free and unfettered with the pounding hearts of the brumbies as they galloped away over the night-dark dunes, tails flying behind them, the wind cool in their streaming manes. Bringing her consciousness back to the clearing, she lay her hand on Dan's strong warm chest and beamed a brilliant smile at the Shiralee team who were charging in to congratulate them.

She was free.

If you liked Shadows in the Dust, you'll love;

Shadows in Deep Blue

Pulled out to sea by a rip-tide, Ebony is drowning. Ex-army Corporal, Jay risks his own life to rescue her. But that's just the beginning of her secrets and lies and soon they're both caught up in a fight for their lives.

Shadows of Red Earth

What if the only thing you wanted in life was your freedom? What if the cost of that freedom was the lives of your family?

The books in this series can be read as stand-alone novels, but are enhanced if you read them together.

Also by Suzanne Cass
NEW

Stargazer Ranch Mystery Romance Series
Combustion: Prequel Novella
Wildfire
Firelight
Snowbound: A Christmas Novella
Snowfall
Cloudburst

Island Bound Series
Books can be read as stand-alone
Bound by Truth
Bound by Silence
Bound by the Stars

Colors of the Earth Series
Books can be read as stand-alone
Shadows in the Dust
Shadows in Deep Blue
Shadows of Red Earth

Romantic Suspense
Single Title
Island Redemption
Glass Clouds
Chasing Bullets

Love in the Mountains Novella Series
Books can be read as stand-alone
Rain on a Tin Roof
Lost and Found
Rescue his Heart

Please Leave a Review
The greatest gift you could ever give an author is to leave a review. You will be helping other people to discover this book and making a difference to me

as an Independently Published Author. If you liked this book and want other people to read it too, please leave a review.

Connect with the Author

I really hope you enjoyed reading Shadows in the Dust. For more action romance info, upcoming release dates, and access to free books join the exclusive Suzanne Cass reader club. As an added bonus, you'll get a copy of my FREE STORY.

Solar Flare

http://www.suzannecass.com/contact/

Or you can stay in touch via my website
www.suzannecass.com
Facebook: www.facebook.com/suzannecassauthor/
Instagram: www.instagram.com/suzanne.cass/
Pintrest: www.pinterest.com.au/suzanne_cass/
Twitter: twitter.com/SusieCass1

About the Author

Suzanne Cass is an Australian author who writes rural romance and romantic suspense abounding with passion and danger.

Her debut novel, Island Redemption, won the Romance Writers of Australia Emerald Award in 2016. Suzanne was also a finalist in the 2019 Romance Writers of Australia RUBY award.

She had always had a fascination with the tough resilience of people who live in our amazing red-dirt outback country. When not writing about the characters that inhabit her head, Suzanne can be found roaming the Perth beaches with her border collie, or encouraging from the sidelines as her two sons play sport.

Acknowledgements

This was the very first manuscript I ever wrote, a labour of love, which has sat at the bottom of my drawer for many, many years. I've taken it out, dusted it off, re-worked and re-mastered it. This story was born because I had to write about all of the characters I met during my years working on a sheep farm as a jillaroo in the Snowy Mountains of New South Wales.

This book is special to me and I need to thank my long-suffering, wonderful husband for living through the ups and downs over the years when I thought this book would never get published. He never lost faith in me or my writing ability.

To my author companions and friends, Rachel, Jillian and Rose, we all share our journey through writing and keep each other uplifted, optimistic and on track. Plus the many other authors out there, without whose help and encouragement I would never have got this far.

There is a small team of people who I also couldn't do without, beta readers (special thanks to Jo and Rebecca) and my ARC team, who are essential to an Indie Author like me.

Thanks to the amazing organization, Romance Writers of Australia, whose volunteers give up their time for the love of books and writing. I've learned so much through my association with them over the past years.

I am so very grateful to all the readers who have bought and enjoyed my books and who will continue to do so. Writing my books for you is what keeps me focussed and invigorated.

And to all those beautiful horses running free and unfettered up there in the Snowy Mountains, may the wind flow forever through your manes and your feet be forever swift and sure.